HOT HIRES

Visit us at www.boldstrokesbooks.com

By the Authors

Nan Campbell
Like They Do in the Movies
The No Kiss Contract
The Rules of Forever
Hot Hires

Alaina Erdell
All Things Beautiful
Off the Menu
Fire, Water, and Rock
Hot Hires

Jesse J. Thoma
Tales of Lasher, Inc.
The Chase
Pedal to the Metal
Data Capture

The Serenity Prayer Series
Serenity
Courage
Wisdom

Romances
Seneca Falls
Hero Complex
The Town That Built Us
Guide Us Home
Hot Hires

HOT HIRES

by

Nan Campbell, Alaina Erdell, *and* Jesse J. Thoma

2024

HOT HIRES

ISBN 13: 978-1-63679-651-2

This Trade Paperback Original Is Published By
Bold Strokes Books, Inc.
P.O. Box 249
Valley Falls, NY 12185

First Edition: June 2024

CREDITS
Editor: Cindy Cresap
Production Design: Susan Ramundo
Cover Design By Inkspiral Design

Acknowledgments

Nan Campbell would like to thank Arturo Leon, a New York City driving instructor so skilled he's been written about in *The New Yorker*. (Look him up!) Thanks for the tips and tricks, Arturo. Thanks also to June—your journey to licensed NYC driver is the inspiration.

Alaina Erdell would like to thank her sensitivity reader, Shraddha Shah, for the gracious education and insightful suggestions, and her partner, for her steadfast support and gentle correction of all things medical.

Jesse Thoma: I'd like to thank C.F. Frizzell for her gracious reading of early drafts and invaluable feedback. To my wife, thank you for being you and choosing me. Finally, to the readers, thank you for continuing to pick up my work.

Hot Hires

NEW YORK IS LOSING HOPE

Nan Campbell

CHAPTER ONE

Some people say New York City is the place you go when you want to remake yourself. I guess all the steel and concrete and summertime hot garbage stink are supposed to scour you clean of all the bullshit you picked up where you were before. But I wouldn't know about that. I've always been here. Born uptown in Columbia-Presbyterian almost thirty-five years ago. Where am I supposed to go when I need a fresh start?

Fresh is not a word I'd associate with my hometown. But by October, the swampy heat is thankfully behind us, replaced by cool, crisp autumn in New York—arguably the freshest time of the year. It's my last fall here, and my absolute favorite season, but it's not quite the roasted chestnut-scented, leaf-shedding, sweater-wearing, *When Harry Met Sally* fantasia we've all been conditioned to expect. That Manhattan exists only on streaming sites nowadays.

Even if it's not some figment of a Hollywood screenwriter's imagination, New York City is a place of change—it's in perpetual motion, and it's constantly forcing you to learn new things. Opportunities for gaining knowledge can come from the unlikeliest of places. Like last week, I learned a valuable lesson while standing on the platform waiting for the Q train. I was listening to my *Veronica Mars* rewatch podcast when my left Airpod popped out of my ear and onto the subway tracks. A rat almost as big as a dump truck leaped over the third rail, skittered over to my poor defenseless Airpod, chomped away for three seconds, and then—I swear by Saint Nora Ephron—it looked up at me and laughed. Where else in the world are you going to get a lesson like that? Definitely not something I remembered from my days at PS 290.

And moments after opening the door of my garden level apartment, I was learning again, whether I wanted to or not. Here to ruin this brisk, sunny, October morning was a biodegradable baggy of poo resting on the lid of one of the empty garbage cans at the curb. So thank you, anonymous Upper East Side resident, for kindly providing me instruction in communal dog rearing this morning. I picked it up with the very tips of my thumb and index finger and dropped it in the bin, and crashed the lid down with a terrific clang.

"It wasn't me! Or Buster. I swear." Mrs. Finkelstein approached with her cocker spaniel straining on his leash as he tried to get near me.

"I'm sure it wasn't, Mrs. F." She'd caught me scowling at an inanimate trash receptacle at 8:40 on a Saturday morning, but what are you gonna do? After I dragged the garbage cans through the wrought iron gate that separated our building from the sidewalk, I bent toward Buster and gave him all the love he deserved. "You would never, would you, Buster, baby? You're a good boy. You don't even poop, do you?"

"Oh, yeah, he does. But I dispose of it properly like any civic-minded dog owner should. Got something warm in my coat pocket right now."

Yikes. This was exactly why I didn't own a dog. The whole poo-handling part. It was infinitely preferable to love on someone else's fur baby rather than care for my own. But maybe getting a pet would be something to consider when I got to Los Angeles. I pressed pause on the Buster love fest and lifted the garbage can lid for her. "Here you go. An easy two points."

"Please forgive me, Hope. I'm sure you don't want to hear about the shit I've been carrying on my person since Seventy-fourth Street. The things we do for our loved ones." Mrs. Finkelstein dropped her baggy in, took a small bottle of hand sanitizer from her other pocket and offered me a squirt before using it herself. "What are you doing out and about so early on a Saturday?"

The front door on the parlor level opened and the woman who gave me life swanned out onto the stoop in her Pucci caftan—the one she reserved for fancy brunches or various moments of high dudgeon. Mom held a bottle of champagne in one hand and a carton of orange juice in the other. "Are you excited, Hope? Today's the big day." She set her beverages on the third step and sat. "Good morning, Minerva. Care to join us for a mimosa?"

"Don't mind if I do." Mrs. F. sat down on the stoop. "What's the occasion?"

"Hope is starting a new phase of life today." She popped the cork on the champagne and poured a measure into three paper cups.

Phase of life? "Let's not get carried away, Mom." She made it sound as if I, at the ripe old age of thirty-four, had finally received a visit from Aunt Flo. I remembered her bursting into dramatic rafts of tears when that milestone had occurred at age thirteen, but right now I detected a subtle, sarcastic edge to her mild words that I really didn't want to deal with right now.

"What? It's not every day a Mason undertakes the task of navigating the city from behind the wheel of a motorcar."

"Nobody calls them motorcars anymore, Mother. It's the twenty-first century." I gave all my attention to Buster again.

Mrs. F. raised her eyebrows. "You're learning to drive? At your age? Why?"

At my age? I was only thirty-four. What the hell was she implying?

"That's what I'd like to know, Minerva. There is no earthly reason for Hope to drive. That's what the subway and the bus and taxicabs are for." She handed a mimosa to her longtime neighbor and tried to hand one to me.

I stood and leaned against the iron newel post. "No thanks."

"Don't slouch, Hope, and take this. I'm trying to be supportive."

My spine straightened as if I were one of Pavlov's dogs, involuntarily reacting to that tone my mother had been using on me since I was five. Then I slouched again just to spite her, like I was five. "I don't think drinking alcohol right before my first driving lesson will endear me to the instructor."

"Oh, right." She stifled a laugh and set the cup on the step next to her. "I didn't think of that. Yet another reason not to drive—you can drink whenever you like!"

"Even at nine in the morning." Mrs. F lifted her cup. "We should toast your new endeavor somehow, Hope. How about a virgin orange juice?"

"Fine." I scanned the street for the driving school vehicle to rescue me, even if it was ten minutes too early.

"This is the Upper East Side," my mother said, as if I didn't know that. "Everything is walkable. You know, Hopey, you live in a very unique city where you don't ever have to drive. There are so many options now, with the Uber and the Lyft and what have you."

"I'm well aware, Mother." She had activated her sermonizing function, and I truly did not have the patience for it this morning. Couldn't she see I was trying to devote all of my mental energy to quelling my driving lesson anxiety? I focused on the unconditional love in Buster's eyes.

"And even before your grandfather bought this building"—she threw a hand toward the facade behind her—"Masons have chosen not to contribute to the auto industry and its outsized carbon footprint. You're finally back where you belong, living under the Mason family roof again, but if he knew about this, he'd be turning in his grave."

Please. As if Grandpa—the loveliest grandpa who ever lived, but let's face it, as timid as the day was long—had the sack to drive in the city. Or had the faintest idea of what a carbon footprint was. He died when I was nine. But I silently endured my mother's lecture because if she knew the real reason I had decided to learn to drive, our morning cocktails on the stoop would turn into the Spanish Inquisition with my mother playing the role of Torquemada.

Of course, I loved my mom and dad. I really did. But the fondness that came with absence was severely reduced by their now very close proximity. When the lease on my East Village apartment expired five months ago, the new terms were four times what I had been paying. Housing was just about the only sector that had bounced back with a vengeance since the pandemic. The garden-level apartment where my grandmother had lived while I grew up in the floors above had been vacant, and my dad offered it to me at an extremely low rent. It was a benefit that diminished my independence in a few very real ways. Not to mention, they wouldn't let me get rid of any of my grandma's furniture.

And now, my mother's third degree was preventing me from achieving the serenity I so desperately needed right now. I was nervous enough about taking to the streets without her passive-aggressive disapproval masked by pseudo-supportive mimosas.

I lifted my gaze from Buster to watch a tall woman walk toward us from down the block. She seemed to be checking the building numbers as she got closer and then zeroed in on us. Yowza. She had thick, long, dark hair tied back in a ponytail, and her features were sharpish—sharp as in angular, high cheekbones but also clear intelligence emanating from her eyes. Tall, dark, and handsome. Her soft butch energy was speaking volumes to me, and I knew I would be staring and trying not to drool at her rangy figure after she passed us by. But then she pulled a piece of paper from the pocket of her black fleece jacket and smiled as she approached.

I don't think I imagined her gaze lingering on me for a moment before she addressed all three of us, referring to the paper. "Good morning. I'm looking for Hope Mason?"

"I'm Hope." I abandoned Buster, who butted his nose against my shin, looking for more attention.

"You're Hope?" The woman tilted her head in what might have been disbelief.

"Yes." I did a quick, surreptitious check of myself. Did I have toast crumbs on my face? Egg yolk on my sweater? No. What the hell?

The woman seemed to quickly recover her confusion and gave a quiet chuckle. Her smile grew wider. It transformed her face. I could easily get lost in a smile like that— so warm and friendly, and sexy. Before I could answer her, mom stood. She had that speculative look on her face that could mean anything from *is this person delivering a subpoena* to *am I looking at my future daughter-in-law*.

"Hello. I'm Cordelia Mason, Hope's mom."

"I'm Hope's neighbor." Mrs. F. added, lifting her cup again.

"And you are?" Mom moved down two steps to get within interrogating range.

"I'm Val Caceres, C&C driving instruction." She pointed at the embroidered logo on the left breast of her black fleece jacket.

Mom put a hand by her ear. "I'm sorry, Valka, is it?"

The driving instructor smiled broadly. "No, Val. Short for Valentina, but nobody calls me that. My last name is Caceres."

"Valentina is a lovely name. You should be proud of it," my mother said.

"Oh, I am, Mrs. Mason. It's just easier for my students to remember." She turned to me. "May I see your driving permit, please?"

While I produced my brand-new permit for her to inspect, Mrs. F. said, "Where's your car? Can't learn to drive without a car." She looked to the street.

Val Caceres hiked her thumb over her shoulder. "I'm parked illegally by the fire hydrant. Not the best move for someone charged with upholding the rules of the road, but this street is narrow and I didn't want to be in the way of traffic."

Mom and Mrs. F. nodded sagely even though neither of them had probably ever given a thought to how narrow the street was.

"Shall we go?" Val showed me that knockout smile again.

We started in the direction of her car. My heart rate skyrocketed at the thought of actually driving, and my palms turned into tiny Slip 'N Slides.

Val glanced behind her. "I'm sorry, but our insurance doesn't cover passengers. Do you want to tell them they can't come along?"

I turned and to my absolute mortification, Mom, Mrs. F., and Buster were following behind us. This was the last thing I needed right now. "They are *not* coming along, but I think my mom is curious. Please bear with her. I come from a long line of proud non-drivers."

"They're proud they don't drive?"

"It's a thing. Don't ask."

She seemed to accept that. We arrived at a black sedan, its headlights blinking and a little sign strapped to the roof that said *C&C Driving School—Confidence on the Roads*. She opened the driver's side door with a flourish and gestured for me to sit, but I opened the passenger side and stealthily slid in. Even though I had bought and paid for this lesson, as well as many more, I had no intention of taking the driver's seat—yet.

Val stood in the street. She bent and gave me a puzzled look through the open driver's side door.

On the sidewalk, Mrs. F. sounded confused. "How is she going to learn to drive from that seat?"

Mom's strident voice was loud even through the closed window. "Yes, what kind of lesson is this? How is my daughter supposed to learn from being a passenger?"

I sunk low in the seat. Had my mother been this embarrassing when I was in junior high? Because that's about how old I felt right now.

"She'll get there. Hope's going to learn about the car first," Val said, and I felt almost boneless with relief when she didn't insist I move.

I pressed the button that lowered the window. "I'll tell you all about it after the lesson, Mom."

"If you live that long," she said ominously.

There was amusement in Val's voice. "I've never had one casualty, Mrs. Mason. Don't worry." She sat on the driver's side. "It was lovely meeting you both."

After I raised the window, I said, "Thank you, and I'm so sorry about them." We were now closed in from the city outside. The interior was spotless and smelled like a pine forest.

"It's fine. Nothing I haven't seen before. Parents are often worried about their babies learning to drive. But their babies are usually sixteen years old. That's why I was so confused before. I thought you were going to be another high schooler. I'm sorry for assuming."

"You don't teach adults?"

"Sure I do, but I haven't had an adult student in a while. It's usually teenagers."

"Got it." I vigorously rubbed my palms on my pants.

Val watched. "This is your lesson, but I'm sitting behind the wheel."

"I didn't realize I'd be driving right away."

"There's nothing to fear. We'll go slow, and I'm right here to help."

My heart was still pounding away in my chest. "Have you ever had any failures?" I can't believe I'd asked that. I'd never failed at anything.

"A few. But don't worry, even if you fail your driving test the first time, we'll instruct you until you pass. Guaranteed. We don't need to think about that just yet, though."

I took a shaky breath. "I'm not ready. Can I ask you a favor?"

"Sure."

"Would you mind if we start this lesson somewhere else? I really don't want these two watching the whole time." I covertly pointed to where my mother and Mrs. F. were still gazing at us from the sidewalk.

Val turned the car on. "Sure. Let's find a quieter, wider street. Please fasten your seat belt, and you may have noticed there is a pedal on the floor on your side. That's a brake for me to use while you're in the driver's seat—in case of an emergency. Please avoid touching it with your foot."

I drew both feet back as if the pedal was covered in cockroaches. Val didn't seem to notice and tapped lightly on her horn and waved at my mom before pulling out. A few moments later we were a couple of blocks away in the loading zone in front of an empty storefront.

"Shall we switch?" Val unclasped her seat belt.

"No." I looked straight ahead. "I just want to say that I don't think I'm ready to drive right now."

"Okay." She was very calm. "Why do you think that is?"

"Look at my hand." I held one up to reveal its slight tremor. "I'm a little nervous—no, I'm petrified, really. I'm a total pedestrian. I've never even ridden a bike. I can count on one hand the number of times I've even been in the front seat of a car. It's just become real, and I can't—I think I'm going to need some time to wrap my head around the idea of actually driving."

Val took the paper from her pocket again. "Well, it looks like you've reserved—whoa—forty hours of lessons—"

Words gushed out of me like a waterfall. "That was the most your website would let me book. Nobody I know drives—at least not in the city. All my practice will have to come from you. Your company, I mean."

"—so if it takes a little while for you to get comfortable, then that's what it takes."

"Oh. Good." I darted a look at Val, whose expression was nothing but kindness. "I'm really nervous. So nervous I almost feel like I'm going to hurl."

"Do you know how to swim?" Val asked.

"Do I—?" What did swimming have to do with driving? Val waited for my answer, her smile serene. "Yes. I started taking lessons at the Y when I was six."

"Too bad." Her expression turned sorrowful. "You almost had the New York City trifecta—no swimming, no cycling, and no driving."

A giggle erupted from me, totally unbidden. "It's true! So many people I grew up with don't do any of those. Who had room for a bike in their apartment? And now all these lunatics on their Citi Bikes? They're just begging to get hit by a cab. And swimming! How many diseases do you think you might pick up from a dip in the East River?"

"At least four, but probably less than six." Val laughed, and it sounded like a child imitating a machine gun. *Hu-hu-hu-hu.* It was lovely and unaffected and made me laugh harder.

"I'm a lifelong New Yorker, but knowing how to swim is a definite strike against me." I sat back in my seat.

"I don't think so," she said. "Knowing how to swim is insurance against whatever life throws at you. It keeps you safer if you somehow do end up in the East River. And that's what driving is too. You never know when having the skill will be useful. And if you ever need it, you and everyone else is safer if you're calm and qualified behind the wheel."

"That is a fantastic argument. I'm going to use it on my parents."

The expression on Val's face said *maybe she really is sixteen.*

"I do walk everywhere though," I rushed on. "And become quietly angry with those glacial-paced slowpokes who get in my way. That should give me at least a little NYC cred."

"Oh, absolutely. Cred that's automatically reduced because you're about to start learning to drive." Val gave me a considering look. "Still feel like you're gonna hurl?"

"No, but now all I can think about is that slick of vomit that would collect in the corner of the pool at the Y. Every single time. Why was that? Swimming lessons must have been traumatic for someone."

"But not for you?"

"No." I thought about those long-ago days when Mona Applebaum and Lauren Havemayer and I took swimming lessons together. "I was the first to jump off the springboard into the deep end. I guess I was pretty fearless back then."

"I'd say learning to drive takes about the same amount of bravery as jumping off the springboard into the pool at the Y. If you had it then, you probably still have it now."

"You think?"

"I do."

"Do you know how to swim?" I didn't know if this breached the instructor-student contract, but call me curious.

"Yes. I also have a bike, and I obviously know how to drive. Plus, I moved away for a while. I invalidated my New Yorker status long ago."

I didn't think this was true. In my opinion, the definition of a true New Yorker was as broad and encompassing as the city itself. There was room for everyone, and if you believed you were a New Yorker then what authority was going to say you weren't?

"I have to ask. Why is someone who comes from a long line of proud non-drivers hiring me to teach her how to drive?"

"Oh." I had only told my closest friends. Revealing the reason to a virtual stranger meant it would be released out into the world. But that's what I wanted, right? I was making a big life change, and this was a necessary step on that path. And driving instructors were a little like priests, right? The car was their confessional. Despite having met Val ten minutes ago, she seemed trustworthy. She should be—I was putting my life in her hands.

"Sorry. You don't have to tell me if you don't want to."

"No, I want to." I took a breath. "I'm moving, and I'll need to know how to drive when I get there."

Val raised her eyebrows. "Giving up that hard-earned New Yorker status? Where to? Jersey? Long Island?"

"Los Angeles."

Val gave a low whistle. "Wow. You're not messing around, and you're right. You'll need to know how to drive in LA."

"That's what I've heard." I didn't sound scared, did I?

"Are you moving for a job?"

"No, as long as I have a computer, I can do my job anywhere." That was as personal as I wanted to get right now. "What does that do?" I pointed to some random button on the dashboard.

Val thankfully picked up on my ham-handed subject change and launched into a lengthy explanation of all the features of the car. This led to her listing all the reasons why I should only use my right foot to operate both the brake and the accelerator, and then an in-depth treatise on the importance of side mirrors. As we sat there, illegally parked on a quiet side street for the entire lesson, I found myself relaxing into Val's calm expertise. It was a relief that I wouldn't be forced to drive today. I could do this. Maybe not right this second, but one day soon, I would be driving.

CHAPTER TWO

The C&C sedan with its rooftop sign was a block away, bobbing along like a buoy among the flotilla of cars on the sea of Lexington Avenue. My third lesson would begin on this blustery, late October afternoon as soon as Val pulled up. I had to admit, I was growing more comfortable with the concept of driving when I was in the car beside my hot instructor. Mind you, I hadn't yet been forced to drive. Up till now, I'd successfully avoided that undertaking, safely observing from the passenger side. As Val braked in an area designated as a bus stop, I once again jumped in the passenger seat before she could even open her door.

The smile she gave me was very cute but also seemed a bit exasperated. "Not again. I cannot continue being your chauffeur, aimlessly driving you around the streets of Manhattan."

I spoke in my most earnest voice. "I really think I need more time to witness your amazing driving skills."

"Flattery will get you some places, but none of them in my car. How are you going to learn to drive if you never sit in the driver's seat?"

I tried my most winning expression, but Val didn't look like she would be won over. She had that same easygoing, laid-back aura I had seen in our previous lessons, but that one raised eyebrow was a definite signal that I had some major convincing to do. "You've been so patient with me, but look at all this traffic. I can't start now. What if I lose control and drive onto the sidewalk and mow seventeen people down before crashing into a lamppost? Then you and I would both be dead because I was not ready to take the wheel."

"Wow. You certainly paint a vivid picture of destruction and mayhem." Val laughed. "I wouldn't let that happen. Not only do you have to trust yourself, you have to trust me as well." She darted a look in her mirror and put the car in gear. "You're lucky we have to get out of the way of the M103 bus." We traveled about two blocks before she said, "We've gone over every inch of the car already. How do you want to spend this lesson if you're not going to drive?"

I was ready for this. "I could still learn a lot by watching you. If I'm ever in a car, it's usually a taxi or an Uber. The only thing I can see is the back of the driver's head."

"Let's make a deal. If you promise you'll sit in the driver's seat and attempt to drive during the next lesson, you can spend this one watching the master navigate these streets."

"Deal." I exhaled with relief. "Is there some sort of survey I need to fill out at some point? Or a manager I need to pass along my compliments to? You're getting five stars."

Val laughed. "Good to know, but I have plenty of job security since my dad is the owner. And I'm currently doing him a giant favor."

"You're not normally a driving instructor?"

"Oh, I am. I started instructing years ago in college—it helped pay tuition, and I was pretty popular with the teens since we were close in age back then. Then I left New York for a while." Val shot a quick look at me. "I came back October of twenty twenty-one. Damn, I've been back two years already."

"Why did you leave and why did you come back?" I was interested. Val was interesting, not to mention very easy on the eyes. But was my curiosity coming across as creepy? "Only tell me if you want to."

"It's okay. I grew up in Washington Heights, and then I left because I finished my nursing degree. I'm a traveling nurse, but I'm taking a break from that." Val tied her history in a brief and neat little bow. "I like what I'm doing right now. It's helping people in a way that's totally different than nursing. And there are fewer bodily fluids." She turned on her blinker. "Now, watch me. I'm making a right. Approach real slow and watch for pedestrians in the crosswalk."

"That's one of the things that scares the shit out of me. What if I hit somebody?"

"If you're paying attention, you will not hit anyone. And if you're behind the wheel, you are—by definition—paying attention."

Perhaps I should embroider that sentence on a pillow.

Val edged forward, then paused as an elderly woman inched across the street with her tiny little Maltese, which looked like a whisk broom on a leash. While we waited, the light turned yellow and then red.

"Never rush. We're obviously in a position to turn. The cars coming across Sixty-ninth will let us go." A large SUV charged past on our left side, immediately disproving Val's claim. "Unless they're assholes." She was utterly calm.

I, on the other hand, had grabbed onto the dashboard so hard there were indentations under my fingertips.

Val proceeded to make the turn and fell in line behind the SUV. "And I have to concede there are a very large number of assholes you'll be sharing the road with." When we came to the end of the block, she put her blinker on again. "Let's try that again. Use your turn signal, slow down, watch for pedestrians." She narrated as she maneuvered the car onto Third Avenue. "When you turn onto a road that has multiple lanes of traffic, try to turn into the closest lane, but be mindful of double-parked vehicles."

I understood all this in theory, but how was I going to do all the things in the correct order so easily like Val did? My eyes caught on something out the window. "Oh my God!"

"What?" Val asked urgently, her eyes scanning all around.

"No, nothing, sorry. Neil's Coffee Shop is closed." I turned in my seat as we drove past. "It looks like it's permanent."

Val took a breath and then shot me a look that seemed to say *And...?*

"My dad used to go there just about every Saturday with his buddies. That place has been open for decades."

"I'm sorry for your loss."

I returned Val's look. "Well, it's more his loss. I haven't been in there since I was a kid. But you don't have to be snarky about it."

"I'm not. I completely understand the shock that comes with something in your neighborhood closing down. It happens all too often these days. When I first came back to the city, I couldn't believe how many of my neighborhood institutions had closed."

"I know. So many since the pandemic."

"A bodega I used to go to every day after school when I was a kid really hit me hard."

"Yeah. One near me is gone too. But a new store just reopened in its place. It's one of those off-license weed-selling places now, with a sideline in snacks from, like, Yemen or Thailand or somewhere."

"I want to try snacks from Yemen."

It had never occurred to me to go in and get any. Now I wanted snacks from Yemen too.

Val kept talking. "But with all those businesses closing, people left too. Their jobs disappeared. So many people from my hood are just gone."

It was the same all over the city. And my ex didn't stick around that long. As soon as the news started talking about lockdowns, she was gone. Among the first to leave. Not because of her job, but because of fear. I stayed through the grimmest months, swearing Covid would never push me out.

"I'm no spring chicken anymore, but I've heard from my younger cousins that nightlife isn't what it used to be either. The city that never sleeps now goes to bed by eleven."

"No. Really? Even the clubs? God, I haven't been to a club in at least a decade." I remembered the occasional night lasting until way past closing time at four a.m.

"What, back when you were thirteen?"

How could Val make me smile with a weak line like that? But there I was, grinning like a fool. It was cheesy, but I could get used to compliments like that.

"And when the clubs close earlier, it's not worth it for the all-night diners and halal carts and delis to stay open. No more greeting the dawn with dosas in Washington Square Park."

I knew exactly which cart Val was talking about. I had probably eaten my body weight in dosas when I was at NYU. But then I'd eaten a dosa about as recently as I'd been in a club. "It's exhausting just to think about it."

The Upper East Side was now my home again for the first time since high school. Even as a teenager, when I escaped it to party in far cooler neighborhoods, I knew it was about as close to the suburbs as you could get while still within the boundary of Manhattan. It had never been known as a late-night destination. At thirty-four, I was officially old, but Val didn't look like a winter hen, or whatever the opposite of a spring chicken was. "You can't be that old. What are you, twenty-five, twenty-six?"

The smile Val threw at me was wide and disarming. "Bless you. I'm thirty-two."

Who knew mutually under-guessing each other's age could feel so nice? Val was dead cute.

"And I get it," she said. "The pandemic took a lot out of the city but the cost of living is the same, if not higher—"

"Oh, it's higher. Totally higher."

"So it's understandable that people left. Look at you, greener pastures in Los Angeles and everything."

Guilt erupted in me. So much for swearing never to leave. Val didn't know how hard I'd tried to make the life I wanted for myself in this city. But I honestly believed living here was preventing me from achieving a happiness in mind, body, and soul that had so far eluded me. Los Angeles could deliver what I desperately sought—fulfillment in my career, a productive life. A girlfriend, a partner, a wife. Family. To be settled with someone I loved with my whole heart. The West Coast beckoned like a shimmering jewel in a distant shop window, shiny with possibility and potential and promise.

But it wasn't New York's fault that my last relationship was cut off at the knees. That was all Covid. And finding someone new had been an impossible task. Dating apps? Forget about it—like finding a needle in a pile of pigeon shit disguised as a haystack. Despite those glowing profiles you see every Sunday in the *Times* wedding announcements, finding true love in New York City was about as easy as finding a rent-controlled apartment. A pleasant, unattainable myth.

Until recently, the city had usually been comforting reliability—like your favorite tweed blazer in the fall, the AC on blast in the summer, commiserating with a bestie over an illicit cigarette in the park during the spring. I hadn't felt that comfort in a long while, but did you abandon your best friend in times of trouble? I gazed out the window without seeing a thing. All the city made me feel now was lonely. "New York is done. It's time to go."

Val frowned. "Is it?"

"It used to be the center of the universe. Now it's not even the center of the US."

"And Los Angeles is?"

"It's better than here."

Val let that one lie. I had no idea if that was true—yet—but I had to feel optimistic about my future home, right? My fascination with Los Angeles began as a tween who watched way too much WB programming. So many early-aughts shows targeted at young people seemed to be set in the sun-drenched shores of southern California, and I ate it up. All those wide shots of the Pacific stretching across the horizon were a revelation to a girl whose bedroom window looked out on a brick wall.

When the Pandemic hit, and with so much time holed up alone in my apartment, I turned to rewatching familiar favorites from my adolescence. Binging entire nostalgic seasons of *The OC, Veronica Mars,* and *Buffy* soothed my soul and sparked a desire for change. I began to see myself inhabiting the bright, vibrant life of a Californian— minus the teenage angst, crime investigation, or demon slaying. Was it ludicrous that old TV shows had incited a desire to upend my entire existence? Absolutely, but it had to be better than doing nothing. Los Angeles was going to open up my life and snatch me off the endlessly spinning hamster wheel New York City had become.

"I had just about the most perfect date in Los Angeles one time." Val sounded wistful.

"Really? What was it?"

"It was a gorgeous, sunny Saturday and we spent it at the Getty. We wandered the galleries a little and had a meal in that nice restaurant they have there, but the grounds were the best part. Beautiful. We pretty much roamed over every inch, getting lost and then finding ourselves again." Val seemed to be caught up in the memory of it. "Then we went back to her place and spent the rest of the weekend in bed."

It seemed like everything came into sharper focus when I heard the pronoun Val had used for her date. *I knew it! My gaydar is still operational!* "That sounds lovely. How long were you together?"

"Um, two days?" She chuckled. "I never said it was a relationship. How about you? Any perfect dates in your past?" Val snuck a look in her side mirror. She did that a lot. What was back there? I'd have to remember to look in the mirror too. But I had lots of time before I thought about actually driving.

"My love life hasn't been worthy of mention in a pretty long time, and perfect doesn't come anywhere close to describing my relationship with my last girlfriend."

She darted a glance at me.

Now you know I like the ladies too, Val.

"Bad breakup?" she asked.

I let out a long exhale before answering. "It wasn't even that bad. It was still new—well, newish. We had been seeing each other for four months but then Covid happened. A new relationship couldn't sustain that, plus she had already skedaddled out of the city before the governor started his daily press conferences. She lives in Indianapolis now and she's engaged."

Val frowned. "This was a few years ago now?"

"Yes. And there's been no one since. I'm talking the driest of spells. I'm convinced the pandemic has jinxed me. Or the city. Or a combination of both."

"No luck on the apps?"

I didn't say anything. Should I admit to hating dating apps with an intensity that rivaled my hatred for bedbugs, the dentist, and dry January?

"Never mind. I retract the question. We both know what the apps are like. And they're just as bad in Dallas, where I last attempted to use them, if not worse. It was like dating on another planet."

"Why?"

She shrugged. "It's very un-New-York-like. Culture shock, I guess."

"What were you doing in Dallas?"

"Working. I was an ICU nurse. That's where I was when Covid hit, so the dating profile was abandoned."

"And that's why you were in Los Angeles too?"

Val nodded. "Yup. A couple of years before that."

I digested this new information about Val's former life. "The ICU. That doesn't sound like the greatest place to spend your pandemic."

"It wasn't." Her smile seemed completely false. "It was just about the worst place to be." The light turned green and Val accelerated.

"Is that why you left nursing?"

"Yeah, eventually. Now I'm going to change lanes. Watch what I do, okay?"

Val narrated the steps and I watched. I had many more questions, but instead I was thinking about how scary those first few months of Covid were, and wondering how Val had the strength to last that long under those conditions.

CHAPTER THREE

On the Saturday morning after Halloween, I was awaiting my doom by the fire hydrant when my dad walked up with an empty shopping bag in his hand. "Hey, Dad."

"Good morning, honey." He gave me a one-armed half hug and kissed my temple. "I'm going to Orwasher's for some morning buns. You want anything?"

"No, thanks. I have a driving lesson."

"How's that going, sweetheart?"

"So far, so good, but I think it's about to get a lot harder," I said, thinking of my promise to Val.

"I'm so proud of you. You're very brave."

Val rolled up and hopped out of the car. "Are you ready? Today's the day!"

"Val, this is my dad, Matthew Mason."

"Hi, Mr. Mason."

"Hello, young lady. Today's the day for what?"

"Your daughter is going to drive today. No getting out of it this time."

"I've been observing Val so far, but today I'll be behind the wheel," I told him.

He must have seen the absolute panic in my eyes. "Courage, ma fille," he said and gave me a kiss on the cheek. He ambled down the sidewalk and called back, "Take good care of her, Val. Without Hope, we are all lost."

I turned to Val. "A well-worn dad joke in our family."

"Wouldn't want to get lost. I'm glad I have Hope." She flashed that confident smile and I couldn't help returning a wobbly one of my own. "The seat's nice and warm for you," she added.

I had made a deal with Val and there was no getting out of it. I took a deep breath and sat in the driver's seat. Just as she reached for her seat belt, Val's phone started to buzz from its place in the cupholder.

"Let me just put this on silent." Val scooped it up. "Oh, sorry. Can I answer this real quick?"

"Take your time." Anything that would forestall starting this lesson was okay by me.

"Hey, Arturo, is Luna all set for tonight?" Her notable excitement dimmed. "Oh no. Poor kid. What are her symptoms…Okay…No, it doesn't sound like it…Lots of rest and fluids…Yeah, it's okay…Tell her I hope she feels better and not to worry, we'll do it another time… Don't worry about that…I'll find someone to take her ticket or sell it or whatever…I gotta go. I'm with a student…I'll call Luna later, okay?"

She seemed lost in thought as she held her phone in her hand, but then she snapped out of it and turned to me. "Okay, you're driving today. What do you need to do first?"

"Shit myself?"

"Incorrect. Try again."

"Throw up?"

Val pressed the button that rolled my window down. "If you feel it coming on, please spew to the left. I have four more lessons after yours and it would really suck for the car to smell like vomit."

"Has that ever happened?"

"No, never. Sweaty palms and foreheads galore, but no puke." Her smile faltered. "The only one getting sick today is my niece. But she's eight. No chance of her getting behind the wheel and tossing her cookies all over it."

"Is everything okay?"

"She'll be fine. Sounds like a touch of gastro. But she won't be able to come to *The Lion King* tonight." Disappointment rippled over Val's face. "It was going to be her first Broadway show. Now, back to the matter at hand. Have you adjusted your mirrors?"

"Wait. You were going to take her to her first show? That's so nice."

"Yeah, I did it for her two older brothers too. They loved it. Luna was really pumped. I feel bad she's not going to make it. Now, enough stalling—"

"I've never seen *The Lion King*. I missed my window. My first show was *Cabaret*. I was seven. Confused isn't even the word for it."

Val laughed. "I have no knowledge of this window you speak of. *The Lion King* is amazing. This will be my fourth time."

"You're a good aunt. I can't imagine seeing a kid's show four times."

"Everyone needs to see *The Lion King*. It's terrific whatever your age. But we're done talking about it. Put your foot on the brake and press the ignition."

I did as I was told.

"See? You took the first step. You can do this, Hope."

I really liked the way Val said my name. It sent a little shiver up my spine.

"This is a perfect day for you to start. Traffic is very light. Now put the car in reverse. You're going to need to back up about two feet before you can swing out of this spot." Val checked behind us. "Now, gently release your foot from the brake and slowly press the gas. Don't worry, I've got you. I can brake if we need to."

I gingerly placed my foot on the gas pedal and pressed down what felt like a centimeter. The car moved backward. "Holy shit."

"Good. You're doing good. Check your mirror. Do you see how you're getting closer to the car behind you? Brake now."

I stomped on the brake and the car rocked with the force of it.

"Good. Maybe not so hard next time." There was laughter in Val's voice. "Okay, now we're going to move the car out into the street. Put your blinker on, check your mirror, put the car in drive, check your mirror again."

With Val reminding me of all the steps, it was like ticking things off a to-do list. "No one is coming."

"Okay. Turn the wheel and give it a little gas. Gently. Slowly."

I didn't know how it happened, but ten seconds later, Val and I were moving down the street approaching the intersection where a red light waited. Sweat beaded at my hairline. Val had been right about that.

"You're doing great. Slow down now for the red. Where do you want to go? Left onto Second Avenue or straight?"

"I don't know," I croaked. My heart was beating as fast as a hummingbird's wings. "Just tell me what to do."

"Fine. Put your left blinker on, we're heading downtown."

"Oh, God." Why hadn't I opted to go straight? Second Avenue was a wide thoroughfare. It was like turning onto the interstate from a country lane.

"It'll be fine."

I made the turn, and there were several cars waiting in three lanes at the light. I aligned the car with the middle lane and left about two car lengths between us and the car in front. The light turned green and suddenly there were cars whooshing past on both sides. I didn't move.

"Press the gas. Let's go." Val's voice was calm and reassuring. It made me believe I could do this.

The car moved as I commanded with my foot. Cars continued to speed past us, and I realized I would eventually have to change lanes to get off this fucking street. Anxiety flooded me and I took my foot off the gas. "I can't do this. How do people do this? How do sixteen-year-olds do this?"

"What's your favorite pasta?" she demanded.

"What?"

"Your favorite pasta. Don't think about it. Just tell me."

"Gnocchi."

"Gnocchi?" Even through my fear, I could hear Val's disbelief.

"What's wrong with gnocchi?"

"Nothing at all. It's delicious, but it's not a pasta. Put your foot back on the gas. We can't stop here. You're doing great. What's your least favorite vegetable?"

"Broccoli." I gave the car a little gas and we picked up speed, but I had no clue how fast we were going.

"Okay, good. Broccoli. Why?"

I answered automatically. "My mother overcooked it every time when I was a kid. I never eat it now."

"Describe what that overcooked broccoli is like."

"I can't. I'm busy trying not to die right now."

"Hope, describe it." Her voice was calm, but it crackled with urgency.

"Pale green! Droopy. Floppy. Limp. Lying on the plate like it had collapsed on a fainting couch."

"Awesome." Val laughed and—unbelievably—I found myself laughing too.

"Why the hell are we talking about broccoli right now?"

I could feel Val looking at me. "It was probably very relaxed resting on that fainting couch of a plate. Don't you think?"

"I guess." I gripped the steering wheel harder and slowed again as a taxi merged into our lane. When was she going to stop talking about—

"You're relaxed like broccoli, Hope."

As soon as she said it, my shoulders dropped from up near my ears. I took a deep breath. I could be my mom's gross, over-boiled, unseasoned broccoli. I eased my grip on the steering wheel.

"Whenever you get nervous—think broccoli. You're loose and limp like broccoli."

"Okay." I bobbed my head like a lunatic. "Broccoli."

"You've got this."

"I've got this."

"Now we're going to move into the right lane."

"I can't."

"Yes, you can. Broccoli." She narrated the steps to prepare to change lanes, and I followed them almost without thinking. Before I knew it, the car had drifted into the right lane.

A man on a bike skittered into my peripheral vision and I flinched. "Where did he come from?" Then I immediately muttered, "Broccoli."

Val nodded, also in my peripheral vision. "Good. Let's turn here. Watch for pedestrians—and bikes."

Somehow, I successfully turned onto a less-busy side street.

"Pull into that loading zone and put it in park."

We sat for a moment. I let my skull drop back against the head rest, my hands unusable rubber appendages in my lap. "Is it over? My lesson?"

"No." Val chuckled. "It's only been about seven minutes."

"Really?" I closed my eyes. Only seven freaking minutes? Then I felt Val's hand rest on my shoulder.

She was looking right at me, grinning from ear to ear. "Take a minute. Bask in your success."

"If you had to grade me, what would it be?"

Val thought about it. "I'd give you a solid B."

I'm not ashamed to admit I'd been a grade grubber all through school. "Not an A minus? Or a B plus?"

Her smile seemed indulgent. "I'm sticking with a B. It's your first time. There's room for improvement, right? But you overcame your fear. You drove and you did so well. I'm proud of you."

Warmth swept through my body. I hadn't felt that in a long time. "Thanks." My cheeks were no doubt a few shades lighter than the color of a beet. "But seriously, can my lesson be over now?"

"Not a chance. Someday you'll thank me for cracking the whip now." Val faced forward again. "Now I want you to pull out onto the street, but I'm not going to remind you of the steps. Let's see how you do. And don't forget—"

"Yeah, I know. Broccoli."

Val laughed. "Exactly."

❖

Forty minutes later, I stopped the car in front of the fire hydrant as Val directed. I had a raging headache and my shirt was damp with perspiration, but I had done it. My head fell against the steering wheel with a thunk.

"You still have a few minutes, but I didn't think you'd mind if we cut it a little short today."

"Mind? I'm putting you in my will. Thank you."

"You did great today."

When my spine could support the weight of my torso again, I sat up and pulled out my phone to check my calendar. "So our next lesson is—"

"Before you go, I wanted to ask you something. I feel like the window is always open for *The Lion King*. How would you like to see it tonight?"

Val's opaque expression was giving me nothing. What was she asking? Did she want me to buy the tickets from her? I had no desire to see *The Lion King*.

Then she started tapping her thumb against her thigh. Was she nervous? "If you don't have plans, that is. I really don't want to sit there alone." She looked away. "And you don't have to pay. You'd be doing me a favor."

Oh. Was this supposed to be like a date? "You and me and *The Lion King*?"

"If you want…"

While I was indifferent to the show, I hadn't really been indifferent to Val since the moment we met. She reminded me of the most popular woman at the hotel pool when I went to the Dinah years ago. The life of the party, talking to every girl, brimming with a confidence no woman could withstand. The one I stared at from behind my sunglasses—not even once contemplating making a move. I never even knew her name. My friends and I took to calling her *dyke in shining armor*. But that woman was a dream, a fantasy, and Val was right here sitting next to me. I liked her. And the idea of expanding our extremely limited relationship was really appealing. But… "Would it be okay?"

A crease appeared between her dark brows. "What do you mean?"

"Well, we have this student-teacher thing. Would we be violating some kind of driving instruction by-laws?"

"Oh." Val's face cleared. "We're both adults, right? I feel like we can see a show and still keep things professional during our remaining lessons together. But if you have a problem, I get it. Never m—"

"No, no problem," I said swiftly. I wasn't an idiot. "I'd love to come. Should I brush up with the Disney cartoon? I don't even remember what the story is."

"No, I think you should go in cold." She put her hand on the door handle. "Thanks for saying yes. Should I pick you up?"

I'd had enough of being inside a car today. I would take the train. "How about I meet you there?"

Val nodded, and we both got out of the car. She switched over to the driver's seat and put the window down, flashing that wide grin that I was starting to get addicted to. "See you tonight."

CHAPTER FOUR

There were about a zillion people outside the Minskoff Theater, funneling into the lobby and past the merch stand where T-shirts and posters and stuffed lions were displayed to be coveted by overstimulated children and purchased by beleaguered parents. I tried to stand out of the way in front of an enormous yellow sign with the stylized lion's head artwork emblazoned across it. You had to hand it to them—there was no company that could sell an experience quite like Disney.

I had purposefully planned my journey so that I had to spend as little time as possible in Times Square. Sure, the area was now better than the scuzzy nineties iteration from my childhood, but its crass commercialism and naked tourism dollar enticements made it a place strenuously avoided by the locals. Sharing the sidewalks with the slow-moving pre-theater crowds was a blatant reminder why I detested this part of midtown. I'd probably see shows a lot more often if most of the theaters weren't located here.

Was accepting this invitation a good idea? Drowning in a sea of tourists consuming the slickest of Disney products wasn't going to add to my store of precious New York memories. It gave me a jolt when I realized I had less than two months until my flight to Los Angeles.

The desire to see and spend time with Val when I wasn't preoccupied with avoiding a painful and fiery accident from behind the wheel of her black sedan had won out. And speaking of my teacher, there she was, walking toward me in her usual jeans and sneakers but with a button-down shirt and satiny-looking bomber jacket replacing her ever present fleece with the C&C logo. I had dressed up a little too. I had chosen a black going-out top and a slim, just above the knee, leopard print skirt—last worn before the pandemic, when I still went to the office.

Val's eyes seemed to be glued to my legs—or my skirt—I couldn't tell exactly where her eyes fell. Was that good, I-like-the-look-of-you staring or was she embarrassed by the way I had styled for the theme? As she approached, I swished my skirt and gave a little twirl. "Well? Suitable for *The Lion King*?"

"I love it! You look fantastic." Val came within two feet of me and stopped in her tracks, her smile turning hesitant, as if she didn't know what to do.

I could relate. Was this a hug situation? A kiss on the cheek seemed too intimate. And not a handshake—God. Val solved the problem by placing a hand on my back and guiding me toward the security check. "It's so cool you busted out the animal print. You'll fit right in at Pride Rock. You didn't do any reading up or YouTubing about the show did you?"

"No. Going in cold, as recommended."

Val nodded, her excitement obvious. She presented her phone to the attendant, and we were ushered to seats about eight rows from the stage. "You sit on the aisle."

"These are great seats." I settled in and noticed children sitting everywhere around us. "I'm so sorry your niece isn't here to enjoy them."

"Luna'll get her chance. Don't worry about her."

"How is she feeling?"

"Poor kid, still fighting a fever. One of her brothers is sick now too. They'll be laying like overcooked broccoli in front of their iPads for a few days." Val gave me a sneaky smile.

"Honestly, if you could taste my mother's cooking you'd understand. But let me ask you—do you have a problem with gnocchi?" It barely registered at the time, but I remembered it later and had to know before this friendship-courtship-whatever-ship went any further. I had strong opinions about gnocchi.

"I have no issues with gnocchi, but whenever I ask that question people usually tell me spaghetti or fettucine or some other noodle that becomes limp and loose when cooked. You're my only student who is not envisioning pasta when I want them to relax."

"So I broke the mold?"

"You did. You're one of a kind."

Val's deep brown eyes held on mine, and my heart rate picked up. For once, I couldn't think of a smart reply, or anything to say at all, and relief flooded me as the lights dimmed and an actor in an elaborate, colorful costume stepped onto the stage. Her opening acapella notes were a clarion call, sending a trill of anticipation right through me. I gripped Val's forearm for a moment and felt her patting my hand.

A repeated chant rose in volume under the vocal, and an enormous sun started to rise over the savannah that the stage had become. And then the animals began to arrive. Ingenious, life-size, human-embodied puppets of giraffes, prancing zebras, trios of leaping gazelles crossed the stage. I understood why Val gave me the aisle seat when an elephant, gigantic and stately, lumbered down the aisle, so close I could reach out and touch her. Her baby trailed behind her, and that's when I realized my eyes were welling with emotion.

The music built to a crescendo as the stage became crowded with the denizens of Pride Rock, all gathered to pay tribute to the birth of a lion cub. It lifted me out of myself. A tissue was pressed into my hand when I wiped away the wetness on my cheek.

"I always cry. It gets me every time," Val whispered in my ear, holding her own tissue, totally unbothered by her free-falling tears.

"Thank you for bringing me here," I whispered back, wiping my eyes.

❖

Disney had defeated my cynicism. I couldn't believe how much I was loving *The Lion King*. Yes, it was very kid-friendly, but the stagecraft was a marvel, and the *Hamlet*-esque storyline appealed to all ages.

During intermission, Val and I stretched our legs and drank overpriced wine in commemorative Lion King cups. Our conversation pinged from topic to topic, and it never became laced with awkward pauses. I was honestly having a great time.

Now, deep into act two, when Mufasa's giant head appeared from out of a starry night sky background during the reprise of "He Lives in You," applause undulated over the audience. The people around me were absolutely rapt with the story unraveling before them, and all of a sudden I was losing a battle with a sob, which came out horrifyingly loud and unbidden. This wasn't the emotion of the opening number, it was a deeper, wrenching feeling that I immediately knew was going to be messy. I raced up the aisle before I made a complete spectacle of myself in front of Val and everyone sitting around us.

In the restroom, there was a mom urging her young daughter to hurry, but once they left, I had the place to myself. I locked myself into a cubicle and let myself weep. It wasn't long before Val's spotless Stan Smiths appeared just beyond the stall door.

"Hey, are you okay?"

No, I wasn't. Couldn't Val leave me to fall apart in peace? I stared at the closed door and wished her away.

"Sorry, dumb question. Is there anything I can do?"

"I'll be out in a minute. Go back and enjoy the show." I tore off a couple of squares of toilet paper and blew my nose.

"I've seen it too many times already. I know what happens. I'm not leaving you."

"You really can, you know."

"Call me stubborn. I'm not going anywhere."

Defeated, I opened the stall door and Val stood before me, hands pushed into her pockets and looking concerned.

"I'm sorry."

"Don't apologize." Val took the bundle of snotty wet toilet paper from me and left for a second to throw it away. It was a kind gesture. Was it the nurse in her that wasn't grossed out by other people's soiled tissues? "What's wrong?"

"Nothing. I'm just being ridiculous." I moved past her to the bank of sinks and washed my hands and face.

Val washed her hands too. "Emotions are never ridiculous," she said. "They're trying to tell you something. I know from experience that you should listen to them."

Something in her voice made me gaze at her through the mirror's reflection. Her eyes were trained on the floor and her expression was closed, but when she looked up and saw me studying her, the smile returned, although it wasn't as wide as before. I stood close to her.

"What do you mean? What was your experience?"

Val shook her head. "We're talking about you."

We stared into each other's eyes. It was probably only a few seconds, but it seemed like the length of Act One. The feeling of comfort Val gave me was fighting with the crickets of excitement leaping around in my belly. Then her eyes dropped to my lips. Was Val thinking about kissing me right now?

Someone burst into the restroom and zipped into a stall, and the spell between us was broken. Val took a step back.

I wanted to know what Val had been thinking at that very moment, and also what she'd meant by her emotional experiences, but now was not the time. Val wouldn't let me veer from the topic of my crying jag in the ladies' room of *The Lion King* anyway.

"Tell you what," I said. "Let's go watch the rest of the show and then let me buy you dinner, or a drink, or something. My head's still a mess but I want to know what happens to Simba. And I have to pay you back for the tickets somehow."

Val gave me a suspicious look.

"We'll talk about it if you really want. I promise." I made for the door and was relieved when Val silently followed.

I took Val to Bar Centrale after the show. It was one of the few places in the theater district I was willing to go to, but then I looked like an idiot when I had to google the number of the building because there was no sign outside. It was small, dark, and quiet—not overrun with tourists.

When our server approached, I didn't have to look at the menu to ask for a dirty Grey Goose martini and an order of chickpea fries for us to share.

"Nothing for me. That wine during intermission was enough. I'm driving," Val said.

"Oh. I didn't realize, but I can't drink while you just sit there. We'll find you something." I turned to the waiter. "Do you have any nonalcoholic cocktails?"

He began describing drinks that would've sounded absolutely delicious if they included a shot of spirits, and Val chose some pineapple spritzy thing.

"How is this paying you back if you don't order anything?" I asked after the waiter left us.

"I thought we were here to talk, but don't worry. I'm hungry. I'll be housing those chickpea fries."

"They're good. And we'll order more food when he comes back. Anything you like." I pressed the menu into Val's hand. "Thanks for the show. I really, really enjoyed it, and I didn't think I was going to. I was biased."

"Against what?"

I shrugged. "Super splashy touristy musicals? The Disney machine? What I perceived as lowest-common-denominator children's entertainment? It was a good lesson for when I move. I need to keep an open mind to new experiences. No preconceived ideas."

Val nodded and waited.

"I guess you want to know the reason for my little breakdown?"

"Do you want to talk about it?"

"It's not really a big deal. You don't have to worry about me, but I guess bursting into class five rapids levels of tears does require an explanation." I took a moment to figure out what I wanted to say. "I couldn't stop looking at people's faces—they were enraptured. Joyful. This musical has been running for decades forty blocks south of where I currently live. An amazing experience for anyone who buys a ticket, and I totally dismissed it without a thought."

Val listened attentively.

"I mean, people travel here from all over the world just to see *this* show. Every night I have the opportunity to watch those talented people tell that story through dance and song, and it took you dropping the ticket in my lap for me to be here. How many other amazing experiences have happened in this city that I've missed?" Embarrassingly, tears started welling again. "And how many will I miss once I leave?"

Val reached out and took my hand. "I get it. Leaving is hard."

"But I need to leave. You left, right? Didn't you say you traveled for your job?"

"It's kind of essential to the traveling nurse thing." Her smile was playful.

She wasn't being snotty, but I felt stupid anyway. "Right. It's right there in your job title. I've never left. Not for anything longer than a week or two of vacation. I always thought the city had everything I needed. People from all over the world come here. I can eat food from everywhere—"

"Snacks from Yemen."

"Right! I haven't had any, but I could if I wanted to. Name a country and their food is here. You can experience every culture here. I never *had* to leave."

"So why do you want to leave now?"

"Ugh, this city. I'm so over it. You know when you're exiting the subway, climbing up the stairs to the street and someone stops right at the top? They're checking the map on their fucking phone while hundreds of people are piling up behind them. Maddening!"

Val gave me a sympathetic look.

"Or when one person takes up the entire sidewalk with those enormous golf umbrellas when it rains? How rude is that?"

"So rude, but are those really your reasons for leaving?"

"I just have to go." These reasons didn't even scratch the surface, and were petty as hell, but pettiness was easier than honesty right now. "Shouldn't I see a bit of the world?"

"You'll be seeing Los Angeles, not the world. You're trading one big city for another." Val opened her mouth but then closed it.

"What?"

"Nothing."

"Tell me."

"It seems to me that you're not running toward Los Angeles. You're running away from New York. What's the attraction to Los Angeles? Why did you choose it?"

There was no way I was telling Val that Buffy and Veronica Mars were making me do it, and that wasn't the whole truth anyway. When I imagined Los Angeles, I saw a clean, white canvas, untouched by my dissatisfaction and restlessness. It felt like my last chance to grasp the things that were important to me and create the life I wanted.

But I couldn't be that vulnerable. "Well, the weather…"

Val chuckled. "Who are you trying to convince?"

"Shut up." I laughed. I couldn't help it. Val was great to talk to, exhibiting no judgment, only curiosity.

She sat back and allowed the server to deliver our drinks. "While I love year-round sunny weather, big salads, and compulsory yoga as much as anyone, if I had spent my whole life in one place, and had a solid living situation and a good job, not to mention close friends and family nearby, those cool things are not nearly enough to make me leave."

"I can do my job anywhere. It's now one hundred percent remote."

"Stability counts. It took me leaving to realize that." Val shrugged and took a long sip of her drink.

"Well, I happen to like sunny weather and big salads. I've decided, and I'm going. I'm a third of the way through my three-month plan, which culminates in an American Airlines flight on January first."

"Three-month plan? Sounds organized and official." She raised her eyebrows. "Tell me more."

"Starting my driving lessons was a major component. I'm giving myself three months to become proficient and licensed."

"Very doable." Val nodded. "You're well on your way."

I paused while the server returned with our chickpea fries. "Thank you. Next week, first week of November, I'm informing my job of my intended change of address—"

"Do you have an address out there?"

"Not unless you count an Airbnb in Silverlake. I want to get the lay of the land before signing a lease."

"Smart." Val dunked a fry into a ramekin of pale green sauce.

"I'm giving work two months of runway. But the transition should be seamless. Then later, in December, I'll start the physical packing up of my life."

"What is it that you do?"

"I'm a digital marketing manager."

"Zzzz." She pretended to fall asleep and I laughed and kicked her chair. "I'm kidding, but you can stare at a computer screen here just as easily as in Silverlake. Still not a reason to leave. It can't only be FOMO. What's really making you so unhappy about living here? Because I can tell you're unhappy, and it can't just be big umbrellas on crowded sidewalks."

"What? Is it written on my eyelids or something?" She can see my unhappiness? How utterly embarrassing. But my snide defensiveness didn't provoke a response from her, and while I stared at her in defiance, she responded with silent amiability. I didn't owe her anything, but under my embarrassment was a desire to be open. Let's not get crazy, though. I didn't want to run pell-mell into true confessions either.

She sipped her faux-cocktail and waited.

Maybe I could open the door a quarter-inch and share a sliver of a reason with her. What possible damage would it do?

I took a deep breath. "I need to find a new dating pool."

Val's brows dipped and she put her drink on the table. "You can't find anyone to date?"

"Does that sound demented? It's true. I haven't been on a date with someone with any kind of potential since before the pandemic. Plus, when I get on the apps—which I can hardly bring myself to do anymore—I see people I already went on coffee dates with or profiles I've already swiped left on."

"So you've had a run of bad luck—"

"No, Val. I'm thirty-four. I'm supposed to already have found my true love. Pickings are seriously slim." I raked a hand through my hair. "I'm ready for forever, but I can't find her. There's no one in New York City. It's time to move on to greener, more western, pastures."

Val put her hands on the table. "Let me get this straight. You're moving because you're hoping to find love? In Los Angeles?"

"She's out there somewhere. All I know is she's not here. I've checked. I've looked in all five boroughs. I even went out to Hoboken for chrissakes."

Val seemed at a loss for words.

"It's a numbers game. She has to be out there," I repeated. "I simply need a change of scenery and a new pond to swim in. And that's Los Angeles. An untapped city full of women who don't know me or my legendary neuroses. There has to be someone there for me."

"And if you don't find her in LA? How much time are you giving yourself to look? Is it a process of elimination?" One side of her mouth lifted in amusement. "Move on to another city after a year? Chicago? Seattle?"

I didn't feel judged, exactly, but I did feel like Val was having a bit of fun at my expense. "It's not funny. You don't understand."

Val sat up straight. "Why do you think that? I know exactly how hard it is to find the one. I'm looking too."

What? I leaned in. This was a damn surprise. "You are? But women must fall at your feet. You could have your choice of anybody. Anybody queer, that is." I thought back to the restroom and our little moment. Val was fantastic-looking, and so cool and collected. My crush on Val would be in full bloom if I wasn't concentrating on the road the majority of the times we were together. But crushing on Val months before I left the city was plain stupid. I mentally pushed her away. "You strike me as a player."

Val was expressionless, but the way she looked away made me think her feelings had been bruised by my assessment. Had I insulted her?

"Maybe," I added hastily. "I don't know. Maybe not. Sorry."

The silence spooled out between us, but I wasn't going to be the one to break it. I'd babbled enough. Thankfully, our server arrived to check on us. I didn't want the night to end this way so I extended it by ordering another drink. "Could we get another round please?" I turned to Val. "Do you want to order some more food?"

"Let's decide after we eat these," she said, reaching for another fry. "Yum."

"Just the drinks then." I watched Val while she ate, unable to tell now if she had been annoyed by the player label. She'd been pretty accepting of my weirdness and then I had turned around and judged her. I sipped at my second martini, which had arrived in record time. The conversation had left me uneasy.

Val paused in her eating. "Tell me what you're looking for in a woman. I had a six-month contract in Anaheim, which is right next to LA, as you may know. Maybe I can hook you up with someone from out there."

"Really? Is that when you had your dream date? What was the name of that museum again?" The story of that date had stuck with me.

She studied me for a second. "The Getty. Yes, as a matter of fact, it was."

"When was this?"

"Years ago, but I still keep in touch with some people out there. So? What are your flags? Red, beige, or any other color."

Was Val serious? She looked so sincere, but I really didn't want to go there with her. Someone I could be interested in would have a personality that was very similar to Val's, but ideally would live somewhere in the greater Los Angeles area and be single and available. I thought for a moment. "Okay. I'm looking for a partner in crime, who's down to earth, and tired of games. She plays hard, works hard, loves to go out, but also loves to stay home. Her friends and family are really important to her and she loves to laugh. She likes candlelit dinners, cuddling in front of the fire, and long walks on the beach. Her life is fabulous—she just needs someone to share it with."

Val sat back and laughed. "You forgot—loves to travel."

"Oh right, everyone has that one in there." Just like that, things were easy between us again. Two veterans of the dating app wars.

"Congratulations, you know your way around the apps. I think you got every profile cliché in there. Now what are you really looking for?"

Christ. Val wasn't going to let this go, was she. I took a deep breath and nodded. "Let's see…She should be in the five to seven range for hotness, not higher because she can't be better looking than me, and I'm objectively at least a seven point five. Funny—but sarcastic funny, not fart joke funny. She should enjoy takeout dinners by the light of the TV and short walks to Anita Gelato or Little Beet since they're near my apartment. She has superficial friendships and hates to laugh." I snuck a glance at Val to see how my list was going down. "Tall but not too tall, not blonde and not a redhead. Well read, a good cook, and makes the bed with hospital corners. That last one's a deal breaker." I punctuated my list with a long swallow from my martini.

Val's mouth was open in shock, and then she closed it without saying a word.

I couldn't help it. I burst out with laughter. "Oh my God, did you think I was for real? I've been trying a long time. At this point I'd take someone with a pulse. That's it. One thing on the list. Be ambulatory."

Val's grin slowly took up her whole face and she let loose that machine gun laugh that I loved so much.

"Oh, and kind," I added. "Sorry, that's two things. Kind with a pulse. Know anyone like that in Anaheim?"

"Kindness? Now you're pushing it."

"That's me. Reaching for the moon." I drank the last of my martini. How had I gotten through it so quickly?

"You had me going there."

"What about you? What are you looking for?"

Val gazed straight into my eyes and said, "Someone who'll surprise me."

I couldn't have responded if you'd paid me several thousand dollars. Her eyes were everything.

She finally broke that thrilling eye contact and looked at her watch. "It's getting late. I have to get up early. Can I give you a lift? My ride is parked at Port Authority."

"Does your ride happen to be a Greyhound bus?"

"Ha, nope. There's a parking garage there too. It's the car you had your breakthrough in today. I picked up a last-minute lesson on the Upper West Side just before the show."

"I can take the subway. I don't want to be a bother."

"It's no problem. You're only a little bit out of my way uptown."

I relented. I didn't want to say good night to Val yet, anyway. "I don't have to drive, do I?"

One last barrage of Val's laughter, and it honestly made me light up to hear it. How could another person's laugh make me feel so good? "No, I'll do the driving."

We huddled close together to combat the November chill on the short walk to her car. The theater crowds had thinned and the streets were quieter. She had parked on the highest level in the Port Authority parking garage—the roof. The bus terminal was not a very tall building, and brightly lit skyscrapers surrounded us on all sides. I had never been up here before. I stepped to the edge of the building. You could see all the way down Forty-second Street almost to Grand Central.

It really was a remarkable street. Chock-a-block with chain restaurants, movie theaters, and souvenir shops, it was a blocks-long high holy temple to capitalism. At almost midnight, the number of lumens pushed out by the overwhelming signage made it appear as sunny as a June morning. I pulled out my phone and quickly panned from left to right, just catching Val on my screen where she stood beside me.

"It's possible I'll even miss Forty-second Street when I go," I said. "Gotta make some memories."

Val propped her elbows on the concrete wall. "There are not many places in the world where you'll see a spectacle like this. Maybe Tokyo—or Shanghai."

"What about Vegas?"

Val didn't turn her gaze from the view. "Okay, Las Vegas too. But that's all Vegas has. There's so much more to New York City."

She was right. And yes, I was swayed by her opinion, but it made no sense to weaken in my dislike of the city now. It fit my anti-New York stance to believe it was just as artificial as the Vegas Strip. I changed the subject. "Have you been to those other places? Tokyo? Shanghai?"

"Yeah. Not for work, though. As a tourist." Val turned toward me, and her face was bathed in the blue fluorescence of the Regal Cinemas marquee. "You have to admit, there is a certain kind of beauty in all of this."

"I can admit it all day long, but it's not going to change my mind."

Val nodded. After a minute she said, "I want to correct the record a little bit."

I studied her profile, but she refused to look at me.

"I was a player. You were right about that. It used to be all about the chase for me. I wasn't interested in settling down with one woman. I liked playing around, and my job also was suited for...short term stuff." Val turned, and her eyes were as serious as I had ever seen. "But that's not me anymore. It hasn't been me for a while."

"I'm so sorry for making that snap judgment. You didn't deserve that."

"But you were right. How'd you know?"

I could say something disingenuous right now, something false, so I wouldn't have to own up to my feelings. But Val had been honest, and she deserved honesty in return. "I was projecting onto you the one characteristic that would make me not be interested in you. If you played around, that would automatically rule you out to potentially date. For me. I mean...I know it's egotistical. I don't know if you'd even want to go out with me—"

"Hope," Val interrupted. "What did you think this was?"

"What do you mean?"

She gave a short laugh. "I mean if it walks like a date, and it talks like a date..."

I shook my head. "No. This was a last minute hey-I-have-this extra-ticket type thing."

Val simply stared at me.

"Oh." I let that sink in. "We're on a date?"

She let out what sounded like an amused grunt. "I'll admit, it's been a while since I've been on one, but I thought this came pretty close to the textbook definition, with the exception of you replacing my niece."

"But I *did* replace your niece."

"Okay, so slightly non-textbook. Anyway, the opportunity presented itself and I went for it." She turned and faced the view again. "The thing is...I like you, but I had no idea you were leaving so soon. Even if I was interested in no strings at one point in my life, my taste for hookups has lessened a lot. So…" Val didn't take her eyes from the McDonald's across the street.

"So this was a date but you're withdrawing your interest in me?"

Val shrugged. "You're about to move across the country."

My heart fell, which was ridiculous because two seconds ago dating Val hadn't even been a notion in my head. I took a step back and crossed my arms. "That makes sense. Good decision. I want you to know that tonight was the best date-that-may-or-may-not-really-be-a-date that I've had in a long, long time. Like before Covid long time." We started back to the car. "I guess that's pretty embarrassing to admit."

"I like that about you, Hope. You say exactly what you're thinking."

That wasn't strictly true. When Val had asked me what I was looking for in a partner, I hedged—twice. Why couldn't I be honest with her? And now I was letting myself think about Val as someone I could be with, and if she might still give us a chance. But I couldn't say that either.

After we got in the car, she said, "And it's not embarrassing. Good dates are hard—and as rare as a winning scratchie. That's why I used to skip them altogether, pick somebody up in a bar, and go straight to the sex."

My skin turned hot as I thought of Val going straight to the sex—with me.

"Our next lesson isn't until Tuesday evening. Think you'll be ready for more time sitting in my seat?"

It was several long moments before Val's question penetrated. "I'll be ready."

Chapter Five

A s soon as I stepped out of my apartment on this chilly November afternoon, I heard my mother calling from above. She must have some kind of sonar that told her when I least wanted to talk to her.

"Do you have any clothes that need washing, Hope?"

"No, Mom. I can handle my own laundry. Is that what you came out here to ask me?"

"I had no idea you were out here. I was checking the weather before your father and I go to our bridge club later, but I'm about to do a load of whites. You sure you don't have anything? I hate to do such a small load."

"I'm sure. Thanks for asking. Have a nice time at bridge."

"Did you eat yet?"

"No. I have a driving lesson. I'll eat when I come back."

"How's that going, dear?"

"It's going well. I actually drove on Saturday."

Mom raised her eyebrows. "And nobody got hurt?" She had so much faith in me.

"Not a single person."

"Well, if you're hungry, there's roast chicken and steamed broccoli. Come get some if you want after your lesson."

I couldn't help laughing. Broccoli just hit different now. "No thanks. I've got some leftovers in my fridge." The C&C sign and the black sedan beneath it pulled in by the fire hydrant. "Oh, there's Val. Gotta go, Mom."

"Be careful. I never thought I'd say this to a Mason, but drive carefully."

My spirits had been progressively lifting as the afternoon wore on. Not even a delay in the product launch I'd been working on for a month straight could get me down when I had a lesson with Val waiting at the end of the day.

She was standing next to the driver's side door and waved me over. "You're getting in here. You're not a scrub. No more passenger side for you."

"I'm not trying to holler at anyone from a car window."

For a moment, Val looked delighted that I caught the reference.

"It's okay. I was prepared for this," I said.

She didn't meet my eyes when we stood close to each other at the driver's side door. "How're your niece and nephew? Are they better?"

"Yes, better. They went to school today." She didn't seem as cheerful today. Her head was bowed as she walked to the other side of the car.

"Is something wrong?" I asked after we were both seated and belted.

"It's been a long day. I'm tired." Val had never said anything like this before.

"Well, all you'll have to do is sit there and look pretty while I drive you around for fifty minutes."

Her lips turned downward. "You'd be surprised how many men say that to me after they've had a few hours of lessons."

"Shit. I'm sorry. I was joking, but I can see it's not funny."

She gazed at me for real this time, and her smile was gentle. "It's okay. I may be feeling a touch sensitive today."

"Still, that was wrong of me." I was about to put my hand on Val's forearm but that would be worse, right? To touch her without consent? "I'm sorry. Is there anything I can do for you?"

Val glanced at my hand hanging there in the space between us like Thing but attached to a brainless idiot. "What do you mean?"

"You seem out of sorts. Do you want to talk about it?"

"No, thank you." She faced forward. "How about you turn on the car and tell me what you're going to do to get out into traffic?"

I felt a little stung, but did as she asked.

It was about fifteen minutes later, when we were sitting at a light, that Val said, "I'm sorry. I shouldn't take my lousy mood out on you."

"It's okay." I was focused on the traffic on Seventy-ninth Street. I couldn't talk about this now. "We can talk about it later if you want.

After I'm finished avoiding an accident with only the power of my mind."

Val chuckled. "You're doing great."

We went all over. The long ride up First Avenue went perfectly because all I had to do was keep the car steady. My heart started to pound when we crossed the Willis Avenue Bridge into the Bronx, but it wasn't that bad, and I even successfully changed lanes a few times without hyperventilating. The best part was we didn't have to merge anywhere. The thought of merging was this petrifying thing looming in my baby driving career and I was going to avoid it as long as I possibly could. I honestly didn't know how I was going to manage it.

Second Avenue was congested almost the whole way back to my block. I didn't mind stop-and-go traffic. Anything that kept my speed low was okay by me. "This is our last lesson before Thanksgiving," I said when we were stopped at a light.

"Right." Val was still moody.

"What do you do for the holiday?"

The question seemed to rouse her from her doldrums. "We get together with a bunch of my aunts, uncles, and cousins at my tia Lupe's house. It's fun—a big potluck-style thing and music and dancing after. We have pernil instead of turkey, and my dad usually makes it—" She stopped talking and looked out the window.

So much for that. At the next red light, I tried again. "Hey, do you have any more lessons today?"

"No," Val said on a sigh. "Thank God you're the last."

"Do you want to get some gelato with me? Spoil your dinner?"

"I don't know." Maybe she was trying to think of a way to politely refuse, but I would be psyched to spend time even with grumpy Val. Maybe I could help her with whatever was bothering her. She rubbed her hands on her jeans. "It's so cold today."

That was the best objection she could come up with? Please. "It's never too cold for ice cream. Come on. Anita Gelato is only a few blocks up ahead."

Val groaned. "How can I say no? It's your favorite."

She remembered. My heart did a little happy dance. But did Val want to say no? To ice cream? "I have many favorites—there are lots of good ice cream places on the Upper East Side. This one is great *and* it's close to my apartment."

"Tell you what. If we can find a parking spot within one block, I'll come. That's honestly the hardest part of my job—finding a place to stash the car when I need to be out of it."

"But we'll never find a spot like that! You know we'll have to drive around a while to find one."

"Those are my terms."

"Will you trade seats with me to park?"

"Nope." She wasn't trying to make it easy for me.

"But I don't know how to park yet."

"No time like the present."

If I could have, I would have looked at Val to gauge her attitude right now. But my eyes needed to stay on the road. "If you don't want to have gelato with me, you don't have to make up an impossible task. You can just tell me."

"It's not that. I was only trying to make it interesting. Let's just see how it plays out, okay?"

My response was pretty damn close to a harrumph, but I had to focus. We were quiet as we passed the gelato place. But then, out of the corner of my eye, just as we approached Eightieth Street, I saw a giant SUV lurch away from the curb. "Val! Val, is that a spot?"

"It is," she replied with disbelief. "Don't rush. It'll be there when you get to it, or it won't."

No fucking way was I losing that spot. I slowed, barely able to contain my excitement, and made the turn. The best part about the spot was that it was just past the no-parking zone, so I wouldn't have to parallel park. I could just slide right into it—which was exactly what I did. Once I put the car in park, I turned to Val, triumphant. "The universe wants you to have gelato! I'm buying."

"You're going to have to learn to parallel park eventually," Val replied with grudging amusement.

Not even that scary thought could bring me down. A few minutes later, we were sitting at a little café table in the nearly empty gelateria with some frozen dairy deliciousness in front of us.

"What did you get again?" Val asked.

I didn't answer. I was too busy watching Val's tongue sensually swipe over the top of her salted caramel and pistachio sugar cone, which I had to admit was a solid combination. Um…what had I ordered again? I dug my spoon into my cup. "Mixed berry pavlova and hazelnut chocolate mousse. Want a taste?"

Val gave me a look. What? Was that gross? Too personal? I'll trade bites with anyone I shared gelato time with.

"No, thanks. I'm busy enough with this." But Val stopped licking and caught my eye. "Thanks. It's exactly what I needed."

"Sure. Gelato cures what ails you, as long as you're not suffering from an actual medical ailment—particularly diabetes. Want to talk about it?"

Val let out a frustrated exhale. "It's nothing you can do anything about."

"But would it help to talk to someone?"

She didn't need much more prompting than that. "It's my dad. I came home to New York for two reasons. The first one is work-related, and we're not talking about that. The second one is my dad's health. He has osteoarthritis in his knees and was in a lot of pain. It took me forever to get him to see someone about it, and then a second forever for him to agree to a knee replacement."

"My dad had one of those too. He loves his new knee. He's sorry he didn't do it sooner."

"Well, my father hates going to the doctor. I've been holding his hand through the whole process, and now that he's done recuperating from the surgery, he needs to exercise the knee. But it's not happening. He sits at home all day while I'm out keeping his business afloat."

"Does he have a physical therapist?"

"Yes." Val's irritation increased. "And he's blowing off the appointments."

"That's not good."

"Tell me something I don't know. I'm a nurse. A medical professional, and he won't listen to me."

"Is there anyone he does listen to?"

"My brother. Sometimes." Val shook her head. "Typical Dominican stubborn-ass."

"Can you and your brother talk to him together about it?"

"We have. I'm at the point where I'm going to block out the times of his appointments so I can personally escort him "

"That will help his healing, but probably not your relationship with him."

Val seemed to deflate. "I know. I don't want to treat him like a baby. Why doesn't he realize this will help him?" She paused to take another long lick of her cone. "Anyway, I had just gotten a call from his physio telling me he was a no-show *again* right before your lesson. I called him and we yelled at each other until he hung up on me. You got the brunt of my mood. Sorry about that."

"Not a problem. And at least your day got better." I waved my plastic spoon between us. "Because gelato."

Val smiled. "You're right. This is excellent gelato. Now let's talk about something else. How are things with you? How's…um…your work?"

"My work? It's fine." I had no idea why Val was asking about this, but then, we knew very little about each other. Might as well start somewhere. Too bad Val wanted to start with the most boring aspect of my life.

"You're in marketing, right? What's that like?"

"It's pretty darn dull is what it is." I thought of something. "Hey, one of my accounts is BMW."

"Nice."

"Are you into cars at all? Besides spending all your time in them and guiding poor incompetent souls like me toward legally taking to the roads?"

Val shrugged. "A little, I guess. My brother is a lot. He works for Tesla."

"Oh wow. This is perfect. I've been invited to this reception for BMW's newest model electric car. We're doing the digital campaign for it. Would you and your brother like to come?" I couldn't have cared less if Val's brother came, but here was a pretty decent excuse to spend more time with Val.

She had leveled her gelato to the edge of the cone, and peeled her napkin away from it. "When is it?"

"Next Wednesday night." Not typically a date night. Which was fine because this wasn't a date.

"Okay, I'm in. I'll ask Arturo. He may be interested. Where is it?"

"At their dealership on the west side."

"He probably won't want to come into the city, but I'll ask."

"Where does he live?"

"In Jersey. Teaneck." Val pointed at my cup. "Your ice cream is melting."

"That's okay. It'll still be good." I had been so invested in arranging this let's-not-call-it-a-date that my flavors had dissolved into near liquid. And Val had finished her cone and was patiently sitting there waiting. When I spooned some more into my mouth, I was reminded how delicious it was and I gobbled up a few more bites before it could melt any further.

When I looked up, Val was staring.

"What? Is it—it's all over my face, isn't it?" I grabbed a napkin, my cheeks burning.

"Relax, your face is fine. You're just really enjoying it. It's nice to see." She cleared her throat. "I'll ask my bro and let you know at our next lesson on Tuesday. Or did you need to know sooner? To RSVP or whatever?"

"Why don't we trade numbers and you can text me when you know?" I didn't need to RSVP. It was a cocktail event and my whole team was invited, but most of them weren't going to stick around for it. And now that I had suggested it, I was desperate to have Val in my contacts.

"I have your number. From when you signed up for your lessons, remember?"

"Oh, right." My shoulders slumped. Of course, Val—or C&C Driving School, rather—had my phone number. I had received multiple appointment reminder texts from them. And here was Val gently reminding me that we were going to remain strictly professional. I had really blown it. Here I was acting like I had a chance with Val when she had expressly told me it wasn't going to happen. And I had to respect that because I was leaving.

I stood, unable to stomach anymore ice cream. "You can let me know whenever. I'm going to walk back to my place from here."

Val stood too, her gaze full of concern. I had gotten her to open up about her problems and now I was going to run off and leave her here. I was a complete asshole. "Wait a second," she said. "What just happened?"

"Nothing happened." That was exactly the point. And nothing was *going* to happen. I backed away. "I'll see you Tuesday. Happy Thanksgiving." And I turned and left.

CHAPTER SIX

Zoom meetings are the fourteenth circle of hell. Currently, one of my direct reports droned on about a problem with a deliverable that was entirely of his own making, and I was attempting to patiently listen without jumping down his throat. It was hard enough to come back from four days off without this bullshit. I was out of coffee, my breakfast had long since been digested, and here he was tap dancing on my nerves. When my phone buzzed with a text, I half expected it to be one of the other meeting attendees suggesting I find a way to shut him down.

But the text was from an unknown number. *Hey. It's Val.*

I unmuted immediately. "Let's put a pin in this, Phil. This doesn't concern the whole team and not everyone needs to hear about your inability to meet a deadline." Harsh, but true. It was hard not to notice how everyone—except Phil—perked up at my comment. "Everyone else, hit me up on Slack with any issues. Phil, I'll call you in ten." I couldn't click *Leave Meeting* fast enough.

Hi, I replied.

A few seconds later, I got another message. *I'm really sorry but I'm going to have to cancel our lesson for tomorrow morning. I have to take my dad to his PT.*

OK. No problem. Disappointment started tugging at my sleeve, but I elbowed it in the neck. It was a little alarming how much I was now looking forward to my lessons. Tomorrow would be seven days without seeing her, and now it would be even longer than that. But I knew how important this was for Val, and I would do my damndest to be supportive.

Another text appeared quickly. *Too bad. Was looking forward to seeing you crush morning rush hour like a boss.* Smiley emoji.

How did that make me grin like a goof? I wouldn't have taken Val for a user of emojis. *Want to schedule something for later in the day?*

Can't. Booked up. The gray ellipsis bounced around for a second. Then: *Next lesson is Thursday at 4PM.*

I texted a flurry of thumbs-up emojis and immediately regretted it. Was that as dorky as I thought it was?

Another message from Val. *Spoke to my bro about the BMW thing. He can't make it.*

Oh. That's fine, I typed. Did that mean Val wasn't coming eith—

But I'm still up for it if that's ok

Sure! I sent the details.

Want me to pick you up?

Yes, I wanted Val to pick me up. I would take any non-instruction time with her I could. But the universe was conspiring against me. *I'll be there all day beforehand for meetings.* Crying emoji. *You can come by any time after 7.*

Sounds good. There was a pause, but the ellipsis was still bouncing. Then—*I'm still thinking about that gelato. So good*

Val wanted to keep texting? I would happily avoid reaming out Phil for a little while longer. *Anytime you want a gelato buddy, I'll be there.*

For the next month anyway.

Why did Val keep bringing up my impending departure? *No. We can have dual coast Facetime ice cream dates. I'll drop almost everything for gelato.*

Val replied, *Good to know. Gotta go. I'm wanted in Harlem in twenty minutes.*

See you Wednesday. Hope it goes well w your dad.

Thanks. CU Wed.

I knew that goofy grin was still plastered on my face. I liked Val. A lot. The abrupt way I had left the gelato place had flitted through my mind repeatedly over the holiday weekend, and I wanted to apologize for that. My mushrooming feelings had no place in our professional relationship. Still, if Val offered a chance at becoming something more for the few weeks I had remaining in the city, I would not hesitate.

I read over our conversation. Did I really suggest ice cream dates—plural? Yikes. At least she had the grace to ignore that.

It didn't matter. Now I had something to get me through the next few workdays and marathon meetings with auto executives. And I needed to give some serious thought to what I was going to wear.

It seemed an age until Wednesday evening arrived. Our pitch had gone well and they liked what we had presented. Everything was on track for their latest luxury electric vehicle's release in six months. The reception tonight was for the auto press and for loyal BMW customers to get a preview of their new product, and they had put out a pretty luxe spread to go with the vibe of the car.

I was here in a purely social capacity now—I had already made the rounds, schmoozing with the C-suite types and the well-heeled guests there to inspect the new release. A few of my team were still here, taking advantage of the canapés and open bar. It was really nice to spend the day with them and work side-by-side instead of interfacing through a two-dimensional screen. These opportunities to interact in a human way with my coworkers seemed fewer and farther between. Once I moved to Los Angeles, they'd probably become even scarcer.

But I didn't want to think about that now. I was ready to have a glass of wine and hang out with Val. The reception was in full swing when she appeared. I tried not to break an ankle in my high heels as I all but sprinted toward her from across the showroom.

All other BMW models had been cleared out and six of the new luxury electric vehicles littered the space—each a different color. There were a few people checking them out and chatting with salespeople and execs, but most were hovering near the food and drink.

I put a hand up and Val saw me. It was as if all the moisture left my body as her dark eyes absorbed me like a sponge. I was glad I'd changed out of my pantsuit and into something more cocktail-ish. My little black dress was a real confidence booster. Val wore all black too. Black jeans with a black T-shirt and blazer. Even her sneakers were black. With her dark hair, she looked sleek and sexy. Very date night.

"Hi, you look fantastic." I leaned in and gave her a kiss on the cheek. I didn't care. I wanted to do it so I did, and it sent a bolt of pleasure through me to see Val's cheeks turn crimson.

"So do you. Gorgeous and a little fancy. I thought this was a work thing." Val looked me up and down again.

"It is." I didn't want to admit to dressing up for Val. And if she took a second to look around, she'd see I was the only one who looked ready for a formal dinner with possibly dancing after that. Everyone else was dressed in workplace attire.

"Well, you look wonderful," she said.

"How was your dad's appointment?" I led her toward the bar where there were pre-poured glasses of wine. "Red or white? Or something else?"

"Red is great." Val accepted the glass. "They worked him hard. He was sweating—as he should be." She looked around. "Are you supposed to be working this event?"

"I'm done for the day. Some of my team is still here, but we're all off the clock."

"Your team? You're the boss, huh?" The way Val said it sounded downright sexy.

"Yes, I am." Even if my job was boring as hell, I'd worked hard enough to take credit for my rise at my firm. "If ever there's some kind of marketing emergency"—I pointed to my chest—"I'm your woman." It worked. Val was now looking at where my thumb pointed. And her cheeks were still rosy. This was fun.

"Let's hope there are no emergencies tonight."

"Spoiler alert—there is rarely a marketing emergency."

Val's gaze rose from my chest to look me in the eye. "I'm a fan of powerful women."

"Good to know." I held her gaze. Our eyes seemed to be having an entirely different conversation than our mouths.

Val looked away first and nodded at one of the cars. "This is the product you're selling?"

"Yes. A new luxury sedan—electric."

"So, it's competing with what? Tesla Model S Plaid? Maybach EQS?" She cast a careless gaze over the vehicles.

"Yes. Both of those." I was surprised Val knew that.

"My brother is an electric vehicle evangelist." Val sipped her wine. "I guess I've passively digested some of the stuff he rambles on about."

"Do you want to check one out?"

"Absolutely. Arturo is going to be jealous."

Val followed me to the car at the far end of the showroom, away from the bar where most people were congregating. We were pretty much by ourselves as Val studied the car. "It's big. Long. Not really digging the color."

I glanced at the sticker. "You're not a fan of Oxide Grey Metallic?"

"Is that what it's called? Looks like sparkly beige to me." Val circled the vehicle. "It's a little odd, isn't it?"

"What?"

"You probably have to know everything about these cars, yet you hadn't driven any car before this month."

"I don't have to drive it to sell it."

Val gave me a thoughtful nod. "Have you thought about what kind of car you're going to buy?"

"Not really. I could probably use your help with that." I gazed at the vehicle in front of us. "It sure won't be this. We're marketing it more toward the busy-executive-with-a-dedicated-driver type person."

"Imagine spending all that money on a car you're not even going to drive." Val shook her head.

"Let's take a look." I pressed a button near the driver door handle and stood back. The door opened by itself.

Val raised her eyebrows. "For drivers without the desire or will to open their own door?"

I laughed. "Here. Sit."

Val got in, and then I pressed the button that closed the door before joining her in the front passenger seat. The dash was sleek and simple and the upholstery was soft leather. It was as quiet as a church inside the car—and although the interior was spacious, it was surprisingly intimate.

Val had her hands on the steering wheel. "Lotta bling. Comfy seats. It's just the teensiest bit nicer than my Camry." She adjusted the seat with the controls at her side.

After about three seconds, I said, "Let's sit in the back."

Val turned, her expression suspicious. "Why?"

"That's where all the fun stuff is."

By the time Val got out, I had hustled around to her side and opened the rear driver-side door, then got in after her, forcing her to move over. She was immediately drawn to the touch screen set into the door. "What is this for? Climate control?"

"Yes, and other things." I pressed the touchscreen on my side to activate theater mode. A screen dropped from the ceiling. It masked the front seats almost completely and spanned almost the entire width of the interior.

Val gave a low whistle. "Gives new meaning to a drive-in movie." She fiddled with the controls and quickly navigated to a panel that showed a range of streaming sites. The dealership had loaded it with all the options. Val clicked on one of them and swiped through a range of new releases. "Oh, *Woman of the Match*! I love that movie. Have you seen it?"

I shook my head.

"We should watch it some time." Val sat back and grinned at me. "Okay. I admit it. That's cool." She pulled her phone out and took a picture of the screen.

"The windows are tinted. You can watch in full daylight, if you want." I reached across her to the screen in her door. "Wait'll you see this."

In a moment, the seat in front of Val started moving forward until it was pressed against the dashboard, and a small footrest appeared. At the same time, Val's seat began to recline until she was nearly lying flat. "Holy shit. This is awesome!"

"Right? Traveling in style." I locked all four doors with a touch of her screen and moved closer.

"Where's the popcorn?" She settled in. "Just picture it. Watching movies back here while we're whisked to our destination."

"Who's driving?"

"I'm going to say her name is Shelly. She's an excellent driver, and knows how to keep quiet." Val laughed. "Can you imagine if I taught lessons in this car? I could get a really good nap in when I have an hour to kill." She gazed at me. "Thanks for this. How long do you think we can hang back here?"

"As long as you like." I had no intention of going anywhere. I rested my head against Val's shoulder and put my hand on her stomach. Val's intake of breath was quick and sharp. "Is this all right?"

After a moment, her stiffness subsided and she relaxed. She pulled me closer, draping her arm around my shoulders. "You know it is." Her voice was low. "That's the problem."

"Why is it a problem?" I curled my body into hers, stretching my knee across her legs, so I was half lying in the reclined seat with her.

She was silent, but at least she wasn't tense anymore.

"I'm trying to throw myself at you, you know."

A laugh sputtered out of her. "Trying? You're a major league pitcher with pinpoint accuracy."

But was she going to take a swing, or was I throwing grapefruits? She hadn't pushed me away yet. "Why can't we just enjoy this?"

"Right now, I have no idea why we can't." Val seemed to search my face for something. "I can't think of anything except for wanting to kiss you."

I didn't hesitate. I pressed my lips against Val's and felt a rush of heat burn through me. Her lips were full and soft. Her breath was warm and wine-scented, and I wanted more—a lot more. Val deepened the kiss, and a moment later I felt her tongue pressed against my bottom lip. I let her into my mouth, my entire existence right now was the silky brush of her tongue against mine.

I could feel the rapid thud of her pounding heart under my fingers. Her hand caressed my calf and slowly moved upward to rest just under my skirt on my thigh.

She pulled away slightly and said, "I've wanted to touch these legs since I saw them in that animal-print skirt. You have fabulous legs."

I wanted Val's hands to remain on my skin pretty much for all time, but I also wanted to touch her. There was altogether too much fabric covering her body, and I sat up to figure out how to remove even one garment, but what I saw in Val's dark eyes almost made me forget that intention.

There was a loud knock on the front driver's side window, and I scooted back to my side of the car so fast it was as if I had been tapped by a cattle prod. I paused for three seconds—running a hand through my hair—before putting the window down.

A man moved to the open window. "Ah, hi there. We wanted to get a look at the navigation system. Can we sit in the front? I think you've accidentally locked the doors."

I glanced at Val, who had figured out how to move her seat back to an upright position.

"Of course. How silly of me. We were about to start watching a movie back here." I laughed, and it sounded ridiculously false to me, but the man nodded and laughed too. I unlocked the door and stepped out.

Val got out of the other side of the car and retrieved our wineglasses, abandoned on a high table nearby. "You think we got away with it?" she murmured.

"Busted. Completely." Who knew—or cared—what those guys thought? I gulped at my wine. "Your face is still pretty red. How come I didn't know you get flushed when we kiss?"

"Because this is the first time we've kissed, but I'm hoping it won't be the last."

I twined my arm around Val's and headed away from the site of our very first kiss. "My God. Necking in the back seat like a couple of teenagers. But you're irresistible. Are you ready to go?"

"Totally ready." The smile Val gave me was sly and flirty. "Where to?"

"Would you think me forward if I said my place?" I asked.

"No, I'd think you were reading my mind."

The showroom was on the third floor of the building, but we still managed to get in one more quick kiss in the elevator. I couldn't get enough of her. "Did you drive?" I asked when we were out on the street. I couldn't wait to be somewhere private with Val again.

"I took the subway."

"Oh." We started walking toward Tenth Avenue.

"What?"

"We can't make out on the subway. Well, we could, but I'm always embarrassed for people who do that. Why would anyone want to kiss where everyone can watch and maybe film you, and where bums have probably taken a piss? But your car would have been a little more private."

"Are you saying that you don't have enough self-control to wait until we get to your apartment? You'd want to ravish me on the way there too?" Val laughed, but then turned serious. "Even though we just made out in a car, and I loved every second of it, I wouldn't want to make out in *my* car. It would color every lesson we have after tonight."

"You're right. How could I concentrate on the road when I'd be so distracted thinking about kissing you?" Val didn't say anything, and I snuck a glance at her face as we walked. Her expression was serious, a little pensive. "Are you okay?"

"I'm fine." Val stopped, and I halted beside her. "But I'm thinking about why I didn't want to go down this road. You're leaving in less than a month. That hasn't changed, has it?"

"No." I drew close and fiddled with the button on her jacket, unable to meet her gaze. "We don't have to do anything you don't want to do. I really like you, Val. Even if all we ever have is one very hot kiss in the back of a too expensive car, I'll treasure it."

"Why did you have to say that?" Val backed me up two steps and gently pressed me against the old, cold bricks of the building beside us. The leisurely, soulful kiss she gave me stole my breath. She pulled away and gazed at me through her lashes. "We're going to have a lot more than one very hot kiss. So many more."

I didn't take my eyes from Val's as I held up a hand and feebly called, "Taxi."

CHAPTER SEVEN

It took what seemed like forever for the cab to get us uptown. We sat close and held hands but refrained from making out. I'm sure the driver appreciated our restraint. But once I got inside, I threw my keys down, flipped on the lights, and shrugged out of my coat all at once. I turned to take Val's jacket from her, but she stood still and beheld the room we had just stepped into.

"Getting organized for your departure?"

"No." My front room had multiples of everything. Two coffee tables, three side tables, two sofas, several easy chairs. Beyond that, in the dining area, there were two dining tables, one shoved against the wall and another antique-looking one taking up the rest of the space. It looked like a furniture showroom. "Sorry it's so cluttered. Only about half of it is mine. The rest is my grandmother's. My parents usually rent this place furnished. They don't want to get rid of any of her furniture."

"You don't mind maneuvering around all this stuff?"

"It won't be for that much longer. Do you want something to drink? Are you hungry?" I pulled her toward the kitchen. "And just think—twice as many horizontal surfaces."

"The mind fairly boggles." Val's gaze returned to me and immediately smoldered. "How many beds do you have?"

"Just one."

"Not Grandma's?"

"No, it's mine."

"Show it to me?"

We bypassed the kitchen and headed for the bedroom. The bed was in its usual hastily made-up state, but the room was otherwise tidy enough. I'm not a slob. Val didn't seem to be looking at the furnishings anyway. We crossed the threshold, and I was in her arms.

"I'm glad we're doing this," she said as we stumbled across the room.

"Me too. I like you a lot." I think I already said that. Was it too much? It was true, though.

She buried her face in that place where my neck and shoulder met and inhaled. "You smell really good."

So did she. Like some kind of exotic flowers. The kisses she began to press along my neck felt delicious.

I slid my hands beneath her blazer. Her body was warm. I pulled her shirt out of her waistband and finally was able to touch her skin. Smooth, silky, and hot. "Can I take these off? I really want to see you." I stripped her of her jacket and tugged at her belt buckle. She put her hands to her sides and let me undress her. I wanted to be quick, but I kept stopping to touch each new body part that was revealed. She ended up finishing the job herself and then turned me around and unzipped my dress. She urged the dress from my shoulders and it dropped to the floor. Her arms came around me from behind, and she pivoted us so we stood facing the mirror above the dresser.

Our eyes locked in the reflection. I reached back to pull her against me. I wanted to feel as much of her as I could. The hooded look in her eyes was mesmerizing, but then they turned devilish and she gave a low chuckle.

"A seven point five," she said with a lazy grin.

"What?" I almost didn't recognize my voice—breathy and high and sort of embarrassing under different circumstances. But it sounded exactly like I felt.

"After the theater. You said you were a seven point five." She shook her head like that was a serious miscarriage of justice.

She cupped my breasts in her hands and then with her thumbs started to tease my nipples through the silk of my bra. But that must not have been satisfying enough for her because seconds later the bra disappeared and my breasts were covered by her hands. Darts of sensation traveled from them straight to my core. My body temperature must have shot up about ten degrees with how hot she was making me feel. I grasped at her thighs, needing to touch her too.

"You're easily a nine point five." She pressed a kiss into my hair.

Oh, how I wanted to believe her. She was doing everything right, and she was definitely going to get laid, there was no question about that. There was no need for extravagant compliments. "Easy now, flatterer. It's like you're trying to get in my pants or something."

I felt her smile against my temple. Both her hands glided over my stomach, and one of them slid about an inch below the elastic of my panties. "I've got news for you," she whispered right in my ear. "I'm already in your pants."

I heaved oxygen into my lungs. "Oh, God."

"Don't you know how beautiful you are?" Her hand dipped lower for one moment, then withdrew. Her fingers grasped my hips and pushed my underwear down my thighs.

With the last remnants of my brain function, I said, "If I'm so beautiful, why am I not a ten?" Seriously? What the hell was wrong with me? My childish need for a perfect score was rearing its head *now*? Of all times?

Val's laughter was like warm honey soothing me from the inside out. "You are one of a kind, Hope." She snagged my gaze and there was nothing but warmth and amusement in her expression, but then her smile lessened by degrees. "I have to dock you half a point because soon you'll be three thousand miles away and that feels really fucking inconvenient right now."

I turned in her arms. "Don't think about later. Right now is all that matters." We stumbled back to the bed and when we landed, I was on top of Val. I was going to make her forget everything except my name.

I woke to the sound of the shower running. A few moments later, Val emerged from the steam in my baby blue moon and stars bathrobe.

"You look so cute in that."

"You look cuter in that." Val nodded toward the bed with the covers all mussed.

"Do you have to go?"

Val retrieved items of clothing from the floor. "Yeah. Believe me, I'd rather stay, but I have a lesson at nine and I'm barely going to make it as it is." She turned her jeans right side out. "These clothes look all right for a second day, don't they?"

"How will your students recognize you without your C&C fleece?" I chuckled. "I'm kidding. Your clothes look great, and you look great in them." I sat up and let the sheet fall.

Val stopped and ogled my breasts. "You're not making this easy."

I heard my front door open. "Hopey?"

"Shit." I grabbed the robe Val had just discarded and scurried out to the living room. My mom was in the process of bringing in several bags from Trader Joes. "What are you doing?"

"You know how TJs is always a zoo. It's less of a zoo if you go early. No lines! Do you have room in your fridge for a few things?"

"It's way too early for this. Can you come back later?"

"Nonsense. This'll just take a min—" She stared at something, or someone, over my shoulder. Her surprised expression transformed into one of delight. "Hello."

"Good morning, Mrs. Mason." Val gave her a sheepish wave.

I stood back so I wasn't in Val's escape path. "You remember, Val, right? My driving instructor?"

"Yes, I do! Valentina. And please call me Cordelia."

"Good. Okay, I'll take care of this, Mom, and you can just go now." I tried to usher her to the door, but she was not having it.

"Just a second. I want to talk to Valentina."

"Her name is Val and she has to go. She has a lesson."

"Is that what she's doing here this early? Giving lessons?" Mom guffawed.

Dad came through the door holding two jars of tomato sauce. "Cordy, I can't find room for these. Should we give them to—oh. What's going on here?"

"Nothing." I exhaled dramatically. "Val was just leaving."

"Hello, Val. Nice to see you again." Dad lodged one of the jars under his arm and thrust his right hand out. "How's our girl doing? Is she getting the hang of it?"

"Hi, Mr. Mason. She's doing great. She'll be more than ready when she leaves for Los Angeles in January."

My parents frowned in unison. They both turned to look at me.

Val continued talking, oblivious. "I bet you're really going to miss her when she moves. But it's really not all that—" She finally picked up on their shocked faces. "Oh, no. Did I—?"

"Mom, Dad, I'm moving to Los Angeles." I held out my arms like a magician at the culmination of a trick. "Surprise."

Dad dropped the jar under his arm. Tomato sauce splattered all over the hardwood floor and everyone's calves. Still, nobody moved.

Val said into the silence, "I'm so sorry."

I grabbed her arm. "Come with me. Mom and Dad, don't move. I'll be back in one minute to clean this up."

Out on the sidewalk, Val kept saying how sorry she was. "I didn't know. You haven't told your parents yet?"

"No. I was working up to it." I bent to examine the sauce spatter on her jeans. Luckily, the drops were minimal and seemed to blend in with the dark denim. "I'm so sorry about your pants."

She ignored that and pulled me up to face her. "But you're leaving in a few weeks."

"I know. I'm actually glad you let the cat out of the bag. I had no idea how I was going to tell them." I darted a look at the apartment door. "I better go back in there. Are we still on for tomorrow?"

"For a lesson? Yes."

I momentarily forgot my traumatized parents. I tried to make my face alluring—like Catherine Deneuve-in-a-sixties-French-movie alluring. "Oh, are we on for something else too?"

"Do you want me to see if I can switch you to the end of the day? Then we can do something after?" She waggled her eyebrows in a corny sexy way.

"Yes! Absolutely. Text me the new time. See you tomorrow." I gave her a quick kiss.

"I'm really sorry, Hope."

"Okay, stop. It's not your fault. It's mine." I kissed her again, not allowing myself to sink into it like I desperately wanted to. "Let me go do some damage control."

CHAPTER EIGHT

I stood, wet and shivering, under the awning of a pizza place on the corner of Seventy-second Street and First Avenue. It was a gray, quiet, Sunday afternoon, and I was worried about driving in the rain. When Val approached, I shook out my umbrella and stowed it in the back before taking the driver's seat. It was a little incredible that I didn't have to psych myself up to do that anymore, but the wet conditions did make me nervous.

After our mutual hellos, the regular click of Val's hazard lights was all that filled the interior before she said, "How are your parents?"

"My mother's not speaking to me right now."

"That sucks. What about your dad?"

"He's very hurt and bewildered, but at least he's mature enough to tell me that. Let's not talk about it right now." I gripped the steering wheel. "Where are we going?"

"I was thinking we could venture out of the city a bit. You up for that? It means the FDR and the GW bridge."

I put my hands in my lap. "Highways? Merging?"

Val nodded.

"Are you serious?"

"You're ready. You can do it. And I'm right here. What do you say?" Val took my hand. It was warm and strong and I didn't really want to let go of it. Would I someday be the kind of driver who could hold someone's hand while driving? Instead of desperately holding onto the wheel as if my life depended on it?

"Now's probably the right time. If I die, my mother won't come to my funeral anyway." I let go of Val and adjusted the mirrors, grimly starting my precheck.

"That's the spirit. I mean about merging, not about your funeral. Now, we'll head uptown and make a right on Ninety-sixth Street."

I started the car. I put it in gear and began to pull away, only for it to lurch to a halt. A car swooshed by.

"I stopped you." Val pointed to the brake on her side of the car, her foot firmly planted on it. "I know you have a lot on your mind, but you have to be fully present when you're behind the wheel. Put the car back in park."

I did as I was told, heat suffusing my chest and neck.

"What did you forget to do?"

"I didn't check for oncoming traffic."

Val nodded. "What else?"

I turned to her, confused. What else was I supposed to do?

"It's raining. You need to turn on your windshield wipers."

"Right." I looked around for where that button might be.

Val pointed to a lever on the steering column. "Here."

I futzed with the switch until the wipers stopped freaking out and settled into serious rain elimination mode. "I'm focused now. I'm not thinking about anything but driving."

"Good. Let's try again."

I had never given a second thought to the FDR, a decrepit highway that hugged the eastern edge of Manhattan. That was probably because I'd only experienced it in the back seat of a taxi. It was a whole new ballgame when I had to navigate it under my own steam. As we approached the onramp, Val talked me through entering the flow of traffic.

"Put your blinker on," she said. "These people in the right lane know there is a constant flow of cars entering the highway here. They should slow down, and if they don't, they're shits who should have their licenses revoked. You're doing great. You've got a lot of room to move over. Here's your chance. Drift over to the left. Good! You did it! You can pick up your speed a little."

I took a breath. I was on the highway! Cars whooshed by on my left.

"You can stay in this lane for a minute, but eventually, you're going to have to be in the left lane to get on the Cross Bronx Expressway—which is a stupid name because there's nothing express about it."

"I have to get across two lanes? Into the left one?" My heartbeat, which had just begun to slow, now amped up again.

"Don't panic. You are broccoli, and you can do anything."

"I'm broccoli, and I can do anything," I repeated. When Val said it, I believed her. My shoulder muscles loosened slightly. And Val was right about the Cross Bronx. We were soon in stop-and-go traffic as we approached the George Washington Bridge, and I relaxed a little more. We slowly made our way onto the upper level of the bridge, where paradoxically, the multi-lane road opened up, and our speed increased. "I wish I could see the view."

Val's gaze didn't turn from the road. "You're not missing anything. It's gray and misty and visibility is terrible. These low clouds have obscured everything. Do you like ramen?"

"Yeah, sure, who doesn't?" I wasn't really paying attention. There was a truck bearing down on us the next lane over and my shoulders started creeping up toward my ears again.

"Don't worry about the truck. He's doing his thing. After he passes you, you're going to want to get over to the left again. After the bridge, we'll be taking Route Nine."

I nodded. Val helped me navigate the tangle of highway exits just after the bridge and guided me onto a lesser traveled local road.

"Welcome to Jersey," she said, after we'd driven for a minute or two. "Let's get an early dinner. What do you say?"

"Oh. We're not driving right back?"

"Do you want to? You're almost at an hour. I thought we'd stop, eat, and I'd drive us back into the city."

"Yes, let's do that." I exhaled with relief, more than ready to get out of this car. Val directed me into the large parking lot of what looked like a supermarket, but its name—Mitsuwa—was nothing I'd ever heard of. I steered the car to the back of the lot where there were a multitude of available spaces. "You don't mind the walk, do you?"

"Of course not. Any chance to get my steps in." Val grinned at me.

We ended up sharing my umbrella and running into the store, which I could see was stocked with all Asian products.

"It's a giant Japanese market, and its food court happens to have some pretty decent ramen. Perfect for a cold, rainy day like today. Why don't you find us a seat and I'll get us some food." Val headed off to one of the food stalls.

I selected a table on the far side of the seating area, right next to a view of the Hudson River and upper Manhattan beyond. And that's where Val found me, sitting with my chin resting in my hand, gazing out at the skyline and the gray clouds that pressed down on it.

"Great table." Val set down a tray with two bowls of ramen and a side dish of several deep green stalks of broccoli drizzled with some kind of brown sauce. "I couldn't resist. Broccoli's been on my mind lately."

"Looks better than my mom's, like there might be a few nutrients left in there, but I'm still dubious." I gave it a wide berth and drew one of the bowls nearer. "Look at the steam. This smells great. Thank you."

"Give the ramen a second. It's probably scalding."

"How do you know about this place?"

"My brother doesn't live too far away. His kids get a kick out of coming here. There's a bunch of claw machines they like to lose his money on." Val nodded toward the offending machines. She snared a stalk of broccoli with her chopsticks and began eating the stem end first. "It's funny because my brother wouldn't eat any of this—no sushi, no ramen, not even tempura. Who doesn't like tempura? All he'll eat is Dominican food, just like my dad." She tilted her head. "He might eat the broccoli."

I warmed my hands on the soup bowl. "What about your mother?"

"She died when I was thirteen. Cancer." Val was matter-of-fact, but there was a subtle change to her demeanor—a closing in.

"I'm so sorry, Val." Despite being at odds with my own mother right now, I couldn't imagine losing her, especially not in my teens. "Is that what made you want to become a nurse?"

Val gave a dry chuckle. "Actually, no. I hated the hospital when she was sick, and for a long time after. I came around about the same time I started watching *Grey's*. Calzona forever." She raised a fist for the pairing. "Then it seemed really interesting and cool. Science was my best subject, but I couldn't see spending so much money and time on med school. So, nursing. When I found out I could travel while doing it, I was sold."

"When do you think you'll get back to it?"

Val looked away. "Not sure. How about some broccoli?" She pushed the cardboard tray toward me.

"Will you stay with the driving school?" I speared a large, flowery piece with a plastic fork. But I had no knife, how was I going to cut it?

"I don't know, Hope." Val's voice had an edge to it.

"Sorry, too nosy. I'll stop." I shoved the too-big floret into my mouth and chewed for what seemed like seventeen years. "This is the most delicious"—I struggled to swallow before continuing—"thing I ever ate."

Val snorted out a laugh. "Unconvincing."

"No, really." My kingdom for a glass of water to wash this broccoli bush down.

"Is it all cruciferous vegetables or is it only broccoli?"

"I like broccoli. Why won't you believe me?" I stirred my noodles with a fork, not wanting to embarrass myself with chopsticks. Val, who sat there grinning at me, seemed an expert with them. If acting the fool with broccoli got me that smile again, I could ignore the damage to my dignity.

"Because of the dead look in your eyes as you chewed for about an hour." Val slurped some noodles then waved her hand in front of her mouth. "Still very hot."

"I didn't mean to pry. I'm sorry."

"It's okay." She clamped a slice of chashu between her chopsticks and held it. "Dallas during the pandemic was beyond hard. It tested my belief that humanity can be rational. It made me doubt my sanity. I thought I would be caring for patients for the rest of my life, but I couldn't deal with all that death, stress, and trauma. It sounds absurd, right? Healthcare means dealing with death."

Her eyes were focused on the bowl before her. My hand reached out to her, but she ignored it. Finally, she put her chopsticks down and looked at me. "A little piece of myself would break off every day. It got to the point where I had nothing left—camaraderie and adrenaline weren't going to see me through one more shift. And when it feels like you have zero compassion for your patients, it's time to hang it up. The hospital made me feel like I was a commodity anyway. It wasn't hard to say good-bye."

I slid closer to her.

She shook her head. "Even though the worst seems to be over, I'm not in a hurry to get anywhere near that headspace again."

"I'm so sorry, Val."

Her eyes seemed bewildered, and she reached for my hand under the table. "I don't know how you got that out of me. I don't usually like to talk about it."

I clasped Val's hand in both of mine. I wanted to hold her in my arms and replace all her heartache with comfort.

"Maybe because you'll be gone soon." She withdrew her hand and nodded toward the window. "Far away from that view. Starting your new life."

Instead of lifting me with hope for my new start, the thought of it brought only bleakness.

"Do you want to talk about how it went with your parents?"

"Not really. I don't want to think about them. I kind of just want us to go back to my place. Or your place. Whatever. I want to be with you. I know we haven't really talked about it, but—"

"What is there to talk about? You're leaving." Her voice was flat, but there was tension beneath it. "Now that we've started something, I'm okay with continuing it, even though it has a January first expiration date."

That was exactly what I wanted. We could subdue all these churning emotions by being as close to each other as we could possibly be. At least for now. "Let's hurry up with this ramen, then."

CHAPTER NINE

Five nights. We'd been together in my and my grandmother's little hybrid apartment for five glorious, deliriously intoxicating nights. By some kind of unspoken agreement, reached via osmosis or symbiosis, or a different -osis I wasn't aware of, we kept ourselves firmly in the present. We cooked and laughed and played together, and exulted in each other's bodies until we quivered with exhaustion. The past and future didn't exist. It was as if the garden level of 392 East Seventy-third Street was a tiny desert island, and we were its only inhabitants.

After that fifth night together, my mother was lying in wait when I walked Val to the door in the morning. She was sitting on the stoop, a black shawl wrapped around her head and shoulders, babushka-style, no doubt trying to make herself look as pitiful as possible.

"Mom, it's freezing. What are you doing out here?"

She refused to look at me; instead, she directed her gaze at Val. "Valentina? Would you please tell me what the going rate is for an overnight lesson?"

"Mother! Don't be rude. You're angry with me, not Val." I linked my arm with hers. "Please excuse my mother, she's not usually so obnoxious. You're just the kind of woman she's always telling me to bring home. Steady job, loves her family, easy on the eyes."

"That's nice to know, but I really don't want to get in the mid—"

"She said she's leaving January first, Valentina. Why would you even want...oh, it's just sex. A knockin' boots call, I think, is how they refer to it."

"If this were 1995, maybe," I muttered. "Do you mean a bootie call? Look, Mom—"

Val interrupted. "I like your daughter a lot, Mrs. Mason. If all I have is a few more weeks, I want to spend as much time with her as I can."

Her sweet words made me want to drag Val through the front door and back into my bedroom, but she had a lesson in forty-five minutes.

Mom sniffed and said, "That's fine. She has no intention of spending time with her family, so you'll be able to see her lots."

Val looked like she wanted to disappear.

"That's not true," I said to her, and then turned to my mom. "If you'd care to have a conversation about this, I'll be back after I walk Val to her car. There's hot coffee inside. Why don't you go in and warm up?" I pulled Val past the stoop and ignored my mom's pointed stare.

Val's car was parked in front of a school two blocks away. Teachers were already arriving to fill the empty spots.

I stood very close as she unlocked her car. "You're lovely. I like you a lot too, you know." I pulled her toward me and kissed her, languid and long.

"Man, if I didn't have to work," Val said. "Same again tonight?"

"Yes, please."

"Be kind to your mom. She feels like she's losing you." Her usual smile was nowhere in sight.

"I'll remember that." I stood there long after she'd departed, my thoughts drifting to how fantastic the last few nights had been. I wasn't avoiding a confrontation with my mother at all.

Since it was nearby, I stopped in at our local bagel place even though my parents usually only ate carbs on the weekends. Both of them were sitting at my grandmother's dining table with cups of coffee when I returned.

Dad took one look at my shopping bag and said, "Did you get lox?"

"And scallion cream cheese." I set about organizing our impromptu breakfast. When we were all quietly eating, I said, "Los Angeles isn't the moon."

"It's a helluva lot farther than downstairs," Dad said with his mouth full. "I can understand wanting to leave the city, but why not Westchester? Long Island?"

"Because it's not far enough," Mom said to him. She started to get up.

"Wait, Mom—"

"We're going to talk about this, Cordelia. Don't go off in a snit." His voice was almost at a shout. My even-keeled father never got this loud. Mom sunk back into her seat.

Dad gazed at me. "Why do you want to go?"

I paused to gather my thoughts. "My dreams were never that grandiose—even as a kid. I really didn't think I was asking all that much—a job that satisfied me, interesting stuff to do when I wasn't working, people who loved me and who I loved back. With the exception of you two, I don't have any of that."

Dad stopped chewing, as if listening and eating were mutually exclusive.

"I feel like my life has gotten very small here. Most of my friends have left. They're all coupled up and starting families. My life has become work and...I don't know, TV, I guess. I rarely leave my apartment. And let's face it, living underneath you two isn't doing much for my independence. I don't think I've bought groceries since I moved back."

My parents glanced at each other, as if this was something they'd discussed before.

"I have to get out of this rut my life has become, and the only way I feel like I can do that is to force myself to leave everything that's comfortable and familiar." I leaned in. "You've got such a good example for me. Don't you realize that?"

Mom wouldn't meet my eyes, and Dad's sorrowful gaze expressed confusion.

"How old were you two when you got married?" I asked.

And just like that, Mom lifted her head. I could see it in her eyes. She understood. "I was twenty-five. He was twenty-seven."

"You had me before you were thirty, Mom. You and Dad created a beautiful family. I should know. You're still taking care of me." I grabbed a napkin from the bagel place and blew my nose.

Mom's chair scraped toward mine.

"I'm almost thirty-five," I said. "I have love to give."

Her hand reached for mine and I held on to it.

"My life doesn't look the way I want it to. There are holes that need filling. And believe me, I've tried to fill them here, but it hasn't happened. I have to leave." I took a breath and said out loud what I'd only admitted to myself while sleepless at three a.m. "I love you, I love the city, but I'm lonely."

"Oh, honey." Mom wrapped her arm around my shoulders. "I don't want you to be lonely."

"I'll come back to see you all the time. You can visit me, too. This has nothing to do with you. I need to do this for me. I need a change."

Dad nodded. "I can understand wanting a change. It might not be what we want, but we have to let Hope live her life," he said to Mom.

"I didn't know how bad it was for you," she said. "I thought the whole driving thing was all the change you would need."

"It's a good change," I agreed. "I feel very empowered when I drive. Still scared some, but I'm conquering the fear. And I'll need to be able to drive when I move."

"Are you going to buy a car?" Dad asked.

"Yes. When I get out there."

"What about Valentina? You like her. I can tell," Mom said.

"I do like her. She's wonderful." Where had she been all of my life? And why was our timing so bad?

"Then why not stay and see what happens with her?"

"This is my plan. I can't just abandon it," I said stubbornly. I wasn't going to be able to do this if they threw Val in my face. Los Angeles had become the ultimate test. Was I strong enough to make a drastic change that I hoped would better my life? The only way I was going to know the answer to that was if I left.

"She seems very nice. Maybe she'll visit you out there." Dad patted my arm before taking another bite of his bagel.

"Maybe." I pressed my forefinger into the errant poppy seeds on the table and brushed them into the bag.

Mom used a butter knife to divide the raspberry cheese Danish I bought into three equal pieces. Like she had done since I was a little girl, she passed me the portion with the most filling.

And just like that, we were back to being an ordinary—conflict-free—family. Carrying on with their breakfast was their signal that they had accepted my decision. They were quiet, but clearly, they got it. For the first time, the thought of leaving my parents filled me with desolation.

"We'll have a nice Christmas together, won't we?" I asked.

"Of course." The cheerfulness in my mother's voice sounded forced. "We'll go to St. John the Divine on Christmas Eve for evensong. It's tradition. If you want, you could ask Valentina if she'd like to come."

"She'll probably be busy." It was one thing to invite Val into my home and cling to her all night long on as many occasions as she would allow until I departed for the West Coast. It was something completely different to impose myself on her Christmas. But if she asked me…No, she wouldn't do that. And anyway, Christmas was for my parents.

The more time I spent with Val, the more I wanted her to stay in my life. But I couldn't allow myself to contemplate a future with Val in Los Angeles, could I? It was an impossible ask. We'd only just met. Besides, she had her job and her family. She couldn't just leave. But it was so easy to get lost in daydreams of the two of us making a life together in the California sun.

No. The most I could hope for was a really nice conclusion to this little interlude of us. She was helping me let go of some of this bitterness toward New York that had become really entrenched in me. I could leave with an open heart. It was the nicest thing she could possibly do.

CHAPTER TEN

"We can't avoid it any longer, you know," Val said, her tone dispassionate.

I was resigned. "I know." I knew this day would come.

Parallel parking.

It was Christmas Eve eve, and Val had scheduled my license exam for December 29.

"If you don't nail parallel parking, you won't pass the road test."

I nodded. I still had a few hours of lessons to use up, and they were earmarked for parking practice and road test prep.

We were parked by the fire hydrant on my block. Val had put bumper protectors on the car. I understood why they were there, but I'd be lying if I said my pride hadn't taken a little hit at the sight of them.

"We're going to drive up to the office. I've set up a little parking practice area there."

This was a surprise. "Your office?"

"Yeah."

"The C&C office? We're not doing it here?" I looked around. There were zero open spots on my block. It made sense. "Where is the office?"

"Washington Heights."

"Near where you live?"

"Not too far." Val looked at the clock on her phone before sticking it in her pocket. "It'll take about twenty or thirty minutes to get up there. Except for giving you directions, I'm going to stay quiet while you drive. Then I'll rate your performance, okay? And the rest of your time will be practice."

"You're going to give me a grade? Awesome." Changing lanes, three-point turns, merging, highway driving—I'd become pretty comfortable with all of it, thanks to Val's excellent teaching. Parallel parking was the final hurdle before the test. "Be prepared to award me your highest score."

"I'll be the judge of that." Val's affectionate grin had me staring, and wanting to sneak a kiss, but then her expression turned severe and she gestured to the road. I focused on getting us there without any mistakes.

The driving school office was about as close to the northern tip of Manhattan you could go without ending up in the Harlem River. We turned onto a side street and on my right side, two black C&C vehicles with student driver signage were parked with space between them marked off with orange traffic cones. "That's where I'll be practicing?"

"Yes." She exited the car, moved the cones onto the sidewalk, and got back in again. "Pull up so that your side mirror is aligned with the second car's side mirror and I'll talk you through it."

"Wait, what's my grade? For driving here?"

"I'll tell you after you practice." She pointed to where she wanted me to go, and I obeyed.

"Parallel parking is a breeze once you have a few rules down. It's all about geometry. How were you with geometry, star student?"

"I aced it, of course." Star student was nice, but I preferred to be teacher's pet.

Val took me through the steps. It was hard to get those angles right. After my third attempt, an older man stopped to watch, leaning heavily on his cane. Val gave him a little wave. I hoped he would move along, but he propped himself against the building and showed every sign of settling in to spectate.

"You were closer that time. Good try. Pull out and do it again." She patted my knee.

"I'm getting a little flustered with an audience."

Val followed my eyes to the man on the sidewalk. "That's my dad. Don't worry about him."

"He's your father? I'm never going to be able to do this now."

"Why not?"

"He's like the principal of the school, right? Talk about pressure."

Val laughed. "He'd love to hear you call him the principal. Throw it in park. You should meet him." She lowered her window. "Pop, come here."

"No, please don't." I wanted to meet Val's dad, but not after failing three times to parallel park. But he slowly shuffled toward the curb, and there was no avoiding it. Val and I got out of the car, leaving it half sticking out of the parking spot.

"Pop, this is Hope. Remember I told you about her?"

"Ah, the one who has to learn to drive before she goes to California." His voice was deep and sonorous, with the lilt of an accent. My hand was engulfed in both of his as he shook it. I now knew where Val got her smile from—his was identical to hers. "Esperanza," he crooned in a smooth baritone.

"Come on, Pop. Nobody wants to hear you sing." Val turned to me. "Esperanza is Spanish for Hope."

"You have a lovely voice, Mr. Caceres." He certainly knew how to turn on the charm.

"Now I know why you are gone all night, Val. Mírala. Tan hermosa. Night after night after night I have the place to myself." He winked at me, and then turned his big smile toward Val, whose cheeks were a very cute shade of red.

"Why is your school named C&C?" I asked him, aiming to put Val out of her misery. "Is it for you and Val? Caceres and Caceres?"

"My wife and I started this business years ago, so it was Cesar y Camila. But now, maybe you're right. It should be papá Caceres"—he pointed to himself—"y hija Caceres." He pointed at Val.

"We can talk about that later, Pop. Hope is still on the clock."

"I'm struggling a little bit here," I nodded toward the awkwardly angled car.

"Do you know about the disappearing triangle?" he asked me. "Did you show her, Val?"

"I was just getting to that."

"Let me." He brushed Val aside, "Get in, Esperanza. Learn from the master."

My eyes blinked open and the clock said 4:12 a.m. As the day of my departure grew nearer, my sleep had gotten increasingly restless.

The middle of the night was now when I became anxious about all the things that were still on my to-do list and how little time I had left to cross them off. At least I had Val's regular breathing beside me to calm me and lull me back to sleep.

I sat up and gazed at her sleeping form. Our evening had been a series of revelations about Val's life. And it had all been wonderful, but I also had to try hard to not let my despondence sweep me away. After her father taught me the trick of the disappearing triangle in my side mirror, I had successfully parallel parked twice. Still needed some practice there.

When my lesson was done, Val had moved the cars into the little lot next to their office, and her father offered to take us to dinner. We slowly walked a few blocks to a restaurant called El Floridita, where her dad was welcomed as if he were the mayor. Curious people stopped by the table to say hello, and Mr. Caceres introduced me as if I were a long-lost family member. The staff gave us the royal treatment with a never-ending procession of delicious Spanish dishes, and eight hours later I was still stuffed.

Mr. Caceres told stories about Val and her brother at Christmas and all the traditions they had with their extended family here in Washington Heights and in New Jersey. It sounded like they had a good few days of eating and celebrating ahead of them. I had laughed a lot, but underneath the joy was a mournfulness that I had beaten back at the time but was now shoving its way to the front of my mind.

This idea I had been toying with—proposing that Val accompany me to Los Angeles—was now obviously a no-go. Even if no one had said it outright, it seemed like her father and everyone in the neighborhood expected Val to take over the driving school. When her dad waxed rhapsodic about finally being able to spend his winters in DR, it was clear Val would be the one running the business. It wouldn't be fair to even ask her.

"Why are you up?" Val's sleepy voice made me jump. She rolled toward me and grasped me around the middle.

"Sorry. I didn't mean to wake you."

"I can hear those wheels turning. What's going on?"

"Nothing. Just thinking about tonight." I scooched down so we were facing each other.

"What about it?"

I couldn't tell her anything I'd really been thinking. "I like your dad. I didn't know we had that in common. Both living with our parents."

"Yeah. You may have heard—it's not easy to find a decent place to live these days."

"Right. I have heard something about that."

"But at least you have your own space here." Val yawned. "It's not bad living with him. He does all the cooking. He's a great cook."

"That's a pretty good deal."

"Yeah, he's already started tomorrow's dinner, and Christmas too. We're bringing all the food and the presents out to my brother's place. Christmas Eve is just Arturo's family, my dad, and me. Then it'll be a big crowd of relatives the next day."

"Sounds nice."

We were quiet, but Val was still awake. I could tell.

"Did you...want to come with me? Celebrate Christmas with my family? You'd be welcome, you know."

"Oh, Val, that's really kind of you, but I can't. I have to spend the holiday with my parents." I moved closer and her arms went around me.

"I figured, but I thought I'd ask anyway. I feel like we have to make every moment count. We're running out of time."

We could have all the time in the world if she would come with me. I drew back so I could see her better in the murky light. Fair or not, I was going to ask. "Would you ever consider coming out to Los Angeles? You worked out there once, right?"

"I'll admit, I've thought about it lately. But I can't. Not for the foreseeable future anyway. I'm sure you picked up on my dad's succession plan. Even if it's not forever, I'm going to have to take over for a while."

I nodded and went back into her arms. Hopes dashed. I would not cry.

"I'm sorry, Hope. You make me think about all kinds of what ifs. But my reality is here in New York."

"I figured," I said. "But I thought I'd ask anyway."

"I'm glad you did." She pressed a kiss against my hair. "This wasn't what I imagined my life would become when I was a kid. I think my father has forgotten that he was the one who urged me to become a nurse, to see the world, to go far away from the neighborhood."

"How do you see your life?"

"I don't know if I'll ever be a nurse again, but I don't see myself teaching people how to drive for the rest of my life either. Right now, I feel like I'm letting life happen to me instead of making a life. Like you are."

"Like I am?"

"Yeah, you're taking control. You're not happy here, so you're taking steps to make your happiness somewhere else. I admire that."

How could learning that Val admired me feel so wretched?

"I just have to trust that I'm doing the right thing for right now." Her voice changed, became breezier, signaling the end of our heavy talk. "Maybe the universe will send me a sign when it has something else in store for me."

Even though we had gone against our agreement to remain in the present, I was glad Val had opened up to me. I felt even closer to her, and it made me want to give her all of myself.

She propped her head on her hand, and her voice was playful. "I'm pretty awake now. How about you?"

How did she know me so well? Here she was giving me the perfect way to express my feelings without saying a word. I cared for her so much. Could she see it shining out of me in this darkened room?

"Yeah, I'm up." I pushed her onto her back and straddled her. "Want to watch TV? Play cards?"

"Maybe later. Any other ideas?" She sounded breathless already.

"One or two." I licked her nipple and then took it between my teeth. Her swift intake of breath sent desire spiraling down into the deepest part of me. Los Angeles had a lot going for it, but it didn't have Val. For the next little while, I wasn't going to think about how much I was going to miss this, and how empty I was going to feel when I left.

A few hours later, after a long shower together, Val had to go. There was only one lesson scheduled today, but it was early.

She waited for me by the door as I threw on some sweats to walk her to her car. I opened a drawer in my grandmother's writing desk and took out a tiny wrapped package.

She eyed what was in my hand and said, "I got you a present too." She tilted her head toward the door. "A car."

"You did not."

She laughed and produced a gift from her pocket about as big as her palm, wrapped in red paper with snowmen all over it. Inside was a matchbox car—a white corvette.

I took it out of the packaging and ran it up her arm. "Vroom vroom."

Her smile faded a little, replaced by an expression I couldn't identify. "This is how I'm going to picture you. Driving along the Pacific Coast Highway or in Beverly Hills or somewhere, your sunglasses on, in a white corvette."

"Remembering to check my mirrors and my blind spot as I do. Thank you. I love it." I handed her my gift. "And here's something for you to remember me by."

She laughed again when she opened the box, but it was more of a sad chuckle. I had searched high and low and finally found it on Etsy. An enamel pin in the shape of a green stalk of broccoli. I had bought two of them.

I fastened one to her fleece, above the C&C logo. Then I put the other one on the lapel of my coat. "You've given me new words to live by—I'm broccoli, and I can do anything. I'm going to remember that forever."

She put her hand over it, her eyes melting with tenderness. "Thank you."

"Merry Christmas, Val." We hugged for so long, she was late to her only lesson of the day.

CHAPTER ELEVEN

Y ou've totally got this." Val's hands were on my shoulders, and her eyes were boring into mine as if she could impart all the wisdom of driving instructors immemorial through them.

I nodded. Val seemed uncharacteristically nervous—more nervous than me. We were standing on a windswept sidewalk in Maspeth, Queens, where many cars were lined up with test takers. Val took all her students here for their tests. She was on at least a nodding basis with most of the examiners and said they were all decent human beings, and fair.

I wasn't worried. I'd always been a good test-taker. And, thanks to Val, I knew my stuff—even parallel parking. We'd spent a lot of time on it over the past couple of days. The week between Christmas and New Year's always meant a lot fewer cars in the more residential parts of the city, and I'd parallel parked all over the upper half of Manhattan.

Yesterday, we'd done several test simulations, and Val drilled me on all the things I was supposed to do. I was remarkably calm. I had this.

"Remember, don't go over twenty-five miles per hour. But don't go too slow either. Keep it between twenty and twenty-five."

"Okay." That was about the fifth time Val had said that today. I was next, and a short man with a clipboard approached us. "Good morning. I'm Hope. This is my driving instructor, Val," I said to him.

"Yeah, we know each other. Hey, Rudy," Val said.

"Hello," he said to us. "Do you have your paperwork? Are you ready?"

I handed it over and followed him to the car. I got in and adjusted the seat, my mirrors, buckled my seat belt—did all the things Val told me were important for the instructor to see. Outside the car, Val gave me a double thumbs up. I smiled and waved at her, and she nodded a bunch of times. Then she stood back and crossed her arms over her chest.

I'd never seen Val like this. Her nerves were on full display. She so obviously cared about the outcome of this test. For me. She wanted only good things for me.

I pictured her with whoever she eventually found to share her life. Bestowing all that attention and concern on some lucky person. What an amazing partner she would be. There was Val and her mystery woman—going to shows with her niece and nephews, eating good ice cream, visiting museums, strolling home after an early dinner at their favorite restaurant on a Sunday evening.

But then I saw them mourning the closure of that favorite restaurant—which always happened to the things you love in this city. I saw them stepping into a brown, slushy puddle at an intersection in the middle of February—a puddle so deep there should be a lifeguard standing by. I saw them enduring delays on the subway, endless lines at Duane Reade, and the aroma of urine that pretty much lingers throughout all of July and August. I saw them walking together at night and both freaking out because a rat darted out in front of them on its way to examine a freshly tossed bag of garbage. And then I saw them laugh about it all the way home.

Well.

It was a good thing I was leaving this place in two days.

"Ms. Mason, did you hear me?"

I turned to the examiner. "I'm sorry. What did you say?"

"Whenever you're ready, please pull into traffic and drive ahead."

I put my foot on the brake like Val taught me and started the car.

Less than ten minutes later, I slowed to a stop right back where we started. I smiled widely at my examiner.

"Your results will be posted on this website by six p.m. tonight." He handed me a card and quickly got out of the car.

Val pushed herself off the wall she had been leaning against and tried to talk with him, but he waved her off after a few short words. She followed him for a handful of steps but then turned back to the car, looking absolutely flummoxed.

I giggled and ran over to her, nearly knocking us both off our feet with the force of my hug. "You're a fantastic teacher." I kissed her hard.

She looked like she maybe wanted to keep kissing me, but her need for information won out and she took a step back. "Rudy said I had some nerve wasting his time with you. What happened?"

"Oh, yeah. I don't think I passed." I grabbed her by her fleece jacket and planted another kiss on her. "Isn't it great?"

"But—"

"Looks like I won't be leaving on the first."

"Yeah." She frowned. "Why do you seem so okay with this?"

"Hey, you gotta move this car!" An official-looking person pointed at Val's car and glared at us.

I playfully dangled the fob from my index finger. "I know you were expecting me to drive us back into Manhattan, but I'm afraid you'll have to do it."

She snatched it from me and stomped over to the car without another word.

A pregnant silence permeated the interior as Val drove away from the testing site. She wouldn't even look at me.

About three minutes into our journey, I couldn't take it anymore. "Somehow I thought you'd be happier about this."

"Happy?" She exhaled violently through her nose. "I had made my peace with this. I was ready to let you go. Now you've just put off the inevitable. You staying around longer is only going to make it harder." Her fingers clenched the wheel like it was all that was keeping her from flying out of the car. "I can't talk about this now. I have to concentrate."

I put a hand on her thigh. "Can you please find somewhere to pull over? We need to talk."

Her mouth was a grim line, but she put her blinker on. "I know a place," she muttered.

She took us to a sprawling park that butted up against the East River. We found a bench and sat, the afternoon air frigid and a weak sun trying to make its presence felt beyond a thin covering of gray clouds. An enormous Pepsi Cola sign loomed behind us, the river and the magnificent midtown skyline in front of us like the establishing shot in the movie of my life. I'd never been to this park, but I'd seen the Pepsi sign countless times from the Manhattan side. Now here I was, with an entirely new perspective on my hometown.

A couple of feet of space existed between us, and Val was looking down at the pavement, oblivious to the view. "Rudy called you Speed Racer, but maybe he was exaggerating. There's still a chance you could pass."

"I don't think so. My three-point turn had about seven points. Must've been that shallow turn radius."

"But you're great at three-point turns." Val seemed dumbfounded.

"I also bumped the curb when I parallel parked and forgot to signal a few times. But what really clinched it was when we were stopped at a light on Grand Avenue and I asked the guy in the car next to me if he wanted to race. I probably hit about forty when the light turned green." I tried to stifle a laugh—Val seemed so agitated—but it came out anyway.

Her eyebrows were up near her hairline. "When you fail, you really fail—in spectacular fashion."

"That's what I'm telling you."

"But now your plans are all messed up."

"Plans can change."

"You're going to have to reschedule, and that won't be quick. You're supposed to be leaving in two—"

"Why would I want to leave when I have one very excellent reason to stay?"

She sat there with her arms crossed over her chest, her expression super serious. How could she be so stern when I was bursting with happiness?

Had she heard me? Did she understand what I meant? "It's you, Val. You're the reason to stay. How could I pass a test that's going to take me far away from you?"

"But Los Angeles."

I scooched over until I could feel her body heat through her jeans. "I needed to change my life, and you showed up. You're it. You're all the change I need." My fingers smoothed a strand of her hair that had come loose from her ponytail and tucked it behind her ear. "Such a good change."

Her deep brown eyes searched mine. "You're going to resent me for making you stay."

"You're not making me do anything. There's no reason to go anymore."

"You say that now." Her mouth was a grim line. How could I convince her?

"Living in New York is hard." I reached for her hand, and thankfully she let me peel it away from her body and hold it. "But it's also pretty terrific sometimes. I imagine the same is probably true of Los Angeles, or anywhere else in the world. Life can be fucking hard."

Val nodded. She seemed to be listening with her whole body.

"But if there's something that makes it bearable, or more satisfying—thrilling even, I'd be stupid not to want to hold on to it." I turned toward her. "You satisfy me, you thrill me, Val. I don't want to leave if you're here."

Her hand tightened in mine. "You're really serious right now?"

I nodded. "Before I took my test, I sat in the driver's seat and thought about who you'd meet after I left, and all the things you and she would experience together. Annoying, aggravating things, sure, but fun and precious and meaningful things, too. I want to be the one by your side through all that. I really want to see how this goes for us."

"I want that too." Val shifted so our knees bumped, and she pulled both my hands into her lap. "I've wanted it for a while now. It was really hard to be supportive when all I wanted was for you to stay."

"And that's the reason why I'm staying. Because you're absolutely worth staying for. It doesn't automatically make my life perfect— far from it. There are lots of other areas I'm going to have to look at improving, like my job, for instance. But staying—holding on to you—makes my life better. I'm sorry it took me so long to realize it." I kissed her, and she kissed me back with a fervor that was equal parts sweetness, sizzle, and sunshine. It felt like a bolt of blue on this gray day. I didn't know quite how to define what I was feeling—I only knew I wanted to keep feeling it.

"It's okay. You did realize it. That makes me unbelievably happy." Her smile seemed to detonate out of her—brighter and purer than anything they have in California, I was sure. She put her arm around me and I burrowed into her.

After a while, Val said, "What are we going to do with the cake that's being delivered to your apartment tonight?"

I sat up. "You got a cake?"

"It says *congratulations* on it and everything." She was rueful. "I jumped the gun. Congratulations are not in order now, are they?"

"Yes, they damn well are! How about—*Congratulations—you're staying in New York because you found an amazing girlfriend, and as for the driving test, well, you'll get it next time*?

Val laughed her awesome laugh. "I think we're going to need a bigger cake." She wrapped her arms around me. "Girlfriend, huh? I really like the sound of that."

"Me too."

We sat for a while. Thinking about all the possibilities that lay before us made me shudder. Or maybe it was just the cold.

"Should we go?" Val asked. "You're shivering."

"I guess. I kind of want to suspend this moment in time so we'll be able to come back and visit it whenever we want to reminisce about the moment we got on the same page."

"I've been on this page for quite a while." Val squeezed me closer. "It just took you a while to catch up to me."

"Now we can read together." I giggled. "Sorry for being so sappy."

"I really don't mind. What do you want to do now?" She stood and pulled me to my feet.

"I suppose I should cancel my flight and that Airbnb reservation."

We strolled toward the car.

"Want to drive?" Val held the fob out to me. "Even if you're out of lessons, you can still drive with a licensed driver."

I plucked the key from her palm. "Don't you have a policy that says if a student fails the test, you'll teach them until they pass? I seem to remember you saying that early on."

"That doesn't apply to people who intentionally flunk it. You were ready. You could have passed easily."

I stopped walking and Val halted too. The sun chose this moment to break through the clouds and it immediately felt warmer. With a hand over my heart, I said, "If you'll take me again, I promise to try my hardest to pass. And I promise I won't use my license to drive away from New York City unless it's something we decide to do together."

Val's arms encircled my waist and pulled me closer. "I think I want to hold you to those promises."

"Hold me as long as you like."

She laughed, and the sun was strong enough that she had to squint as she smiled at me. "I'm going to want to hold you for a long, long time."

"That sounds perfect."

And we got into the car and drove off into the sunset.

Two Women, Two Weddings

Alaina Erdell

CHAPTER ONE

A arti snapped the run of show back into the binder after she'd finished reading through the details of her sister's wedding for maybe the hundredth time. Everything looked perfect. It had to be. This was her big chance to prove herself as an event planner to her parents.

She'd followed her family's tradition of becoming a doctor, but her heart had always pulled her toward organizing and overseeing the momentous celebrations in people's lives. Her mother had never seen Aarti's dream as anything more than a hobby, though, and in their family, that made it so. Maybe *this* would change things.

Nearby, her phone rang. The name Taylor Mobley, the chef doing the catering for the wedding, appeared on the screen. A chill rushed over her. They'd long ago established what time Taylor would arrive, and Aarti had texted her the address days ago. "Hello?"

"Aarti. It's Erin Rasmussen."

She froze. It wasn't Taylor who greeted her, but her wife. Aarti closed the sliding glass door so she could hear over the crashing waves. Even in nice weather in the Hamptons, the swells rushed the shoreline, though they tended to be more bark than bite.

"What's wrong?" She grasped the back of a chair for support, her mind already spinning with potential issues and ways to rectify them.

"Taylor broke her leg."

This couldn't be happening. A bit offshore, a few surfers straddled their boards, waiting. "What do you mean?"

"And fractured her wrist. A gutter overflowed and rainwater accumulated on the restaurant's loading dock. She slipped and fell. We just got the imaging results. She wanted to inform you, but they've given her something for the pain, so I thought it better I break the news." The weariness in Erin's voice bled through the line.

Another time, Aarti might've inquired what type of fracture, but more important questions needed answers. In the background, Taylor pleaded for the phone.

"No, darling, you won't be able to do it." Erin's muffled voice was barely audible. "I'll tell her the plan. Just rest."

With a hand on her forehead, Aarti paced the small living room. Late afternoon sunlight glinted off the waves as they tumbled toward the beach, and a few fishing vessels sat offshore. But the stunning view didn't give her its usual solace. Not after this. "I'm sorry she's injured. Where are you? Is there anything I can do?" She tried to focus, but her mind raced. Maya's wedding was mere days away. What was Aarti supposed to do? As the event planner, she needed to figure out something fast.

"We're at Lenox Hill. It wasn't too busy when we arrived, so they saw her within an hour." Again, Erin spoke to Taylor in a soothing voice.

Aarti pressed two fingers to her carotid artery and watched the clock on the mantel. Great. Tachycardia.

In the background, Erin assured Taylor that she wouldn't be fit to cook for over a hundred guests, and no, she wouldn't hand over the phone.

Aarti assumed Taylor's medications had kicked in. "Well, let me know if I can reach out to any of my colleagues."

"Thank you, but everyone's been quite attentive," Erin said, her attention on Aarti once again.

"Good." Aarti had been so excited to forget the hospital on her vacation week, not that she wouldn't still be working, just a different kind of work. The fulfilling kind. But her heartburn flared as she contemplated the problem. "You mentioned you had a plan?"

"Yes, I spoke with the executive chef of our second restaurant. Josephine Samuels. We're sending her in Taylor's place. Her sous chef can handle everything while she's gone. It'll be an excellent test for him. Meanwhile, Taylor's sous chef can cover for her with my help. I've gotten quite adept at expediting. We'll manage without Jo this week."

"Erin, I respectfully disagree. She might be good, but this is an enormous problem, and I'm not comfortable throwing someone new into an event this important." Aarti pulled her hair from her ponytail and shook it out. A headache pressed against the back of her eyes. "I'm not sure how much Taylor shared with you, but she told her cousin she'd be here herself overseeing the food preparation. Jackson and my sister have planned not one wedding, but two, with Christian and Hindu ceremonies, and there are separate menus for everything." She threw the hair tie. "Catering one wedding is hard enough. How am I supposed to deal with an unknown chef? I can't serve pigs in a blanket at the reception when everyone will be expecting traditional Indian food." Even as she finished her tirade, she couldn't come up with a better solution.

"Yes, yes, of course. That's the good news. Jo helped Taylor choose the Indian dishes for the menu."

Aarti bit her lip. What choice did she have? If they trusted this Jo woman, maybe it wasn't quite doomsday yet. "But what about the rehearsal dinner and the rest of the week's meals? What about supervising the catering team and setting up the outdoor kitchen?" She turned back to the view. Dark clouds to the north threatened rain. Fine, it could rain all it wanted today, but if a drop fell the rest of the week, she'd have something to say to more than one deity.

"Jo's seen all the menus, and she can cook anything. And remember, the catering team under her will remain the same, so you'll have that consistency. Taylor worked for the owner when she was in school. They're professionals and do this all the time. Hold, please." Again, Erin spoke to Taylor in a hushed voice.

Aarti drummed her fingers against the window.

"Taylor says they know how to erect the outdoor tent and kitchen faster than, well, she mentioned some elephant and circus analogy that would make more sense if you could see the state she's in."

Aarti pressed her forehead to the cool glass. Maya would never consider postponing the wedding, not with so many relatives flying in to attend. "We don't have any other options, do we?" She'd hoped this event would go off without a hitch so her parents would respect her talents. How foolish she'd been.

Erin sighed. "I could drive Taylor to the Hamptons and park her on a stool to bark orders, but she'd be limited in what she could do. I think Jo's a better option, and selfishly, I think Taylor should take it easy."

"You're right. Taylor needs to rest and recover." Aarti rubbed her temple. "I'm sorry. I'm trying to wrap my head around this and make sure the event is successful. I'm sure Taylor wants that, too."

"She does." Erin said. "Jackson's her favorite cousin, and she feels terrible—*yes, darling, I just told her he's your favorite cousin. No, I'm not telling her that*—and she wanted to be the caterer as her gift to him. We still plan to attend the weddings, or at least as much of the day as she can handle. I'm going to rent a wheelchair for her."

"He'll be glad to see her. Have you told him yet?" Aarti hoped she didn't have to be the one to break the news to Jackson and Maya.

"Yes, I spoke with him right before I called you."

Aarti turned from the window with its graying sky and sank into a corner of the sofa. "When can I expect Jo?"

"She plans to be there at nine, just like Taylor had. I'll run the binder with the run of show, menus, and recipes over to her once I get this one home and settled, though I'm sure Jo knows them by heart." Erin cleared her throat. "I know this development makes things stressful for you, but know we're sending you the next best."

"Thank you." She appreciated the sentiment. "If Jo's as good as you make her out to be, we should survive."

"I think you'll do better than that, but you'll meet her tomorrow. I'm sorry, they're getting ready to release Taylor, so I need to go, but please call me if I can be of any help."

Erin recited her number, and Aarti saved it to her phone.

"Give Taylor my best. And thanks for finding a solution." Aarti hung up and leaned against the sofa's arm. She'd done minor events, even a few weddings, but this was her biggest function to date. It was supposed to show her family how capable she was, how organized, how she'd spent months, even years, planning the smallest detail. And now, it appeared to be in limbo.

Perhaps Taylor was right. It seemed like a circus.

The crunch of gravel alerted Aarti a car had arrived at the guest cottage on her parents' Southampton property. After checking the buttons of her blouse aligned with the fly of her slacks, she stepped onto the small porch and shielded her eyes from the glare of the sun off the SUV's window.

A woman, presumably Jo Samuels, retrieved something from the rear seat, and her form-fitting jeans concealed little of her muscular physique. Aarti's gaze traversed tight thighs and calves and stopped at the most audacious socks peeking above the woman's Crocs. Fluorescent yellow, dotted with unwrapped Hershey's kisses, or—Aarti blinked a few times—nope, poop emojis.

It was going to be a long week.

Jo straightened and swung the door closed. She held a large duffel and a tote with a binder protruding from it. Her black tank hugged her torso, revealing she wore no bra, and an electric guitar decorated the front, the neck curving over one breast. Her hair, light brown at the roots and blond at the tips, shot out haphazardly in various directions in a manner that seemed intentional. Her piercing blue eyes claimed the status of most striking feature and seemed to take in Aarti much like she'd done moments before.

"I was told to stop at the little house. Am I in the right place?" Jo halted a few feet away. Her eyes were even bluer this close, like the depths of a drop-off beyond a sandbar.

Aarti snapped to attention and extended her hand. "You are. I'm Aarti Singh, the event planner."

Jo shifted the tote, so both bags hung from one shoulder. "Jo Samuels. Nice to meet you. I'm filling in for Taylor."

Her grip was firm, as if daily use had strengthened her hands. Aarti's fingertips grazed over small callouses on Jo's palm as she pulled away. Her runaway mind went to what they might feel like on other parts of her before she shoved the thoughts aside.

She focused. "I'm sorry to hear about Taylor. Thanks for volunteering."

Something passed over Jo's face. "I'm not volunteering. Taylor and Erin are my bosses. I go where they say."

Aarti bristled. "Well, I'm sorry to inconvenience you, but—"

"That came out wrong." Jo leaned against the handrail. "I'm happy to do what they ask. They've been generous, and if I can help you out this week, I'm glad." She slowly smiled. "Even more glad now that I'm here."

Was she flirting? Aarti took a step back. It was going to be difficult getting through the next handful of days working with a woman she was attracted to. She didn't need Jo hitting on her to complicate matters.

"Let me show you where you'll be staying." Aarti crossed the porch and opened the door to the second unit, identical to the one she'd exited. Once inside, she turned in a circle. "It's not huge, but you have it to yourself. As you can see, there's a kitchenette, not that you'll probably want to cook once you're done for the day. Snacks are in the cupboard. And there's a king bed and a full bath through there."

Instead of checking out the bedroom, Jo dropped her bags on the floor and wandered through the living area to the sliding glass doors. "Whoa, look at that view. I'm staying here?" Her expression held childlike wonder.

Aarti had to smile. "Yes, it's my parents' guest house." She opened the slider, and they stepped outside. "You're welcome to use the deck." She motioned across a low wall covered in wooden shakes, splitting the area in half. "I'll be staying on the other side if you need anything."

Jo glanced past her, where her bikini hung over a chaise lounge. "Is that yours?" The gleam in her eyes returned.

Aarti's cheeks warmed. "It needed to dry. Let's go back inside."

Jo tested the thick cushion of the lounge chair. "This is almost as big as a twin bed." She trailed her hand over the headrest. "I might sleep out here so I can hear the waves."

As they stepped inside, Aarti shook away the image of Jo sleeping a dozen feet away, only a pane of glass between them. "Why don't you get changed? I'll be next door. Just knock when you're ready."

But before they reached the middle of the room, Jo bent over, and unable to stop in time, Aarti grabbed Jo's hips to keep from slamming into her.

"I'm so sorry. I didn't know you were stopping."

A subtle scent surprised her, a perfume but not floral. Its notes were fresh and redolent of cardamom. Aarti glanced at her hands, still holding onto Jo's jeans. She ripped them away.

Jo straightened, shook out a chef's coat, and shrugged into it.

Aarti, mesmerized, watched her deftly push knots through buttonholes and then roll the sleeves over her sculpted forearms. Tattoos she hadn't noticed marked the soft insides of Jo's arms. Two crossed knives and what looked like an herb.

Aarti gave a start. She'd forgotten she was supposed to be leaving. When she looked up, Jo grinned. It seemed too late to do anything besides hope the burning tips of her ears weren't evident.

From her bag, Jo withdrew a bandana that matched her eyes, folded it against her thigh, and tied it on like a headband. After retrieving a long black case from her duffel and the binder from the tote, she nodded. "I'm good to go. Put me to work."

"What's the black thing?" Anything to stop the intense eye contact.

Jo ripped open the Velcro flap. She'd slotted a dozen shiny knives under elastic straps. "My babies." She rolled it up. "Where to?"

"I'll give you a quick tour. Hopefully, Taylor mentioned you'll be doing on-site catering. The rest of the crew, minus the servers, is due this morning, along with the appliances for the outdoor kitchen. You'll be in charge of all of it."

"Whatever you need. I'm yours this week."

Aarti clenched her jaw as she opened the door. At any other event, she wouldn't mind working together because she couldn't seem to keep her eyes off Jo. However, her parents would be scrutinizing her every move in the next few days, and she had important things to do. *Whatever you need. I'm yours this week* was the last thing she needed to hear from a woman she found attractive.

They picked their way up the path toward the contemporary house her parents had built. Had it already been a dozen years ago?

"Seating for both ceremonies will begin a few yards past the swimming pool. During the Christian ceremony, the couple will be married under an elaborate trellis with the ocean as the backdrop. Did you find the run of show in Taylor's binder?"

Jo shaded her eyes. "Yeah, though I focused on anything food-related and only skimmed the rest."

"That's fine." She glanced back. "I'll give you an updated ROS later. I need to be down here to direct arriving deliveries this morning."

Jo stared at the water. "I can't get over this view. It's gorgeous here."

Aarti looked out over the water and took in the scenery with her. Strands escaped her ponytail and blew across her eyes. She tucked them behind her ear. "After the Christian ceremony, you'll serve food during the intermission while we switch décor." She gestured to the seaward side of the house. "The procession for the Hindu ceremony will start over here, meander around the exterior, and end over there."

"What about a mandap? Are you planning to use the trellis for that, too?"

Aarti caught her toe as she cut across the lawn, but regained her balance. She stopped to look at Jo. "How do you know about that?" Most of the non-Indian Americans she knew had no idea of what took place during an Indian wedding, let alone knew the name of the structure under which the bride and groom were married.

"I was an exchange student in France my junior year. The family I lived with owned a popular Indian restaurant in the 10th Arrondissement. Their eldest daughter's arranged marriage took place while I was there."

"Is that how you learned to cook Indian food?"

"Yeah. I quickly learned to make the family's favorites. When Mademoiselle Mathur noticed my interest in cooking, she took me to work with her when I wasn't in school and taught me how to make the restaurant's dishes." Jo rubbed her forearm and grinned. "I didn't have hair on my arms for months because of the tandoori oven. But I got paid in kulfi or pretty much any food I wanted."

Her smile was pleasant, and Aarti returned it. Jo's abdomen didn't look like she indulged in sweets. "Ice cream, huh? You're easy to please." Trained in Indian cooking? She wanted to shake her head. Erin could've mentioned that. Still, dishes varied across India, let alone in other countries. She'd judge for herself.

"I'd like to think so. I'm pretty laid-back. Not much rattles me."

She hoped that was the case because Jo was about to get very busy, and she'd better be able to handle it. "You say that now, but I hope you realize Indian weddings are multi-day affairs. As in, many people are going to need to eat all throughout this week. And almost nothing is more important than the quality of the food served."

"Got it, boss."

She prickled at the moniker. "Please call me Aarti." It would be refreshing to hear someone use her first name, since so few did. "Here, between the house and the ocean, they'll erect the reception tent where the guests will dine and dance. Because we'll be so spread out, I'll give you a walkie-talkie so we can communicate." She headed toward the large deck off the kitchen.

"Can't we just call each other?"

Aarti climbed the stairs. "I need instant communication. If you don't hear your phone ring or vibrate, I can't be running back and forth to get an ETA on the food or tell you what I need." She gestured. "This is where you'll set up the outdoor kitchen. The tent is almost the same size as the deck, and the wood grills and tandoori ovens can go on the pavement. All the other appliances should be electric. We'll be using multiple generators, both here and at the reception tent."

"What about more lighting?" Jo glanced at the two security lights below the eaves.

"You'll also have generator-run lights, inside the tent and out, for after the sun sets."

Jo dropped her knives and binder on the table, leaned on the railing, and looked out toward the cottage. "Thanks for letting me stay here. I'd hate to drive over four hours round trip to Manhattan each day or try to find a vacant room with such late notice."

With the sun on her face and the wind rippling her hair, she was even more striking.

Jo turned. "I'm sure your guests are occupying most of them around here."

Caught staring, Aarti startled. "You're welcome. And yes, they are. Many are staying at a resort, but some opted for Airbnbs." She looked toward the horizon. "Like you said, the view is gorgeous, and I hope you find time to enjoy it." She faced Jo. "One thing though, while I realize there's a lot to do, I need you to follow labor laws, both for yourself and those working for you."

"Not an issue. My staff would tell you I'm a stickler about that." Jo folded her arms. "There's a difference between being laid-back and taking advantage of people. But if I feel the work can't be done with the number of people I'm given, we'll have to discuss bringing on another person or two."

While she agreed, Aarti didn't want the cost of the event to increase. Showing her parents she could operate under budget was essential. Taylor hadn't charged them for her role, calling it her wedding gift, and Aarti doubted she'd rescind her offer because she couldn't personally cater it. Jackson was her cousin, after all—favorite cousin, Erin had said. And he'd told Aarti that Taylor had been the person who supported him the most after his accident.

"Do you think the staff we have can handle food for six hundred and forty-five guests?" She kept her expression stoic.

Jo swayed and grasped the railing. "Taylor said a hundred."

"Just testing your inability to be rattled." Aarti grinned. "Yes, it'll be around a hundred guests. Ready to see the main kitchen?"

Jo blew out a breath and slapped her hand over her heart. "The restaurant only does a hundred and fifty covers on a busy night. You scared me. Mean." She winked and picked up her belongings.

Not mean, but against her better judgment when she needed to keep things professional. What had possessed her to flirt, especially being so out of practice? At least Jo's wink had held amusement.

❖

Aarti's parents had remodeled the kitchen last winter, though they claimed it wasn't because of Maya's nuptials. She knew better. They went to great lengths for their younger daughter who did no wrong.

Yesterday, Aarti had brightened the lifeless stainless steel appliances and granite countertops with large bowls of lemons and limes, and arranged overflowing bunches of cilantro on the island workstation, in the small breakfast nook, and on the sideboard coffee station. A citrusy fragrance filled the air.

"You can leave your things here. Family members might pop in to make themselves coffee or tea, but no one will disturb them. And there's a mini fridge with milk and creamer," she opened a cupboard, "so they have no excuse to be underfoot over there."

Jo wandered around the island. She opened the refrigerator, glanced inside, then closed the door. She gestured toward the pantry with its frosted glass window. "May I?"

"Go ahead."

Jo stepped inside. "Wow. This is half the square footage of my apartment."

She laughed. "Obnoxious, isn't it? If my parents ever filled it, they'd look like those people with bunkers loaded for the apocalypse. At least you'll have plenty of room for the dried, canned, and jarred goods." She grew serious. "Which reminds me. I have until two today to place my food order for a next-day delivery. Let me get my laptop so we can determine what you need."

Jo shut the pantry. "I made a list last night, so you'll just have to input the items."

Aarti stared at her. "What time did Erin call you?"

"I don't know." Jo shrugged. "Five?"

Impressed only scratched the surface. "You somehow wrote your order, packed, and arranged a rental car between five and whenever you went to bed?"

Jo tilted her head. "No, I worked last night and didn't get out of there until eleven, so I did it after that."

"I appreciate your initiative." She touched Jo's arm to convey her sincerity. "That's enormously helpful. May I see it?"

While Jo found her list, Aarti ducked into the formal dining room to retrieve her laptop. Neat piles of paper covered the table. While the arrangement might not make sense to anyone else, it did to her. She'd threatened her family, including Jackson, if they moved anything.

When she returned, Jo sat at the banquette in the breakfast nook. She'd laid out two sheets filled with small, neat handwriting.

Jo turned the lists toward her. "Taylor said the wedding cake and the Indian sweets were special order."

"Yes, and the chocolate truffles. But you don't have to worry about those."

"Not even plating them?"

"Nope. I've hired an Indian bakery. What they can't make ahead, they'll finish on site. For instance, they'll serve the gulab jamun and halwa hot. I plan to station the two of them in the downstairs kitchenette so you won't be competing for space."

Jo's expression held a hint of amusement. "Of course, there's another kitchen. And the wedding cake?"

"I've hired a bakery that blends Eastern and Western concepts. Maya and Jackson chose a pistachio flavored cake with mango filling and saffron buttercream. The bakers will cover it with edible paper designs resembling the henna patterns brides have painted on their skin."

"Sounds delicious." Jo leaned forward. "I hope I get to try it."

Aarti smiled. "With kulfi?"

Jo licked her bottom lip. "I never turn down ice cream."

Aarti thanked Krishna she was sitting, or her knees would have given out at the sight of Jo's tongue making that sensual sweep. She pulled up the food distributor's website. "In the meantime, use what you find in the cupboards, refrigerator, and pantry. I want you to prepare six Indian dishes, all savory. I'd like three of them to be vegetarian. The others may contain chicken, turkey, or fish."

"Why those three?" Jo didn't seem to flinch at being asked to cook on the spot.

"Because I'll be the one determining how well you cook Indian food, and those are my preferred animal proteins." She began to input the order.

Jo hadn't moved. "Are you sure? I make a great goat—"

"I'm a cardiologist, and I've seen enough heart disease. I eat those three." It came out sharper than intended.

Jo's back hit the banquette. "You're a doctor?"

She seemed to care more about that than which types of meat have the most saturated fat.

"Yes." Aarti typed basmati rice in the search field.

"Planning a wedding, let alone two, is an enormous task. What made you offer to do that for your sister?" Jo shook her head, as though in disbelief.

Afraid of making an error on the order under Jo's questioning, or simply by her presence, she pushed her laptop away. They didn't need enough rice to feed all of East Hampton. "I didn't. I've been an event planner for a few weddings, and I've done other events as well. It's always something I've been interested in."

"But you became a cardiologist." Jo's eyes narrowed.

Aarti refused to have a prolonged conversation about this volatile topic in her parents' kitchen. "I'm the Indian daughter of two surgeons. And the eldest, which comes with even greater pressure." She shifted in her seat. "So, it's complicated. Now, how about those dishes?"

Jo seemed to take the hint. "Got it. Sorry, boss—Aarti." She stood. "Do you have any requests? Most of what I know how to make are North Indian dishes. Are those acceptable?"

Aarti tapped the touch pad to wake the screen. "Yes. I gave you my requirements. The remaining decisions are yours." She wanted to see how Jo responded, if the head of her catering team could think on her feet.

Within minutes, Jo had emptied the refrigerator of half its contents. Aarti hadn't moved. She hadn't even looked away, though the island had blocked most of her view of Jo's jean-clad lower half. All her stuff was in the dining room, but something made her stay besides being able to watch the driveway for deliveries. She rested her chin in her hand. Besides flirting like a hormonal teen, something made her want to be near Jo.

CHAPTER TWO

From the breakfast nook, Aarti had watched Jo cook without being too obvious, impressed by the speed with which she retrieved items from around the kitchen. Jo even found the paneer, chicken, ground turkey, and halibut she'd placed in the lowest refrigerator drawer last night.

When Aarti returned inside after signing for the helium tanks, her mother's entire spice rack appeared to be in use, and the aromas made her mouth water. While outside, she'd received emails from the florist and fireworks companies. After sending a quick response threatening to reject the entire flower delivery if she found a sprig of baby's breath, she assessed the food preparation.

Jo sprinkled what looked like cilantro over a dish. Alongside it, five others wafted steam into the air. A few smaller bowls accompanied the larger platters.

Aarti came closer. "Are you ready, or do you need more time?"

Jo rushed around the island and pulled out a stool. "Here. Please, sit."

"What did you make?" Aarti recognized the dishes, but enjoyed hearing Jo's husky voice.

Jo scooped a spoonful onto a plate, added a fork, and set it before her. "First, the biryani." She dabbed some raita next to it.

"Malai kofta and dal makhani."

Aarti savored each taste, and Jo added items, occasionally bumping her arm.

A spoonful of basmati rice Jo brought from the stove landed beside the dal. She'd cooked it to perfection, each grain separate.

"This is a turkey and potato samosa with green chutney." Jo placed another scoop on the plate. "And this is a coconut-based fish curry. I also made the people's favorite, chicken tikka masala, because if I can't get that right, send me home now. And of course, no Indian meal is complete without lemon pickles. The dosa and coconut chutney are simply to impress you."

Impress her? As a chef or for another reason? She took bites of the remaining items, including the raita, chutney, and pickles on their own. The dosa was splendid, thin and crispy, just how she liked it. As she enjoyed it, Aarti also admired the length of Jo's eyelashes and the way they swooped outward, then upward. Jo was attractive *and* talented. It was then she realized Jo watched her with amusement.

For crying out loud. Caught staring again.

Aarti looked away, swallowed, then stood. "This'll do. You have an hour to clean up before the catering team arrives. Please advise them to set up the outdoor kitchen to your specifications." She needed to put some distance between them.

A crease formed between Jo's eyebrows. "Got it."

Aarti took her laptop to the dining room. Why had Jo looked so disappointed? Had she expected her to eat a full meal? It wasn't even noon.

When she returned to the kitchen after regaining her sensibilities, the sink was filled with soapy water, and Jo had put the spices away.

"There's a dishwasher."

Jo spun around. "I know, but I need to hand wash the pans and my knives."

Aarti respected that Jo wasn't too proud to do a bit of clean up. "Please leave the food on the table. I'll let my family know it's available, or they'll wander in when they catch a whiff." She turned to leave, then backtracked. "Jo?"

Jo looked up. "Yeah?"

"Can you please put some biryani and curry aside for me?" Aarti snuck a fried onion from atop the rice dish. "They're delicious. I'll reheat them for dinner." She headed toward the door but not before Jo's mouth curved into a smile. Aarti found more gratification in Jo's happiness than she had from the scrumptious food.

While Aarti answered an email before finding her family, Jackson and Maya wandered into the dining room. Jackson's Under Armour tank showed his muscular pecs, and the stump of his left knee peeked from beneath the hem of his black shorts. He wore his sports joint prosthesis, meaning he likely planned to go for a run soon. Purple-red scars covered his other leg, and a significant divot interrupted the otherwise smooth bulge of his calf. His dark hair stuck up at the crown like he'd forgotten to comb it, but his dimpled grin was firmly in place. Maya, a head shorter, wore a bright yellow sundress with her shades perched on her straight, dark hair.

Jackson sniffed. "What smells so good?" He maneuvered around the table, careful to clear the chair legs with the prosthetic's base shaped like the number seven.

Maya tugged her ponytail as she went by. "She's busy. Leave her be."

"It's all right." Aarti rose. "Come and meet Jo. She'll be cooking the food."

"Thank goodness. I freaked out when I heard Jackson on the phone with Taylor's wife. She could've mentioned up front she had a replacement. Talk about burying the lede." Maya followed Jackson into the kitchen. "I've been worried enough about my shoes arriving in time."

Aarti kept from rolling her eyes because Jo was watching her. Maya looked the antithesis of a stressed bride. "I tracked them earlier. They'll be here today." Aarti had also been concerned whether the bespoke red shoes would arrive on time, not that she'd admit it. "Maya, Jackson, meet Jo. She's the executive chef at Taylor and Erin's newest restaurant."

Jo smiled and stepped forward. "It's a pleasure."

Jackson shook her hand. "I'm sorry my cousin is such a klutz, but we're thrilled you're here. I don't know what we would've done without you. And your food smells fantastic. I'm sold."

Maya laughed. "I agree." She leaned over the curry and inhaled. "Is this spoken for? Could we have a bite?"

"Aarti taste tested it, and I'm ninety percent sure I passed. You're welcome to whatever is left." Jo pointed to a stack of plates.

Ninety percent? Had she been unclear?

"Your timing is perfect. I'm starving." Maya slid into the booth and spooned rice onto a plate. "Have you eaten? You're welcome to join us."

Jackson sat beside her, playfully making her scoot further in with a bump of his hip. He took a samosa.

Jo looked at Aarti. "Is that okay? I'll be quick."

"Of course. It was thoughtless of me not to offer." Jo's presence and her own fear of embarrassing herself by gushing over the deliciousness of the food had distracted her. She hadn't considered whether Jo might be hungry. She turned away to hide the flaming in her cheeks. "I'll see if Mom and Dad want some."

She found her mother on the deck outside her parents' bedroom reading the *Journal of Thoracic and Cardiovascular Surgery.* "Hey, Mom. Where's Dad?"

Her mother was one of New York's most respected cardiothoracic surgeons, and her formidable demeanor didn't diminish when she left the hospital, the same one where Aarti worked. For a moment, she wondered how the hospital was managing with both of them away, but her concern was brief. Other matters required her attention.

Her mother looked up. "He's on the court hitting some balls. Why?"

Even here at the beach, her mom wore her hair in a low bun. It might be necessary when wearing a scrub cap, but Aarti didn't understand why her mother never let her hair down, literally and figuratively, while at home. "The chef heading the catering team prepared some dishes. She learned to cook while staying with an Indian family." Jo appeared to be in her late twenties, and she'd bet Jo had continued to cook Indian food since her time in France. Her skills were too refined. "I was a little wary of what to expect, but I sampled them, and she's quite good. They're in the breakfast nook if you're hungry." On second thought, setting her mother on Jo wasn't the best idea. She'd tag Jo as a lesbian on sight, and who knew what might happen. "Why don't I bring you a plate?"

Her mother rose. "I'll go with you. I need fresh tea." She tipped the contents of her mug into the shrubs.

"What article had you so engrossed you let it go cold?" It wouldn't be the first time.

On her way through the bedroom, her mom set the journal on her nightstand. "How they're improving lung cancer diagnoses with advanced imaging modalities. Dr. Stedham, the new attending in oncology, mentioned it."

"Vidya?" Her father turned the corner, tennis racket in hand, and almost collided with them. Sweat drenched the ring of gray hair that extended from ear to ear, and the bald top of his head shined.

"Slow down." Her mother patted his chest.

"Hi, Dad. The chef's here, and she prepared some samples for us to try. Hungry?"

"Hello, love." He pulled his damp shirt away from his body. "I'll be down after I shower. What'd she make?" Her dad squeezed past.

"Samosas, malai kofta, curry, dal makhani, tikka masala..." She tapped her forehead, trying to remember. "Oh, and biryani."

He made a guttural sound she recognized as excitement. "Vegetarian?"

"Half are."

"Go make sure that boy doesn't eat everything. I'll be right down."

Her mother scoffed. "It's Maya you should worry about where curry is concerned, Rakesh, not Jackson."

Maya had always been fond of spicy dishes. Aarti made a mental note to tell Jackson the story of when their mother caught Maya standing on a chair at age three with one knee on the front burner sampling a pot of curry simmering on the rear. Maya had always been the adventurous, rambunctious, entertaining child and Aarti the responsible, pensive, rule follower.

Her mother lowered her voice as they passed through the dining room. "Can this chef handle this?"

"She can." It was the truth. Jo had handled her test with panache, and the dishes had been extraordinary. When had she last eaten Indian food this good? Most restaurants seemed to temper the spice for more sensitive American palates. What she'd eaten during her trip through India might be the only food she'd rate higher than Jo's.

Aarti stared at Maya and Jackson, whose faces hovered inches above their plates. Based on the amounts before them, they were both on second helpings. Jo stood by the coffee station beside a plate on which only smears of sauce, a few grains of rice, and a fork remained.

"Jo, this is my mom, Vidya Singh."

Her mother stopped in the doorway.

Jo crossed the room, hand outstretched. "It's a pleasure, Mrs. Singh."

"*Doctor* Singh." Her mother didn't offer even a slight smile. She stared at Jo's socks and scrunched her nose like she could smell the tiny emojis on them.

Maya glanced up from her food. "Geez, Mom. So formal. We're at home."

Jo dropped her hand. "I'm sorry. Dr. Singh, it's a pleasure to meet you."

"Yes." Her mother stepped around her and peered at the dishes. "Where did you learn to cook like this?"

Must she treat Jo with such disdain? For someone so entrenched in science and medicine, she ought to know lesbianism wasn't contagious. After all, Aarti had never infected her, not that her mother liked to be reminded of her sexuality. "Mom, I explained. She learned to cook from an Indian family she stayed with."

"What part of India were they from?" Her mother's eyes narrowed.

Jo shifted from foot to foot. "Uh, it was a long time ago." She scratched her head. "I forget. Somewhere in northern India."

"Good." Her mother moved around the pieces of halibut and vegetables in the curry with the serving spoon as if searching for something. "Plate?"

Like touched by a live wire, Jo darted toward the pile.

Aarti jumped into action. "I got it." Jo had been hired to cook, not wait on her mother. Their hands landed on the stack at the same time. "I got it," she said again. Backup beeps sounded outside. "Please see if whoever has arrived is the rest of your team."

Jo's shoulders slumped, and she stepped back. "Sure."

Aarti brought her mother, who sat across from Maya, a plate and fork. As she passed the windows, she breathed in relief at the arrival of the outdoor kitchen. Jo would be busy coordinating the erection of the tent and setting up the appliances, not cornered by her mother and obnoxious questions.

"Can you go easy on her, Mom? She's stepped in during an emergency to help. I can tell you're impressed with her cooking. Everyone will judge the food we serve and talk about it for years. If you can find someone better than her before guests arrive, let me know who."

"What kind of meat is this?" Her mother poked at the innards of a samosa with her fork.

"Turkey."

"Why would she put turkey in a samosa?" Her mother glared at the pastry, clearing offended by it.

Aarti struggled to maintain her composure. "Because I told her to, and I'm in charge of this event. If you'd like to volunteer to oversee some tasks, I'd be happy to assign you something. Otherwise, please respect my decisions."

Her mother laid down her fork and the muscles around her eyes twitched. "Don't act like you're inconvenienced. You're thrilled to pretend you're a wedding planner for a week, so enjoy it while you can. Life will be back to normal before you know it."

Jackson shifted in his chair, eyes downcast, like an intruder in a private matter.

Welcome to the family, buddy. "I'm going outside to check on them." After all these years, she didn't need a reminder. She was all too aware of the speed with which she'd be whisked back to an existence she didn't care to lead. If not for her dedication to her patients, she wondered how she'd stomach it. Here she was, forty years old and with little control over her life. She ground her molars since she couldn't even produce a retort about how they'd saved thousands of dollars using her instead of another wedding planner. Her mother had paid more for the espresso machine.

❖

After seeing the catering team depart for their hotel, Aarti switched off the exterior lights. She looked toward the ocean, but only the pounding waves signaled its existence in the darkness. As balmy an evening as it was, she'd been ravenous since early afternoon but hadn't had time to eat, so enjoying the outdoors would have to wait.

In her parents' kitchen, the glow below the microwave dimly lit the room. She opened the refrigerator. A few Pyrex dishes held her mother's overnight oats, what looked to be the remains of the dal, and canned peaches Jackson had opened a few days ago. The curry and biryani she'd asked Jo to set aside for her were nowhere to be found. She sighed. Either Jo had forgotten, or someone had eaten it.

If the dal hadn't remained, she'd wonder if her mom had instructed Jo to discard any leftovers. She disregarded the thought. Her mother might be rigid, but she wasn't spiteful. Yet, marooned in the ever-growing distance between them, Aarti struggled to recall a time when they'd been close.

She slipped outside and found the path to the guest cottage by habit. At least the light beside Jo's door gave her something to aim for. Her side of the duplex was unlocked, as it always was. She kicked off her shoes, switched on lights, and opened a bottle of sauvignon blanc. With a glass in hand, she stepped onto the deck where the cool salt air refreshed her as much as her first sip. While she hadn't planned to drink her dinner, at least she had the wine. She'd needed it since the tense exchange with her mother.

As she settled into her deck chair and pulled a blanket over her legs, her stomach rumbled. She imagined she could smell Indian food. How cruel of her subconscious to tease her with the delicious aromas from all those hours ago. Why hadn't she eaten more at the time?

"Hi."

Aarti jumped, and the contents of her glass sloshed all over her lap.

Jo helped her stand. "I'm so sorry. I thought you heard me come out." She shook out the blanket and hung it over the railing. "Is that wine I smell?"

"Yes, would you like some? It's a sauv blanc." Her heart still raced.

"I just wanted to know if it was red so we could rinse it out before the stain set." Jo moved closer. "I didn't hear you come in. Your slider squeaks, or I wouldn't have known you were here at all." She took her by the elbow. "Come inside. I've been waiting for you. Your food is in the oven."

Jo hadn't forgotten about her. When Aarti entered the space glowing with light and laced with mouthwatering scents, pleasure suffused her. Not only had Jo set food aside, but she'd reheated it for her.

"You seem tired. Here, sit."

Still surprised, Aarti nodded. "Yes, but I can get it."

Jo gently stopped her. "Come sit." She squeezed her shoulder before turning her toward the table. "I'll get it for you."

"You've been working all day, too." Aarti relaxed into the chair, stretched out her calves, and wiggled her bare feet. Had she sat more than ten minutes since she'd sent the food order this morning?

Jo fixed her a plate. She set a generous portion in front of her along with cutlery and a napkin. "May I get the bottle of wine?"

"Only if you agree to share it with me." At the first forkful, she closed her eyes and moaned, then covered her mouth with her hand. "How is it even better than before?" When she opened her eyes, Jo wore an expression she'd yet to witness.

Jo's focus seemed to be on Aarti's lips. "I think I do need wine." She returned with the bottle and another glass moments later. "I'm surprised you drink alcohol. I wasn't sure."

"Because I'm Indian or because my family is Hindu?"

"I don't know." Jo tilted her head. "How does that work?"

Though tired, she enjoyed talking to Jo and didn't mind explaining. "While the law varies state to state in India, many Indians drink alcohol, both here and there. As far as religious customs go, some conservative sects of Hindus forbid it, but they're few, and it's rarely followed in reality." She refrained from shoveling the fantastic food into her mouth and took a dainty bite.

Jo raised her eyebrows. "I didn't know that."

"My family's been in the US for three generations, and they've assimilated to the culture. We'll have alcohol at the wedding, though not everyone will drink."

Jo's forehead wrinkled. "I'm trying to remember if my host family drank or served alcohol in their restaurant. Cooking must have fascinated me too much to notice."

Aarti laughed. "Spoken like a true chef."

Jo filled their glasses and sat beside her. "I'm guessing Maya's marriage wasn't arranged?"

"Correct. Not all Indian marriages are, even in India. It's more common in rural areas and a few states. In urban centers and most other states, there are no such rules or rigidness." Aarti picked up her glass. "My parents had a love marriage, and that was over forty years ago."

Jo smiled. "I'm learning so much."

"While I love many of our culture's traditions, I'm happy they didn't want to choose my sister's husband, especially considering how madly in love she is with Jackson." Aarti sighed. "Although, it's often stomach-turning to witness the goofy eyes they make at each other." She ate a bite and took her time savoring it.

"You've never looked at someone that way?" A smile tugged at the corners of Jo's lips.

Aarti had never gotten to that stage in her relationships, if she could even label them that. She should've had more dalliances while away at med school and during training, but when would she have found time? "No, I don't think so." When Jo opened her mouth to speak, Aarti quickly changed the subject. "Are you hungry? Did you eat?" Once again, she'd forgotten her manners.

"I ate with your dad at the house."

She did a double-take. "My dad?"

"Yeah, the curry seemed to be his favorite, too. If I hadn't smuggled this out earlier, I'd be sharing my morning protein bar with you right now." Jo leaned back in her chair. "We had a pleasant chat. He mentioned your sister's a doctor, too. Your family could open a hospital of their own."

"Yes, Dad's a neurosurgeon, Mom a cardiothoracic surgeon, and Maya's an orthopedic surgeon." The conversation had veered right into yet another uncomfortable territory.

"So, you're a cardiac surgeon?"

There it was, the question everyone asked. "No, a lowly cardiologist, the black sheep of the family." She cleared her throat. "By the way, I want to apologize for my mother earlier."

Jo pulled the bandana from her hair and mussed her short locks. "Do you control her behavior?"

Aarti managed to shake her head despite being thrown by the response.

"Then there's no need." Jo shoved the folded fabric into her pocket.

Aarti blinked a few times before shoving a piece of chicken into her mouth. How rare for someone to see her as an individual.

"Anyway, your dad sounded so proud. How did it happen, both you and your sister becoming doctors? You said it's complicated earlier. Did you want to go into medicine to be like them, or did they pressure you to become a doctor?" Jo rested her chin in her hand.

Was this idle chitchat until she finished her meal and retreated to her half of the cottage, or was Jo's interest genuine? If the former, she assumed Jo would let her finish eating so she'd leave sooner. Jo must want to know.

"Like I said, it's complicated. It's a stereotype that all Indian parents want their children to become doctors because, like any other ethnic group, the people within it are diverse and don't all hold the same beliefs. Indians are no exception, whether they live in India or any other country." She paused to enjoy the curry's flavorful sauce. "However, *my* family does, for several reasons. My parents care less about social status and more about how it reflects well on them that their children followed in their footsteps and were intelligent enough to do so. Our parents wanted us to be educated, financially successful, and have a career with longevity. Doctors have been around, and will be around, for a very long time."

"But you hoped to be an event planner?"

She stared at a carrot. "Yes, and specifically weddings. I suppose I've always been a hopeless romantic." Too bad she had zero romance in her own life.

"Did you tell them that's what you wanted to do? You still could have gotten an education. I'm sure degrees like business administration or hospitality would've come in handy." Jo propped her foot on the rung of Aarti's chair, her knee almost brushing Aarti's thigh.

"When it came time to apply to colleges, I tried." She set down her fork. "The conversation was a non-starter. I was a teenager with no income, and my parents were clear about their expectations. I didn't push the issue because I feared...well, many things." She turned toward Jo, and this time, their legs touched. Jo didn't move away, so she didn't either. "You should understand, it wasn't as simple as expecting me to become a doctor. If I'd become a general practitioner, I would have embarrassed them. They expected us to board in two or preferably three specialties. I did, but even that wasn't enough. My mother wanted me to become a surgeon like her, but I'd gotten older and brave enough to put my foot down for once. It's strained our relationship ever since. Maya though, found her passion in orthopedics and adores what she does."

Jo studied her. "How long has your relationship with your mom been difficult?"

Aarti considered how much to share. "Well, I turned forty this year, and she caught me kissing my friend Tiffany in high school." She did the quick math. "So, twenty-four years, give or take."

"Ouch." Jo softly laughed. "I meant about being a surgeon, but you two haven't seen eye to eye in some time."

She'd caught how Jo's eyes had widened when she'd mentioned the kiss. Why *had* she mentioned it? "I was twenty-six when I decided not to go into surgery, and that definitely made things even worse between us."

Jo scrunched her brow. "I forget. Is Jackson a doctor, too?"

"No, he was a medic in the Army. But two months before the US pulled out of Afghanistan, his convoy came across a boy covered in blood. Jackson got out to help and triggered an improvised explosive device. His body armor protected his torso, but his legs took the brunt of it." She took a sip of wine. Jo ignored hers, seemingly riveted, but Aarti assumed her interest to be in the story. "His platoon had a jammer, but it must have been a pressure plate rather than a remote detonation."

"And the kid? Did he live?"

This part angered her as much as Jackson's injury. "It was a setup."

Jo blew out a breath and downed a mouthful of wine.

"The boy jumped up and ran off, according to Jackson's CO." The depravity necessary to force or entice children to fight in a war never failed to shock her.

"Was Maya his doctor? Is that how they met?"

"No, they met at a fundraiser for the Special Olympics, where he'd been training athletes. He receives his medical care through the VA." She leaned back in her chair. "And doctors aren't allowed to date their patients, despite what you see on TV."

"Is that so?" Jo swirled the wine in her glass.

"It's part of the Code of Medical Ethics."

A small dimple creased Jo's cheek. "Then I hope I don't need a cardiologist anytime soon."

Wait. What? Did that mean Jo intended to ask her out? The oven must've still been on because Aarti half expected the heat in the room to blister the paint on the walls. She rose, holding onto her chair, and sweat gathered along her hairline. She needed air. "Let's go outside." She refilled her glass and topped off Jo's without making eye contact. "Thank you for dinner."

On the deck, a cool breeze ruffled her hair, fanning her neck, and a rising crescent moon offered a bit of light by which to see. She leaned on the railing. The tide had withdrawn, leaving long expanses of wet, sandy beach.

Beside her, Jo rested her glass on the wooden plank.

Aarti touched the blanket hanging over it. Still damp from her spilled wine.

"It's too bad this is here." Jo rapped her knuckles on the dividing wall. "We can't sit on the lounge chairs and talk with this stupid thing between us, and there's not room for two chairs on one side."

"We could share one." What made her say *that*? Apparently, coming outside hadn't been the brightest idea.

"Here, hold this." Jo handed Aarti her wine glass and ducked inside. She returned with the bottle and a dry blanket and sat on the lounger and spread her legs. "Come here."

Aarti froze. "I'm not sitting there." Even in the feeble moonlight, she saw Jo grin.

"It was your idea. What are you afraid of?"

"I'm not afraid. We've only known each other since this morning. Do you always operate at this speed?" A chilly gust of wind raised the fine hairs on her arms. As warm as she'd been inside, now she needed a sweatshirt.

"Sometimes." Jo made a come-hither motion with two fingers.

Aarti didn't doubt it. An attractive woman like Jo would have no trouble finding women to share her bed. "I don't think so."

"I'd just like my wine, please."

Grateful for the darkness that might mask her blush, she handed Jo the glass.

Jo set it on a small table beside her. "I know you're cold. The sooner you sit, the sooner we can be under this blanket. It's nipply out."

Was that a word? And was Jo insinuating she could see her nipples? They *were* hard, and Aarti wanted it to be from the cold. The frigid air must also be causing her hand to shake, sloshing the contents of her glass, because she refused to believe otherwise. While Jo might *sometimes* move quickly, Aarti didn't.

Jo unfolded the blanket. "It's okay."

Something in her voice eased Aarti's fears.

She sat on the edge of the lounger and placed her glass beside Jo's. "What're we doing?"

"We're getting warm." Jo wrapped her arm around Aarti's waist and pulled her between her legs.

Aarti stiffened as Jo swung the blanket over them and flinched when she tucked it around their legs.

Jo encircled her in a loose embrace. "Lean back. You won't hurt me."

It wasn't hurting Jo she was worried about. Aarti tried to relax into the warmth of Jo's body, the softness of her breasts, and that intoxicating scent she wore. When Jo rubbed her arms, her rigidity melted by degrees until she'd molded herself to Jo.

"That's better." Jo's breath feathered against her ear. "Warmer now?"

The heat radiating off Jo did more than warm her.

"Yes." This wasn't how she'd envisioned her evening, but she had no complaints.

"What are all those lights out there? Yachts?"

She laughed, and so did Jo, her abs flexing against Aarti's back. "Maybe some, but most of them are commercial fishing vessels."

Jo trailed her fingertips, slow and lazy, over Aarti's arm. Definitely not an attempt to warm her, at least not in the conventional way.

"What do they catch?"

"Lobsters, crab, halibut, striped bass. Probably other stuff."

"I should've worked a local dish into the menu." Jo sighed, the exhalation warming Aarti's ear.

Aarti readjusted, leaning her head against Jo's solid but soft shoulder. "You only received the menu last night." She turned to Jo, only to realize how close their faces were.

"Actually, I helped Taylor create it. You distracted me this morning, or I'd have thought to add some fresh local fish to the order."

Aarti shook her head, careful their lips didn't brush, and wondered if she'd been a pleasant distraction. "There's no shortage of places nearby to get local seafood. If I don't have time to run out, I'll send you."

Lines curved around the corners of Jo's lips as she smiled. "I like the sound of that, being your errand girl."

The comment made Aarti tense, but Jo's splayed hand across her stomach eased her bunched muscles, and after a few seconds, she relaxed again. Above her, more stars dotted the sky than those visible above Manhattan. It was breathtaking, with only a few thin wisps of clouds.

Her body had warmed being sandwiched between Jo and the blanket. The last time she'd been in a woman's embrace had been with

Leticia. "So, about tomorrow." She turned, but this time, her lips came into contact with Jo's. A voice in her head screamed for her to retreat, but Jo's lips were so supple, so soft, and Jo hadn't pulled away.

When Jo moved her lips over hers, Aarti gasped. Again, Jo's palm against her stomach steadied her. Aarti closed her eyes, not sure she wanted to see what Jo's eyes might hold. Jo was gentle but insistent, nipping now and then, and when the warmth of her tongue skimmed Aarti's lips, Aarti opened to her.

Unhurried, Jo cradled the back of her head and explored her mouth until Aarti lost herself in the haze of sensations. She hesitated, then stroked her tongue along Jo's, and Jo's soft moan broke her reverie. What was she doing? She jerked away. "I'm so sorry." When she sat up and the blanket pooled at her waist, Jo didn't try to keep her in place. She didn't make her do anything.

"I'm not." Jo passed Aarti her glass and took a sip from her own.

Aarti waved it off, unsure if her hands were steady enough to hold it.

Without a word, Jo returned it to the table.

Aarti stood, caught the blanket, and laid it beside Jo. "I'll be up at seven. Breakfast tomorrow will be at nine for the immediate family." Jo would, of course, already know all of this, but she had to say something to distance them from the kiss. "Lunch will be on the oceanfront deck for close family members, about twenty people. It should be in your binder. I can give you a wake-up call if you'd like."

Jo laced her fingers behind her head, displaying her tattoos. Her hardened nipples showed beneath the thin material of her tank. "Are you sure you don't want to roll over in the morning and wake me?" This time, no playful grin accompanied her question.

"No. I mean yes. I mean no, I can't. And yes, I'm sure." For crying out loud. Every week, she gave patients unpleasant diagnoses without stumbling over her words, yet she couldn't answer a simple question from an attractive woman. Even if she found Jo charming and sexy, Aarti was sure she was the latest in a long line to be propositioned by her. A deep inhalation only slightly calmed her. "Do your abysmal lines work on other women?"

This time, Jo grinned. "Sometimes."

Aarti handed her the blanket. "I'll see you in the morning."

Jo didn't answer, but Aarti sensed Jo watching her until she ducked around the wall. Once inside, she flopped onto her bed fully clothed.

Her reluctance to take Jo up on her offer had little to do with propriety. Technically, she wasn't employing her. Jo probably wished she was at her restaurant, not hours away performing a favor for her bosses. Perhaps Aarti should've accepted. She needed to keep her happy since it'd be disastrous if Jo walked away. Aarti covered her eyes with her arm. No. Sleeping with Jo to insure the event's success was going too far.

She needed to get a grip, though, because letting something like fleeting attraction divert her from her goal wasn't happening. This was her chance to prove to her family, especially her mother, that she had skills beyond medicine. Besides, her parents would be around all week witnessing everything she did, wedding-related or otherwise. She'd be remiss to remind her mother of her sexuality at a time she hoped to impress her. Even if Jo was hot, sleeping with her was a terrible idea.

CHAPTER THREE

B ehind Aarti, someone entered the dining room, and based on the clacking of sandals on the hardwood floor, it was Maya.

She leaned over Aarti's shoulder, appearing to read her laptop screen. "You weren't at breakfast. Problems?"

"No. Just sending reminder emails to vendors."

Maya plopped into the chair beside her and glanced at the papers spread over the long table. "You missed out. Jo ran an omelet station. She also baked a coffee cake and cut up fresh fruit. I felt like I was at a resort."

"Sounds delicious, but I was fine with coffee this morning." Aarti tried to focus on her email to the DJ.

"Your loss." Maya crossed her legs. "I drank two mimosas. Didn't I, Jo?"

When Aarti looked up, Jo stood in the doorway in her white coat and black pants. Today her socks featured frogs wearing rainbow roller skates.

"You're entitled as the bride-to-be." Jo sat opposite Maya, but turned toward Aarti. "The food delivery arrived while you were on that call. I inventoried and signed for it, and the crew put everything away. Geri and Larry—"

Aarti glanced up

"It's true." Jo grinned. "Those are their names. I can introduce you to everyone or be the go-between. It's up to you. Anyway, they helped me sort which foods to keep in here and what to put in the low-boys and the reach-in outside." She moved, and her knee came into contact with Aarti's, but she kept talking. "They've started lunch. Geri is grilling chicken kabobs and veggie burgers, and Larry is making the salads."

Maya lit up. "Ooh, I love veggie burgers."

"Yeah, they look like good ones." Jo turned back to Aarti. "Anyway, we're on schedule. Since the servers won't arrive until tonight, is it okay if we set up a buffet inside? Everyone can still eat on the patio."

"That's fine." Aarti eyed the table. "This is the best place to do it. Let's stack the chairs against the wall, so you can use both sides. I'll clean up my mess." She closed her laptop.

"I don't want to displace you. We can probably fit the food on the island, but it might get crowded in there with that many people, and it won't be clean because we're prepping."

She rose. "No, it's fine. I'll move to the breakfast nook, unless it'll bother you." She missed the contact with Jo's leg.

Jo also stood. "No bother. If you're within sight, I can make sure you eat something." She squeezed Aarti's forearm.

Maya looked between them, but Aarti couldn't read her expression.

Jo moved chairs against the wall. Aarti gathered her papers, turning each pile ninety degrees, so they stayed separate. Maya watched them.

Aarti hugged everything to her chest. "I'm going to put these down. Then I need to make sure Dad relocated the trash and recycling bins so we can make a staging area for the elephant."

Jo dropped a chair with a thud. "Did you say elephant?" She waved her arm in front of her face like a trunk.

"Yeah," Maya said, "Jackson will arrive at the second ceremony while riding it. It's a South Indian tradition, not even a North Indian one, where our family came from. And it's rarely done anymore, but my father's wanted this since his parents refused to do it for his wedding." She waved her hand. "He's obsessed."

"So, what did North Indian grooms use?" Jo's eyes widened like she expected almost any animal to be named.

"Horses," Aarti said. "Now most couples opt for luxury cars for the groom to make an entrance, but my dad insisted on springing for an elephant. He likes the theatrics of it." She leaned closer. "He's vicariously living out his own fantasy through Jackson. It's only a matter of time before he's up there taking a ride."

Jo laughed, then blinked a few times. "Where did you rent an elephant?" She held up her hands. "Never mind. I don't want to know. I don't have to prepare food for it, do I?"

Maya stood. "I'm pretty sure they eat hay or grasses, so you're safe. Besides, it'll have a handler to care for its needs." She dragged her chair against the wall. "I'll come with you, Aarti."

It surprised Aarti that Maya had exerted herself enough to move the chair, let alone want to accompany her. Not much had concerned her thus far other than the status of her shoes. If it wasn't for the impending lunch, she'd be poolside. Aarti wasn't complaining. She loved coordinating these things. Perhaps Maya's disinterest was her way of demonstrating confidence in her.

They left Jo to the chairs, and Aarti dropped her stuff in the kitchen. "Who's here so far?"

Maya held the back door open. "Nani, Nana, Grandma Singh, Jackson's parents, his brother, Uncle Naveen, Sundar, Harini, and Amala. They're all on the ocean deck. Pradeep called and said he'll be late. They're hounding me with questions about how soon I expect to be pregnant, so I escaped for a bit."

They walked around the perimeter of the outside kitchen. Based on the gurgling of her stomach after catching a whiff of the wonderful aromas coming from the grill, Aarti needed to eat. Besides, working or not, she'd offend her extended family if she didn't spend time with them.

"What was going on in there?" Maya lowered her shades to study her.

"I was working." Aarti emphasized the last word. Maya should've deduced that after outscoring Aarti soundly on the medical licensing boards.

Maya flicked her arm.

"Ow!" Aarti rubbed the sore spot. "What was that for?"

"Because you're clueless. Jo was flirting with you, or are you too absorbed with deliveries and trash cans to notice?"

Aarti glanced around. "Can you not? All I need is Mom or Dad overhearing you, and this week won't be about your wedding or my event-planning skills. You know how they feel about that."

"I know how *Mom* feels about it. Dad just follows her lead."

They rounded the corner of the garage. "Oh, good. He moved the bins and even attached a hose to the spigot. Nice."

Maya put her hands on her hips. "What are you going to do with the elephant during the fireworks? I don't want it to be stressed."

"He won't be here." Aarti began walking toward the house. "The handler said she wanted to get him here early to make him comfortable, but she'd take him elsewhere for the hour of fireworks. I guess he likes to go for rides."

"Huh." Maya's expression appeared to change from wonder to mischief, and she lowered her voice. "So, what about Jo?"

Aarti had forgotten how annoying having a younger sister could be, but her irritation was minor. She recalled her elation when her parents had told her they were having a baby when she'd been eight. While she and Maya had been too far apart in age to fight as kids, apparently they'd saved their bickering for adulthood. "I'm not going to do anything about her. She has a job to do, and so do I."

"Yes, but you're sharing a cottage." Maya's sing-song voice accompanied a poke in the ribs that Aarti brushed away. "And Mom and Dad have no reason to go down there."

Maybe little sisters got worse with time, the opposite of a fine wine. "Maya. Seriously."

Maya put an arm around her. "I love Jackson, and I'm lucky to share my life with him, but I want that for you, too. I hope this week's not difficult for you, being so involved."

Aarti squeezed Maya's hand. "I chose to be. I want you to have the best wedding day imaginable. But I also want to show Mom and Dad that I'm good—great—at what I do, and that this makes me happier than reading EKGs or echoes."

"Well, I love that you're doing it for me. It's reassuring knowing you won't overlook any details." Maya wiggled her eyebrows. "So no funny business in the guest cottage? I think you're missing a prime opportunity."

Aarti put an arm around Maya's waist. "Let's see if Jo has any mimosa ingredients left."

Maya held up her hand. "I already had two. Keep in mind, I have to sit still for hours soon for the peethi and henna to be applied. I don't want my bladder to explode halfway through. But what bride doesn't want glowing skin? My designs will pop."

"I never said the drink was for you." While Aarti was happy for Maya and Jackson, it was difficult to witness the love they shared, a love she'd never experienced in her forty years. But nothing had ever been equal between them. Aarti had been the only child and then the older child, the weight of expectations heavy. As an adult, she'd barely done enough career-wise to satisfy her parents, and with regard to her sexuality, she doubted she ever could.

Maya had come along, the girl who radiated brightness and exceeded expectations. She'd succeeded where Aarti had failed. The way their family rallied around her for this special occasion should have made Aarti bitter, but it didn't. Maya deserved it. Aarti simply wanted a little slice of her family's adoration and well-wishes. Was that too much to ask?

Aarti surveyed the property from beside the outdoor kitchen. The small bus hired to shuttle guests between the house, the resort, and two other locations turned down the driveway with its first transport.

She checked her iPad. The henna artists should arrive soon. Nearby, three caterers had their heads down under the tent as dinner preparation reached a peak. Geri, whom she'd met earlier, wore Ray-Bans and worked the grills, moving between the two with ease while facing the western sun and singing in her delightful Caribbean accent. Was the song true? Would every little thing be all right? Aarti hoped so.

The wind changed direction, and smoke wafted her way. She retreated inside since she didn't want to smell like mesquite chicken for the rest of the evening.

In the kitchen, Jo and two other caterers danced around one another in a manner that appeared choreographed. On the largest deck visible through the living room windows, catering staff dressed in black and white made final touches to a long buffet and a dozen round tables, all laid with golden tablecloths.

"How's it going?" Jo looked up from where she piped filling into deviled eggs.

The food for the party featured an array of eclectic small bites, both Eastern and Western, and just seeing some of them made Aarti's stomach rumble. "So far, so good. Who's in charge of the rental staff?" The truck needed to be moved off the grass as soon as they finished unloading the chairs, or it would leave indentations in the lawn. She didn't want her grandparents, or anyone else, tripping.

Jo made a slicing motion near her lower back. "Megan, the one with braids down to her waist."

"Thanks." Aarti headed for the deck.

"Hey."

Jo's voice made her stop.

"You look nice."

The other two caterers didn't look up, but Aarti feared she might wobble on her heels if she moved with Jo's gaze upon her, so she took a moment to glance at her bright red blouse and apricot-colored pants. When she raised her head, Jo hadn't moved. "Thank you. It's tradition to wear bright colors for the mehndi ceremony."

Jo seemed to weigh her words, presumably because of the two people listening. "Those colors suit you." She touched her lip with a finger.

Without thinking, Aarti mirrored the movement until she realized she'd almost disturbed her cherry-red lipstick. Was that what Jo was trying to communicate, that she liked her lip color? She gave a small nod and smile in understanding. She flicked a finger at Jo's bright yellow bandana. "You're also wearing an appropriate color."

Jo looked up, as though trying to remember what color she'd chosen. She smiled. "Oh, yeah. Are you getting a henna design? You're allowed, right?" Jo finished piping the remaining eggs, and the man beside her whisked them away. She wiped her hands on a towel and came around the island.

Despite the competing aromas from the kitchen, the delightful scent Aarti had noticed on Jo last night made her breathless. How could it affect her like that? Maybe it was one of those fragrances containing pheromones. So unfair.

"Yes, everyone can, but the difficulty varies. I've booked three henna artists. I've dedicated one to Maya. Her designs will take four to six hours." She motioned to her own arm. "Her hands and arms to her elbows, feet and legs to her knees. Close family members will have both hands painted, and so will I, if there's time. Or I'll just get one done. Relatives get it on their palms."

"Just one, huh?" Jo lifted Aarti's hand and caressed its back with a finger.

Tingles shot up Aarti's arm. She pulled away with a glance at the caterers, who hadn't been watching.

Tiny creases around Jo's mouth belied her nonchalance. "Do you think I could see Maya's design when she's finished? I love trying to find the partner's name hidden in the artwork."

Aarti glanced at the deck where the truck hadn't moved and lowered her voice. "After your crew has left and you're done for the night, you're welcome to enjoy the music and dancing."

Jo moved closer. "How long will you be occupied?"

"Until it's over."

"I'll stop by after we've prepped for tomorrow and the team has gone to the hotel. I'd like to see Maya, but I don't know how long I'll stay. Come to me when you get back to our place."

Our place. Aarti hoped the men hadn't overheard Jo's comment or her own heart beating against her ribs. "It might be late."

"That's okay. I bought us dinner on my errand today. Knowing you, you won't eat during the event, and I won't have time, so we can enjoy a late meal." Jo reached out to touch her cheek, but seemed to think better of it and dropped her hand.

"Should I bring candles?" Aarti immediately wanted to take it back. What was wrong with her?

Jo's beaming smile indicated she enjoyed the banter. "I'd settle for another bottle of white wine. I bought the most gorgeous, succulent scallops." Her face fell. "I forgot to ask if you even like scallops. I just assumed because you said you eat fish. Do you?"

Jo's sudden insecurity made Aarti smile. "They're one of my favorite foods, and I stocked up on wine on my way here."

"Oh, good. I didn't charge them to the wedding budget, in case you were wondering. But they were too tempting to turn down."

"I wasn't, but that was kind of you." Aarti glanced outside again. "I have to go, but I look forward to dinner."

"Yeah, me too." Jo grasped her apron, and her eyes crinkled at the corners. "Did I mention you look really nice?"

The compliment heated parts of Aarti that hadn't been warm, well—since last night's amazing kiss. Her coloring probably matched her shirt. But she could play, too, at least when her parents weren't present. "Aren't you supposed to be cooking or something?" As she passed, she caressed the back of *Jo's* hand.

CHAPTER FOUR

Aarti drank a glass of wine while appreciating Jo's tight backside with a tiny twinge of guilt, especially when Jo had retrieved the plates warming in the oven. She'd enjoyed a second pouring with the mouthwatering scallops, root vegetable puree, and sauteed mushrooms. How Jo had whipped together such an exquisite meal in the dinky kitchenette with its poor lighting and ancient stove was beyond her.

Tonight she didn't argue when Jo straddled the lounge chair and made room for her, but simply toed off her shoes and climbed on. Under the blanket, Jo seemed to enjoy the silkiness of her shirt, each move causing delightful prickles to erupt on Aarti's arms.

In the distance, the DJ announced the last song of the night to a few groans. Most of the party goers had already left or taken the shuttle. Only Maya, Jackson, his brother, and their friends had remained when Aarti had bid them good night. She admired the young people's stamina. The bar closed in a few minutes, and the party would quiet down soon to respect the noise ordinance.

"I'm sorry I was running around all night. The DJ didn't bring an extension cord long enough, the shuttle driver took a wrong turn, and whenever I passed the bar, someone would beg me for a bucket of ice. I'll have to come up with a solution before tomorrow. Did you find Maya?" Aarti angled her head to look at Jo.

"Yeah. I found Jackson's name hidden in her mehndi design. Her henna artist was talented. It took me a while."

"I'll have to get you some hidden object books so you can decrease your time before the next wedding." What was she saying? There'd be no next wedding.

Jo didn't respond, likely thinking the same thing. Aarti pretended to stargaze to lighten the mood.

"Hey." Jo turned her face with a finger to her chin. "I wouldn't mind catering another wedding. It'd give me an excuse to see you again." She moved closer until her face blurred.

Aarti closed her eyes, feeling Jo's warm breath, waiting for the contact of Jo's exquisite lips against hers. Dismayed when it didn't come, she closed the distance, angling her head when Jo opened her mouth and welcomed her.

When Jo worked her hand beneath Aarti's shirt to caress the muscles of her lower back, Aarti let her lips linger a moment, then drew back. "I get the feeling you do this often, which is fine. I'm not judging." She ran her finger over one of Jo's eyebrows. "You're very charming, but a one-night stand has never appealed to me." When Jo didn't respond, she continued. "We're different. You're impulsive and go for what you want, while I'm a planner and constrained by perception." A planner she may be, but she hadn't planned on Jo Samuels.

"We all have to deal with perceptions."

"Sure, but I'm not sure you understand the high expectations of my parents."

Jo looked thoughtful. "I did used to be a bit of a player in the past. I enjoyed women, but I wasn't looking for anything serious. Even though I was out to have fun, I was respectful and let them know beforehand it was just sex." She gazed upward. "But something always happens when we aren't looking for it, doesn't it?"

"Like someone special?" Aarti shifted to see Jo better. She'd be off the lounger in half a second if Jo had a girlfriend.

"Yeah. I met a woman named Sophie who worked for one of our vendors. I don't know what it was about her, but I was the one wanting more for the first time. My interest in playing around vanished. We dated for a bit, but she was young and still trying to figure out what she wanted. She floated from job to job, and then a friend in San Francisco offered her a position co-running a bakery."

"Oh." Aarti relaxed. Sophie didn't sound like a current girlfriend.

"I love sourdough as much as the next gay, but I wasn't about to move across the country when Taylor's been so good to me. She and Erin were just about to open their second restaurant, and I had a chance to make a name for myself. Until that point, I'd always shied away from the limelight. I was Taylor's sous chef for years, and maybe I needed that time to work up the confidence, but I was ready for the opportunity." Jo gave a hollow laugh. "Sophie went to San Francisco, and I stayed in Manhattan. Part of me hoped she'd change her mind, but she didn't seem to have the reservations about us parting that I did. She didn't even mention trying to make it work long-distance. One day she was here, and the next gone. It devastated me."

Aarti touched Jo's cheek. "I'm sure it did." She couldn't be certain in the darkness, but there seemed to be a glimmer of tears in Jo's eyes.

"My point is, I'm willing to date and have a proper relationship if the situation is right."

The conversation had turned so fast, Aarti had whiplash. She dropped her hand and sat up. "I apologize if I made it sound like that's what I'm looking for. I'm afraid I can't have a relationship with you, or any other woman, for that matter."

"I'm not talking about moving in together, just dating. We both live in the city. Why not?"

Aarti hated having this conversation. "It's not possible."

"Because of your religion?"

"No." Aarti wasn't sure how to explain the convoluted answer. "Hinduism as a whole isn't against homosexuality, although some Hindu communities don't support it." She missed Jo's warmth and leaned against her again. "I would shame my parents. Family is everything, and I'd be disrespecting them." She shivered.

Jo rubbed her warm hands along her arms, making the silk slide against her skin. "How often do you see them? My mom lives in the city, and I see her twice a month max. Why can't you date and not tell them about it?"

"I work in the same hospital as my mother, and it's a horrid gossip mill. I ate lunch with a physician's assistant from the neuro ICU a few times, and my mom heard rumors."

"Simply over lunch with a woman?"

Aarti shook her head. "No. We'd been sleeping together for a few weeks, though we'd never stayed overnight. My parents live nearby and often drop by without notice. But even being seen having lunch together had my mother's hackles raised. She complained her colleagues were talking about us, so I ended it." Aarti recalled being upset, not because she'd been in love with Leticia, but because of her inability to even have a delightful fling without her mother finding out. She should've known better, dating someone from the hospital, but where else was she supposed to meet women? She spent most of her time at work.

Jo wrapped her arms around her and squeezed. "I'm so sorry. Do they expect you to be celibate?"

"I don't know. That would involve acknowledging my sexuality." Aarti touched the fine gold necklace she'd worn for the mehndi ceremony. "I'm forty years old, and I've never lived my life."

After a moment of silence, Jo shifted behind her. "Then let me give you this week." Jo moved her hair aside and pressed a kiss to her neck. "I like you. You're interesting and the most beautiful woman here. I found you everywhere you went tonight and not because of your red shirt. You're smart, driven, and really good at what you do. But from this moment on, I won't look at you unless you speak to me. I won't start a conversation with you outside of what I need for the event, at least until we get back here each night. Once here, I'd like to give you everything you need."

Aarti's stomach did cartwheels. Jo found her that attractive? Not her sister, resplendent with intricate henna designs adorning her extremities? Aarti had opted for one hand painted because of time constraints. Why her and not any of the gorgeous young women at the party? Jackson's cousin Veronica starred in a commercial for lululemon, and one of Maya's friend's success as a social media influencer likely only happened because she looked like Bollywood star Alia Bhatt. Yet it was *her* in Jo's reassuring arms, not them, as unreal as it seemed. She closed her eyes as Jo kissed her neck. When Jo kissed along the line of her jaw, Aarti turned, and their mouths met.

In her twisted position, Jo held her like a dancer dipping a partner. Aarti tried to recall a time she'd ever felt so safe, so cared for, as she did in Jo's arms. The fine hairs at the nape of Jo's neck delighted her, and contrasted with the soft crunch of hair product when she grasped a handful of locks.

As Jo sought new depths of her mouth, she flattened her hand against Aarti's stomach much like she'd done the night before, then slid it upward until she cupped Aarti's breast. A firestorm raged in its path. The cool ocean breeze and salty air had blown away, replaced by Jo's warm hands, hot mouth, and that intoxicating scent of hers.

Aarti floated on a sultry sea of pleasure, first from the kiss, then from Jo's hand inside her shirt, then under her bra. She ignited when Jo rolled her nipple between her fingers, and she opened her eyes. Above, in the inky sky, the stars shone, but when Jo kissed down her chest and sucked her nipple, the universe spun, arcs of light created around a single point. She closed her eyes to the dizzying sensation.

Jo moved her hand downward, hesitating at the waistline of her tailored pants in a nonverbal question, but Aarti had already grabbed her wrist, stopping its trajectory.

"The sky won't fall if you have an orgasm in my arms tonight." Jo nuzzled her ear. "No one is around, and if someone comes down the beach, I'll see them. And those fishing vessels would have to have some pretty sophisticated equipment to see what we're doing." Jo kissed her temple.

No, the sky wouldn't fall, but Aarti couldn't afford for anything *else* to either, like her. Because while she'd admitted right away she found Jo attractive, Jo's concern about whether she'd eaten and genuine interest when they talked had only made her interest deepen. She enjoyed being around Jo, watching her cook or listening to her. And Aarti had shared more with Jo than she had with anyone in a long time. She never discussed her personal life with her colleagues, and rarely even did with Maya.

The ease Jo had around her family and their customs surprised her. While Aarti didn't expect a non-Indian woman to know how to cook traditional dishes or assume she'd been to a Hindu wedding, Jo's knowledge of Aarti's culture and willingness to ask questions earned her points. It seemed they'd known one another so much longer than a few days after all they'd shared.

Despite that, Aarti knew the possibility of her parents accepting Jo was almost nonexistent. That should've stopped her, made her remove Jo's hand altogether, but she didn't. While maintaining eye contact, she released Jo's wrist and unbuttoned her slacks.

"You sure?" Jo didn't move.

"Yes, but please keep it low key the rest of the week." Aarti smoothed the hair above Jo's ear. "No appreciative glances and no innuendo. And when the week is over, we go back to our lives. Can you do that?" She expected a quick answer, but it didn't come.

Instead, Jo brushed her thumb over Aarti's cheek. "I'll agree to no glances or flirty talk, but I want to save the last item and revisit it at the end of the week. Can you do *that*?"

Aarti hadn't been aware this was a negotiation. Did that mean Jo was serious about wanting to date her, or at least have sex, back in Manhattan? From the little Aarti knew, chefs worked long hours, and so did she. If she rushed from work with no explanation, or couldn't attend dinner with her parents without a legitimate excuse, her mother would see right through her. But she might manage one night a week. Still, Jo had offered to give her time to consider it. And she'd need to know what she was agreeing to before deciding. "I'll concede to your stipulation. We'll talk about what comes next when the event is over."

Jo's face transformed into a smile. "Yeah?"

Aarti slid her finger along the excited curve of Jo's lips. "Yeah."

Concern twisted Jo's features. "Did we lose the moment?"

"A kiss or two will bring it right back." Aarti pulled Jo down until their mouths met. Who was she, half-clothed and making out with a gorgeous woman on a deck overlooking the ocean? She'd never had sex outdoors before, and the thought excited her. Come to think of it, she wouldn't need two hands to count the times she'd had sex outside a bedroom.

Minutes later, Jo had somehow undone her bra to provide more room to leave searing kisses on her breasts. Even the slip of silk against Aarti's skin seemed to burn her. The calluses on Jo's hands only added to the sensations and reignited the fire that shot straight to Aarti's core. She moved Jo's hand lower.

The music had stopped, the party goers retiring or catching the shuttle. Aarti didn't care. All that mattered was Jo's mouth on her sensitive skin, and how the damp trails from Jo's tongue shot like heat lightning across her abdomen when the wind gusted. She held Jo to her breast and scanned the beach, but no one occupied it.

Jo raised her head, and Aarti's wet nipple stood erect in the cool breeze. "You're absolutely gorgeous, and I'm enjoying watching you, but I've got one eye on the shore." She ran her fingers through Aarti's hair. "Your job is to relax."

When Aarti reclined, Jo kissed her again, letting her lips play against hers, her tongue flicking and withdrawing as if teasing and beckoning her. After hesitating, Aarti licked the roof of Jo's mouth, and her low moan did things to Aarti's insides that shouldn't be legal. Jo traced the skin atop the waistband of her underwear, and when

Aarti curled her fingers around her wrist, not to stop her, but to ground herself, Jo lifted Aarti's hand.

For a few moments, she studied the mehndi design, then kissed the painted swirls on Aarti's skin. "I love that."

Aarti had forgotten it was there.

Jo turned her hand over and kissed her palm. "Will you stay the night with me?"

Aarti bit her lower lip. On the off chance her mom or dad knocked on her door in the morning, she'd need to be up early, which shouldn't be an issue. Even with the assistant she'd hired, she'd require every minute to ensure the day proceeded as planned. "Yes, but I need to be awake by six." While eager to spend the night in Jo's arms, she didn't want Jo to ask her inside, at least not yet. She wanted her to finish what they'd started right here.

Jo combed her fingers through Aarti's hair she'd straightened for the occasion. "I love your hair down. You're so beautiful." With a glance in both directions to make sure the beach was clear, she bent and licked first one nipple then the other, then dipped her fingertips under the waistband of Aarti's underwear while studying her.

Aarti lifted the material so Jo could slip her hand inside. Her mind went blank at the feeling of Jo's fingers sliding through her wetness. No, not blank. Too full to form thoughts. She blinked back tears at the absolute exquisiteness of Jo's touch. Jo must have noticed because she kissed the corner of Aarti's eye, and the press of her lips left a wet mark where she'd caught it. They found a rhythm, and Jo's hips surged beneath her. Jo's caresses grew firmer, then she pushed her hand deeper, creating room inside the confining material. When she swirled a finger around her entrance, Aarti nodded, breaking their kiss. "Yes."

Jo slid inside, just one finger, if Aarti had to guess, but her mind was such a kaleidoscope of colors and sensations, she wasn't sure. It didn't matter because Jo soon added another, and the stretch made her gasp. Then Jo pressed the base of her palm against her and curled her fingers. Aarti forced her lids open, needing to see, the fractured colors behind them replaced by a twinkling skyscape and Jo's stunning blue eyes. She hooked her arm around Jo's neck, her breaths coming in shallow pants. Hopefully, the crashing waves would hide any sounds she couldn't contain, because she was about to lose control.

"I—"

Jo nodded, her eyes full of awe. "I know, beautiful."

Aarti's insides clenched. The sheer pleasure coursing through her left her breathless. She arched against Jo's arm as her orgasm hit, but Jo held her, sure and steady, even as she pulled the last euphoric jolts of pleasure from her trembling body.

With a shaky sigh, Aarti went limp, her mind jumbled and broken, only semi-aware of Jo removing her fingers, pulling her close, and throwing the blanket over them. She buried her face into Jo's neck, comforted by the racing pulse against her cheek. Somehow, her hand had landed on a strip of exposed skin between Jo's tank and pants, and she brushed her thumb over it, the simple contact seeming so intimate.

Jo traced Aarti's necklace, tickling her collarbone and making goose bumps rise on her chest. She seemed unhurried, though she had to be aroused. Aarti would have bet her life on it based on the movements of her hips a few minutes ago.

She pulled back. "Hi, you."

Jo kissed her, a simple press of lips. "Hi, yourself. Feel good?"

"Amazing." She nuzzled into Jo's neck again and tasted her skin. Then she sat up and swung her legs to the deck. "Lean forward." Jo did, and she lowered the backrest to a flatter angle. "There."

Jo reclined, her eyebrows twitching a bit. At first glance, she looked relaxed, but her fingers gripping the edge of the cushion betrayed her. Aarti retrieved the now-dry blanket from the railing and folded it. She dropped it on the floor next to the lounger but sat beside Jo, facing her.

"Hi." Jo's voice had taken on a huskier tone.

Aarti ran her hands up Jo's thighs until they rested at the junction of her body. She stroked her thumbs in slow arcs as she lowered her head to kiss that exposed strip of skin. Excitement flowed through her when Jo jumped. "Easy, tiger." She kissed her way up Jo's abdomen, probing the taut muscles with her tongue. When she pushed Jo's tank over her breasts and swirled her tongue around a nipple, Jo gasped. Aarti sat up to check the beach, but it was still clear.

She turned back, covering Jo's body with her own until their lengths met. Their kiss had none of the tameness of a moment ago. While she led the dance of lips and tongues, Jo responded with so much urgency Aarti thought she might come again without even being touched. Jo spread her legs so one of Aarti's fell into place, and Aarti pressed into her. This time, Jo's moan was loud enough that Aarti jerked upright. The beach was still unoccupied.

"You'll have to be quiet, or we need to take this inside. Which is it?" Aarti let her hair brush over Jo's breasts.

Jo dug her fingers into Aarti's hips and pulled her hard against her. "I'll try. You're driving me crazy."

Aarti couldn't contain her smile. How exhilarating, for her to elicit such sounds from Jo. Maybe Jo said these things to all the women she slept with, but her expression appeared genuine.

With her fingers rolling a nipple, Aarti sucked and nibbled until Jo surged against her leg. Aarti slid lower, unbuttoning Jo's pants and pulling them off. She dropped off the lounge chair and onto the folded blanket that would cushion her knees.

"Oh, God." Jo watched, rapt and breathless.

Aarti tugged Jo's hips. "Slide closer." She kissed the skin above the rainbow waistband of Jo's fitted boxers.

Jo wove her hands into Aarti's hair, then gathered and flipped it to one side, presumably so she could watch.

Aarti wished she had a hair tie, but she wasn't about to stop and search for one. She traced a finger down the fly, feeling the soft rise of hair beneath, then cupped her hand over Jo's sex. Dampness met her fingers, and when she pressed a kiss there, Jo jolted. Aarti tugged on the waistband, Jo lifted her hips, and her boxers hit the deck. Gently, Aarti kissed Jo's inner thighs and spread her legs until one fell over the edge of the chair. Jo angled her body toward her, and Aarti moved into the opening, pressing her stomach against the cushion.

Another scent replaced the one she'd come to know as Jo's, still intoxicating but richer. She drew her nose through Jo's light curls and pressed kisses along the crease of her leg. Jo's hand dove into her hair, not pressing or holding, but as though she needed another point of contact. When Aarti glanced up, Jo's eyes were closed, and she'd never seen Jo look more stunning, her small breasts exposed, her dark nipples hard and pointed skyward, and her stomach muscles quivering as Aarti tasted her. Jo's hand in her hair tightened, a thrilling response to her touch.

Aarti closed her eyes, reveling in the taste and scent of her, the smoothness of her sex and her soft, murmured exclamations. Where prior lovers might have urged Aarti to hurry, Jo didn't, though Aarti didn't doubt her need. The wetness coating her chin provided evidence of that, but Jo seemed content to let her take her time. And while Aarti could do this all night, she wanted to give Jo more.

"Can I be inside you?"

"God, yes."

Jo's back left the lounger when she entered her. Aarti waited, enjoying the feel of her against her tongue until Jo relaxed. When Jo tried to take her deeper with a thrust of her hips, Aarti moved, drawing her fingers out until the tips remained, then pushing in again. She ran her tongue around Jo's clit as she increased her speed. As the sound of Jo's panting mingled with the sound of the surf, Aarti smiled against her, and Jo twitched. Jo cradled the back of her head, her hand tangled in Aarti's hair. With each faster thrust, Jo's hips met her. Aarti sucked her clit and flicked it with her tongue. Jo went rigid, and with a guttural, muffled cry, collapsed against the cushion. She lifted Aarti's chin away when Aarti took one last, selfish lick.

While Aarti had been too preoccupied to notice before, her knees now screamed in pain. She rose, only to fall atop Jo, almost crushing her with her entire weight.

Jo caught and held her. "Stay. I like the feel of you on top of me."

Aarti tugged the blanket at their feet over them. She entwined their legs and kissed Jo, languid and soft, the play of tongues slow and lazy. When they'd satisfied themselves, Jo held her.

When Aarti opened her eyes again, she expected to see the pink hues of an oncoming sunrise, but the sky was as dark as India ink.

Jo spoke, her voice sex-drunk and raspy. "I'd love to be the hot, muscular woman who picks you up and carries you to my bed, but I'm afraid I'd drop you. You wrecked me. And both of us have too much to do tomorrow to deal with an injury."

Aarti cupped Jo's breast beneath the blanket. "Look at the stars with me for a few more minutes, then you can take my hand and lead me inside." Warm lips against hers made her forget everything else.

CHAPTER FIVE

"Hey," Jo called from the kitchen as Aarti passed through the dining room.

Aarti detoured and stepped inside.

Jo dried her hands on a towel. "The staff has almost finished cleaning up the rehearsal dinner. Only the dessert table remains, and they're moving it to one side for the dancing."

Aarti knew this because it was her plan in action. "That's great. Let's send people home, but keep one or two to clean up at the end of the evening, please." She glanced around. The bakers had made the pastries and sweets off-site and done final preparations downstairs, but even so, the indoor kitchen looked nearly spotless. The open door to the deck showed staff loading the commercial dishwasher, scrubbing grills, and wiping off surfaces. Jo was all but finished with her responsibilities, at least for today. Tomorrow would call on all her talents to pull off catering breakfast, the intermission, and reception.

"I want to prep a few things tonight. Once they're finished out there, I'll ask Geri to stay and help me make the doughs and pre-measure the spices for tomorrow's dishes. We had some extra time today, so we've already broken down the proteins and marinated everything." Jo leaned against the island. "When I'm finished and you're no longer needed, would you like to take a walk on the beach?"

Aarti glanced at her phone. "I need to touch base with the DJ, the photographers taking candid shots, and the head of the fireworks crew. And I promised my aunt she could tell me about her prize-winning roses. I'm exhausted and have no interest in dancing, but I need to appear for an hour, for Maya's sake. After that, I can slip away."

"Too tired to walk?" A hint of a smile played on Jo's lips.

Is that what they were calling it now? Aarti's mouth watered. "No."

Jo leaned closer but still maintained a respectable distance. "Come to me," she whispered.

Aarti's entire body buzzed as she slipped her phone into her pocket. "It'll be at least ninety minutes." They both seemed to understand she'd agreed to more than a walk. Something swelled inside her. Nervousness? Anticipation?

Jo tossed the towel on the counter with a grin. "See you then."

It turned out, Jo didn't have to wait that long. Aarti Venmoed the photographers their payment and reminded the DJ and the fireworks tech of the noise ordinance. Her aunt Kavita had gushed for twenty minutes about a new variety made by crossing existing rose species, but Aarti couldn't complain. It'd saved her from dancing with her male cousins or Jackson's handsy army friend.

She and Jo had agreed to meet at the cottage, but Aarti hadn't expected to beat her there. Instead of wondering where Jo might be and appearing as though she had nothing better to do than wait around, she showered and changed. Twenty minutes later, as she considered which bottle of wine to open, a light tapping at the sliding glass door made her turn. With a wave, she motioned Jo inside. "Wine?"

Jo closed it behind her. "No, thanks. You've changed. Does that mean you're in for the night?"

"No, I still want to walk with you." Aarti abandoned the wine and grabbed a hoodie from the back of a chair.

Once on the sand, she directed them away from the house and the music. The sky had turned a purplish-black while she'd showered, casting everything in shades of gray. Jo walked beside her, both of them barefoot, and waves washed over their feet. They'd spoken little since Jo had stripped off her chameleon socks on the deck.

"You're quiet tonight."

Jo turned to her, and the lights from the nearest house glinted off her beaming smile. "I'm sorry. I've been lost in thought." She took Aarti's hands in hers. "I've met someone."

Aarti pulled her hands free and tucked them beneath her arms. "What?"

"Yeah, he's amazing." Jo turned over a shell with her toe.

He?

"He's tall," Jo held her hand far above her head, "and broad shouldered. And he loves it when I feed him." She grinned. "Such a hungry boy."

Aarti let her arms drop. "For fuck's sake, Jo. Are you talking about the elephant?"

Jo had already taken her by the waist, and she twirled them around. "His name is Jasper. His handler let me feed him watermelon. He ate it right out of my hand."

Her ebullient laughter made Aarti join in. She put her arms over Jo's shoulders. After a moment, they no longer spun but swayed side to side. "That wasn't very nice." She wove her fingers through the short hair at the nape of Jo's neck, the indentation from the bandana Jo had been wearing still crisp.

"I thought you'd see through me when I said *he*." Jo touched their noses together. "Were you jealous? You dropped my hands like they were on fire. Does this mean you like me, Dr. Singh?"

Did it? Or had she slept with Jo because she'd recently turned forty, had been surrounded by romance all week, and wished she had what Maya had found with Jackson? Clearly, it was more than just sex, or they'd be in bed right now, not taking a moonlit walk on the beach. She wouldn't dare define it as something more profound than all those things, certainly not this early.

"Fine, I like you." Aarti pressed her fingers to Jo's chest. "But this is as good a time as any to inform you that I don't share."

Jo covered her hand. "I don't either. Like I said, I've gotten serious about my life the last year. I've matured. I'm not hanging out in bars on my nights off looking for a woman to take home." She moved their joined hands over her heart. "I accepted more professional responsibilities instead of hiding behind Taylor like I had been. Hell, I even gave up cigarettes."

"I'm glad, because cardiologists aren't fans of smoking." In this position, with Aarti's hand clasped in Jo's, her fingers tangled in Jo's hair, swaying side to side to the faint beat from the party, it almost felt like dancing. Except it felt nothing like times men had grasped her, forcing her this way and that while she fought to keep some distance between them. "Are we dancing?"

Jo glanced at their bare feet as an incoming wave soaked them to their ankles. "I suppose we are." She pressed her hand against Aarti's lower back until their bodies met. "Is that all right?"

"It's nice." Understatement of the year.

A piercing shriek shattered the night, then burst into sparkling diamonds above. More fireworks exploded, and a few houses away, the guests in attendance exclaimed in delight. Then Jo kissed her, and while Aarti could still hear the fireworks, she no longer saw them, no longer needed to. Everything of brilliance was in her arms.

Jo broke the kiss and dipped her, almost dangling her hair in the water. Aarti squealed and laughed as Jo helped right her. Then Jo became serious, touching her face and lips, softly, reverently. Another languid kiss made them sway like the ebb and flow of the waves at their feet.

When the finale ended and muted cheers erupted, Jo entwined their fingers, her stronger ones alternating with Aarti's. Her lips tickled Aarti's ear as she whispered, "How's that for romance, my hopeless romantic?"

My? Is that how Jo saw her? After only a few days? A lump formed in her throat and a fiery ache burned lower.

Jo's question hung in the air. A walk with her lover on the beach, a slow dance in the waves while the sky exploded above, and kisses that made her convinced she didn't need oxygen to survive. What would Jo think if Aarti told her it was the most perfect, most romantic night she'd ever experienced? Too afraid to speak those words, she kissed Jo's cheek instead. "Wonderful. Thank you." She led them toward the cottage.

CHAPTER SIX

A arti tapped at the bedside table until the offensive noise stopped. Through the sheer curtain, dawn glimmered in the east. The nondescript room looked much like hers except for the chef's coats and pants lying rumpled on the floor. *Jo's.* And Jo's arms in which she'd awakened.

Jo groaned and held her tighter. "Five more minutes. I'll help you shower, for speed, of course." She kissed her shoulder.

Aarti swatted her hip. "Liar. I'm on to you." She rubbed her eyes. Despite her intentions to jump out of bed, Jo's hand caressing her side lulled her into relishing a few more moments. She'd savored plenty the night before, and the amazing memories came rushing back, accompanied by a new twinge of arousal. It would have to be ignored until later. Aarti turned toward her, and losing Jo's warmth along her back made her shiver.

Jo kissed her. "Good morning."

"Mmm, it is." Aarti grazed her teeth over Jo's lower lip. "I'd love to stay and do more of this, but I can't." As she sat up, the contents of Jo's open duffel caught her attention. "Wow. How many pairs of socks did you think you'd need?" Bright, funky colors and designs filled half the bag.

"I like to have choices based upon my mood. Same for my bandanas. A chef's uniform is boring, so I spice mine up." Jo flashed her a sheepish grin. "No pun intended."

"My mother's expression was priceless when she saw your socks when you arrived." Aarti smiled in remembrance. "Which ones are you wearing today?"

"How about," Jo leaned over the edge of the bed, "these." She dropped a rolled pair into Aarti's palm.

"Purple eggplants?" Aarti covered her mouth with her hand. "Oh, no. Please tell me you won't."

"But look." Jo unrolled them and held them up. "The ones around the ankle have googly eyes." She erupted in a fit of laughter. "*Your* eyes are enormous right now."

Aarti shook her head. "You're awful. Even if my mother doesn't get the joke, others would."

"What do you mean? They're eggplants. I'm a chef." Jo's grin pulled her mouth to one side before she leaned over again. "These would be appropriate for today." She handed Aarti a pair of bright red and brown socks.

"Peanuts?" Aarti unrolled them but found no googly eyes or other surprises.

Jo flopped back on the bed, her arms crossed behind her head. She didn't appear self-conscious of her half-naked state, and Aarti let her gaze roam. The view was delightful.

"You know, because elephants like peanuts." Jo wore a proud expression.

"Ah, such a comic." Aarti rolled the socks and tossed them at Jo's stomach.

Jo made no move to catch them, and they bounced off her abs, reminding Aarti how firm those muscles had been under her touch. Damn, she needed to get out of this bed.

"Well done. I'm impressed. Now I," she leaned close to kiss her one last time, "need to shower. Next door. Alone."

Jo watched as she searched for her clothing. "When do you get dressed up? I assume you'll need to change and have your hair and makeup done, right?"

"I scheduled time. My assistant has worked on a few events with me, so she'll handle anything that comes up while I'm changing or with the stylist. I'll apply my makeup." She buttoned her shirt, pulled on her pants, and balled her bra and underwear in her hand.

"Come here."

Aarti tilted her head. "I really need to go, and I'm not sure of your intentions."

"One more kiss. I promise. It's going to be torture without being able to look at you or touch you all day." Jo extended her hand.

"One kiss, and no innuendo. I need to trust you." Aarti came closer.

Jo curled her fingers around the back of her neck, and the kiss almost had Aarti ripping off her clothes and leaping back into the bed. It hadn't lasted thirty seconds, but she pulled away breathless, almost wishing she'd said no and left. Jo could kiss, and she couldn't afford to be rendered so defenseless, not now.

"I can't wait to see your outfit." Jo licked her lower lip in an absentminded sort of way. "Dress or pants? No, wait. Don't tell me. I want to be surprised."

Aarti retrieved her phone from beside the bed. "I doubt it'll be what you expect."

"I expect you'll look gorgeous, but I'll behave myself and keep my glance quick. You could text me a selfie, or better yet, stop by the kitchen and ask why I chose rumali roti when it's so time-consuming to make." Jo wiggled her eyebrows. "I'll give you a very detailed answer while I appreciate your attire."

"You've put some thought into this." Yet she warmed under Jo's appreciative scrutiny, even while standing in yesterday's clothing. Again, what did Jo see in her? "Keep in mind I'm not the typical wedding guest. Even though I'm Maya's sister, I'm working, so I don't want you to be disappointed."

Jo ran a hand through her hair, a glimmer in her eyes. "Not possible, Dr. Singh. Not even remotely possible."

Aarti glanced at Maya, who sat on the bed. The room had been Maya's since their parents had built the home in the Hamptons. Maya's hands shook. Beside her, their mother seemed unsure what to do.

Aarti keyed her walkie. "Bree, I need a bottle of water. Oh, and ask the chef to make a pitcher of iced tea and bring it up. Hurry with the water."

"Okie-doke. Roger, over and out."

Aarti cringed. While over the top at times, at least Bree got things done.

While waiting, she glanced around. Unlike her quarters, Maya's room looked like a field of wildflowers had exploded, even on the lacy curtains. Jackson was staying in what had been Aarti's old room. With its off-white walls and simple blinds, it was as uninteresting as her. She'd used the guest cottage for the last ten years because of the view and its privacy, something she valued even more this week. But now was not the time to fixate on why she appreciated no prying eyes.

Aarti regretted barking orders at Bree, something she never did. But they hadn't had a bride hyperventilate from a panic attack either. Now her primary focus needed to be making sure the two wedding ceremonies occurred.

Her mother rubbed Maya's back. "Just breathe."

Maya needed time and a dose of logic, both of which Aarti would provide. The three of them sat quietly for a bit.

Maya's ashen face and terrified expression contrasted with the festive designs covering her arms and feet. She twisted the comforter between her fingers. "What if I'm making a mistake?"

Their mother scoffed. "It's normal for a bride to feel this way. I was a mess before I married your father."

"But after today, it's official, and I don't know if I'm ready for that." Maya wailed the last word, and tears rolled over her cheeks.

Aarti touched her leg. "You're just nervous and stressed, darling. Try not to cry, or your eyes will swell and be red in your photos. Remember, you love Jackson, and he loves you."

"What do I have to be stressed about?" Maya gestured at her. "You're taking care of everything. How are *you* not stressed?"

Aarti's stomach churned. She hadn't been expecting this from Maya. This delay threw off her entire schedule, but unless she got Maya to come around, it wouldn't matter if things happened on time. There'd be no wedding.

Bree ran in out of breath, her blond ponytail swinging, and handed Aarti a bottle of water. "Chef said she'll make tea. The linens just arrived, so I'll be downstairs. Call me on my walkie if you need me."

Aarti thanked her, and Bree closed the door behind her. "Here, drink this." Aarti uncapped the bottle and pressed it into Maya's hand. "This is what I do. I'm not stressed because I have a solid plan, I realize unexpected things happen, and I'll do my best with what I'm given. I've had no major hiccups yet, and you will not be my first. The two of you spent more than a year imagining this, incorporating traditions that mattered while making it all your own. No one will ever have a wedding day quite like yours. You're just nervous, sweetheart, and I'm sure your gorgeous husband-to-be is, too."

Her mom studied Aarti, but her dark eyes provided no clues to her thoughts.

"Yeah, you're right." Maya sniffed, then laughed. "He's usually the emotional one, and I'll hide your favorite stethoscope if you tell him I said that."

"There's no shame in having nerves. It's emotional. If it wasn't, it wouldn't hold the same meaning." She tucked Maya's hair behind her ear. "But you two adore one another, and you're going to have the most amazing day."

Maya smiled, her sniffles turning to hiccups. "Yeah, we are, aren't we?"

Her mother mouthed the words "thank you" from Maya's other side.

Pride suffused Aarti. It had been some time since she'd impressed her mother. Would this be the first step toward mending their relationship? She luxuriated in the feeling while Maya tried to tame her hiccupping.

Someone knocked, and Maya called, "Come in."

Jo peered around the door. "Hi, I hope I'm not intruding. I brought tea."

Aarti stood, moving bottles of perfume to make room on the dresser for the tray. When Jo set it down, her heart sank. After solving one issue, Aarti was about to have another. Out of the corner of her eye, she saw her mother stand.

"That's not iced tea."

Jo smiled, but it wasn't the same easy-going smile she gave Aarti. This one looked forced. "No, I made iced chai for you instead. Would you prefer black tea?"

Her mother inspected the glass pitcher, picking up the long metal spoon and stirring the contents. "I prefer my chai hot."

"I don't." Maya rose and poured herself a glass, splashing tea onto the tray as ice cubes rushed over the rim of the pitcher. "You should drink some, Mom. It's already warm in here."

"Yes. Why is it?" Her mom fanned her face.

Jo stepped forward to pour her a glass, and Aarti held her breath. Her mother held very strong opinions on her favorite drink, and no one ever made it right, Aarti included. She'd long ago quit wondering why her mother continued to order it from places she knew would disappoint her.

"Where did you find chai? I thought I was out." Her mother's eyebrows had formed a V.

Jo handed her the glass. "I didn't. I made it."

Her mom paused, the glass halfway to her mouth. "What do you mean?"

"From scratch, with the spices you had and those I'd brought or ordered."

Jo shrugged as if to say it hadn't been a big deal, and Aarti was sure it hadn't been.

Maya made a noise, and Aarti looked at her. Her eyes had nearly rolled back in her head. "That's fantastic." She pressed the glass to her cheek. Her hiccups had subsided.

Her mom turned to Jo. "You know, if you add spices, technically that makes it—"

"Masala chai, yes. I should have said that, and I used whole milk like they do in India."

Her mother's expression softened, though she still held the concoction in midair. "Well." She took a sip, her eyelids fluttering, then swallowed, licked her lips, and stared at it. "That's rather good." Another drink followed. "Yes, that's very good. Not too sweet. Sometimes I order it and worry I'll have a cavity by nightfall. Did you toast the spices?"

"Yes, in a skillet for speed. It sounded like you were..." Jo glanced at Maya, then to Aarti, her eyes wide like she'd realized she shouldn't mention Maya's breakdown. "Parched."

Maya twirled her hand in a small circle. "Yes, I was having a moment, but I'm fine now. This helps." She added more to her glass.

"I prefer toasting them in a pan." Her mother drank a sizeable mouthful and closed her eyes as if to savor it. She made a smacking noise. "Delicious. Is that lemongrass?"

"It is." Jo seemed to grow two inches.

This was going far better than Aarti had expected. She was afraid to move and break whatever spell Jo had cast over her mother.

"Would you like some?" Jo picked up the third glass.

"How can I not after the rave reviews?" One sip told Aarti why her mother and Maya were acting like toddlers experiencing their first taste of ice cream. "They're right. It's very good." Not too sweet, creamy, and spicy. Addicting. She couldn't look at Jo. If she had, everyone in the room would see her starry-eyed admiration and more.

"I should get back to the kitchen."

Jo made it as far as the doorway before her mom spoke from where she'd perched on the edge of the bed. "Jo? It's Jo, isn't it?"

"Yes, Dr. Singh." Jo nearly stood at attention.

"Or do you prefer Chef…" Her mom waved her fingers as if trying to recall Jo's surname, not that she'd ever known it.

"Samuels, but Jo is fine."

"Call me Vidya."

Aarti consciously closed her mouth.

Her mother gestured to the nearly empty pitcher. "Could you please bring more of that around in an hour? It'll be twenty degrees warmer in here with the stylists and their equipment."

Aarti almost interjected. Jo wasn't here to wait on them, but when she glanced at Jo, she appeared so elated. And her mother had said please. Plus, who was Aarti to judge? She'd just ordered Bree around in the same manner. Perhaps she wasn't so dissimilar to her mother after all.

"I'd be happy to, Vidya." Jo picked up the tray.

"Here. Top me off." Her mother held out her glass. "No reason to waste that."

Aarti stared at the ice cubes floating in the top of her drink until Jo had gone. How surreal.

❖

Aarti surveyed the enormous, three-peaked tent with its stunning ocean view and the hundred-plus guests dining beneath it. She'd scheduled an intermission and light meal between services so the staff could transform the décor from the pale pastels of the midday wedding to the bright colors of the Hindu ceremony.

From her quick foray through the tent, she'd heard nothing but delighted comments about the food. Two long buffet tables on each side held an array of small bites. She'd admired the tempting finger foods, including many vegetarian options. Even the pickiest eater would find something delicious.

An attractive woman in a wheelchair caught her eye. So did the striking woman with long, dark hair pushing her. Aarti recognized Taylor from their one face-to-face meeting and then Erin from the few times she'd seen her on television. They were a very good-looking couple.

"You made it." Aarti took in Taylor's cast and wrist splint, then the gorgeous diamond on her left hand. "How are you feeling?"

"Better, thanks. The meds help. This is my wife, Erin Rasmussen."

"It's a pleasure. " Aarti motioned to the lawn. "I'm sorry you have to navigate over the grass."

Erin smiled and toyed with Taylor's hair. "I don't mind. It's a good arm workout."

"I can assign one of the staff to help you." Aarti glanced around to see if any of them were available.

"Thank you, but we don't need to do much moving around." Erin rested her hands on Taylor's shoulders.

Taylor covered one of Erin's with hers. "I wouldn't mind touching base with Jo after she's finished with the reception. I'm sure she's in the thick of it, but so far, I think she's done a better job than I could've. I hope you feel the same."

Aarti didn't want to reveal her true opinions of Jo, so she stuck to the safe topic of the menu. "The food has been fantastic. My entire family is going to lose their minds over her Indian dishes. Consider increasing her salary now before some of them band together and poach her to be their private chef."

Taylor beamed. "I'm so glad. This whole situation," she waved at her cast and splint, "made me feel terrible about not being able to do this for Jackson and Maya."

"You're here for them today, and that's what counts." Aarti glanced between them. "I hope to see you two on the dance floor tonight. Make Jackson teach you how to do a wheelie." She gave them a fond smile, promised to chat with them later, and headed for the house.

After telling the same staff member for the second time where the flowers from the Christian ceremony should be kept, she headed for the kitchen. As she passed the mirror above the entryway table, she smoothed her saffron-colored suit.

"Aarti, what's your twenty?"

At times, Bree got a little too excited about using the walkies.

Aarti keyed her mic. "Main house."

"We have an issue." Bree sounded breathless. "They're erecting the canopy for the mandap, but they can't get the trellis inside the garage because it's too tall."

"Have them leave it on the side." She assessed her hair in the mirror. The stylist had done a marvelous job, and a finishing dose of extra-hold spray had made sure nothing had moved. Would Jo like her hair up like this? It differed from her usual ponytail, especially with the soft tendrils framing her face.

"That's where they're readying the elephant."

"Oh, right. Behind the garage then. If that doesn't work, have them store it next to the tennis court near the stand of trees."

"Got it." Bree sounded relieved.

Aarti hadn't seen Jo since Maya's incident. While she shouldn't bother her, she couldn't help herself. And Jo had wanted to see her attire. With a palm on her chest, she tried to steady her breathing.

When she entered the kitchen, a flurry of activity greeted her. Jo had her back to her, shaking a pan of something on the stove. Geri skewered miniature sandwiches with toothpicks and cherry tomatoes, stabbing them with dizzying speed.

Larry burst in from the outdoor kitchen. "Fresh ones." He slid a hotel pan of something fried on the end of the island.

Jo turned and saw Aarti. Her eyes widened, and she fumbled the sauté pan. It clattered to the floor as she danced her feet out of harm's way. What looked like sliced almonds dotted the tile.

A guy from the catering team had just slipped behind. He spun, and his mouth dropped open. "I'm so sorry, Chef. I should've said behind."

"It's fine. It was me." Jo turned the burner off and bent to retrieve the pan.

"I got it, Chef." He grabbed a handful of paper towels.

Jo handed him the towel she'd been using to protect her hand from the heat of the pan's handle and stepped around him. "Did you need something?"

"I wanted to speak with you. First, you've chosen to serve rumali roti when it's time-consuming to make. Why?"

The corners of Jo's mouth twitched. "Rumali roti, yes." She licked her lower lip as she slowly took in Aarti's attire. "Many cooks find it finicky, but all it takes is practice. I've made hundreds of them in a single day. My host mother even gifted me a tawa for my birthday. I decided a wedding of this caliber deserves such a delicacy." Jo didn't make eye contact with her until she finished. Intense eye contact.

Aarti's skin probably emitted as much fiery orange as her outfit. She forced a swallow. "I also noticed an issue with something you've stored in the pantry." Even though she hadn't raised her voice or intended it to sound accusatory, those in the kitchen scattered and found a task that seemed to need their undivided attention.

"The pantry?" A divot appeared between Jo's eyebrows.

Aarti opened the frosted glass door and motioned her inside. She followed and closed it behind them.

"There's no issue in the pantry, is there?" A slow smile formed on Jo's face. "And wow, you look fantastic." She took another appreciative glance at her outfit.

"Oh, there's an issue." Aarti was conscious of how little time she had and how badly she needed this. Backing Jo against the shelves, she cupped her face and kissed her. "I've been wanting to do that all day."

Jo grasped her hips, keeping a few inches between them. "I might have food on my apron. I don't want to ruin your sexy suit."

Aarti pressed their bodies together. She needed to feel her. "I don't care. I'm taking it off soon."

Jo groaned. "You are?" She slipped a leg between hers. "Why?"

"This is what I wore for the first ceremony. I'm changing soon for the second."

Jo's eyes gleamed. "Oh, you didn't tell me this was only the appetizer."

Pure desire laced their next kiss.

"Hey."

They jumped apart at Bree's voice in the small space. It was Jo's walkie, not hers, Aarti discovered when they pulled them from their pockets.

"I'm in the tent. The south buffet is out of crab rangoons, Chef, and both are out of fondue."

Jo quickly kissed her. "I gotta go." She keyed her mic. "Rangoons are on their way." With a step around Aarti, she exited the pantry. "Fondue is five minutes out." Jo slipped the walkie into her pocket, motioned to a member of her crew, and shoved the hotel pan at him. "Take these to the south buffet and refill the chili sauce. Geri, I need that fondue stat."

"It's ready, Chef."

For a few seconds, Aarti watched Jo manage her team. It appeared Jo had forgotten she was there, but Aarti doubted it. The lingering tingle would remind her, and hopefully Jo, of their kiss for some time. Yet, many hours remained before Aarti could claim the event a success and hurry to the cottage and into Jo's bed. She slipped out the side door. First things first. A wardrobe change was in order.

CHAPTER SEVEN

A arti surveyed the reception from the rear of the tent. A shocking amount of fairy lights crisscrossed high above the heads of the guests, all of whom appeared to be enjoying themselves. Maya and Jackson drew her attention, grinning as they danced as husband and wife for the first time. Around the room, caterers removed abandoned dessert plates and half-eaten slices of cake. Those drinking, mostly Maya and Jackson's friends or invitees from Jackson's side of the family—though a few from hers—sipped on expensive champagne or the occasional cocktail.

Jackson stood out, tall and handsome in his pineapple-yellow silken pancha dhoti. He appeared mesmerized by Maya, resplendent in her bright red and gold lehenga, a vermilion streak of sindoor marking her forehead. She wore the mangalsutra he'd given her during the ceremony, the delicate black and gold necklace catching the light. As they danced and turned, pure joy upon their faces, they appeared more like one entity than two, much like the necklace signified. A heaviness filled Aarti. Would she ever know that feeling?

The song ended, and the DJ segued into the next, a lively hit popular at weddings. People crowded onto the dance floor.

"Excuse me, Dr. Singh?" Jo stood beside her in a pristine chef's coat minus her apron.

Aarti backed a few steps away, although the couple remaining at the nearest table had their attention on the dance floor. "Yes?"

Jo pointed toward the house. "Do you have a spare minute?"

"Of course." Her heart sank. Was something wrong? Everything had gone so well until now. The elephant had waited to do his business until after the ceremony, the wedding cake had arrived in perfect condition, Maya hadn't had any more nervous episodes, and the guests had raved about the dinner to the point she'd worried whether Jo's cooking might've overshadowed the vows.

She followed Jo onto the main deck, then around the corner, but Jo didn't go inside. Instead, she held Aarti at arm's length under the glow of the security light.

"Jesus, you should've told me you'd look like this." Jo appeared to admire the long, flowing folds of her turquoise saree, pausing when she reached the small amount of midriff exposed between Aarti's blouse and the drape.

Incapable of moving or speaking, she let Jo look until their gazes met again.

"Your hair." Jo touched a tendril. "My God, you look stunning."

Aarti raised her hand to her hair, though it likely didn't need fixing, but it gave her a moment to unstick her tongue from the roof of her mouth. "Thank you. You think so?"

Jo inhaled. "I can't even find the words to tell you." She ticked each of Aarti's gold bracelets with her fingertip. "Look at you."

Praise like this from Jo rendered Aarti speechless. Had someone ever impaired her ability to think or speak? Her first days of residency and fellowship had seen her more confident and articulate than this, and she hadn't a clue what she'd been doing then. Something about the wonder in Jo's appraising eyes and the reassurance of her words and touch made Aarti believe it. Jo found her beautiful. *Her.*

"I was dying to see what you wore. When I did, I had to have a few minutes alone with you, even though I promised to be good." Jo shuffled her feet. "I'm sorry. This is your sister's wedding. That was selfish."

"You're fine. It's nice to see you for a few minutes." Aarti touched the knotted buttons on Jo's coat.

The song ended, and a microphone screeched. "Sorry. Sorry, folks."

Jackson's amplified voice reached them where they stood. Aarti curled her fingers into Jo's jacket and fought the urge to rush to the tent. This wasn't on the run of show. What was he doing?

"This guy will play more music for you in a minute," Jackson said. "I know the official speeches are over, but I need to tell everyone how much this woman means to me. Right before I met Maya was one of the lowest periods of my life. I wanted to be strong and fight through it, but the darkness kept pulling me down. My therapist suggested turning my efforts toward helping others versus dwelling on my situation. That's how I ended up at the fundraiser the night we met."

She and Jo hadn't broken eye contact the entire time he'd been speaking. Jo rested her hands on her waist, and the warmth on Aarti's exposed midriff made her tremble. She draped her wrists over Jo's shoulders.

"So, my point is—"

"You have one?" A heckler—probably his brother and best man—interrupted him, and the guests broke out in laughter.

"Yeah, I do. My point is, if I had to choose between Maya and being able to walk, I'd happily sacrifice my other leg. She's my everything, now and forever."

A chorus of sappy sounds and clapping hands followed Jackson's impassioned speech. Then an upbeat song took over.

Aarti's blood whooshed in her ears. "Is that what it's like? Love?" It embarrassed her to ask, but she needed to know if that's how it felt, and whether the wonderful emotions she'd been experiencing might be somewhere in the vicinity, not there yet, but like a moon orbiting a planet, growing ever closer.

Jo blinked. "Why are you asking *me*?"

"Sophie. Weren't you in love with her?" An ache formed in Aarti's chest. She wasn't sure which answer she hoped to hear.

"I thought so at the time, maybe until recently." Jo adjusted her bright green bandana with one hand. "Now I...I'm not sure what to think."

"Oh." Aarti looked away.

"What is it?"

Aarti closed her eyes. "I don't know. Perhaps these weddings are getting to me. All this romance is a reminder of what I've never had."

"Never?" Jo's soft question held no derision or judgment, only sincerity.

"No." Could Jo see her blush in the light from the bulb above them?

Jo brought her mouth to Aarti's ear, so close her breath sent goose bumps sprouting upon every inch of Aarti's flesh, exposed or not. "Last night was pretty romantic, if I remember correctly. And it was ours, no one else's."

With her arms around Jo, Aarti closed her eyes. "Yes."

Jo moved a curl aside to brush her lips below Aarti's ear. Then she kissed a path to the corner of her mouth. "I might not be able to answer your question, but I'm certain we can conjure up something romantic later."

The kitchen door opened, and they sprung away from one another.

Her father stepped outside and halted when he saw them. "Oh, sorry. I needed my pill. Aarti, a word?"

"Excuse me." Jo passed her.

After the door closed, her dad scratched his head, then smoothed his hair into place. "So, you seem to get along well with the chef."

She swallowed. "Yes, she's very capable."

"I'll say." His features softened. "Her curry is something else."

"Yes, all her food is excellent." She wanted to hide until Jackson and Maya drove away in the Rolls Royce to the honeymoon suite at the resort where they'd stay until their flight tomorrow. Maybe her father would forget anything he might've witnessed amid the farewells. How much had he seen?

He scowled. "Don't disappoint your mother right now, beta, not after everything you've worked so hard for. This is Maya's time, and the moon shouldn't outshine the sun."

Acid surged up her esophagus at his words, even though she knew he often invented sayings to make a point. "I understand." She might, if she thought she'd ever have a time. Sure, if she'd wanted to date Jamal in radiology or Harini's son, like her mom had suggested, then she might've had a time to call her own. But a lesbian daughter who'd developed feelings for an out and proud chef wouldn't be given time in her family.

Her father turned the corner. Aarti counted to twenty, wanting to avoid any continuation of the conversation, and followed. She was tempted to let Bree handle most of the remaining tasks. Her father's decree had sucked everything from her.

She'd lived and breathed the preparation for this event, and now she just wanted it to be over. That said, she didn't want to face what would happen once she and Jo went back to Manhattan, when their fling would likely end and Jo would vanish, leaving a crater the size of Columbus Circle in the center of her chest. How could she go to Jo tonight now, even if they did nothing more than talk? What would happen if her parents found out?

Aarti dismissed those thoughts. The evening wasn't over, and things still needed to be done. If she expected her parents to respect her as an event planner, she needed to end tonight on a high note.

❖

Aarti entered the cottage and tossed her phone on the table. She hadn't been able to forget her father's admonition. As she'd watched the last shuttle bus depart, she'd made a decision. She'd shower, eat the crackers in her purse because she'd been too busy to enjoy the buffet, and go to bed. Perhaps have a glass of wine. What she definitely shouldn't do was leave her cottage before ten the next morning. Everything had gone so well. Jeopardizing her success in her parents' eyes by doing something stupid was an enormous risk.

Based on the light she'd seen coming from the windows of the opposite unit, Jo was awake. Had she heard Aarti come in? In the darkness, Aarti flipped the lock on the slider and drew the blinds. She leaned against the adjacent wall. There, Jo wouldn't be tempted to knock now. The only way to be more clear would be to hang a sign that said Go Away.

She massaged her forehead. After the spectacular feat she'd just pulled off, she'd expected to be ecstatic. Sure, one member of the crew seemed incapable of following simple directions and spent more time vaping than unfolding chairs, but otherwise, everything had gone according to plan. According to *her* plan. She'd been the organizer, vetted the vendors, and made sure that she gave both ceremonies equal time and respect. Maya and Jackson had articulated their wishes, and she'd made them happen. So, why did she feel like the elephant had trampled on her stomach?

She pushed away from the wall, stepped out of her flats, and unwound her saree. It had been a long day and night, and she should shower, but Jo might hear through their shared wall. Aarti paused. Did she intend to hide until Jo left? How rude after everything Jo had done for her family. What then? She tossed the saree over a chair and rooted around in her purse. The crackers had been smashed to crumbs, and she threw the mangled package toward the trash. Fuck this. Yes, it was stupid, and she'd probably regret it, but this was her chance to talk with Jo, to determine what they would do after tomorrow. In the bathroom, she turned on the water.

As it heated, she put on her robe and flicked on lights on her way to the living room. She retracted the blinds and unlocked the slider, the ocean a sea of blackness beyond the short deck.

Hot water sluiced over her body in the shower. Steam filled her nostrils, and she closed her eyes. With her hands flattened against the wall, her thoughts drifted to Jo and whether Jo could hear her. Had she noticed Aarti's attempt to lock herself away?

When the water cooled, she got out. Steam covered the mirror, and the unusual impulse to write something in it, like initials or a heart—or both—was only quashed with her finger a few inches away. Was she twelve?

In the bedroom, she pulled on sweats and a T-shirt, then paused. The place hadn't smelled like this before her shower. She wandered into the living area where the aroma grew stronger. Jo stood in front of the stove, stirring something in a small saucepan. The microwave dinged.

"What are you doing?"

Jo jumped. "I didn't know you were out already. That's a noisy microwave." She turned off the burner. "I'm making us dinner."

"You've been cooking since early this morning. I'm sure you're exhausted." Aarti peered into the containers.

Jo tucked Aarti's damp hair behind her ear. "And you worked all day. If yours was anything like mine, and I know you, you didn't stop to eat anything. So, I brought leftovers for us. I hope you don't mind."

"Mind? I could kiss you." Her words didn't register until Jo touched her cheek.

"Please do." Jo hesitated, only a few millimeters separating their lips.

But Aarti didn't. Trembling shook her limbs. "I don't know what I'm doing," she whispered. She'd kept her emotions at bay until now, but whether because of fatigue or Jo's presence, she no longer could.

Instead of kissing her, Jo pulled her into a tight hug. When Aarti buried her face in the crook of Jo's neck, the fresh scent almost made her weep. Jo also must have showered. With occasional kisses to her forehead, Jo rubbed her back.

After a minute or two, Aarti collected herself and straightened. Jo held her by the shoulders. "You okay?"

"I'm sorry. I don't know what came over me."

Jo led her to a chair, sat, and pulled her sideways onto her lap. "Is this related to your dad finding us on the deck?"

Aarti nodded and recounted the conversation. "So, I shouldn't be here with you."

"Is that why you pulled your blinds earlier?" Jo squeezed her knee.

Aarti couldn't contain her self-deprecating laugh. "I tried to stay away from you, but I didn't last ten minutes." She caressed Jo's cheek. "What is it about you that makes me keep coming back?"

Jo took her hand and kissed her knuckles. With a serious expression, she said, "My food."

Aarti laughed but quickly became serious. "I'm a mess."

"The loveliest one I've ever seen." Jo gave her a quick kiss, then tapped her leg.

Aarti stood.

"Splash some cool water on your face, and when you come back, we're going to eat dinner and relax."

With the steam now dissipated, Aarti recoiled at her reflection in the bathroom mirror. Jo *must* like her because she looked frightful, hair frizzing as it dried and dark circles below her eyes she hadn't noticed earlier. She did as Jo suggested and then pulled her hair into a ponytail.

When she returned, plates of food awaited her. Jo might've been ambitious in her estimation of how much they could eat, but Aarti planned to give it her damned best. Her stomach had been rumbling since the intermission.

"Wine?" Jo held open the refrigerator.

Around a mouthful of naan, Aarti managed a noise that must've sounded like an affirmative because Jo selected a bottle.

When she joined her, they sat cross-legged in front of the coffee table. The guests had been right. Jo's food was delicious, and her thoughtfulness to set some aside almost made Aarti choke up again. She leaned her head on Jo's shoulder as she chewed a bite of palak paneer. They ate in near silence, no TV or music, not even the slider open to allow the lulling sound of the ocean in, just the two of them enjoying a quiet meal. What Aarti wouldn't give to replicate this scenario most nights of the week.

As Jo put the remaining food away so Aarti could take it back to Manhattan, she refilled their glasses. They moved to the deck where Jo snuggled behind her and pulled a blanket over them.

Aarti tilted her head to look at her. "I agreed to your demand that we revisit things when the week was over. So, now what?" Her stomach churned as she wondered whether Jo had changed her mind in the interim.

Jo kissed her temple. "What do you think, Dr. Singh?"

Aarti angled her body so she could rest her cheek against Jo's shirt. "I like you, and I'm attracted to you, as you've probably noticed. If I was another woman from another family, I'd say, 'Let's make a go of this. I might not have a ton of free time, and you run a brand new restaurant, but maybe we can find one night a week to spend together.'"

Jo stiffened. "But you're not another woman from another family."

"No." Aarti squeezed her eyes shut.

"Yet your event was a smash. If we were to see each other in the city, it'd no longer steal Maya's thunder." Jo gently rocked her.

"No, but my mother and I work together." Aarti opened her eyes to find Jo watching her. "She insists that what I do in my personal life reflects on her and the family."

"Still, we should be able to coordinate one night a week. I'd like to explore what's between us. I guess the question is, are you willing to sneak around?"

In the distance, the lights of fishing vessels flickered. How had she and Jo been strangers a few short days ago? It didn't seem possible. What small percentage of the time since then had she spent in Jo's arms? Whatever the answer, it'd been too short. "Yes, but will that be enough?"

She listened to Jo's heart beat as she waited for her to answer. Seven strong beats. It was a minuscule amount of time each week. Could they manage?

"It has to be." Jo's voice had become gravelly. "I'm not willing to walk away from finding out what this is. So if one night a week is all we have for now, we'll make it work."

Aarti liked Jo and might be falling for her, but she needed to have realistic expectations. "This means we won't be hanging out with my family and can't go places where medical professionals frequent. And my mother and I usually walk to work together. When you and I have sex, it will need to be at your place, and I'll need to go home at a reasonable hour."

"I hadn't thought about that."

Fear crept up Aarti's spine. Did that mean Jo didn't want to go through with it? Her eyes stung, and she started to stand, but Jo caught her.

"Hang on. I didn't say I was reconsidering. I simply said I hadn't thought about it." Jo kissed her cheek. "How do I keep you from running when you're afraid?"

Aarti leaned back and allowed herself to relax before she answered. "I'm sorry. I don't have much experience with any of this."

Jo tipped her face up. "I want to be the person you run toward, not from."

The kiss that came next should have calmed Aarti, soothed her fears, but that wasn't the effect it had, and the throbbing between her thighs made her squirm. She twisted to face Jo, and when she couldn't get close enough, she straddled her. Their tongues battled, and she tore at Jo's clothing.

Jo broke the kiss and grasped her hands. "Easy, easy. I want to take it slow tonight because it's going to need to last me until I can see you again." She kissed her knuckles. "Come on, Dr. Singh. Let's go to bed."

Aarti studied Jo for a moment, caressing her face and running her fingers through her damp hair. She liked this woman, this understanding soul who was compassionate and kind, and willing to put up with her silly insecurities. "After you, Chef Samuels."

As Jo led her to the bedroom, a flash of something bright and pure speared Aarti. How long had it been since she'd known what hope felt like? Since she'd felt the sheer thrill of anticipation that marked something good? Yes, it was about time she did what she wanted with her life.

CHAPTER EIGHT

Aarti took a bottle of water from the refrigerator in the doctors' lounge, stifled a yawn, and claimed her favorite table by the window while her stir-fry reheated. She liked the view, even if the brown vinyl chairs on this side of the room had torn seats. Finally getting to eat almost two hours past noon at least provided quiet.

She pulled a fork rolled in a napkin from her bag. Jo often packed her a lunch after a night of cooking for her, and Aarti wondered if Jo made extra just so she could. Upon unrolling it, a flash of red caught her eye. She smoothed the paper to find a heart drawn in marker. When she turned it over, it was blank.

A heart? Jo had drawn a heart for her?

They'd been sneaking around for months, scrambling to find rare nights and even rarer days in which to spend with one another. Jo didn't work on Mondays since it was her least busy day, but even taking one day off from a new restaurant was often difficult.

A heart.

What had Jo meant when she drew it? Aarti traced the red ink with her fingertip. Did it mean Jo loved her? Exhilaration surged through her like she'd gotten an amp of IV epinephrine. While Aarti had suspected her feelings had been heading that way for some time, and she knew Jo cared for her, she hadn't assumed Jo felt the same. They'd never said the words. Were they in love? Were they even in a relationship? They hadn't used the term girlfriend, but then again, so few people knew about them, they hadn't needed to define what they were to each other.

The buzz of the microwave startled her. She carried her food to her seat. Once she'd settled, she slid out the napkin and looked at it again. Their time together was precious, and seeing Jo was the highlight of every week. In such a short amount of time, Jo had gotten to know her better than anyone, could read her better than her family or colleagues, and had become the most important person in her life. Aarti's chin quivered. Someone so dear, something so precious, shouldn't have to be kept a secret.

She stabbed a piece of tofu and stared out the window at nothing in particular. Her morning had been hectic, but the empty lounge gave her uninterrupted time to consider what might have inspired Jo to do this. Or it did until her mother entered and scanned the room, her eyes brightening when she saw her.

Aarti quickly folded the napkin into her hand.

"Good afternoon, Dr. Singh."

"Hi, Mom. How's your day?"

Her mother gestured toward the opposite chair. "May I join you?" At Aarti's nod, she sat and unwrapped her sandwich. "Difficult surgery this morning. Couldn't get her heart started off pump and ended up losing her."

Aarti knew the death of a patient, especially in the operating room, always affected her mother. She squeezed her hand. "I'm sorry, Mom."

Her mother skated past the platitude and eyed Aarti's lunch. "That looks healthy. Did you make it?"

Aarti pushed a mushroom aside and speared a snow pea. "Yes, healthy but delicious." In truth, her only contribution had been rinsing the rice, at least until Jo had slid her hands under her shirt from behind. The next thing Aarti knew, her back was on the tile with Jo's head pressed between her thighs. Later, when they'd sat down to eat and uncooked grains of rice had fallen from Jo's hair, they'd laughed until they cried. The memory made her smile.

"What's that about?" Her mother circled a finger in front of her face. "You seem to be enjoying something amusing."

"It's nothing." Aarti wasn't about to tell her mother about the memory. She crushed the napkin tighter.

"You had that fortieth anniversary this weekend, right?" Her mom extricated an onion from her sandwich and set it aside. "Are you looking so vibrant because it went well?"

Aarti's stomach tightened at the dozens of lies she'd told her parents since Maya's wedding. She hated dishonesty. "Yes, they were quite pleased." While true, it wasn't the entire reason for her demeanor. "I don't know how you find time to plan events around all this." Her mother made a sweeping motion. "Or why you'd want to. You're going to exhaust yourself."

Her mother was partially right. Aarti often had trouble finding enough hours in the day, sometimes using her lunch to return calls or send emails to her clients. In this month alone, she'd planned the anniversary, a bat mitzvah, and a birthday party. She couldn't recall the last time she'd enjoyed a free weekend, but it was worth it. The high of doing what she loved was difficult to replicate. "I'd like to do even more events."

Her mother made a choking sound and reached for Aarti's water. She took a long swallow and returned it. "And how do you plan to do that?"

"My contract is up for renewal soon, and I plan to negotiate." Aarti had discussed it with Jo last week. "I'm going to ask Jeff about dropping to three-quarter time." She tensed and waited for her mother's response.

"No longer full time? Perhaps your father and I made a mistake in gushing about how well Maya and Jackson's wedding went. You did an outstanding job, but leaving cardiology to do *that?*" Her mother's nose and upper lip scrunched. "We paid good money for your education."

"I'm not leaving cardiology, just reducing my hours."

Her mom opened her sandwich and redistributed the vegetables. "I hesitate to tell you this now because I don't want to validate your decision, but I recommended you to Susan this morning."

"Susan?" Aarti thought she knew the members of her mother's team, but that aside, her mother was referring clients to her?

"The new anesthesiologist that started a few weeks ago. She's engaged, and they want to set a date for next fall."

"Who's she marrying? Does he work here, too?"

"No, she's a paralegal or something." Her mother glanced at her, but quickly looked down.

She? "Oh." Her mother was sending a same-sex wedding her way? "Thank you. Susan knows how to contact me?"

"I gave her your number." Her mom wrapped the rest of her sandwich. "That doesn't mean I approve of your plan. What am I supposed to tell people? 'My daughter who followed in my footsteps would rather plan baby showers and quinceañeras'?"

Her mother's vitriol stung. Yes, Aarti had chosen cardiology to please her, but then she'd disappointed her mom when she hadn't become a surgeon. "Let them talk. It's not a reflection on you. Give the rumor mill half a day, and they'll have something else to focus on."

"Indeed. Like how my single daughter who never dates is planning a lesbian wedding."

Aarti sighed. "You referred Susan to me. Besides, I *am* a lesbian." She'd never responded like this to her mother before, and it showed in the way her mom's eyes blazed.

"You know how I feel about that." Her mother quickly glanced around, likely to ensure they were alone.

Aarti slipped the remains of her meal into her lunch bag and stood. "I do." She clutched the napkin in her hand. "But it doesn't change the facts." Aarti paused beside her. Yes, they were at odds, but she wasn't heartless. "I'm sorry about your patient this morning." With her lunch and the precious note in one hand, she squeezed her mother's shoulder with the other.

Back in her office, Aarti smoothed the wrinkled piece of paper. She wasn't sure how to interpret Jo tucking a heart in her lunch, but it had to be positive. Warmth spread through her. Even the unsettling encounter with her mother wouldn't dampen her spirits today.

CHAPTER NINE

Don't stop. Please, don't stop." The pillow muffled Aarti's voice, and she hoped Jo had heard. Since Jo didn't stop plunging her fingers into her, Aarti settled into the oncoming pleasure of her orgasm. Jo kissed the base of her spine and rubbed her clit, and it was over. Aarti's world exploded into a million tiny, breathtaking pieces. She met Jo's thrusts until her legs faltered, then collapsed in the middle of the bed.

She hadn't been aware of moving, but when her mind cleared, Jo held her, and a sheet covered them. Her head rested on Jo's chest, and she kissed the side of Jo's breast. The lazy motion of Jo's fingers on her back made her want to succumb to sleep.

The lamp beside the bed—the one with the broken shade—cast a warm glow over Jo's skin. Aarti trailed a finger around Jo's nipple and watched it harden. She strummed the pert peak with her thumb until Jo squirmed beneath her. Carefully, she rearranged her lower body so her hand moving down Jo's rippling abdomen had room to maneuver. When her fingers reached Jo's slick, swollen folds, Aarti licked her nipple.

"No foreplay needed, baby. I'm too close." Jo bucked against her. "Please."

Aarti didn't disagree. While slow and sensual was nice, she liked it fast, at least when it meant watching Jo lose it. And that's exactly what was happening under the rhythmic motion of her fingers.

She grazed her teeth over the tip of Jo's nipple, then sucked it, making her moan. As Jo's panting grew louder, Aarti nuzzled her face against her breasts, and Jo rocked into her hand. "Inside?"

Jo grabbed her wrist, keeping it where it was. "Too la—" Her head pressed into the pillow, and her legs went rigid.

As Jo recovered, Aarti covered their damp bodies with the blanket. A surreptitious glance at Jo's bedside clock showed it was after midnight. She never stayed this late, but she was also no pillow princess. Still, she needed to be up for her shift in less than six hours.

It'd been two months since she'd renegotiated her contract. Jeff had balked at seventy-five percent but agreed on eighty. At least it had given her more time for event planning. In those couple months, she'd picked up eight new clients, including two gay weddings, and the couple whose fortieth anniversary she'd done had asked her to plan their retirement party. If she didn't count the uncle of one bride getting drunk and falling into the wedding cake last month—and she didn't—all her events were successes, and her clients had raved about her in online reviews.

Aarti covered Jo's breast with her hand. Work had been uncomfortable for her mother, or at least that was her mom's story. When Aarti cut back her hours, it had surprised her coworkers, and questions had ensued, but she didn't mind explaining. Her mother, however, complained about the supposed rumors.

Despite the positives, an unsettled feeling ate at her. She didn't enjoy being at odds with her parents, though her dad had seemed fine at dinner last week. It was her mother who was unhappy. And even though Aarti now had more time for her hobby, as her mother called it, she wanted more. More time to take on events and more time with Jo.

Aarti dreaded crawling from Jo's warm embrace each week to take the train home, but they couldn't have sex at her apartment. If her parents dropped by and Jo was there, she didn't know what might happen, but she knew she feared the encounter. And if she wasn't at home in the morning to walk with her mother, her absence would be telling. Would they disown her? She tried to imagine life without her family, as fraught with difficulty as their relationship was, and she couldn't. Despite everything, she loved them. Would Maya support her, or would she side with their parents to stay in their good graces?

Jo's breathing steadied, but Aarti knew she wasn't asleep. Now and then, Jo ran her fingers through Aarti's hair. She gave Jo's breast a squeeze and brushed their lips together.

Jo opened her eyes, but they looked flat, with none of their usual sparkle. "You're leaving, aren't you?"

"Yes." Aarti slid from the bed. "You know I don't want to."

"Then don't." Jo turned on her side as Aarti dressed. "I wish you didn't care so much about what your parents think, especially at your age."

Aarti shot her a look. "Watch it." She pulled on her pants.

"You should fight for your happiness." Jo got out of bed and pulled on sweats like she always did to walk her out. "In all these months, you've never stayed the night. I've seen your apartment one time when we ran in to get your laptop. Once!" She ripped a sweatshirt off the back of the desk chair. "Can't you ask for your spare key back or change your locks?"

"Do you think this is easy for me? There are things you don't understand. My parents have always been this way." Aarti scanned the bedroom. "Where's my bra?"

Jo ignored her and stepped into her Crocs. "You've given up your right to happiness because of their expectations, both in your career and your love life. I want more with you, but you're not willing to press the issue." Her shoulders drooped. "I'm basically your dirty little secret."

Love life? Aarti should have paid heed to the rest of Jo's diatribe, but there was that word again they'd had yet to say. It'd frozen her in place. Why was Jo doing this now? Aarti didn't need to feel more misunderstood.

Jo watched her from the foot of the bed. "That's all you have to say?"

Aarti held up her hands. "What do you want from me?" She couldn't breathe.

Jo stared at her, her lips stretched tight. She didn't respond, and truth be told, Aarti didn't really want to know the answer. It was likely something she couldn't give. Her entire life was about meeting people's expectations. Work, her family, her mother, and now Jo. And despite her best efforts, Aarti continued to disappoint all of them. She pulled on her clothing, grabbed her phone, and went to the living room to find her bra. Jo didn't follow.

After searching everywhere, Aarti sank onto the sofa. She was tired of this. Tired of trying to make everyone happy. Tired of not having anything left for herself when it was all said and done. Life shouldn't be so difficult, not when it came to whom she had feelings for, yet she couldn't seem to escape it. The heaviness of the situation made her plant her palms on the couch and stretch. Her fingers tangled in something at her hip. Her bra. With a yank, she tugged it from between the cushions and shoved it into her bag.

Jo hadn't left the bedroom. Hadn't come to see if she'd found her things. Hadn't come to walk her out. Aarti had known it was only a matter of time before Jo tired of all this. Of her. It'd actually lasted longer than she thought it would.

She grabbed her jacket, shouldered her bag, and quietly shut the door behind her.

Her footsteps echoed on the linoleum stairs. Even as a child, she'd never been much of a crier. When Maya was six, Aarti had taken her to Central Park and gotten lost, but she hadn't broken down, even when it grew dark. When her beloved Grandpa Singh passed away, she hadn't shed a tear despite being heartbroken. That ability to lock away her emotions and focus on what needed to be done was part of what made her a good doctor. Even when the heartache and pain were nearly debilitating, she still needed to do her job.

This, however—losing Jo—exposed her to her core and left her raw. She fought off the stinging in her eyes and blinked to clear her vision. It had finally happened. Jo had had enough because Aarti was too afraid to make her a priority. Deep down, she'd known it would happen. She'd tried to warn Jo in the beginning, but obviously, Jo had been no more able to walk away than she had.

When Aarti stepped outside, the freezing wind whipped at her clothing and bare neck, making her gasp. She pulled her collar higher. The sickly stench of sewage wafted through the air. Up ahead, a cloud billowed from the orange and white steam stack in the street. Shoulders hunched, she hurried down the sidewalk and took a right at the shuttered MoneyGram place.

Even though turning the corner had changed the whipping wind into a chilly breeze, the contrast between the frigid air and the hot tears on her cheeks made her come to a stop. Why now? When she never cried, why now? Ending things with Leticia, who'd been kind and good in bed the few times they'd had together, hadn't felt like this. Aarti cared about Jo in ways she wasn't sure she understood.

Across the way, a young couple laughed as the man ushered the woman inside a twenty-four-hour convenience store with a protective arm around her. Even the bitter cold didn't seem to affect the eyes they had for each other as the grimy glass door clanged behind them.

Aarti let her hand fall from where it grasped her collar. That's what love did, and she was pretty sure that's what made her heart swell when she thought of Jo. Love had the ability to mute the negatives, to make the daily simplicities of life seem wondrous and new. Even tribulations were more manageable when it was two against one.

She wasn't sure how long she'd stood there, but the young couple came crashing out of the store with a pint of ice cream. The woman stopped to feed the man a glop on a wooden spoon. Ice cream? Aarti didn't even want to extract her hands from her pockets. Weren't their fingers freezing? They grinned at one another as the woman wiped a drop from his lip with her thumb.

Her parents still looked at each other like that. Forty-plus years into their marriage, and they were one another's best friends. Anyone could see the love they shared. Where would Aarti be when they were no longer here? What would she be left with? Was it so wrong simply to want what they had?

As the couple grinned at each other and shared a kiss, Aarti slowly turned and faced the corner from which she'd come. Some might desecrate the feeling by calling it limerence or rose-colored glasses, but it wasn't those things. At a cellular level, Aarti knew one thing to be true. She was in love with Josephine Samuels, and she wasn't about to walk away from that, from them.

Ten minutes later, in the hallway outside Jo's apartment, Aarti hesitated. She had a key she'd been given months ago, but the thought of using it now made her chest tight. Leaving like she did had changed things, so she knocked instead.

When the door opened, Jo stood before her, looking as weary as Aarti felt. They stared at one another.

"You came back." Jo's gaze flicked to the ice cream in Aarti's hand.

"Can I come in?"

Jo stepped aside.

Aarti set the pint on the coffee table. "I owe you an apology." She stepped closer. "I'm sorry for leaving like that. I know you're frustrated with me, but I should have stayed and talked to you instead of bolting."

"What changed your mind?" Jo shifted from foot to foot.

"Come sit."

They faced one another on the couch, one of Aarti's legs tucked beneath her.

"You're right." Emotion welled within, and Aarti covered her face with her hands. Those damn tears again. "You're right about everything, right to be upset, but I'm not sure I know how to fix it."

Jo gently pried her fingers away. "Yes, I'm upset, but it's because I haven't had the pleasure of watching you sleep or waking up next to you since the Hamptons."

Aarti laughed but fresh tears fell. "You watched me sleep?"

"As often as I could. I couldn't help it. Sometimes I think back on our time there, and even though I only got a dozen hours of sleep that week, it was still the best time of my life." Jo brushed Aarti's hair back from her face. "I can't do this anymore, not like this."

Aarti's dinner threatened to reappear. She stood.

"Hey, hey." Jo gently tugged her hand until she sat beside her again. "What I meant is we need to come up with a solution. This isn't working. I need to see my girlfriend a hell of a lot more than this."

The word girlfriend made Aarti's eyes sting even more, and she wiped at her tears with her palms. "I don't know what to do about my parents."

"I've been thinking." Jo caressed her knee. "Your mother's biggest issue seems to be related to your shared workplace. What if you didn't work there?"

"You mean do event planning full time? She'd never talk to me again."

"No, what if you worked at a different hospital or joined a private practice? Wouldn't you be happier out from under her shadow? It'd allow us more freedom, too."

Aarti sniffed and considered it. "I've worked at Lenox the entire time I've been an attending, but maybe. I'd have to get out of my contract though."

"Are you willing to try?"

The vulnerability in Jo's eyes eviscerated her. "For us? Yes." Aarti squeezed Jo's hands. "I'm not losing you, and it's about time I stood up for myself."

Jo's smile lit her entire face. The intensity of the kiss they shared could have powered the Empire State Building for an entire month.

"What now?" Aarti laced her fingers behind Jo's neck.

Jo glanced at the coffee table where frost now covered the outside of the pint container. "Let's have a spoonful or two of ice cream, and then, if you're serious about us, come back to bed. Okay?" She traced Aarti's lip with her thumb.

Aarti kissed it. "Okay." She produced a single wooden spoon from her pocket.

Once again, Jo's steady, comforting arms wrapped around her. "We're going to figure this out."

CHAPTER TEN

A arti fidgeted in the restaurant's plush chair and tapped her shoe against the table leg as she strained to see the entrance. Her mother had questioned having brunch somewhere other than their favorite place but had agreed she and her father would be there. If a scene occurred, Aarti wanted her parents to be comfortable returning to their treasured establishment. There she was again, worrying about them and not herself. It would take some time to break that mindset.

She'd spent yesterday planning what she would say, but now, when they were due to arrive, perspiration formed on her upper lip. If only she could postpone the conversation until she felt more ready, but she couldn't. Jo was too important, and Aarti needed to make changes. Too bad knowing what she must do couldn't ease the apprehension that made her hands tremble in her lap.

The server offered her a Bloody Mary or a mimosa, but she declined, and when she turned, her parents followed the host across the room. Her father wore his typical Sunday tennis shirt, and her mom had accessorized her tight bun by tying a colorful scarf around it. After they'd hung their jackets on a nearby rack, Aarti hugged them, and they sat.

Once they'd ordered, the conversation became stilted, so Aarti jumped in. "I asked you here because I have something important to tell you."

Her mother shot a glance at her father before asking, "Are you pregnant?"

Aarti shifted in her chair. So, this was how it was going to be. "I have some things I'd like to share with you, and I'll be happy to answer your questions, but it'd be easier if I could talk for a minute."

Her father took her mother's hand and his knuckles whitened. "But you're not sick, just tell us that, beta."

"No, Daddy. I'm healthy." She drank some water to give herself a few seconds to organize her thoughts. "I'm planning to leave Lenox, and before you say anything, I'm not leaving medicine. I've been looking at cardiology positions, both at other hospitals in Manhattan and at private practices, but not full time."

Her mother's rapid blinking might have been disbelief or to hide her tears of disappointment. Aarti couldn't be sure. To her mother's credit, she allowed her to continue. Aarti danced her fingers on the tablecloth, unable to contain her anxiety. "I haven't been happy. I don't know if I've *ever* been happy." She looked up. "Until this year."

Her father squirmed, and her mother opened her mouth but closed it.

Aarti took a deep, steadying breath. "Do you remember the chef that catered Maya's wedding?"

"Jo." Her mom glanced at her dad. "Right?" Her hesitance made it sound like she waited to be chastised for speaking.

"Yes. We've been seeing one another since then." Aarti tried to gauge their reactions, but neither moved. "I haven't told you because I know your feelings on the matter, especially with you and me working together, Mom."

Her mother started to say something, but the server arrived with their food. When Aarti chose the location, she traded interruptions for the convenience of discussing things somewhere her mother wouldn't cause a scene. She cut into her eggs and spread jam on her toast, even though she couldn't imagine eating anything, but it gave her parents time to sample their meals.

"I liked Jo."

Aarti almost snapped her neck meeting her mother's gaze. "You did?"

Her mom chewed the bite of Belgian waffle. "Yes, remember that iced masala chai she made from scratch? I asked her for another pitcher, and when she brought it an hour later, she'd baked vanilla cardamom scones to go with it." She sipped her coffee. "Sometimes late at night,

I crave her cooking and wish I could transport myself back to that reception buffet."

Aarti grasped the edges of her seat to keep from falling from her chair. "You do?"

Her dad laid his fork on his plate. "Your mother knows I saw you and Jo together on the deck." He took her mom's hand again. "We don't keep secrets from one another. There's been a noticeable change in you since, and we wondered if she might be why, but we weren't sure. We figured, if she was important, you'd tell us when you're ready." He glanced at her mom.

"I thought you'd disown me." The words were out before Aarti knew it. She wrapped her arms around her middle. "You're already disappointed I've cut back my clinical hours. I knew admitting it would bring shame to the family." How much had her father witnessed? Had it affected her parents' silence on the matter since?

This time it was her mother who shifted in her seat. "You're right. I don't like it. I wish you hadn't chosen to go down this path, and I hope you'll still try to be discreet wherever you end up. As you know, the medical community is close-knit."

Aarti sat straighter. "It's not a choice. I'm a lesbian and always have been. I've tried to make you happy, and I've lived half a life." The decades of unshed tears trickled down her face. "I can't do it anymore."

Her father took her hand. "Beta, we would never disown you. Yes, we struggle with what you want, but you're our daughter." His eyes seemed to glisten for a moment. "But I don't think we realized how unhappy you've been."

Her mother blinked rapidly. "All I've ever wanted is the best for you. I worry you'll never find it with everyone always whispering about how you lead your life. You make things difficult for yourself." She sighed. "Even so, you're very good at what you do, be it medicine or event planning. What you did for Maya and Jackson was monumental, especially after Taylor's accident. Yet, you gave them the wedding of their dreams and served food guests are still talking about."

"Thank you, but Jo deserves all the credit for the menu."

Her mother signaled their server and pointed to her mug. "It's not what I want for you, Aarti, but I suppose if you insist," she switched to a whisper, "on dating a woman, you could do worse than Jo. And I believe you leaving Lenox is for the best. I'm sorry the rumors and talk bother me, but they do." She dabbed at her lips with her napkin.

"So..." Aarti searched for words. "We're okay?"

Her father leaned his arms on the table. "You lied to us, even if by omission, and you know I don't like dishonesty. We're disappointed but not mad. You've drifted away from us, even from Maya, and we miss you. If this means we get to see you more, and hopefully see you happy, then I support you." He kept his gaze on Aarti.

Her mother stared at him but remained quiet.

In retrospect, Aarti had avoided their possible questions by making herself scarce. The few blocks she and her mom walked to work went by quickly, and when she saw her mother during the day, they never had the time or opportunity for personal conversations. Now she craved that conversation to know where her mother stood. "And you, Mom?"

Her mother thanked the server who refilled their coffees. "Does Jo know you're changing jobs?"

"Yes, of course."

"And she still wants to be with you?" Her mom took a sip. "Even though you won't be a full-time doctor?"

Aarti bristled, then composed herself. "Jo doesn't want to be with me because I'm a doctor, and I'm not full-time now. She suggested I focus all my energy on event planning if that's what makes me happy, but I'm not ready for that. I care about my patients, and I'm sure I'll care about my new ones, wherever I land. I'm in no hurry to leave medicine, and I might never be. Even if it wasn't my first dream, I worked hard to get where I am, and I'm proud of that."

Her mother shrugged. "If you're expecting me to do a one-eighty today, you're going to be disappointed. Here I'd hoped to get to retirement before all this cropped up, but I guess that's not going to happen." She dropped her napkin beside her plate. "I don't want you to hate your life, but I also don't want to be miserable in my workplace, to be embarrassed in front of my colleagues and staff." She looked at Aarti. "Let's see where everything settles once you leave Lenox."

It wasn't the answer Aarti had hoped for, but it wasn't the worst either. She nodded. "I plan to give my notice this week."

Her mother looked to her father. "Well, I suppose we should meet Jo again, properly this time. Dinner or something."

Her dad leaned back in his chair, his lips twitching with a smile. "That would be the polite thing to do, but you can't ask her to cook for you, Vidya. Not yet."

"Rakesh." Her mother shot him a look from beneath lowered eyebrows.

The trembling in Aarti's hands had stopped. She bit into a piece of toast as her parents' conversation drifted to Jo's curry.

They hadn't exactly met in the middle, but they'd taken steps toward each other, and that pleased Aarti. She'd feared other possible outcomes. As they finished their meal touching upon lighter subjects, she found herself wishing Maya was here. Jackson and Jo, too. Imagining them all together one day didn't seem so unfeasible, considering the progress they'd made. Her parents were who they were, and so was she. Maybe she imagined it, but an unspoken agreement seemed to exist between them to move toward, not away from one another, even if the steps were small.

She couldn't wait to tell Jo everything.

Aarti held the bag containing the bacon, egg, and cheese with avocado sandwich she'd ordered to go. It was Jo's favorite. Her parents had hugged her, her dad twice, before they'd left her outside what they'd called their new brunch spot. Despite hoping her mother would continue to make strides toward fully understanding her, only Aarti's toes had touched the pavement on her walk to Jo's restaurant.

She pulled open the front door, unwound her scarf, and stopped at the host stand. Even in winter, the bright space appeared welcoming, and the ever-rotating paintings by local artists that adorned the walls had changed. She admired a still life of cheese and fruit by Casey Vaughn.

"Table for one?" A young man picked up a menu and wine list.

"No, I'm just here to see Jo. Is she available?"

"Let me check." He strode through a swinging door in the rear.

Bringing Jo food when she could make whatever she wanted seemed foolish, but Aarti wanted to give it to her, so she was stuck holding it.

The young man returned. "Please, come with me." He led her through the doors and into the kitchen.

Aarti hadn't expected it to be so big or bright. Every surface seemed to gleam. Despite more than half a dozen people working at various stations, no one raised their head to look at her. She followed the host down a back hallway where he stopped outside a door.

"Right through here."

Aarti entered the small room. "Hi."

"Hey." Jo glanced up, then returned her attention to her laptop. Then she seemed to recognize her and jumped up, crushing her in a hug. "Oh, my God. What are you doing here? Trevor said a woman was here to see me, and I assumed you were a vendor. You'd be the sixth one today, so forgive me for not appearing more excited at first."

"Forgiven." Humored by Jo's rambling, Aarti gave her a quick kiss, unsure how much affection Jo was comfortable with at work. "I brought you your favorite sandwich, avocado and all."

Jo grabbed the bag and had the box torn open before Aarti stopped speaking. "This looks amazing. Where did you get it?" She returned to her seat behind the scuffed desk and motioned for Aarti to sit in a folding chair.

"Where I asked my parents to meet me for brunch a few blocks away to talk."

At that, Jo dropped the sandwich in the box. "Talk?" She swallowed the bite she'd taken. "About?"

Aarti shrugged as if it had been nothing. "My job." She'd often heard people say they felt like a weight had been lifted from their shoulders, but she'd never understood the sentiment until now. "And us."

"You didn't mention this." Jo came around the desk and pulled her up. "You told them about us?"

"I did. I wanted to surprise you, make you proud." That's when Aarti felt them. More tears. Who had she become?

"Sweetheart, what happened?" Jo grasped her upper arms.

"It's okay." Aarti laughed. "It went better than expected. They already knew about us, at least about us at the wedding, because my dad saw us. But I confirmed we've been seeing one another since then, and we're in a relationship. And I told them I've decided to leave Lenox, and they didn't disown me or cause a scene. If anything, *I* might have by crying in the middle of the restaurant. I told them I'm happy for perhaps the first time because of you." Even more tears fell.

Jo wrapped her arms around her, not seeming to mind that her chef's whites might get wet.

Why hadn't Aarti cried before? Who knew it was so liberating?

"My mom's not fully on board, just so you know, but I think we've come to an understanding. I think our relationship might improve once I leave Lenox."

"I'm so proud of you. So damn proud." Jo kissed her temple. "Do you know where you want to work?"

"Not yet." Aarti sniffed and pulled back. "I'll need to see who's willing to hire me part-time. And I'll need to find another apartment because mine will be too expensive once I drop my clinical hours. I don't have the client base as an event planner yet to afford it."

Jo tensed.

She put her hands on Jo's chest. "What's wrong?"

"What do you think about finding a place to live together? With as busy as we both are, it would allow us to see each other every day, and you'll no longer need to be within walking distance of the hospital."

"Oh, yeah?" Aarti smiled. "I'd love living with you." She rested her arms over Jo's shoulders and gave a soft laugh. "You wouldn't believe it. My mom brought up your iced chai and some scones I didn't know existed. Then they reminisced about your food for a good ten minutes."

"Really?" Jo beamed.

Aarti nodded. "They'd like to have dinner with us soon, to get to know you now that you're more than just part of the catering team. Maybe we could get that out of the way and wait to address our living arrangements until I see where I end up."

Jo pulled her closer. "Absolutely. You've been doing what others expect of you for too long. Why don't you tell me whenever you think you're ready." She smiled. "As long as I have plenty of opportunities to wake with you in my arms, I'm happy."

"Same, sweetheart. Same." Aarti kissed her, then guided Jo back to her seat. "Please don't let me keep you from eating."

Aarti stayed for another ten minutes, and as she watched Jo, she marveled at how lucky she was to have her as her rock, her champion, her support, and the woman who meant more to her than anyone. By the time Jo finished the sandwich, Aarti had relayed most of the brunch conversation.

Not wanting to keep Jo any longer, she rose to leave. "Have a great service tonight, and text me when you're finished. Maybe we can meet for a late drink to celebrate." Aarti kissed her, capturing Jo's lower lip between hers before letting it go. At the door, Aarti turned back. "By the way, there's something else in that bag."

Aarti waited just long enough to see Jo's expression when she found the napkin on which Aarti had drawn a heart.

FOR LOVE OR MONEY

Jesse J. Thoma

CHAPTER ONE

Bang! Bang! Bang!

Dakota Osborne startled awake from her ratty, threadbare recliner she refused to throw away. She fumbled for her gun but couldn't immediately locate it. The banging on the door continued so she pulled her knife from its sheath at her ankle and crept to the front of the room.

Her heart was pounding loudly in her ears, but her mind was clear. She stayed out of the line of fire of the doorway, in case whoever was outside decided to blast their way in, and ran through a mental list of everyone who could be pissed enough at her to be outside assaulting her entry. Admittedly, the list was longer than she'd like, but that was because usually she was the one kicking down doors as part of her job as a bail enforcement agent. She was a bounty hunter and the job was as kick-ass as it sounded. Except for right now when it might kick her ass.

Almost as abruptly as the barrage on her door began, it stopped. She listened for the sound of a cocking firearm or the ragged breathing of a nervous assailant. Instead, a woman, perfectly calm and friendly called out. "Ms. Osborne, you prefer to be called Oz, am I right? I'd like a moment of your time. I know you're in there. Whatever weapon you have pointed at me, please lower it. I'm unarmed."

"What the ever-loving fuck." Instinctively, Oz followed the woman's request and lowered the knife before catching herself. "I'm supposed to believe that? My door would disagree that you're harmless."

"I tried knocking politely, but you didn't answer. I thought maybe you were in the bathroom or asleep in your armchair."

Oz spun to look at the windows facing her recliner. The shades as always were drawn. How could her mystery guest have known that? She wanted to ask so the woman would keep talking. She sounded pretty which was absolutely not a reason to strike up conversation. Jesus, she needed to get laid.

"Are you going to let me in? I'll put my hands on my head or against the wall or whatever you need to feel comfortable." There was amusement in her tone now.

Oz pressed her fist to her forehead, nearly slicing her eyebrow in the process. She struggled not to think of the hot woman she imagined with her legs spread and her hands against the wall. Before things got more out of hand than they already were, Oz threw caution to the wind and yanked the front door open.

For the love of God, please be ugly.

The woman on her front stoop was not only not ugly, she was stunningly beautiful. She had the kind of effortless style that would look at home on the streets of Paris and was of a kind Oz knew she'd never be able to pull off. The woman's hair was cut in a choppy short pixie and her makeup was understated but gorgeous. She looked startled by Oz's sudden appearance but recovered quickly.

"You're not ugly." Oz nearly facepalmed at her lack of filter.

Instead of slapping her, the woman smirked and looked her up and down. "Neither are you, stud." She looked over her shoulder, tension creeping into her previously cheeky expression. "Mind if I come in?"

"I don't usually let people in…" Oz trailed off as the woman breezed past her and into the house. "Sure, come on in."

"Thank you. Do you mind locking the door? I'm Frances, Frankie, Sender by the way." Frankie looked nervous.

Oz did as requested, not liking being told what to do in her own house one bit and also intrigued that Frankie was able to get her to comply so easily. She told herself it was how scared Frankie suddenly looked, but Oz wasn't sure that was really the reason. She took a seat in her recliner and grabbed the TV remote. She'd nodded off halfway through the season finale of her current favorite show.

"What are you doing?" Frankie put her hands on her hips.

Oz paused the TV. "You crashed into my house and seem to think you're running this show. I figure you'll get around to telling me why you're here when you're ready. In the meantime I'm going to finish my program." She pressed play.

Frankie snatched the remote from her hand and turned the TV off. "I need your help. No, that's not right. I want to hire you."

"Are you a bondsman?" Oz sat up and looked at Frankie more carefully, far from a hardship. She didn't look like any bail bondsman Oz had ever met.

"What?" Frankie looked horrified. "God, no."

"Then I'm afraid I can't help you. Wikipedia can explain what bounty hunters do. I'm not private security. You can look up Holt Lasher and her team if that's what you're looking for."

Frankie made a face. "I'm not interested in her or her team. I'm sure she's very qualified, but I'm not looking for the top dog. I want someone with more to prove and a disgusting recliner they can't afford to replace."

Oz held up a finger. "Hold on, I know you just insulted me, I need a minute to figure out how badly."

"Get over yourself. You're a little pip-squeak of an operation, barely surviving. Holt's got a huge team, all the bells and whistles she could ask for, and a beautiful wife and family." Frankie ticked off Holt's assets on her fingers.

"So you're offering yourself up for marriage? We don't even know each other. What's your favorite bagel flavor? Which side of the bed do you sleep on? What's your mother's name?" Oz knew she shouldn't enjoy Frankie's look of annoyance that grew more pronounced the longer she talked, but damn if she did anyway.

"I'll marry you the day you get rid of that recliner."

Oz knew Frankie wasn't serious, but she was tempted to consent just to see how Frankie responded. "No deal."

"Enough nonsense. I told you I need to hire you. Will you hear me out? I promise it will be worth your while." Frankie cast around until she seemed to find somewhere she was willing to sit and perched on the edge of Oz's coffee table.

The house wasn't dirty so Oz wasn't sure what the problem was. It seemed like Frankie was spontaneously uncomfortable in her skin, not just in the house. Oz rolled her finger indicating Frankie should continue. The least she could do was hear her out. Then maybe she'd leave and Oz could get back to her show.

"I'm due in court in three days and I have no intention of making my appearance." Frankie picked at her fingernail but looked Oz in the eye.

Oz sat up and leaned forward. This was intriguing. "I've never had a skip come to give me a heads-up. What's stopping me from keeping you here until you've missed your court date and hauling you back in?"

Frankie gave her a withering look. "The kidnapping charge I'd imagine."

Oz waved her hand trying to make it seem like such things were a minor concern to her. Frankie was right though, without bond paperwork she had no ability to keep Frankie, regardless of her declared intentions related to her court date.

"Out of curiosity, what are you charged with?" Oz schooled her face into casual disinterest.

"Murder." The corners of Frankie's mouth quirked up.

"Lovely." Oz had no idea what look crossed her face before she could regain control of her expression.

"I didn't do it." Frankie sounded like Oz should have already surmised as much.

"Obviously."

Frankie looked deflated. "You don't believe me."

Oz shrugged. "Occupational hazard. Plus, I don't know anything about you. No reason to think you couldn't commit murder. No reason to think you could, except that someone said you did."

"Well, this would have been easier if you'd given me the benefit of the doubt, but it doesn't matter either way. I need you to keep me alive until I can prove my innocence and finish my investigation into the company that's framing me. As soon as that's done, I'll let you bring me in and you can collect the bounty for me missing my court date. I promise it's worth it to you. My bond was *extremely* high." Frankie's face was cool and matter-of-fact, but she wasn't able to mask the hope in her eyes.

"No." Oz didn't hesitate.

Frankie gaped at her. "You don't know how much money you could make."

"I don't care. I'm not protecting a murderer." She paused when Frankie glared at her. "Alleged murderer. I'm not protecting an alleged murderer and helping you evade the law. It goes against everything I stand for."

Oz saw the moment Frankie's anger turned to fear and then desperation. What had Frankie expected? There was no way she could agree to what Frankie had proposed, which made it all the more annoying when her heart tugged at Frankie's clear distress.

"I'm sorry I can't help you. You're welcome to anything in the fridge before you head back out. There's coffee and I think I have some tea."

Oz could hear her mother's voice ringing in her head scolding her for her poor life choices and being a disappointment to the family. If only her mother could see her now, offering tea to a murderer. *Alleged* murderer. She looked over her shoulder at Frankie looking lost standing in the kitchen. Why was there a piece of her that would be sad to see her go?

CHAPTER TWO

Frankie stood in Oz's kitchen taking deep breaths, trying to calm her heart rate and regroup. She considered making tea to buy herself more time. Her first attempt to win over Oz hadn't worked, but she needed to try again. What other option did she have? It was a miracle she'd stayed alive on her own as long as she had, but her luck would run out eventually. One didn't take on a corporation like InvestBioX and live to tell about it if they were motivated to shut you up, and InvestBioX was very motivated to keep Frankie quiet.

For the hundredth time, she considered whether she'd be safer in jail before reminding herself, for the hundred and first time, that she'd be shivved within an hour of her stay. At least on the street she had a fighting chance. Getting bail was the only break she'd gotten since InvestBioX had framed her for murder. If she'd been smart she would have stopped digging into the company and enjoyed a life with all of her limbs and a beating heart, but smarts weren't ruling the day. She couldn't let them off the hook when she was so close to nailing the bastards.

Frankie yanked open Oz's fridge expecting to see moldy takeout and an empty bottle of ketchup. She wasn't prepared for the beautifully stocked shelves filled with fresh fruit, yogurt, hummus, vegetables, cheeses, and almost anything else her stomach could wish for.

"You're a foodie?" She turned to get a better look at Oz who was once again settled into her disgusting recliner.

"No, I'm a person who likes to eat and respects my body. There's a difference." Oz raised her voice over the sound of the television.

Frankie had been living off fast food and what felt like table scraps since she'd been released so she fixed herself a heaping plate. Oz did say she could help herself. Once that was done she returned to her perch on the coffee table. She crossed her legs and balanced the plate on her knee.

"I think we got off on the wrong foot. Let's start over. I'm Frankie Sender. I'm a short seller and I've been investigating InvestBioX. I think their supposed new drug is smoke and mirrors to cover up some shady finances. They're the ones who framed me for murder and it turns out they're also trying to kill me." Frankie took a few bites while she let that sink in. Oz didn't turn her way but Frankie could see she was interested.

After a long pause, Oz answered. "I'm still not helping you." Another long pause. "What's a short seller?"

Bingo.

"I thought you only cared that I'm a murderer." Frankie took a bite of carrot and chewed slowly.

"I thought it was alleged murderer? Ready to plead guilty?" Oz had the slightest hint of a smile.

"When I'm not, allegedly, relieving people of their pulse and earthly soul, I bet on companies to fail. Most people make money on the stock market when stock prices rise, I make money, lots of money, when those stocks bottom out." Frankie scrutinized Oz's reaction. She seemed intrigued, not put off. Frankie still had her on the hook.

"I know what you're doing. It's not going to work." Oz turned back to the TV.

So much for the hook.

"InvestBioX is trying to kill me. They didn't expect me to get out on bail. They're not going to stop what they're doing, and a lot of people are going to get hurt."

Oz turned fully to her now looking unimpressed. "Which is it, getting rich or the greater good? You need to get your story straight."

"Who says it can't be both? I can expose misdeeds and also make a ton of money. I learned to walk and chew gum a long time ago."

Oz didn't respond with anything more than a noncommittal huff. Frankie munched another carrot, evaluating her next move when the glass of the closest window exploded inward. Something hot whistled by her ear and thudded into the wall across the room. Another window shattered. Frankie knew she should do something, anything, but felt frozen in place.

"Get down." Oz grabbed Frankie by the front of the shirt and yanked her to the floor. "Kitchen, now. Stay low."

Oz's command broke Frankie out of her daze. Frankie crawled, glass crunching beneath her hands and knees, toward the kitchen. She kept as low to the ground as she could while also moving like hell to get out of the living room. As Oz had pulled her to the floor, she'd realized it was a bullet that had nearly collided with her skull. The sound of them peppering the house was terrifying and a great motivator.

She risked a look behind her, hoping to see Oz following her, scared she'd witness her last moments, or worse, see her bleeding out on the floor. Thankfully, Oz wasn't dead. She was tucked behind her damn recliner reaching into the drawer of the side table nearest the windows. If she was looking for the television remote, Frankie would tell the gunman where to aim.

Relief rushed through Frankie like the first sip of a cool drink on a hot day when she saw Oz retrieve a gun from the drawer and make her own way toward the kitchen.

"I'm assuming these are the people who want to kill you?" Oz checked her weapon and grimaced. From her seat on the floor, she opened kitchen cabinets and blindly fished into drawers until she came up with two more magazines and a pen that looked like something a spy might find useful. She tucked her finds in her pocket.

"Unless you were expecting guests." Frankie flinched at another burst of gunfire.

Her nerves felt exposed to air, raw and alight.

"No, but they seem to keep showing up anyway." Oz motioned Frankie to follow her. "They're going to get tired of shooting at us from outside pretty soon. They'll need to come in and make sure we're dead. We can't be here when they do or we will be."

Frankie didn't like the sound of staying put or leaving the house. Hiding in one of the kitchen cabinets seemed like an option they should consider.

"Come on, you tried to hire me ten minutes ago to protect you from exactly this. Don't get cold feet on me now." Oz made the universal "hurry up" sign.

"I'm not." She totally was. "I'm reevaluating if my trust in you was misplaced. How do I know you'll keep me safe?"

"You don't. But they definitely won't." Oz pointed in the direction of their assailants.

"Fair point. Off we go then. What's the holdup?" Frankie shooed Oz along. Whether Oz knew the banter was the only thing keeping her from completely losing it, she allowed Frankie to boss her right out the back door and into the side yard.

Oz pushed her against the house, and they inched along, pressed flat against the siding, until Oz could peek at their attackers. "You sure brought a party." She pointed back the way they came and they made the slow shuffle back. "We're going over the fence. My neighbor's got a motorcycle we're going to borrow. It's parked next to his garage."

Frankie stopped abruptly and turned to Oz. "You can't steal your neighbor's motorcycle."

"Your moral compass is very confusing." She gave Frankie a little shove, which got them both moving again. "When I tell you, go over the fence. I'll give you a boost. The keys are under the rock by the front tire."

When they reached the fence, Oz hoisted Frankie then followed with a graceful leap. Frankie ran to the bike and retrieved the keys. "Do you know how to drive this thing?"

Oz tucked her gun in her waistband and looked behind her warily. "It can't be that hard."

Frankie would have taken more time to explain the intricacies of riding a motorcycle but no one had time for that. "I'm driving. Hold on and don't throw off the balance."

She straddled the bike and motioned Oz to get on. Oz started to protest. Frankie pulled the gun from Oz's pants and handed it to her. "If anyone follows us, shoot them. You can't do that if you're up here."

That seemed to appease Oz enough to climb behind Frankie as she started the bike. It roared to life between her legs and she peeled out of the driveway. Oz snaked an arm around her waist which was unexpectedly distracting. How could she notice something like that while running for her life? Her multitasking skills were next-level.

"They're coming." Oz was barely audible above fear, adrenaline, and wind whipping by as they flew down the road.

Frankie's heart rate, already dangerously high if the palpitations she felt pinging around her chest was anything to go by, kicked up another two or three levels. Who the fuck was coming?

"When I say, make a hard U-turn so I can get a better shot. Then head for that alley we just passed." Oz tapped her on the shoulder to make sure she understood.

Why would they head back toward the people with guns and a murderous attitude? Didn't an alley mean a dead end? She didn't want to end up dead. In a stack full of shit days, this one was starting to set itself apart. Not to mention Oz was asking her to do the near impossible.

"You know it's nearly impossible to do what you're asking me to do without dumping the bike and getting us killed?"

"You wanted the keys, I don't want to be dead. Don't dump us." Oz tightened her grip around Frankie's waist.

It probably wasn't worth arguing, but Frankie had a strong urge anyway. Before she could, Oz squeezed her tighter and yelled "now." Frankie assumed that was the signal so she closed her eyes against the sight of instant death and spun the bike. As she expected, it took everything she had to keep the bike and the two of them upright.

She didn't know what gunshots felt like, but she hadn't noticed passing over into the great beyond so she opened her eyes and hit the accelerator.

"You're doing great. Hard right into the alley in three, two, one, now!" Oz fired at their pursuers as Frankie made the turn.

As soon as they were in the alley, Frankie's vision narrowed until all she could see was the wall looming at the end of the pavement in front of them. "Now what, Oz? We're trapped in here."

"Hey, it's okay. We're not trapped." Oz squeezed Frankie's waist gently. "After the dumpster, make a hard left. You're going to have to keep your speed so we can make it up the stairs."

"Dumpster? Stairs?" Frankie's hands were trembling where she gripped the handlebar. Without realizing, she slowed the bike.

"Don't slow down." For the first time Oz sounded uneasy.

The sound of metal pinging off metal a foot to their left was all Frankie needed to gun it again. Oz returned fire. Frankie jumped every time a shot rang out and Oz's twisting and turning made controlling the bike difficult.

"Here's our turn. Hold on." Frankie hoped Oz heard her so she wasn't the victim of centrifugal force.

Another barrage of gunfire chased them as they exited the alley. Oz crashed into her back and grunted loudly. She held tightly to Frankie as they bounced their way up steep stairs that seemed to climb well into the rapidly darkening sky.

Frankie white-knuckled the handlebars as they climbed. It felt like trying to hold an over-caffeinated jackhammer. Her jaw slammed shut so rapidly on one particularly violent bounce she immediately tasted blood and worried about the state of her tongue.

Keeping control of the bike as they pounded and caromed up the stairs would have been an unbelievable challenge under any circumstances, but having Oz plastered to her back proved a special kind of test. Perhaps sensing the precariousness of their relationship with the laws of physics, Oz was holding tightly to Frankie. With each jarring jolt, they moved as one on the bike which Frankie found weirdly intimate and distracting as hell.

After what felt like an eternity in a rock tumbler, they finished the ascent and emerged onto a deserted street lined on each side by warehouses and office buildings. Frankie didn't recognize anything despite being nearly on top of where they'd started. Frankie slowed the bike and looked around. No gunman in sight. She took a real breath. The oxygen felt sweet in her lungs.

"We only have a few minutes until they figure out where those stairs lead. First right, then second left. Park the bike behind the shipping containers and we can walk from there." Oz's words were clipped and raspy. "When we get there you can tell me where the hell you learned to ride like that."

Frankie's urge to know where they were going was overruled by her overwhelming desire never to be shot at again. She revved the engine and followed Oz's directions. When they reached the shipping containers she cut the engine and walked the bike behind the first row, making sure it was out of sight from the road.

Once off the bike and on the move, Frankie realized there were hundreds of shipping containers, stacked three or four high, in neat rows, stretching for God knew how far. She was immediately lost, but Oz seemed headed somewhere specific so Frankie followed.

After a long jog, much longer than was appropriate for Frankie's footwear, Oz finally slowed. It wasn't until they crossed into the glow of an overhead light that Frankie noticed the blood dripping down Oz's arm, snaking along her fingers, and oozing over her gun.

"Why are you bleeding?" Frankie didn't mean to sound so histrionic or be so loud.

Oz glared at her. "It's what happens when you get shot."

Frankie took a deep breath and looked skyward. "You got shot? Were you planning on telling me?"

"I'll probably need your help getting patched up, so yes. But not until we're both safe. You're not someone who faints at the sight of blood, are you? I'll quit if you faint while stitching me." Oz motioned Frankie to follow and they darted to a set of containers set off by themselves.

Oz looked around quickly then turned the combination and unlocked the heavy padlock securing the door. She pulled Frankie inside and secured the door behind them.

"You can't quit if you haven't been hired. Does that mean you're taking the job?" Frankie crossed her arms and tried to look like the answer wasn't more important to her than anything else in her life.

"I take umbrage at my house being used as target practice. And like you said, you're only an alleged murderer. I'll keep you alive until you can either prove you didn't do it or I see compelling proof you did. After that, you turn yourself in." Oz rummaged in a cabinet and pulled out a surprisingly large first aid kit. She pawed through it with her uninjured arm, the conversation seemingly over.

Frankie took a deep breath, then another. Oz was going to protect her. Suddenly she felt wobbly. Her nerves felt as jangly as the bike bouncing up the stairs. She looked around the small space for something to calm her rattled system. It looked like a survivalists dream. Food, sleeping quarters, you name it, it was here. What was this place?

She looked at Oz, hoping for answers. All she got were more questions. Why was one look from Oz enough to settle her anxious thoughts? Why could she still feel the heat of Oz's hand on her stomach? Since when did she have a thing for badass women who knew their way around a gunfight? And most importantly, why was she thinking about any of that when there was a price on her head?

CHAPTER THREE

Oz grunted and fought every instinct to pull her arm away from Frankie's ministrations. "Ow. The treatment isn't supposed to cause more harm than the injury. Have you ever done this before?"

"Yes, badass, you picked the one short seller with a side hustle patching up gunshot wounds." Frankie paused mid stitch and gave Oz a look.

"That was pretty badass, wasn't it? I felt like a freakin' action hero. Although the real star of the show was your driving. Are you lying to me and you're really an international spy or a superhero?" Oz winced again as Frankie made another pass through her skin with the needle and thread. She'd kill for anything to numb the wound, but she hadn't found anything useful.

"I'm exactly who I said I am. As for you, action movie heroes don't get shot." Frankie's hands trembled as she tightened her stitch.

"Pfft. It all happens off camera. Seeing all this would slow down the plot." Oz turned her head to look at Frankie. "Although if they had someone as beautiful as you stitching up their hero, they'd be sure to show it, so maybe you're right."

Frankie laughed and the fear melted from her eyes. "Don't think for a second your sweet talk is going to keep me from sticking this needle right back through your arm. I have two more stitches to go. Don't be a baby, I'm almost done."

Oz snapped her fingers on her free hand. "It was worth a shot. Although I stand by my assessment."

"I've moved up from 'not ugly' to 'beautiful'? What heights will I climb to next?"

"Let's see." Oz tapped her chin. "I bet you were gorgeous in an orange jumpsuit. If you'd stayed on the street alone much longer, I'm sure you would have been the most stunning corpse in the morgue."

Frankie groaned. "This is why the heroes never get shot. They're good at their action part, but when they have to talk to a smoking hot woman it all falls apart."

"Let's not forget you banged down my door and *begged* for this." Oz gave her biggest, most winning grin.

"You'll never let me forget it if I'm reading this situation correctly." Frankie tied off the last stitch.

Oz flexed her arm. It felt better than she expected. Thankfully the shot had only winged her. "Damn right."

While Oz cleaned up the medical supplies she watched Frankie as she took in the small shipping container.

"I'm having trouble reconciling your ratty recliner and your tricked out hidey-hole." Frankie gently tapped a pistol hanging on the wall.

"This place?" Oz pointed abstractly around her as if she didn't know what Frankie was talking about. "Oh, this isn't mine."

Frankie looked like a cartoon with her eyes practically bugging out of her face. "Excuse me?"

"You borrow things to do your job, I borrow things to do mine." Oz motioned Frankie to a stool and pulled up a matching one across from her. She could tell Frankie wanted a better answer, but they had more important things to discuss. "Tell me everything you've got on this company that's supposedly trying to destroy the world."

"Do you think our hosts would mind if I sampled some of their copious canned goods? Come to find out, motorcycle chases make me hungry." Frankie's stomach growled on cue.

"Help yourself, but if I were you, I'd steer clear of the Spam and canned beans and hit up that little cabinet over there." Oz pointed to a metal footlocker stashed under the pegboard of weapons.

Frankie returned with a bowlful of peanut M&Ms, pretzels, and cashews, a bag of chips, and a handful of dried apricots. "Why all the canned goods and this gold mine?"

Oz shrugged. "The longer you stay in here, the more questions you'll have. Better to stick with the task at hand. Eat and talk."

Frankie looked around one more time before opening her bag of chips. The first loud crunch nearly obscured her words. "InvestBioX.

Evil incarnate and not just because they're after me, although that does complicate my feelings toward them. They're new to the pharmaceutical business, but since they turned their attention that way, they've been active. It started with acquiring small companies with existing patents on rare, not widely prescribed drugs. I watched the prices of those drugs skyrocket as soon as InvestBioX took over ownership of the patents."

"Why the rare meds? Couldn't they make more money by gouging something everyone takes?" Oz helped herself to some of Frankie's snacks and received a slap on the hand for her efforts.

"The more common the med, the more people are making it. You can't get ahead of the market or no one will buy your product. The rare drugs might only have one option and no easy alternatives. Most of the ones I watched were lifesaving or life-sustaining medications. People would literally die if they stopped taking the meds and so they'd pay whatever the price." Frankie wrinkled her nose as if she'd smelled something rotten.

Oz's cheeks warmed until they felt on fire. It was something that happened when anger slowly burned a pit in her gut until it seeped into her blood and out every pore. "Is any of what they're doing illegal?" She could already guess the answer.

Frankie shook her head sadly. "It makes them shitty people, but they're allowed to do it. Before you ask, I'm not on their hit list because they're not nice, well, not only for that reason. About three months ago, there was, out of nowhere, a ton of buzz about a new product InvestBioX was developing. They've never shown any interest in creating anything, only squeezing every cent out of desperate people."

Oz shrugged. "Their business model could have changed. You haven't convinced me they'd care one bit about you or your Googling." She tried again for snacks and was rebuffed again.

"You're so cute giving a big horrible corporation the benefit of the doubt." Frankie patted Oz on the cheek. "New drugs take years, sometimes decades, to develop and even if they'd gotten the research from one of the companies they acquired, they fired nearly all the scientists as soon as the ink was dry on the ownership transfer. Plus, I forgot to mention that when talking about InvestBioX, you also have to consider the hedge fund owned by their CEO." Frankie looked a little smug.

Oz was happy to meander along the evidentiary path Frankie was leading her down, but she'd better have one hell of an ace up her sleeve.

Before Oz could push for more information, an insistent beeping started across the small space. Oz rushed to it, her heart rate climbing the closer she got.

"How did they find us so fast?" She had five solid seconds of blind panic before her instincts kicked in. She cast around until she found clothes folded neatly in vacuum sealed bags. Each was labelled with a size and the contents. The pristine organization was nearly enough to make her puke. She turned to Frankie and tossed her the bag. "Don't argue with me. Strip down and change every piece of clothing. I think these should fit. Shoes, socks, bra, all of it. And anything you carry with you like a wallet or phone." Oz pointed to the floor where she wanted Frankie to pile her things.

"This chitchat took an unexpected turn." Frankie put her hands on her hips. "I'm not getting naked for you for any reason."

Oz bit back a reply that was far too suggestive for the situation. She could see the same emotions swimming in Frankie's eyes. "How about to stay alive? Your fan club has arrived and the only way they could have gotten to us this quickly is if you are wearing a tracker. I'm giving you the benefit of the doubt and assuming that's not intentional."

Frankie rolled her eyes, but the saucy gesture didn't hide the anxiety that had crept into her countenance. "How generous of you. Turn around and no peeking."

Despite her joking tone, Oz noticed Frankie shucked her clothes with remarkable speed.

"What do we do now?" Frankie was eying the pile of clothing and personal items on the floor like one of the bad guys might crawl out of a pocket.

"Only choice is to get out of here." Oz helped herself to another gun and a jackknife.

She slipped the knife into Frankie's jean pocket and pulled her to the door. "Just in case you need to rescue me." Oz still inched out slowly. "We need to get to the train tracks and we need to do it without getting caught by your friends or the container yard security." Oz considered taking Frankie's hand but figured that would likely get her a sucker punch to the gut. Frankie was no damsel in distress as she'd proved on the motorcycle. She didn't need Oz's coddling.

"I didn't expect being on the run to involve quite so much actual running." Frankie took a deep breath and rolled her shoulders. "Let's do it."

They dashed and darted in and amongst the containers stacked high all around them. Oz felt like a rat in a maze. If she hadn't spent enough time here to know her way around she would have been well and truly lost.

"Are you sure you know where you're going?" Frankie sounded more worried than Oz was comfortable with.

A flash of light reflecting off something nearby caught Oz's attention. Without processing, she grabbed Frankie in her arms and spun her against the side of a container. She shielded her with her body as the staccato ping of bullets on metal filled the air around them. She watched the corrugated wall of a bright blue container pockmark with each impact, inches from where they'd been a moment before.

"Holy shit!" Frankie clung to Oz tightly.

It wasn't the appropriate time to notice, and Oz certainly didn't want to notice, but she was, for the moment, still breathing and Frankie felt damn good in her arms. Things like that were hard to ignore, even when there were bullets zinging all around.

"That was too close. We have to keep moving." Oz's heart was beating as rapidly as the gunshots had impacted the metal next to them. She took off again, and this time she did take Frankie's hand and dragged her farther into the maze.

Oz urged Frankie in front of her, directing their madcap dash while also protecting Frankie from assaults from behind. They turned a corner and Frankie pulled up short and backed up two steps into Oz.

A man with a terrible haircut and a nasty snarl turned the corner, his gun aimed at Frankie's forehead. "Little bitch. You thought you could run forever?"

"Mind your manners, barnacle. That's no way to speak to a lady." Oz pulled Frankie behind her and took her place in the line of fire.

"Oh, for fuck's sake." Frankie exhaled loudly. "He doesn't look like a barnacle. Sorry, sir, my friend here forgot her manners."

Oz shushed her. "You didn't hire me for my pristine etiquette. Give me a minute."

As soon as she said it, she lunged at the man's hand and pushed his weapon skyward. It discharged with a loud "crack" which seemed to startle him as much as anyone. Oz took advantage of the momentary distraction and drove her shoulder into his chest, sending both of them flying into the dirt.

Once they landed, Oz on top of the assailant, it became a mad, desperate, scramble for the upper hand. Oz landed two punishing body blows before the man kicked her off of him. The boot to the gut knocked the wind out of her. There wasn't time to wait for it to return. Her opponent lunged for his gun which had fallen from his hand during Oz's initial assault.

Before he reached the gun, Oz jumped on his back and wrapped her arm around his neck. He clawed at her forearm and kicked his feet wildly. Even though Oz had an advantageous position, he had size and strength on her and was able to plant his feet enough to roll them both, pinning Oz to the ground. She held on tightly, her arm still around his neck.

Oz didn't want to harm him, she only needed him to pass out so they could continue to the train, but she struggled to maintain her grip. She felt him losing his fight, but before she could finish the job, he slammed his head down on her face. She instinctively loosened her hold, which was enough for him to slither free.

Liquid, Oz couldn't tell if it was blood or snot gushed from her nose. Sweat from her forehead ran into her eyes making them burn. She dragged herself upright and grabbed the man by his booted foot, tripping him and stopping his forward momentum.

"Get off me." He kicked back viciously but this time missed Oz's face.

One last surge and he reached the gun still lying in the dirt. It felt like a slideshow clicking together into a whole as Oz watched him lunge, his hand reach the gun, the flash of steel in the sunlight, and a knife plunge into the man's hand, pinning it to the ground.

"Fuck." Frankie and the man yelled simultaneously. Frankie put her hand to her mouth, her eyes wide with horror.

Oz scrambled to her feet and pulled her own weapon. She motioned Frankie to retrieve his. Once it was secure, she gave him a quick, sharp blow to the back of the head, knocking him unconscious.

"Don't say anything." Frankie looked shell-shocked.

Oz nodded. She pulled the knife from the man's hand and wiped the blood on his shirt. He had a bandana in his pocket which she wrapped tightly around his hand. It was quickly blood-soaked but he wasn't bleeding enough to be life-threatening.

Her hands shook slightly as she placed a nine-one-one call and reported his location and condition. He was a hired hand like she was. No need for him to lie out here in pain longer than necessary.

"Time for us to catch our ride." Oz took Frankie's hand again.

"You need some clean up. You look awful." Frankie squeezed Oz's hand.

"Thank you. I do what I can to impress." Oz wiped her free hand across her nose, trying to staunch what she now knew was blood. She urged Frankie on.

"Thank you." Frankie's voice was serious and sincere. "You saved my life."

"Don't thank me yet, we still need to get out of here." Oz pointed to the train tracks close by.

They didn't have far to go now, but there were more people in this part of the yard and they needed to wait for a train. Frankie fidgeted next to Oz as they lurked in the shadows cast by the towering stacks. A train whistle sounded and Oz saw it slowly groan into motion. "That's our ride. Follow me." She stuck as close to the container walls as possible, but they had to risk being seen to make sure they made it.

She approached the moving train with Frankie right behind and raced alongside. The train was picking up speed, and soon it would be out of reach. "You have to jump and grab there." Oz shouted as loudly as she dared and pointed at a three-step ladder on the end of the nearest rail car.

Frankie looked terrified but did as instructed. She reached for the first rung and missed. She stumbled and Oz let out a horrified squeak, but thankfully Frankie stayed on her feet. Oz silently urged her to try again, quickly. They didn't have much longer. She looked behind her and saw three men burst from one of the rows. Oz angled as best she could to shield Frankie from the imminent barrage of bullets, but it was difficult while sprinting all-out.

On her second attempt, Frankie grabbed the ladder and scrambled up. Oz chided herself for noticing Frankie's ass. Better to fill her mind with smut than the fact that what she was about to attempt was insane and would likely kill her.

The train tipped over into moving faster than Oz could keep up with. It was now or never. She lunged and caught the ladder and was immediately pulled off her feet. Her arm screamed its protest. She bounced uncomfortably off things not meant for human bodies. She heard Frankie calling her name. All she could do was kick and claw her way back to the ladder. The muscles in her hands and forearms were burning, but she held on for dear life until she was, finally, able to get her feet back on the lowest rung.

She held on, hugging the ladder and not moving, for what could have been miles or only the blink of an eye. When she stopped shaking enough that it felt safe to move, she pulled herself the rest of the way up and joined Frankie on a small deck just above the coupling connecting the cars in front and behind.

"Don't do that again." Frankie's eyes still held the shadow of anxiety and adrenaline. "You're too hot to get smashed under a train. Someone like you deserves an open coffin."

Oz barked out a laugh. Frankie's dark humor was exactly what she needed to release some of her own fear. "I make no promises and it's all your fault. My life was boring until I met you."

"The pleasure is all yours." Frankie held out her hand as if offering it for a kiss.

"Somehow I don't doubt that." Oz took her hand and brought it close to her lips. She didn't kiss her hand, although she wanted to, but she played along with Frankie's game.

It worked. Frankie batted her eyes and laughed, as close to relaxed as Oz figured was possible on a train running for her life.

"What does the hedge fund have to do with InvestBioX?" Oz shifted so she was more comfortable. Her thigh brushed against Frankie's. It sent a shiver through her stomach.

Frankie made no move to put distance between them. Oz tried not to read into it.

"I don't know, yet. I have a theory, which is why I need you to keep me alive, something you're doing a very good job of, by the way."

Oz tipped an imaginary hat. They rode together in silence as the miles flew past. Oz wasn't sure where they were going or how to get the proof Frankie needed, but for now they were safe. Until the train slowed, they were at the mercy of the tracks. Protecting Frankie felt a little like this ride. Life had thrown her onto a moving train with no map or schedule and expected a miracle. Oz looked at Frankie, her profile framed artistically by the setting sun. She shouldn't, she couldn't, but damn if she wasn't starting to enjoy the ride.

CHAPTER FOUR

Frankie dared a look across the street at the bail bond office hoping to see Oz exiting. She felt exposed sitting in the Laundromat alone. The red plastic chair was uncomfortable and creaked ominously when she fidgeted, something she was doing quite a bit of while she waited for Oz.

To keep her mind off all the ways things could go wrong, Frankie was picturing the two of them still riding the rails, the air filled with the smell of freedom and adrenaline. Neither she nor Oz would have chosen to come back to town after they'd worked so hard to narrowly escape, but Oz needed to get bond apprehension paperwork for Frankie so she could officially bring her in and get paid when this was all over.

By the time Oz finally emerged, Frankie had made a list of all the destinations she'd like to visit if she ever took a cross-country train trip. Now that she had, she cursed her reality that made that currently impossible. Maybe someday. And maybe she'd invite Oz. Because she'd proven useful, of course, not for any other, less practical reason.

Frankie watched Oz jog across the street and couldn't help the smile. Who was she kidding? She'd ask Oz along so she could look at her. The woman was gorgeous in a butch, capable, save the world kind of way and who in their right mind could help but find that attractive?

"Why are you looking at me like that?" Oz settled into the chair across from Frankie and put the paperwork she'd collected on the table between them.

"That chair might dump you on your ass. It's wobbly." Frankie pulled the paperwork closer so she could read it. She frowned. "It's all so contractual, how boring."

"Did you expect a 'wanted dead or alive' poster?" Oz's eyes danced with laughter.

"Maybe I did. To feel special." Frankie slid the papers back to Oz who folded them and put them in her back pocket.

"You don't need a poster to be special." Oz squeezed Frankie's hand.

"What are you doing?" Frankie pulled her hand away.

Poor Oz looked confused. "Is 'comforting you' the wrong answer?"

"Yes. No. As long as you weren't considering flirting. We don't have time for that, no matter how cute you think you are."

Oz put her hand over her heart. "I would never insult you in such a way. Although." Oz tilted her head as if thinking deeply. A strand of hair fell across her eyes. It was hot as hell. "You did tell me I wasn't ugly, so I think you started it."

Frankie wagged a finger. "Oh no, that was you. You need to work on your hostess skills. I hope that's not how you greet all your guests."

"Only murderers who invite themselves over." Oz raised an eyebrow.

"Alleged murderer."

A woman doing laundry nearby pushed her cart a little farther away.

"Of course. That's what I meant."

Frankie groaned at her own inability not to take the bait every time. She knew Oz was teasing her. The fact that she was still around and working so hard to hide a smile now gave her away.

"Can we get back to the flirting?"

Oz did smile now. "I thought you were against any of that nonsense."

"Talking about it, not doing it." Frankie felt her cheeks heat. "It's not allowed. We're in a stressful situation and it would be too easy for you to fall in love with me." Frankie tried hard to keep a straight face. She almost succeeded.

"Oh, is that right? I'm not that impressionable. What if you fell in love with me?"

Frankie shook her head. "I play cat and mouse with the stock market for a living. I'm not going to let your charms get to me. Besides, I have enough admirers."

Oz crossed her arms and scowled. "For the record, I'd be a much better suitor than the people who keep trying to kill us. Although I do admit it's a low bar. But I'm a damn good girlfriend."

"I don't know how you can say that with a straight face when you own that recliner."

Oz laughed aloud. "What did you have against my recliner? May it rest in peace."

Frankie sobered. "I'm sorry about your house. That chair needed to be put out of its misery, but I'm sorry about the rest of it."

"You shouldn't be. If you hadn't stopped by I don't think your day would have ended all that well." Oz waved her hand as if her house getting sprayed with bullets was no big deal.

Frankie shuddered. That was probably true. After the last few days it felt like even more of a miracle she'd survived as long as she had on her own. "Now that you have the paperwork you need, what's our next move?"

Oz drummed her fingers on the chipped table. "I was hoping you'd have the answers to that. Back in the container yard you said InvestBioX fired all the scientists and there was a hedge fund to consider. What did you mean? Are you saying this new product is made up?"

Frankie leaned forward and lowered her voice. "No, I don't think the new product is made up. It exists, but I don't think it does what they say it does. I think they're using the buzz to raise a huge amount of money." Frankie held up a hand to stop the questions she could see percolating. "I know what your next question is going to be. Since when is it illegal to want to raise a lot of money." Oz nodded her affirmation and motioned her to continue. "Look, I'm very good at what I do, and part of that is piecing together clues, no matter how well hidden. InvestBioX *is* out to make a lot of money. I think this product launch is specifically for that purpose, but not for the reasons you think. All that money they made ripping off everyday people needing medicine? It's gone."

Oz's eyebrows shot up like she didn't expect Frankie to say that. "What do you mean, gone?"

"I mean it's poof." Frankie made an exploding motion with her hands. "It's like it never existed. At least not in the accounts associated with InvestBioX."

"Hedge fund?"

Frankie nodded. She was impressed Oz had put the pieces together so quickly.

"Don't hedge funds make their own money? Why would money be transferred?"

"Hedge funds should make their own money from their investments and fees." Frankie felt the same excitement she had when she'd first made this discovery. There was something sketchy going on, she just needed proof.

"So why did they need all the money from InvestBioX?"

"Exactly. They shouldn't. But when I followed the trail of their clients' investments, you'll never guess what I found."

Oz looked like a lightbulb went off. "That money's gone too, isn't it? So InvestBioX is raising money to pump into the hedge fund? Why?"

"I don't know. Yet. But I'm sure answering that question will explain why InvestBioX is trying to kill me." Frankie whispered that last part so quietly she wondered if Oz had even heard her.

"Okay, so we need proof. I'm also going to get us some new clothes and some cash while we're still in town." Oz nodded matter-of-factly like that made any sense to Frankie.

Oz got up and spoke to the woman manning the cash register. Frankie couldn't hear what they were saying, but the woman looked at Frankie with a sympathetic look. She turned around and collected a large box overflowing with clothes. She handed it to Oz who returned to the table. "Lost and found. She said we can take whatever we want."

They sorted through the box and took everything that was close enough to their sizes. Oz returned the box when they'd finished.

"Wait here, I don't want you seen on an ATM security camera."

Before Frankie could protest, Oz was out the door and jogging across the street. She disappeared from sight, but Frankie could see the recognizable logo of a large bank reflected in the windows across the street. At least Oz hadn't gone far. She checked the clock. Three minutes had passed. It felt ten times that.

Oz reappeared with a dirt-covered backpack and a satisfied look. "I got us some traveling money and traded one of my credit cards for this backpack from a gentleman camping in the bank parking lot."

"You gave away your credit card for a backpack?" Frankie realized she was talking too loudly for the small space and lowered her voice. "Why?"

"We needed something to carry our clothes and anything else we stock up on and I don't need my cards anymore. Can't risk using them." Oz began to shove the clothes haphazardly into the backpack.

Frankie snatched the bag from Oz. "I might be forced to wear this monstrosity." Frankie held up a flowy blouse covered with an extra large floral print in colors that should never have been matched. "But it doesn't have to be wrinkled too." Frankie folded their new wardrobe and packed the pack neatly.

"It could be worse." Oz patted a pair of aggressively orange joggers.

"I like those. I'll never lose you unless you squat down next to a stack of traffic cones." Frankie packed Oz's new pants. "So tell me again why you ditched your card? He's going to use it since you gave it to him."

Oz nodded seriously. "That's the point. I'm going to pass out my others too. Charges will show up all over the city and either they think we're still in town and they waste a lot of time tracking all the purchases or they know we've left and have to spread their resources thin finding us."

"What if we let them think we've skipped town but hide out here? Do you have another hidey-hole you can borrow from someone?" Frankie's stomach seized when she thought of running again.

"I could find us something, but then we'd never collect your evidence." Oz looked sympathetic as if she could read Frankie's mind.

Frankie sighed. "Fine. You're right." She tried to ignore the feeling of warmth in her chest at Oz's kindness. "We need to get to New York and track down a former employee."

"Let's get going." Oz stood so quickly her chair nearly wobbled itself to pieces. "We need a couple pre-paid cell phones, but we can get those on the way."

Frankie stood as well and followed Oz out the door of the Laundromat. They both waved their thanks to the woman behind the counter. Hopefully, they hadn't made such an impression that she would bother remembering them in a few days if anyone came asking.

"Are you thinking train again?" Frankie fell into step next to Oz. "Less security than an airport and you don't need an ID like we would for a plane or to rent a car."

"Good point. What was the name of your first pet?"

"I didn't have any pets growing up. My parents weren't animal people. Why are you asking?"

Oz looked horrified. "Not animal people? Those actually exist? That's okay, I had an abundance of pets so we'll use one of mine." She was silent for a moment or two, clearly thinking. "What street did you grow up on?"

Frankie stopped and stared. "Are you doing the porn star name thing right now? Or are you trying to get answers to my security questions so you can clear out my bank accounts?"

Oz laughed, took Frankie's hand, and pulled her back in motion. "We need names for our train reservation, why not make them fun? But if you want to give me your bank information, I'm happy to help you spend some of your riches."

"If you must know, I grew up on Supreme Court. It was someone's idea of a democratically inclined inside joke I guess." Frankie stifled a groan as she thought of all the jokes she'd endured as a kid related to her street name.

"We might have to retire the game after this. No one will ever beat that street name." Oz's azure eyes lit up. "Goldie. That's the one. You're now Goldie Supreme. I'm Archie Ridgeway."

Now Frankie did groan. "Those are awful. Shouldn't we go with something a little less memorable?"

"Fine, but this officially makes you no fun." Oz looked too full of mirth to be taken seriously.

Frankie didn't mind the teasing. In a less life-or-death situation she'd be the first one to travel under a name as fantastic as Goldie Supreme. Goldie probably wasn't afraid of anything and certainly wouldn't require a bodyguard to stay alive.

Frankie looked at Oz and momentarily wondered what Archie Ridgeway was like. It caught her by surprise when she realized she didn't care. She did want to know more, but about Oz, not the made-up Archie. She chalked it up to her predilection for research and getting to the core of things. She did it every day for work, of course she'd want to do a deep dive on Oz as well. Except the usual thrill of discovery wasn't ping-ponging around her system. Instead, there was longing, a hint of arousal, and curiosity. She didn't need to know Oz for their arrangement to work. She *wanted* to know her and that was a much scarier proposition.

CHAPTER FIVE

Oz startled awake, initially unsure where she was. Frankie sleeping across from her and the rhythmic clacking of the rails grounded her. She spent a minute or two chiding herself for falling asleep and leaving them vulnerable and then decided it wasn't worth it. Nothing bad had happened and she needed to sleep. Since the moment Frankie arrived at her door she'd been running, planning, and trying not to let either of them die. Her arm throbbed and she was exhausted.

She checked her watch. She'd only been asleep an hour, but she felt much better than when she'd landed in her seat. The scenery flying by out the window was beautiful. She took a few minutes to enjoy it. Looking at the world pass by was calming enough she could almost forget the dire straits she and Frankie were in.

As if on cue, Frankie whimpered in her sleep, pulling Oz's attention away from the window. Frankie didn't wake, despite her furrowed brow and tight set jaw. Oz took the opportunity to study her more carefully without being caught. Her initial assessment of Frankie as "not ugly" now seemed comical. Frankie was exquisite. Her hair was no longer styled as it had been when they'd first met and her makeup was long gone. If possible, Oz liked this version even better than the chic, runway-worthy version that she'd first met.

Oz's mind strayed to what Frankie must look like fresh from bed, rumpled and relaxed. She chided herself. *Keep your clit in your pants, Osborne.* It really had been too long since she'd seen anyone except her own reflection in the early morning hours.

"You can stop staring at me like you're slowly undressing me." Frankie didn't look like she'd opened her eyes, but her smirk said she knew exactly what was going through Oz's mind.

"How do you know I wasn't thinking about my grocery list or what chance I have of solving the Sunday crossword this week?" Oz put her feet up on the seat next to Frankie and stretched.

"If you get that look from thinking about produce, canned beans, and a half gallon of milk, I might take my chances with the bad guys." Frankie finally opened her eyes and she too stretched.

Oz licked her lips before realizing what she was doing. Why was she acting like a high school boy who'd never seen boobs before? She returned her attention to the landscape outside.

"I used to love riding the train." Frankie sighed.

Oz could hear the melancholy and stress in Frankie's voice. "Come on, this trip isn't so bad. No one's shot at us, we got a little sleep, and you get to hang out with me. Where's the issue?" Oz held her hands out to the side, feigning innocence.

"If you could go on any train trip, what would you choose?" It was Frankie's turn to look out the window pensively.

"I don't know. I've never considered a train as anything more than a way to get where I'm going. What trip should I choose?" Oz leaned forward in her seat bringing her closer to Frankie.

Frankie was quiet, clearly pondering. "I've always wanted to ride the California Zephyr. I've heard it's the most beautiful train ride in America. I'd also like to go on a Grand Canyon tour by train."

"Aside from the guys with the guns and getting arrested for murder, what's stopped you?" Oz gave Frankie her full attention.

"I don't know." Frankie hesitated then continued. "That's not actually true. I could use the excuse that I work too much or now's not the right time, but the truth is I don't want to do them solo. I want to have someone to share the experience with. There hasn't been anyone I want to make those memories with so I haven't gone. Sounds a little pathetic when I say it out loud."

Oz reached across the space between them and squeezed Frankie's hand. "It's not pathetic at all. Surprising that you haven't already been snatched up, but not pathetic."

After a spell of companionable silence, Frankie broke the quiet. "Why are you doing this for me?"

Oz shifted in her seat, uncomfortable under Frankie's penetrating, searching stare. "Who says I'm not doing it for me? You promised me gobs of money and I need to buy a new recliner."

"Oz." There was warning in Frankie's voice.

"Okay, okay. I don't know is the best answer I've got. Trust is a funny thing, and for some reason I trust that you aren't actually a murderer, or at least you don't have your eyes set on me as your next target." Oz shrugged. "And the asshats after you shot up my house. That pissed me off. Between you and me, I'd probably still be at home dozing in my chair if the trigger-happy hitmen hadn't stopped by."

Frankie looked unsatisfied. "You were pretty set on showing me the door."

"Hey, I fed you first. I have a few manners." Oz grew serious. "Why are you trusting me?"

Frankie shrugged. "I have a pretty finely tuned gut. It doesn't usually steer me wrong. I'm used to taking calculated risks and you seemed like a safe bet."

Oz couldn't decipher the look that passed swiftly across Frankie's face. Was it longing? That couldn't be right.

"In order to keep my reputation intact, I'll be offering full service this ride. Can I get you something from the dining car?"

"Full service you say? What other services do you have to offer?" Frankie raised one eyebrow in challenge.

"Your wish is my command." Oz made a show of bowing grandly.

"I love hearing a woman tell me that." Frankie grinned widely, the joking making her face light up and her eyes sparkle. "For now though, some food would be great. Can we afford to eat on the train? I know our funds are limited."

"I think we can splurge for overpriced underwhelming train food. I'll be right back." Oz pushed through the door of their private room and went in search of the dining car. She jumped when her cell phone rang loudly. She jerked it out of her pocket and answered quickly. "Hello."

"Ms. Osborne, thank you for taking my call. Please do not alert Ms. Sender who you are talking to until you've heard me out." The man's voice was calm and matter-of-fact. He sounded like a stereotypical movie villain with an unbeatable master plan. It put Oz on high alert.

"I don't know who I'm talking to so it would be hard for me to alert anyone of anything. Who are you and what do you want?" Oz stepped into a small alcove at the end of the car and leaned against the luggage rack.

"My name is Jordan Minor and I am representing InvestBioX in this conversation."

Oz yanked the phone away from her ear and stared at it before returning to the call. "Then you and I have nothing to discuss unless it's how to compensate me for my holey house."

"I'm sorry about your property. It was an unfortunate misunderstanding. Before we get riled up about a few stray bullets, let me present my offer."

There was silence on the line. Oz let it drag. The man could say what he wanted to say and then she'd be free to end the call.

Finally, the man spoke again. "Right, okay. I'm assuming since you're still on the phone that you are willing to listen. We, InvestBioX, would like your assistance in bringing Ms. Sender into custody. We know you have the bond paperwork and her intention is to skip her court date. Frankly, she's become a nuisance to the company and we'd like to see her where she belongs, in jail."

"Says you." Oz's mind was whirring. What was this guy's angle?

"You're right of course. Except you've been getting Ms. Sender's version of events and now I'm taking the opportunity to present mine. Ms. Sender is a dangerous criminal who took another's life. We want justice to be served."

"Again, so says you. Why are you involving me in all this?" Oz was getting impatient.

"You were an unanticipated wrinkle but one that I think can be mutually beneficial. We'd like your help bringing in Ms. Sender and handing over any evidence she thinks she has. In exchange we can compensate you handsomely. Ms. Sender offered you the money from bringing her in after she completes this mission she thinks she's on. Is that correct?"

Oz nodded before realizing he couldn't see her. She grunted an agreement.

"We'll triple it." There was no hesitation on the other end of the phone. InvestBioX, or someone, had deep pockets to be offering that kind of money.

"You don't have to give me an answer right now. I'll be back in touch. Just remember you would be getting a dangerous criminal off the streets. I know your moral compass points true. In the meantime, keep an eye on her. If there is more out there that she's collected, we want that as well. I'm counting on you. And please don't share this information with Ms. Sender. I don't want to have to take more drastic measures."

"How much more drastic can you get?" There was no one on the other end of the phone. The man disconnected and was gone.

Oz stared at her phone and shook her head slowly. *How much weirder can this crap get?* Her first instinct was to give a middle finger salute to Jordan Minor and his overlords, but she hesitated. All she knew about Frankie was what she'd provided. Oz wanted to trust her, her gut told her to trust her, but what if she was wrong? What if she'd let a pretty face and a sad story cloud her judgment?

Thankfully, the line to order moved at a glacial pace so Oz had plenty of time to think before returning to Frankie. Should she tell Frankie about the call? Ask for more proof of her innocence? Pretend the call never happened? Each option had pros and cons.

After torturing herself with question after question all throughout ordering and waiting for their food, Oz finally returned the her seat and to Frankie. She pushed open the door and was met with a wide, welcoming smile. It lit Frankie's whole face and seemed to melt the worry away, if only for a minute. Her smile faded though as soon as Oz sat down heavily. Whatever look was on her face, Frankie had deciphered it. The smile evaporated and fear dominated her features.

"Are they on the train? Do we need to run again?"

"No. They're not here." Oz let Frankie search her face. It pained her how Frankie was now stalked by the specter of menace.

Frankie crossed her arms, pulling herself inward. "Then what's wrong?" Oz must have hesitated too long because anger flashed across Frankie's face. "Don't you dare lie to me. Whatever it is, spit it out."

Oz took a deep breath and opened her mouth to speak. She had no idea what was about to come out. "There's a reason I'm asking what I'm about to ask and it doesn't mean I don't trust you, but I need to know. Do you have any proof that you didn't do the things you were arrested for?"

Frankie's jaw tightened and her body stiffened. "Do I have proof I didn't murder someone? Is that what you mean?"

"Yes. I guess that is what I mean." Oz's insides felt wriggly in an unpleasant way.

"I'm not a murderer, Dakota Osborne." Frankie's voice was ice. "But if you need to know, the man I'm accused of murdering was an executive at InvestBioX. Appointments and invites were added to my calendar without my knowledge showing multiple meetings with him even though we'd never met. Around the time of the murder I was at the gym in a body combat class. The police never interviewed a single participant from that class or checked the security camera footage from the gym. I asked around." Frankie stopped and took a slow breath. "They supposedly recorded a phone call of me arguing with and threatening the victim, but the conversation never happened. I recognized my end of the recording as part of an argument I had with another short seller. The part where I said 'I'm going to kill you' is so poorly spliced it sounds like the voice of a phone tree from the late nineties." Frankie paused for a moment. There was still fire in her eyes. "All of that and the guy I supposedly killed was well over six feet tall and weighed two hundred and sixty pounds. He was an amateur weightlifter and was working toward his black belt in karate."

Oz swallowed hard. "How do they say you killed him?"

"Strangled him. With my bare hands." Frankie sat back in her seat and crossed her arms. "If you're having second thoughts, get out now. I can't worry about them and about you."

"Whoa, I told you there was a reason I was asking and there is. I got a phone call."

Frankie dropped her head back against the seat and groaned. "I should have known they'd come after you. You're a problem for them and an asset to me. What did they say? Not to trust me, I'm a liar and a killer?"

Oz tilted her head side to side. "Something like that. And they offered to pay me to betray you."

Frankie sat up. "How much?"

"Triple the amount for bringing you in."

"Holy shit." Frankie looked startled at how loudly she'd exclaimed and clapped her hand over her mouth. "Holy shit." She used a quieter voice. "I'd toss me to the wolves if I were you. You could buy a whole furniture store filled with nothing but ugly recliners with that kind of money."

"Oh, shut up. I'm not betraying you or taking their money. But I think we should let them think I am." Oz's gut settled. This felt like the right move.

Frankie motioned her to continue so Oz explained her plan. With Frankie's help, she'd hand over shreds of information to look like she was making a good faith effort to keep her end of the bargain. In return she'd try to pry as much out of them as she could. It was risky, but to Oz it seemed like a line worth casting.

Although Frankie agreed, she looked hesitant. Maybe she was overwhelmed with yet another wrinkle or maybe she didn't fully trust her. It surprised her how much that thought bothered her. Despite being incredibly hypocritical given her questioning of Frankie, it still stung. More than it probably should. As long as she didn't let her desire for Frankie's approval cloud her judgment. Sure, right, that wouldn't be a problem. Oz rolled her eyes. This job just got a whole lot harder.

Chapter Six

Frankie was annoyed by the pit in her stomach. She stared down the ups and downs of the stock market without blinking for a living. She was used to playing with high stakes and she never flinched. Now though, it seemed she'd been given a murder charge with a side of anxiety. It made logical sense that she'd be skittish given her current predicament, but it still frustrated her. She prided herself on not getting rattled.

Maybe she'd have had more luck if Oz hadn't told her about the phone call. It didn't seem like Oz had been tempted by the offer of truckloads of cash, but what if that changed? Or what if Frankie was wrong in her assessment? She sighed. There was no point second-guessing now. She'd taken a calculated risk contacting Oz, something she did for work all the time, now she'd have to live with the consequences.

"You okay?" Oz looked concerned.

"Fine, why?" Frankie tried to keep her voice light.

"Because you've been huffing and puffing and sighing dramatically since we got off the train. It seems like something's on your mind." Oz shot her a half grin.

Frankie debated how much to share before she spoke. In for a penny, in for a pound. "I was thinking about you actually."

"Oh shit. That's not good. Too much sighing, not the good kind, for that to be good. What did I do?" Before Frankie could answer, Oz held up a finger. "Wait, I know. It's the phone call. You're wondering if you can trust me. Am I right?"

Frankie harrumphed. "So what if you are?"

Oz's gaze softened. "Then I'm not doing something right. You have enough on your plate without also having to feel like you're looking over your shoulder with me. Ten thousand years ago when this thing started between us, I told you I'd keep you safe until you proved your innocence or I brought you back to jail. There's no amendment to our deal."

"There's no 'thing' between us." Frankie pointed between them and bit back a smile.

"You're wrong. There's definitely a thing."

Frankie couldn't help but notice how the light played in Oz's eyes, like tiny fireflies sparking mischievously. She had dimples that only appeared when a smile captured her whole face, and she was solid and strong and all the things Frankie needed to believe in at this moment.

"No thing." Oz didn't need to know Frankie enjoyed the teasing and found Oz wildly attractive.

"There's a thing." Oz mouthed before turning more serious. "Do you know where we're going?"

Frankie nodded. It was good the man she'd come to talk with lived close to the train station. It made it easier to avoid unnecessary interactions and also saved them money by not needing a ride. She pointed to a tidy colonial painted a tasteful light gray with yellow shutters.

They climbed the three steps to the front door. It was ajar. Something felt wrong. Goose bumps erupted on Frankie's arms. Oz clearly felt it too because she stepped in front of Frankie before slowly pushing the door open.

"Hello?" Oz peered in, one arm holding Frankie behind her.

There was no answer. Oz took a step in the house and called out again. Frankie followed. No way in hell she was going to stay out on the porch alone.

Once inside, she wished she'd stayed outside. "Is that blood?" Frankie looked at the red drops on the floor and a red handprint smeared on the wall.

"Stay here and don't move." Oz was deadly serious now. She drew her weapon and crept down the hall.

Frankie waited, torn whether she should do as Oz instructed or follow her farther into the house. Either way, she'd feel vulnerable, but she opted for active motion and picked her way through the blood droplets after Oz.

Before Frankie caught up, Oz stopped abruptly and lowered her gun. "Oh holy hell." She held up a hand. "Frankie, don't come in here. You don't need to see this."

Frankie's breath hitched. She knew what was on the other side of the door but didn't want to believe it. There was too much blood sprinkled around the hall leading into the living room for the scene to be anything other than a nightmare.

"Is he dead?" Frankie needed the confirmation.

Oz was pale when she turned back to Frankie. "Someone is. I don't know what the guy we were meeting looked like, but it's probably safe to assume it's him."

Frankie's pulse began to race. Someone was dead, which made her heart ache, but she couldn't help but think of the implications for her as well. This guy had valuable information she needed. Plus, they were standing in the middle of a crime scene. She couldn't get caught here. She'd already been accused of one murder she didn't commit.

"We have to get out of here. You can't be seen here." Oz took Frankie's arm and pulled her back toward the door as if reading Frankie's mind.

Against every instinct screaming for her to leave, Frankie hesitated. "No, not yet. Trust me, I don't want to be here either, but this guy knew things about InvestBioX. Everything I've learned points to him getting ready to blow the whistle. That's why I wanted to talk to him and probably why he's dead right now. But a guy who's ready to take on InvestBioX doesn't leave anything to chance. He's got receipts and I want to find them."

Oz looked disgruntled. "There's nothing in here worth dying for. Or ending up back in jail."

Frankie crossed her arms, annoyed. "What he has might be the best shot I have of staying out of jail. You can wait outside if you want. I need a minute." Frankie turned back to the interior of the house and tried to think.

"Fine, but we have a timer and it starts now." Oz checked her watch. "What do you know about this guy?"

"He's a midlevel accountant. He lives alone. Unmarried." Frankie ticked things off on her fingers.

Oz looked around the house. "What else? Anything more personal?"

"He's an avid fly fisherman if his social media is anything to go by. He's in an online group for people with dog phobias, an unfortunate fear for him since InvestBioX allows pets at work. Judging by the high-end knives in the kitchen over there, he's a decent cook or at least wants to look like one." Frankie stepped into the kitchen, careful not to step in any bodily fluids.

Oz followed. She glanced at the knife block. Frankie noticed one missing and shuddered. She didn't want to spend a lot of time thinking where it might currently reside.

"Don't let your mind run away with you, okay? Let's focus on why we're here." Oz's voice was gentle.

Frankie nodded. She looked away from the counter and scanned the rest of the room. They probably needed to explore upstairs, but her desire to stay and search was quickly waning. The longer they were here, the more likely they got caught. Oz interrupted her inner conflict.

"Didn't you say this guy lives alone?" Oz was staring across the kitchen, a confused look on her face.

"Not even a pet, why?" Frankie moved next to Oz to try to see what she was looking at.

Oz pointed. "Then why does he have a bag of dog food in the pantry?"

Frankie felt the jolt of excitement she got at work when she had a promising lead. Could this be her break?

They picked their way across the kitchen, careful not to disturb anything. Oz gently unsealed the bag and looked inside.

"I can't decide if I want to curse you for finding it first or kiss you right now." Frankie felt her cheeks heat to blast furnace temperatures. "It's a figure of speech."

"So I shouldn't pucker up then?" The mischief was back in Oz's eyes.

"Maybe I'll reconsider if you find me what we came for." Frankie peered into the bag again.

Oz looked a little shocked. "Well, if that isn't motivation, I don't know what is." She winked and turned her attention back to the bag.

After a minute of digging, Oz triumphantly pulled a cylinder covered in duct tape from the kibble. It looked like a paper towel tube that had been taped over completely.

"This has to be it. I think we've pushed our luck being here this long. Let's sneak out and hope no one saw us come in." Oz handed their find to Frankie and pulled her toward the door.

Frankie took one last look around before following Oz back into the sparkling, sunshiny day. It felt jarring to see the sun and cloudless, impossibly blue sky, after experiencing such a grisly scene inside the house.

"Walk casually. People will take note if we run or look nervous. We're two women out for a walk in this beautiful neighborhood, nothing more." Oz slowed her pace. Her body looked relaxed.

"I'm having a little trouble with that. Every instinct is telling me to run." Frankie gripped the duct-taped treasure tightly, her hands shaking.

Oz nodded. "You can do this." She took Frankie's hand and held on. "Hold on to me. We're fine."

Frankie immediately felt calmer. Oz's strength was contagious. Why did she feel so comfortable hand in hand with Oz? Frankie didn't want to probe too deeply into her feelings. For now, she was content to walk and enjoy the feeling.

Chapter Seven

Oz walked with no destination in mind. Normally, she wouldn't complain about an aimless stroll holding hands with a beautiful woman, but her nerves were humming and her mind filled with images of the dead man. It would take time to get the sight of his bloody, lifeless body from her head.

A small park came into view, and Oz led the way to a bench, set back from the road, under the protective canopy of a large elm. They sat without speaking for a few minutes, each lost in their own thoughts. Frankie scooted closer until their thighs met along their length. Despite the horror movie playing in her head, Oz wasn't immune to the electric tingle that shuddered through her as soon as Frankie's leg contacted hers.

"I'm having trouble juggling my emotions right now. I want to be happy because we found this." Frankie held up the cylinder. "But its owner was murdered."

"You were really brave back there. Probably braver than I would have been in your situation." Oz squeezed Frankie's hand which was still joined with hers. "I don't know how you're managing to do any of this, honestly."

"Is that a line? Are you buttering me up for something?" Frankie smiled wearily.

"Not even a little. Simply an observation." Oz was impressed with Frankie's fortitude.

"That's too bad. Maybe it's the fact that we were creeping through a murder scene and life seems fleeting all of a sudden, but I'm finding it hard to not vomit out everything that's on my mind." Frankie pulled her hand from Oz's and toyed with a loose piece of duct tape.

"Don't let me keep you from sharing freely." Oz leaned forward and rested her elbows on her knees. She turned to get a better look at Frankie.

"I'd be a hypocrite if I did. I was very clear there was to be no flirting between us. Too risky for you." Frankie raised an eyebrow as she caught Oz's gaze.

"We were in a very stressful situation. You can be forgiven for a little contradiction." Oz raised a corresponding eyebrow.

Frankie laughed and sat back. "That was my whole point. Our situation heightens everything, including how damn hot you are."

Oz felt both her eyebrows shoot up this time. "Is that right? So you're saying if we met at a bar you'd blow me off? It's only when dodging bullets and discovering dog food disguised as treasure that I turn your head. Good to know. Good to know." She was joking but her stomach also cartwheeled at Frankie's words.

Frankie tilted her head back and forth. "I'd probably still notice you without the bullets."

"Please be careful. My ego is going to be too inflated to fit through doorways." Oz fanned herself dramatically.

Frankie reached out and stroked Oz's cheek. "Thank you for all you're doing for me. Are you okay? After what you saw at the house?"

Oz stilled. She ran her hands through her hair. "No, not really. I'm glad you didn't see it too. No one should have to see something like that. How could InvestBioX do that to another human being?"

Frankie scooted closer still and put her arm around Oz's shoulders. "I'm sorry I got you into this."

"No. I don't want to hear that again. Bullets started flying ten minutes after I met you. I knew what I was getting into." Oz pointed to the cylinder. "And we're not done yet. Should we open it?"

Frankie pulled at the duct tape, slowly unwrapping it. "This better not be a vintage playboy or his nana's secret casserole recipe." She yanked one particularly stubborn section and the end cap came off too.

They both peeked in the tube as if the contents would speak directly to them. Frankie gently eased out the rolled up stack of papers. Oz could feel her practically vibrating with energy as soon as she got a look at what they contained.

Oz was lost as soon as she took in the first page. It was full of spreadsheet data and graphs. Handwritten notes were scribbled next to a number of columns of data. Frankie seemed to know exactly what she was looking at and muttered exclamations to herself as she took it in. It wasn't hard to tell Frankie liked what she saw.

When Frankie flipped the page, Oz felt a flush of understanding surge through her. The second page didn't contain numbers, but a description of a drug, including side effects, mortality rates, and chemical composition. There was a note in the corner in all caps that said "KILLER."

"Is that what I think it is?" Oz pointed at the paper.

Frankie nodded absentmindedly and flipped the page again. More spreadsheet data. Frankie sat back and whispered "whoa."

"Do you know what this means?" The excitement was impossible to miss in Frankie's voice.

"Not a clue." Oz turned the page back to the previous one. "But I can tell this isn't good."

They both stared at the stark warning about InvestBioX's mystery drug. Frankie shook her head slowly. She flipped the final page and gasped. No commentary was needed. The page contained two photographs of a computer screen. On the first screen was an email with the subject line "Frankie Sender." The message went on to describe Frankie as meddlesome and a problem to be contained. The second screen, also displaying an email, was a reply to the first email.

Oz couldn't stop reading and rereading the third line of the missive. "We have a body that will work. She'll be in prison until she rots." A note in the corner of this page read simply "Find Ms. Sender."

"This is it. It proves I'm innocent." Frankie looked skyward, her eyes welling.

"To me it does." Oz tread carefully. "But I'm not sure it does legally."

"What is that supposed to mean?" Her tone was defensive and accusatory.

"Hey, I'm on your side." Oz risked taking Frankie's hand. She didn't pull away. "But a defense lawyer could argue we obtained this illegally or we photoshopped the whole thing. Those spreadsheet numbers might mean something to you, but we could have created them ourselves and printed it out."

"No, actually we couldn't." Frankie pointed to the corner of one of the spreadsheets. "See that watermark? I've seen it on other InvestBioX pages. It's how they protect their documents and authenticate them if needed. It's probably how they found the guy who printed these." Frankie squirmed. "What I don't understand is how he was able to get them out of InvestBioX offices to begin with. The watermark usually prevents printing and downloading."

Frankie turned back to the spreadsheet data. She ran her finger down one column, then another. Her eyebrows scrunched together. Oz wanted to ask questions, but Frankie looked like she was lost in the numbers. Oz drummed her fingers on her knees waiting for an explanation. She looked skyward. The blue above was pristine. There wasn't a cloud or bird marring the azure expanse. It didn't seem possible something so wondrous could exist in the same world as the scene she'd stumbled upon back at the house.

She turned her head and looked at Frankie. The sky was not the only thing of beauty to remind her not everything was gunshots and bloody corpses.

"What are you looking at?" Frankie looked up from her spreadsheets with a puzzled look on her face.

Oz stammered. She hadn't meant to stare. "I was looking for the beauty in the world to remind me everything is not awful."

"So you turned your head my way? A murderer on the run?" Frankie turned more fully in Oz's direction.

"Alleged murderer." Oz pointed to the stack of papers on Frankie's lap. "Unless you want to tell me those are a lie and confess."

"Oh, shut up."

Oz suppressed a laugh. The moment felt charged, and she had a surprising urge to lean forward and capture Frankie's lips. Where the hell had that come from? Oz sat back and looked once again to the sky. Frankie had been clear about flirting. Oz assumed kissing was off the table too. If only Frankie hadn't confessed to finding Oz attractive.

"Whatever's going on in that head of yours, snap out of it. I have something to show you." Frankie poked Oz in the shoulder, then flipped through the pages. "Look." She pointed to a column of numbers that meant nothing to Oz. "This new wonder drug isn't technically an InvestBioX product. They've spun off another company."

"I don't know why that matters." Oz stared at the numbers, but they still might as well be abstract art.

Frankie was quiet a moment then sat up straight as if poked with a cattle prod. "I need to know if this new company is trading on any of the major indices. Those phones you got us have internet, right? Can you look it up?"

Oz did as Frankie asked. "I found it. The stock price is—"

"The price doesn't matter. Is it up or down?" Frankie didn't look up from the pages she was once again poring over.

"Up." Oz felt like a cartoon with her eyes bulging out. "By a lot. Is that good or bad?" Excitement tickled Oz's insides. She might not know how to interpret the details, but she knew when a solid lead was right in front of her.

"For the world? Bad. For us? Maybe not so bad."

Oz recognized the look on Frankie's face. She was like a dog on a scent. The chase was on.

"I think I know what they're planning." Frankie looked like she'd smelled something distasteful.

Oz urged Frankie to continue. She'd try to keep up.

"First, how much is InvestBioX's stock up?"

"How do you know it'll be up?" Oz tapped on her phone to pull up the information. Frankie gave her a look. "Because you're a brilliant boss ass bitch. Of course."

"Don't you forget it." Frankie patted Oz's cheek. "The stock?"

Oz didn't hide her confusion. "It's up, but not very much. Two and a half percent."

"Tricky bastards. They're driving up the price of this new company's stock with all this press and fanfare. I bet if it craters it won't impact InvestBioX's stock long-term. They'll have some built in excuse why it's not their fault." Energy and excitement was emanating so strongly from Frankie Oz was afraid of getting knocked over by a shock wave.

"You've lost me completely. I don't understand why that matters." Oz's brain felt like it was being stretched and pulled uncomfortably. This was not her wheelhouse. It almost made her miss the bullets and foot chases.

"I don't have proof yet, but I think someone at InvestBioX is driving up that price. If I were them, I'd push it as high as I could and then short the stock. They know they are sitting on a turd. It's going to fall." Frankie's eyes were glimmering. She was extremely sexy talking numbers.

Oz pinched the bridge of her nose. "I'm afraid to ask, but how do they do that? Why not buy the stock when it's low, let it go as high as it can, and then sell it?"

Frankie leaned back and casually crossed her legs. She stretched an arm out on the back of the bench. With the sun catching the highlights in her hair, she looked like she was posing for a high-fashion magazine. Oz was breathless.

"They can't buy and sell normally without hanging a big flashing sign on their door that screams insider trading. They know the two companies are legally separate, but regulatory bodies won't see it that way. If they have insider knowledge that the stock is going to crash, they can't get caught making a shit ton of money by selling before anyone else is aware."

"Getting arrested isn't so bad. It did wonders for you." Oz pointed both thumbs at herself.

"Offering your services to the enemy now? Waiting eagerly for the next mystery phone call?" Frankie's words were joking but her voice was tense.

Oz took Frankie's hand and leaned toward her. "You hired me and I'm loyal. I'm like a German shepherd or a Rottweiler."

Frankie tilted her head back and forth, clearly thinking. "Labradoodle. I won't offend you by saying Chihuahua with a hero complex."

"I've plotted daring escapes, dodged bullets, and discovered spreadsheet treasures. How exactly does that scream Labradoodle and not pit bull?" Oz pulled her hand from Frankie's and crossed her arms, mocking disgust.

Frankie smiled wickedly. "It's the poodle in you. They're insanely smart, athletic, and versatile. If any dog could pull off all that, it's a poodle. And the Lab is for this cute face." Frankie gently pinched Oz's cheek.

Oz swatted her away. "Fine, Labradoodle. I wear it with pride. Now back to short sales. How do they work and what do we do now that we know about it?"

Frankie sobered. "We don't know yet. It's what I think is happening, but I could be wrong."

"Are you wrong?" Oz shot her a pointed look.

"I am not. It's their only play." Frankie tapped the pages on her lap. "Imagine you had stocks that were worth twenty-five dollars each. If I want to short them, I would borrow, say one thousand, of your stocks at the twenty-five-dollar price. So now I hold the stocks and their twenty-five-thousand-dollar value. But." Frankie held up a finger. "I'm sure these stocks are going to crater. So I hold onto them until I've reached the limits of my nerves or the price reaches zero. If, in our scenario, I hold until the stocks are five dollars a piece, then I have to close the position by buying the stocks I borrowed. In this case, I only have to buy them for five thousand since the value decreased. My profit is the amount I received when I borrowed them minus what I paid to close the position, so twenty thousand dollars."

Oz's head felt like it was being crammed with sharp-edged figures intent on maximizing pain. "Okay, I think I followed about sixty percent of that, which I'm damned proud of. These guys are going to wait until the stock is at its highest and then short it and wait until it bottoms out? Is that more or less what you're thinking?"

"Yes, exactly." Frankie gave Oz a high five.

"What do we do about it? Go to the police, the government watchdogs, what?"

A predatory look flitted through Frankie's eyes. "No, we short them first. This shell company and InvestBioX too. We'll hurt them by taking their money."

Oz exhaled slowly. It was hard for her to be as jubilant as Frankie because she didn't have a clue how they were going to accomplish what Frankie suggested. Frankie had trusted her with her life, it was time for Oz to do the trusting. If taking their money was the way to make InvestBioX hurt, then it was time to make them bleed.

Chapter Eight

Frankie plopped into her seat on the train, closest to the window. Oz insisted on being on the aisle so she could protect Frankie from anything that came their way, but Frankie was pretty sure she liked the option of stretching her legs out further in front of her.

No sooner had the train started moving and Frankie was able to take a deep breath again after the fear and excitement of the last few hours, then Oz's phone rang. She yanked it from her pocket and looked at the screen frowning.

"Must be a wrong number. No one knows about this phone." It was clear she wasn't really talking to Frankie.

"What if it's the Caller." Frankie kept her voice low but couldn't keep the slightly screechy worry from slipping in.

Oz accepted the call and held it to her ear. She didn't say anything. Frankie could hear someone talking on the other end. From Oz's suddenly rigid posture and deeply furrowed brow, it was easy to connect the dots. InvestBioX was reaching out again.

"How did you get this number?" Oz demanded.

A passenger behind them hissed an aggressive "shhhh."

Oz stood and glared at the man behind them before moving up the aisle toward the open space in front of the lavatory. Frankie had no interest in being left out this time. She stood quickly and followed Oz. Before she could catch up, Oz stepped into the lavatory and closed and locked the door. What the hell?

Frankie tried not to make a scene by banging on the bathroom door, demanding to be let in. She wanted to and allowed herself thirty seconds to picture going full superhero and breaking down the door with her otherworldly strength. Back in reality, she leaned against the luggage rack, arms crossed, and tried not to huff and sigh so loudly the entire train could hear her.

Seconds dragged, minutes crawled. She couldn't hear words, only Oz's indistinct side of the conversation. Questions flew through her head so fast she barely registered one before another elbowed it out of the way. They all vied for top billing on her worry list and got more wild and extreme the longer Oz stayed holed up in the bathroom. What did InvestBioX want? Was Oz considering their offer? How did they know how to contact Oz? Was this all one big setup?

"Excuse me, are you in line?" An impossibly tall, slim man tapped Frankie on the shoulder.

"Try the next car. She's been in there for ages." Frankie made a gagging motion and pointed at the bathroom door.

The man's eyes grew wide and he scurried back the way he'd come. Apparently, the idea of visiting a bathroom after someone trying to hit a toilet bowl on a moving train was enough to calm his bladder. Hopefully, his quick retreat would discourage anyone else looking to relieve the call of nature.

Just as Frankie was considering testing whether she actually did have some super strength lying dormant in her muscles and kicking the door once or twice, Oz emerged. "What the hell?" Frankie punched Oz in the shoulder, harder than she intended.

Oz didn't flinch. She motioned Frankie back to their seats. Once they were settled again, she leaned close and whispered, "Your friends got in touch again."

"Oh, you don't say? Why else would you be hiding in the bathroom if you weren't talking to them?" Frankie knew she sounded salty. She didn't like being shut out when it was her life on the line.

"How do you know I wasn't talking to my secret girlfriend and didn't want you to know about her?" Oz looked too amused to be taken seriously.

"Easy. You have good taste in women." Frankie moved her hand in front of her own face down to her lower torso. "So if you had a girlfriend, there's no way that recliner would have been at your house."

"What do you have against that chair?"

Frankie put her hand over her heart. "Nothing now that it's dead. Now tell me what InvestBioX said this time."

Oz sighed and scrubbed her face. "First, I locked myself in the bathroom to keep them from knowing you were next to me and to try to disguise the train noise. Even in the bathroom it's hard to hide the sound of the rails, but I didn't need a conductor demanding tickets or noisy neighbors in the background."

Suspicion crept into Frankie's thoughts unbidden. She didn't like the feeling of turmoil threatening her gut. Oz had been her Hail Mary, her last option. What if she betrayed her? "Why didn't you want me to hear what they said to you?"

Oz's eyes softened and she covered Frankie's hand with her own. "That's not what I said. I wanted them to think I was alone. If they don't believe I'm considering their offer, we can't get any information from them. I needed them to think I snuck off to talk behind your back."

"You did sneak off to talk behind my back." She wasn't letting Oz off the hook yet, but the churning in her stomach lessened at Oz's explanation.

"You chased me all the way. I hardly snuck, but that's not the important part." Oz lowered her voice. "They upped the ante to try to get me to buy in. They implied there's a lucrative job waiting for me at InvestBioX after we get your situation squared away."

Frankie sputtered, unable to spit out her rage, frustration, fear, and a sentence simultaneously. "My situation? You mean me being killed or ending up in prison for the rest of my life?" If she had daggers to shoot from her eyes, they'd all be aimed squarely at Oz's chest.

Oz squeezed Frankie's hand, still protectively encased by Oz's. "Hey, I'm on your side. I'm only reporting what they offered."

Frankie pinched the bridge of her nose. "I know. I'm sorry. So let me see if I understand what you're saying. InvestBioX first offered you three times what I did to turn me in? Now they're sweetening the deal by offering you a job kneecapping senior citizens, punting puppies, and framing people for murder?"

"We didn't get into a scope of work, but I assume those things are in the job description somewhere." Oz grinned cheekily. "I know you have to be worried about the money they're offering me. I can't make you trust me, but I'd take a lot more bounties if I only wanted to get rich. No matter what happens, I'm not going to sell you out to InvestBioX."

Frankie wanted to believe her. She was desperate to believe her, but she couldn't get all the way there. "You're an idiot for turning down that much money."

"Not if accepting it meant you rot in jail or a coffin." Oz pulled her hands into her lap and picked at a nonexistent hangnail.

"Sweet talker." Frankie turned to the window and watched the landscape fly past as they barreled down the track.

"Not my best material but you get the idea." Oz rested her head on the seat back and closed her eyes. When she opened them she leaned close to Frankie, a concerned look on her face. "What I want to know is how they had my number. I wonder how much they paid the guy I bought them from to sell us out? I thought I'd been careful enough. Damnit. I'll get a new one when we're off the train, but we need to be even more careful. If you see anything even remotely out of place, you let me know."

Frankie nodded. "Right, up the paranoia to unhealthy levels. Not sure how much higher I can push it to be honest, but I'm a striver."

Oz looked amused. "I'm glad you're keeping your sense of humor."

"Is that what that was? Better than flop sweats and panicked screaming." Frankie worked at relaxing her shoulders which were up around her earlobes.

"We should keep the panicked screaming to a minimum. You are a wanted fugitive from justice after all."

Frankie tried to remember the date. "I was supposed to be in court today, wasn't I? Now I'm really at your mercy. You can bring me in anytime and I'll go back to jail or you could accept a huge payout to turn on me." What a sobering thought.

Oz scowled disapprovingly. "I'm not going to betray you, Frankie. I'll keep proving it. Until then, I guess you have to trust me."

Despite the pressure and uncertainty, Frankie laughed. "I showed up on your doorstep and begged you to save me, not to mention sharing a lot of information and running from the bad guys. I do trust you." She waited for Oz to make eye contact. Hopefully, Oz believed her. "You said we can use InvestBioX or whoever is reaching out to you. How?"

Oz shifted in her seat. She looked uncomfortable. "I've been thinking about the evidence we found and your theory on InvestBioX's malfeasance. I'm not sure how to get around the chain of custody issue with the papers, and shady stock trading doesn't prove they framed you for murder."

Frankie had always pictured marching into a police station, thrusting open the door with such force it banged against the wall, and presenting dramatic evidence against InvestBioX clearing her name. Was Oz saying that was impossible? "What are you suggesting?"

"We need a confession. It's the way to get you off the hook and if we leak it to the right people, maybe it will also tank their stock?" Oz went back to picking at her cuticles.

Frankie felt her brows raise and her eyes widen. "How the hell do you plan on getting them to confess?"

Oz shrugged. "I'm still working on that. In the meantime, what do you need to do your short shrift, sale, thing?"

Frankie tried not to roll her eyes. She couldn't tell if Oz was being purposely obtuse to give her something else to think about, or if she really was clueless. Frankie hoped it was the former. "The Wi-Fi on this train isn't good enough for me to do the trading I need. I'll have to be somewhere with a good signal for a computer and cell phone. You'll have to make sure I have plenty of time to work." Frankie paused. "I guess you'll have to get me a computer too since everything I own now is in that backpack.

"I can do that. As soon as we're off the train, let's find you some internet and a place to trade." Oz nodded like that item had been checked off the to-do list.

Frankie watched as Oz slowly gave in to exhaustion and fell asleep. Maybe she should have felt more concern or vulnerability with her bodyguard asleep, but instead she was taken by Oz's rugged good looks. She really hoped Oz was as honorable as she insisted she was. Despite her warnings, rules, and best efforts, Frankie was beginning to care for Oz. Before she could stop it, an image of Oz naked in her bed flashed through Frankie's mind. Annoyance quickly flared which Frankie had come to realize was usually a sign that she needed to pay more attention. What was it about Oz that was setting her defensive systems to high alert? Frankie studied Oz's profile, worry free in slumber. She was smoking hot for one. Kind, compassionate, brave, and noble.

Frankie groaned. Here she was mooning over a woman she'd hired to keep her alive. No one was flawless. Hell, she probably put soy sauce in her cereal or knocked ice cream cones out of the hands of children. Frankie let out a frustrated sigh. Who was she kidding? She was going to enjoy Oz and her company for as long as they were together. She'd told Oz there was no flirting or falling in love. She hadn't made a rule about window shopping. Surely there was no danger in that.

CHAPTER NINE

For the second time, Oz snapped awake after falling asleep on the train. This time however, her return to consciousness was much less peaceful. Frankie was nudging her aggressively. It took a few blinks before Oz realized Frankie was also trying to talk to her but she was whispering and Oz had to strain to make out her words.

"Oz, wake up. Wake up. I need you."

Despite the undertone of fear in Frankie's voice, Oz couldn't help but thrill at Frankie's statement of need. She wanted to feel strong and powerful and needed.

"There's a guy a few rows behind us that's been moving seats closer for the past thirty minutes. He keeps staring at me." Frankie had both hands wrapped around Oz's biceps as if clinging on for dear life.

Oz tensed. Frankie was far from histrionic. If she felt threatened, Oz was going to pay attention. She couldn't casually turn around to get a look, it would be too obvious. She needed to figure out another way to see the mystery man.

"Give me your cell phone." Frankie held out a hand. "They already know about yours so no need to hide it."

"Why do you need this?" Oz handed over the phone, not trying to hide her confusion.

"Smile." Frankie held the phone in front of them and snapped a series of selfies of the two of them.

When Frankie was done she scrolled through the pictures. There wasn't a single one that was prize-worthy. Their chins were at the bottom of the frame and they weren't centered.

It took a minute, but finally Oz caught on. "You cut off my head, take another one." Oz said it loudly enough for the passengers around them to hear. "I'll do it. I have longer arms." She positioned the camera at a different angle, cutting off even more of the bottom of their faces this time, but giving a very clear picture of the three rows behind them. She snapped a few shots and then she and Frankie huddled over the camera again.

"That's the guy," Frankie whispered, pointing to the screen.

Oz zoomed in on the man in question. She wasn't able to see much more than his head and shoulders, but he certainly looked the part of a hired killer. She studied the photo more closely, squinting as if that would help her decipher the image.

"What do you see right there?" Oz centered the part of the photo in question.

Frankie looked closely now too. "Is he wearing suspenders?"

The man was wearing a jacket, but peeking out beneath the collar was a small section of exposed leather. "I think it's a shoulder harness. I don't like an armed, mean-looking dude two rows behind us. Too much of a coincidence."

"You have your gun too, right?" Frankie sounded worried.

"I'm not going to get in a shootout on the train." Oz considered their options. They didn't have luggage or anything that couldn't be left behind if needed. "Let's go get a snack." She stood abruptly and pulled Frankie to her feet after her.

Frankie looked like she was about to question Oz's sanity. Oz shook her head as subtly as possible and pasted on a smile. Whether Frankie figured out what Oz was up to or was willing to trust her, she too smiled and gave Oz a playful push into the aisle.

"You promised me food ages ago but then fell asleep. As punishment, you're buying."

Oz took a step down the aisle away from their seat to allow Frankie passage. As she did so, she glanced back, getting a better look at the man of mystery. He was watching them but quickly averted his gaze when Oz turned his way. He also adjusted his jacket to cover what Oz was now sure was a shoulder harness. Suspicion confirmed, she swung her backpack over one shoulder and followed Frankie toward the dining car.

"Okay, now what?" Frankie turned enough for Oz to hear but kept walking quickly away from danger.

They made it to the next car before Oz risked looking back. The man was halfway from his seat, heading their way.

"Keep going." Oz pulled the backpack to her front and fumbled with the zipper. Her hands were shaking. There weren't many places to hide on a train. "Here, hold this." Oz slipped Frankie a sweatshirt from the lost and found at the laundromat. "As soon as we're in the dining car we'll have a minute out of sight. Get that on as fast as you can." Oz pulled out a sweatshirt for herself as well.

Frankie nodded and picked up the pace. She hit the button opening the doors between train cars and rushed through. They were in the dining car. The kitchen and counter took up a lot of the first half of the car, making the walkway narrow. It also meant on the other side of the kitchen was a blind spot they could slip into momentarily.

As soon as they were out of line of sight, Frankie and Oz pulled on the sweatshirts. Frankie pulled up the hood on hers, hiding her hair. Oz heard the door to the dining car swoosh open. Frankie must have heard it too because she looked at Oz, panic clear in her eyes.

Without thinking, Oz pulled Frankie into line for refreshments, pressed her against the side of the car, and kissed her. The moment their lips touched Oz didn't care about bad guys, short sales, or InvestBioX. All she could feel was Frankie. The kiss reverberated through her like dipping into a glacier-fed stream. The sensation started slowly and built until it quickly overwhelmed her system. She'd never felt such a crackling intensity connecting with another person.

Oz's moment of wonder was interrupted when Frankie pulled away, looking over Oz's shoulder as she did. "I don't know why you did that, but it worked. He passed us." Frankie took her hand and pulled her back the way they'd come.

"Most people don't stare at public displays of affection. It's uncomfortable so people look away." Oz's brain was going a million miles an hour. "You didn't feel anything back there?"

"I was scared we were about to get caught. Were you feeling something different?" The hint of want in her voice made Oz question how unaffected Frankie really was.

"Of course not." Oz needed to tell the lie to get her mind focused on their current predicament. "It's not going to take long for that guy to figure out we're not in front of him anymore. We need a plan."

They walked as quickly as they could without making a scene. Oz's mind raced. Where could they safely hide?

"Why don't we lock ourselves in one of the bathrooms and wait until our stop?" Frankie looked back longingly at the toilet that smelled of too many hours in use.

"Because then we're trapped with no way to see what's happening outside that door. I don't want to risk walking you into a trap once we try to leave." Oz put what she hoped was a comforting hand on Frankie's back. Frankie turned and rewarded her with a megawatt smile, so apparently it worked.

Before Oz could take another step she was hit hard from behind by something large and heavy. She crashed into Frankie, knocking them both off balance and onto the floor of the train car. Oz wasn't able to turn over or get to her feet fast enough. The feel of someone grabbing the back of her sweatshirt and pulling her roughly upright sent fear skittering along her spine. The feeling intensified to near panic when her assailant pressed something hard into her back. She'd never had a gun held to her spine, but it wasn't hard to fit the pieces together and get a read on the situation.

Frankie was still lying on the floor of the car, staring up at Oz, her face tight with anxiety.

"Is this the stalker who was bothering you before?" Oz tried to keep her voice light and steady. She held Frankie's eyes and did her best to ignore the unsettling jab of the gun when she started speaking.

"No. This train is full of unfriendly people." Frankie looked to her right and left and mumbled a "sorry" and "no offense" to the passengers on either side.

If the situation weren't so tense and threatening, Oz knew she'd find it funny how many people were trying to pretend she wasn't being held at gunpoint feet from where they sat. Some people couldn't look away while others seemed intent on keeping their gaze out the window. No one seemed a likely candidate to come to their aid.

"Shut up." Finally, the man spoke. His voice was deep and rough.

Oz looked out the window. The train was slowing. A bell started ringing from the locomotive. A platform was visible in the distance. They were entering a station, but given the ringing, it wasn't a stop on this route. In the distance, the track curved, giving her a view of what was ahead. Not far past the station, the track crossed a bridge. A wild idea popped into her head. It was dumb and probably too risky. Oz looked at Frankie lying vulnerable on the floor. Risky and dumb might be their only hope.

As subtly as possible, Oz formed her hands into a circle and mouthed "kick him in the balls" to Frankie.

Frankie shook her head, her eyes widening.

"Trust me." Oz mouthed again.

Without warning, something impacted hard against the back of Oz's head. It wasn't enough to do damage or threaten her consciousness, but it hurt like the devil.

"Hey." Frankie's expression was pure fire. "Grow a pair and fight her face-to-face." Frankie lunged forward and kicked upward, hard. Her shin hit Oz in the crotch but from the grunt and whimper behind her, Frankie's foot connected solidly between their assailant's legs.

Oz spun and wrested the gun from his hand while he was preoccupied with the pain in his balls. He lunged at her with the hand not cupping himself, but missed. She delivered three quick strikes to his nose and one to his throat. He dropped to a knee, gagging and wheezing.

She didn't wait to see how much fight he still contained. Oz grabbed Frankie's hand and pulled her to her feet. They raced along the aisle, trying to put as much distance between them and their felled foe as possible. Oz checked the location of the train as they ran. They were passing through the station. They'd soon be picking up speed. It was now or never.

"Do you trust me?" Oz pulled Frankie to a stop in the enclosed space between two cars.

Frankie didn't hesitate. "Yes."

"I'm sorry about this. Try not to tense when you land." Oz opened the door usually reserved for platform exits and entries and shoved Frankie out. She leapt after her.

The train had been moving more quickly than Oz assumed, or maybe jumping out of a moving train was always going to hurt, no matter the speed, but it took a few seconds for Oz to complete a systems check and realize she wasn't injured. She scrambled to her feet and ran to Frankie who was still lying in the grass. She dropped to her knees next to her, suddenly desperate to know she was alright.

"What the fuck, Oz?" Frankie looked mad enough to spit venom. "You threw me off a train."

"I did do that." Oz looked Frankie over inch by inch, not seeing any signs of obvious injury. "And I'm sorry about it."

Frankie raised herself onto her elbows and narrowed her eyes. "You don't look very sorry."

Oz grinned. "I am, it's just that I saved us and made sure the assholes couldn't follow us." Oz pointed at the train already on the other side of the bridge. If either of the two men on the train had tried to follow them out the door, a long drop would have been their reward.

"You didn't save us. I'm the one who kicked him." Frankie allowed Oz to help her to her feet. "I will give you credit for the dramatic exit and excellent use of topography."

"Madam, you flatter me." Oz tipped an imaginary cap.

"What's your plan now that we're off the train?" Frankie quirked an eyebrow.

Oz couldn't help but smile. It was probably the adrenaline from being held at gunpoint and their desperate leap, but Oz was giddy with emotions. Surprisingly, many of them centered around Frankie. It was heady and uncomfortable.

"It's time to find a place to hide and let you be the Wall Street wizard you claim to be."

Frankie cracked her knuckles. "Finally, it's my turn to show off."

They headed back in the direction of the station and the surrounding town. There had to be somewhere for them to hole up so Frankie could work. As they walked, Frankie took Oz's hand. As their fingers intertwined, Oz was struck by how natural it felt, like a puzzle piece snapping into place.

The feel of their kiss rushed back. Oz's lips tingled at the memory. She knew she should pull her hand away, keep the distance Frankie had insisted was necessary, but she couldn't force herself. Right here, right now, Frankie's rules be damned, Oz was enjoying the moment.

CHAPTER TEN

Frankie flopped into the faded and cracked diner booth, exhausted and sore. It was still hard to believe she had survived a leap, a push really, from a train. It didn't seem like something that happened outside of movies and books, but she'd now not only jumped onto a moving train, but off of one as well. Her life had changed drastically from her days sitting at a desk focused on making money.

Oz flagged the waitress. She looked like a woman who'd seen it all in this diner, but, despite her knowing eyes, Frankie doubted she really had any idea of the mess they'd been through.

"Can you start me with three coffees?" Frankie's eyelids were heavy and her brain felt like a dirty pair of glasses. It was still functional, but everything was slightly out of focus.

"Refills are free, dear." The waitress's eyes were kind, like the best type of television grandmother.

"If I have three, I don't have to pause my consumption. Unless you have an IV drip? That would also work." Frankie attempted a smile, but was too tired.

"I'll bring you over a mug and I promise to stay close with a hot pot. You won't reach the bottom." She patted Frankie's shoulder and nodded to Oz.

"I like her." Frankie rested her elbows on the table and her head in her hands.

"Are you okay?" Oz looked concerned. "Maybe we should be focused on finding a place to sleep for a few hours."

Frankie's fuzzy brain was now a direct result of looking at Oz. She was overwhelmed with gratitude. How would she ever repay her? The bond bounty seemed piddly after what they'd been through together. And then there was the matter of the kiss. Logically, she knew Oz was only doing what needed to be done to keep them safe, but there wasn't one part of her body that cared a bit what her brain thought. Her nervous system felt like a flashing neon sign screaming "kiss me again."

She tried to remind herself of the warning she'd given Oz about getting attached. They were in a stressful situation with heightened emotions. As an example, Frankie wasn't confident she would stop herself from proposing to the waitress if she brought a big enough cup of coffee. Despite the risks of runaway emotions, being around Oz felt different. Instead of heightening everything, Oz seemed able to slow things down, calm her fears, and make her feel safe. Oz looked at her like she *saw* her. Frankie couldn't remember the last time that was true with anyone. And good God, the kiss.

Oz looked really concerned now. She reached across the Formica tabletop and took Frankie's hand. "I know this is a lot. I can only imagine what's on your mind. Tell me what you need."

Frankie stopped just short of rolling her eyes. If only Oz knew what was on her mind she wouldn't be asking her what she needed, she'd be stripping her bare and helping her forget the mess her life had become.

She dropped her head to the tabletop. What was the matter with her? She refused to be the subject of a tragic headline "accused murderer found dead, naked, in arms of a bounty hunter."

Oz looked startled when Frankie snorted out a laugh. She probably thought the fall had jostled a few screws loose in Frankie's brain.

"I need to not get thrown off any more trains."

"I am sorry about that." Oz looked chagrined.

Frankie waved her off. "I should rephrase. I need to not need to be thrown off any more trains. Or get shot at, or find dead bodies. I like having you around, maybe too much, but I'd like the time we spend together to be a little less violent. We could try something normal, like have dinner or catch a movie."

"Like a date?" Oz's brows stitched together and she looked perplexed.

Frankie sat up. "I never said anything about a date."

"You just did. Dinner and a movie. Stereotypical date." Oz raised an eyebrow. It looked like a challenge.

"I said dinner or movie." Frankie felt some of the tension melt away. Their teasing was a balm to frayed nerves.

"Close enough." Oz's eyelids were heavy now too. Frankie couldn't tell if it was from exhaustion or desire. It was probably the former, but she wanted it to be the latter.

"I never took you for a stereotypical kind of woman." Frankie held the just delivered mug of piping hot coffee between both hands before taking a careful sip.

"You were the one who suggested the stereotype. My game doesn't need to fall back on what everyone else does." Oz mimicked dusting off her shoulder before they both erupted in giggles.

"I'd bring up the recliner again, but it's starting to feel like the argument's done all the work it can." Frankie turned serious. "Why are you single?"

Oz looked surprised by the question.

"I'm sorry. It's none of my business." Frankie felt her cheeks flush. She needed to get a hold of herself.

"Please." Oz's smile spread slowly, creeping across her face as if in slow motion. It was annoyingly sexy. "You're allowed to ask me anything. My job isn't filled with unicorns playing the harp at the top of a rainbow. I'm stuck seeing how shitty people can be to each other every day. I guess that's made me less willing to compromise or settle in my personal life. I'd rather be alone."

Frankie's teed up sarcastic response died in the back of her throat. That kind of honesty didn't deserve a quip. "I respect that. You deserve more than settling."

Oz looked slightly uncomfortable. "What about you? Why is the intelligent, beautiful, rich Ms. Sender not tied down?"

"I never said I was rich."

"You damn well better be because we're staking a lot on you being good at your job. Doesn't gobs of money come with being exceptional in your field? Besides, how else would you have made bail? Now stop deflecting and answer my question." Oz stole a sip of coffee while she waited.

Frankie sighed. "Fine, yes, I have plenty of money and I could continue my cliché streak and say I work too much to have time to date, but that's only part of it. I guess I haven't found the woman who makes me want to work less."

It looked like there were more questions on the tip of Oz's tongue, but they were interrupted by the waitress returning to take their order. They made small talk and enjoyed companionable silence while they waited for their food. After the food arrived, they were both too busy eating to continue discussing their nonexistent love lives.

"It's not really any of my business, but I'm going to ask anyway." The waitress was back with the coffee pot and a concerned look. "Do you two have a place to stay tonight? You look a little worse for wear and I haven't seen you around before. At this hour almost everyone is a regular."

Oz narrowed her eyes and tensed. The waitress might not have noticed the defensive posture, but Frankie had seen her in action enough times now to know Oz was on guard.

"I'm only asking because I know a place if you're looking to get a few hours' sleep." She put a gentle hand on Oz's shoulder.

"Does it have Wi-Fi?" Frankie went with her gut, which was telling her to trust this woman.

The waitress looked surprised at the question. "It's a barn, but a modern one. There's internet and an apartment over the tack room. I don't have anyone staying there right now. It's yours for the night if you need it."

Frankie was overwhelmed with gratitude. She looked to Oz, to gauge her reaction. Oz nodded subtly.

"That is so kind. Can we pay you for the night?"

"Leave a big tip and we'll call it even." She walked away and returned a minute later with a pen and paper. She wrote down an address and slid it to the middle of the table. "I'm Carla by the way."

Frankie started to respond but Oz cut her off. "Jen." Oz pointed to herself. "And Sarah." She pointed to Frankie. "Really appreciate your hospitality. I do have a favor to ask. If anyone comes around asking about us, do you mind forgetting you ever met us?"

Carla nodded sagely. "Trouble with one of your fellas?"

It was difficult to stifle the laugh brought on by the thought of Oz having a fella. She oozed so much butch sex appeal Frankie wasn't sure how every woman they passed wasn't left drooling.

"Something like that, yeah." Oz looked earnest and sincere.

"I promise as soon as you leave here, I'll never have met you." Carla winked. "I'll be right back with the check. No rush of course." She topped off Frankie's coffee as she left.

"I've never slept in a barn. You're expanding my horizons left and right." Frankie pulled the paper with the address closer to her. It meant nothing since she didn't know the area.

"Hey, the barn wasn't my idea. Will you be able work your magic there?" Oz pushed her plate away and used her napkin to wipe her mouth.

"Hopefully, but we don't have a computer and I'm dubious about the connection speed of these phones." Frankie wouldn't know until she was able to connect to the internet. She needed a connection that didn't cut out repeatedly.

Oz dropped some cash on the table, including a large tip for Carla, and helped Frankie to her feet. The coffee and food had helped, but Frankie still felt like she'd gone through the spin cycle of an industrial washer.

They were both quiet as they left the diner and made their way to Carla's barn. It was a risk trusting her, but it didn't seem any riskier than other options they could have considered. She'd watched enough movies to know the bad guys always checked cheap hotels first.

Frankie thought back to Oz's comment about the crappiness of her job and the people she met. Which side of the crappy equation did she fall on? She wasn't in control over the situation they were in so it shouldn't have mattered, but it was important to her. The kiss was still fresh in her mind and she realized she didn't want Oz lumping her in with all the other bail jumpers she encountered. Oz wasn't likely to kiss her again if she saw Frankie as part of the morass of her daily grind. And kissing her again was something Frankie really wanted to do.

CHAPTER ELEVEN

Oz paced, too anxious to be standing still, waiting. She'd insisted she and Frankie wait for their rideshare tucked away in a narrow alley between two buildings, but Oz still felt vulnerable. She stole a glance at Frankie. She looked calm, but the tension in her shoulders belied her nerves. Oz knew they'd both feel better once the short sale was complete and they could focus on ensnaring InvestBioX.

"Explain to me again how the short sale works." Oz needed something to take her mind off their current situation. Frankie probably did too.

"Are you trying to distract me?" Frankie's shoulders relaxed minutely.

"Of course not." Oz moved closer to Frankie. It was impossible to stay away. Frankie was magnetic and Oz was scrap metal. "But if I were, how am I doing?"

Frankie moved into Oz's personal space. She wrapped her arms around Oz's waist and leaned her head on Oz's chest. "You haven't made a wrong move yet."

Oz stifled a sigh. How was she supposed to function with Frankie so near? She took Frankie in her arms and held her close. Any doubts she'd harbored about her growing feelings for Frankie were banished the moment she returned the embrace and held Frankie tight. Both she and Frankie relaxed. The proximity seemed to be what both of them needed.

"You might be more dangerous than anything InvestBioX can send after me." Frankie pulled away with an exaggerated look of horror on her face. "Do you secretly work for InvestBioX and you were sent to woo me?"

Oz couldn't keep a straight face to play along. "Woo you? How is that done exactly? I thought you were immune to my charms."

Frankie snuggled back against Oz. "I thought you wanted to know about short sales."

"Did I? Why would I care about something like that?" Oz was having a hard time concentrating. Frankie felt too good resting her head on Oz's chest, her breath tickling Oz's neck.

"Oh no, I told you, no finding me irresistible. Keep your head in the game." Oz could feel Frankie laughing silently.

Oz held her closer. "Go ahead, let's talk work."

Frankie pulled away and picked up a rock from the ground. "Pretend this rock is a stock I'm interested in shorting." She handed the rock to Oz. "You own the rock but are willing to let me borrow it."

Oz handed Frankie the rock. "Why would I want to give up a beautiful rock?"

"You're not giving it up. I'm borrowing it while you're not using it."

"Fine, why do you want the rock?"

Frankie's eyes lit up. "Because I'm going to sell it to that squirrel over there." Frankie pointed at the rodent hopping along a branch. "Say I sell it for one hundred dollars. Now I'm richer than I was before I borrowed the rock."

Oz was confused. "But what about me? Why do you get to make money off my rock?"

Frankie wagged a finger. "I haven't actually made any money yet. I can't pay off my debt to you until I get the rock back. Since I've done my research and am positive the value of rocks is going to fall off a cliff, I'm happy to wait until the rock price is very cheap."

"How cheap is very cheap?"

Frankie's face was full of verve. She clearly lived for this. "That depends on how long I want to wait and if I think there's a chance the value will go back up. I don't want that."

Now Oz was confused. "Why exactly?"

"Because I still have to repay you. But squirrel has my rock. So I need to buy it back and I want to do that at the lowest price possible." Frankie tapped the rock still in her hand. "Let's say the rock now costs five dollars. I buy it back from squirrel and return it to you. Our business is now done."

Oz held up a hand. "Wait, but what happened to the money you got from selling the rock to squirrel?"

"That's my profit. My original sale minus expenses for the short is how much I take home. In this simplified example, I would have a profit of ninety-five dollars since I sold the rock for one hundred and bought it back for five." Frankie's face was flushed with excitement. She was astonishing.

"Final question." Oz took Frankie's hand, eager to reconnect. "Why are we going back to our city? InvestBioX has to be watching everything familiar to us."

Frankie ran a hand through her hair. "I'm not happy about it either, but the asshole who's going to do my sell orders is insisting I come and finalize the transactions in person."

Oz startled. "Has he never heard of the internet? Email? Zoom?"

"He's being a jerk because he can. I'm sure he knows he wasn't my first choice and I'm desperate if I'm calling him."

"So he makes the rules?"

"Afraid so." Frankie looked disgusted.

Oz gave Frankie's hand a little tug. "Our chariot back to the lion's den has arrived." Oz led the way to the electric blue muscle car waiting for them at the curb.

They climbed into the back seat and their driver, Fox, introduced himself. As he pulled away from the curb, Oz tried to let go of some of the tension gripping her. She couldn't. She had an intransigent sense of dread.

"Any chance you ladies are in some kind of trouble?" Fox looked in the rearview mirror and caught Oz's eye.

Oz was sure her blood pressure spiked twenty points. "Why do you ask?" Oz worked to keep her face calm and neutral.

Frankie squeezed Oz's hand, hard, but she too kept her facial expression under control.

"Well, you see, this big SUV pulled away from the curb at the same time we did. He's been following us ever since. He's staying back, but I can see him." Fox looked concerned.

Oz weighed a response. Frankie beat her to it.

"We're not in a position where we'd like to be followed. You're good at spotting a tail, any chance you could lose them?"

Fox looked like he could wiggle out of his seat with delight. "Yes, ma'am. I've been training for this moment for years."

Oz started to inquire how he'd been training, but her inquiry died on her lips as Fox hit the gas and took a left turn on two wheels.

"My favorite video game trains you to become a spy. The driving training is my all-time favorite. I've played it probably a thousand times. You're in good hands." Fox looked in his rearview mirror and cursed.

A video game driving course didn't set Oz's mind at ease. She stole a look out the back window. A large black SUV was closing fast. She watched, horrified, as an assault rifle appeared out the passenger side window. "Turn right, Fox. They're about to start shooting."

"I can do better." Fox yanked the wheel hard and accelerated into his skid. "Shoot at this, assholes." Fox flipped off the SUV as he tore off down the road in the opposite direction. He side-swiped a bus stop but didn't slow.

"Biscuits and chili cheese fries." Frankie was gripping the door with one hand and Oz's wrist with the other. She was holding on hard enough to leave a mark.

"I was going to say 'fuck,' but chili cheese fries works too." Oz looked behind them again. The SUV had managed to turn around and was in pursuit. "Don't crash for the next thirty seconds, Foxy, I'm coming up." Oz unbuckled her seat belt and shimmied into the front seat.

"Get back here." Frankie sounded four notches above scared.

"I'm not going to shoot back at them with you right next to me." Oz drew her weapon and rolled down the window. "They're going to shoot at what's shooting at them."

"Oh shit. Now we're talking. You're like my badass bodyguard. This is so awesome." Fox slammed his hand on the wheel a few times and pumped his fist.

Frankie muttered something under her breath that Oz couldn't make out. It didn't sound polite. "She's spoken for. Hire your own bodyguard."

"Hey, sorry. I didn't realize. I've got no designs on your lady."

Frankie didn't correct him so Oz let it go.

"They're coming up on the right." Frankie slid across the back seat to the left-hand side of the car. Smart woman.

"Shoot out their tires or disable their engine." Fox sped up. The SUV didn't counter their speed immediately and fell behind.

"That's not as easy as it looks in a game." Oz spun in her seat so she could see out the rear. "Let them get closer. When I give you the signal, change directions as fast as this muscle car will go. Got it?"

Fox looked a little pale, like all the fun and games had taken a turn toward misery and work.

"Can you handle this, spy master, or do you need me to drive?" Oz didn't like conscripting a stranger to help them stay alive, but she didn't currently have a lot of options.

"Of course I can, boss. Give me the word." Fox gripped the steering wheel even harder than he had been. His knuckles were white. He slowed as Oz requested and they all watched the SUV approach.

Oz fought every instinct to tell Fox to turn. She needed the SUV closer, but closer meant more danger. She looked at Frankie in the back seat. That was a mistake. Her heart double-timed and she had a quick flash of Frankie covered in gunshot wounds. She gritted her teeth. It was up to her to make sure that didn't happen.

"They're almost here, Ozzie. Tell me when." Fox's voice was high-pitched and screechy.

The SUV closed fast. Maybe they mistook them for a weakened opponent or maybe they were eager to finish the job. Oz counted down from five silently.

Oz braced herself and relaxed her shoulders. She tightened her grip on her gun. "Now, Fox!"

Fox held his nerve and pulled hard on the wheel. "Fuck, yeah. Get 'em, boss."

As they spun, Oz sighted and pulled the trigger. She didn't want to hurt anyone, but she wasn't going to let InvestBioX kill them either. Her shots shattered the front windshield and blew out a tire. She missed her target on the engine block. The SUV returned fire, peppering the rear passenger's side.

Oz looked to the back seat, panicked. Frankie looked shaken but unharmed. She returned her attention to their assailants.

"I've always wanted to try this." Fox kept his foot on the gas and the wheel cranked. The car continued its circular skid.

The right side of the SUV came into Oz's line of sight. She took aim at the right front tire and fired. It blew and the SUV veered before the driver regained control. Sparks flew from the wheel, now scraping along the ground.

Fox grunted and held the wheel. His car had made a half circle around the SUV and he kept accelerating.

Oz waited until they had nearly completed the full circle before firing again. She took out another tire and ducked when they returned fire. More bullets sprayed along the rear of the car. She checked on Frankie again. She was still unharmed.

"Coming around again." The muscles in Fox's arms were straining and he had his tongue out in concentration. "Don't miss this time, boss."

"Do you want to do the shooting?" Oz shot back.

"Can I?"

"No." Frankie and Oz echoed each other.

Oz sighted the engine block as it came back into range. She squeezed off three rounds. Steam erupted from under the hood and the SUV slowed and came to a stop. They were dead in the water.

Fox pulled hard in the opposite direction and then evened out. They rocketed away from their attackers. Oz slid into the seat, breathing heavily. She glanced back at Frankie who was still bracing herself, one hand against the back seat, the other on Fox's headrest. Her eyes were wide, but when they met Oz's she smiled.

"I guess you're earning your money, stud." She blew out a breath and slowly lowered herself back to seated, facing forward.

"Did you see that spin? I can't even pull it off in my game. That was some next-level shit." Fox's words didn't match his pale face and trembling hands.

"I'd say you passed your tactical driving test, man. You were awesome." Oz patted him on the shoulder. "You can let us out anytime."

Fox looked horrified. "No way. We're almost to your destination. I got you."

They were all silent the rest of the way. Fox overshot the curb when they arrived and smashed into a bollard. They all lurched forward. Oz caught herself on the dashboard. She glared at Fox who looked at her sheepishly and reversed before cutting the engine.

"Sorry." Fox hopped out and pulled open the door for Frankie.

Oz's legs were wobbly when she stepped out of the car and her heart felt like it was tapping out a double-time tango. She stumbled and landed against the side of Fox's car.

"Hey, careful, Ozzie. I don't want any dents in the shape of your ass on my baby."

Frankie looked like she was having a hard time not laughing. Oz decided not to point out the crumpled front end, scraped sides, and bullet-hole-dotted rear quarter panel.

Oz took Frankie's hand. She told herself it was to comfort Frankie and keep her close, but in truth she craved the contact as well. "Thanks for the ride, Fox." Oz didn't know how to express her gratitude for what Fox had done for them.

Frankie did a better job. She pulled him into a tight embrace and gave him a kiss on the cheek. Fox immediately blushed deep scarlet. "Any spy agency would be lucky to have you."

It didn't seem possible, but Fox turned an even deeper shade of red. A wide grin lit up his face. "You keep her safe." Fox gave Oz a hard stare. "And don't forget to leave a five-star rating on the ride." He hopped back into his car and was gone in a busted up blue flash.

"I wonder what rating he'll give us." Frankie still looked a little dazed.

Oz couldn't help it, she laughed. Then she couldn't stop. Frankie joined her. "We didn't get him shot so I think we're still in line for five stars. Man, did we hit the jackpot with that guy picking us up. He was almost better than you on that motorcycle."

Frankie looked affronted. "Excuse me?" She gave Oz's shoulder a gentle shove. "Watch your mouth."

"Pardon me, ma'am, what was I thinking." Oz extended her hand in an exaggerated invitation for Frankie to lead them inside.

"Damn right." Frankie pulled Oz after her and inside.

Oz stuck close while Frankie found the man they were meeting and signed his paperwork. Adrenaline was still surging through her. They'd need to find somewhere safe after this so they could both rest when the rush was gone and they crashed. She stuck her hands in her pockets to try to calm them. Somehow the pen she'd taken was still there. She pulled it out and clicked the top a few times. It did look like a spy pen. She should have given it to Fox.

Her mind wandered while she aimlessly played with the pen. Now that they were safe, she allowed herself the space to replay their wild ride. Her stomach seized painfully when she realized how close they'd come to dying. How close Frankie had come to dying. The thought sent chills through her.

What would I do without her?

The thought was formed before she had a chance to squash it and now that she'd thought it, the truth was impossible to deny.

Chapter Twelve

Frankie looked around the posh hotel room Oz had secured. She'd never stayed in a place quite this high-end. "Was this worth the money?" She hadn't had reason to question Oz's choices so far, but this felt like a large splurge.

"It's only for one night." Oz came out of the bathroom, towel drying her hair. "We need to hide from InvestBioX and they won't check the luxury hotels right away. Everyone knows we're not rolling in money so cheaper places make more sense."

"I never thought I'd agree with InvestBioX on anything." Frankie's worries were driven away by wet, towel-clad Oz. "Are you trying to distract me?"

Oz looked at her cheekily. "No, I'm trying to get dressed. She tossed her towel on the bed. "Look away if you don't want to see."

The problem was Frankie very much wanted to see. She tried to look away, but it proved impossible. Oz naked across the room was something she was sure she'd never be able to look away from. She was a harmonious balance of sculpted muscle and feminine curves. Frankie's mouth went dry and her clit throbbed.

"You shouldn't look at me like that." Oz's voice was low and rough.

Frankie took a step closer. "Why not?"

"Because you told me we couldn't." Oz made no move to cover herself.

"Well, that was stupid." Frankie closed the distance between them and pulled Oz to her. Their lips met in frantic, passionate kisses. All the pent-up chemistry between them made for an explosive meeting.

Frankie couldn't get enough now that she'd given herself permission. Oz seemed to feel the same.

Oz pulled back, a look of concern on her face. "Is this only because of the high of the car chase? I don't want you to regret anything."

Frankie kissed her quiet. "Shut up." She gave Oz a shove, landing her on her back on the bed.

With more calm than seemed possible given the rat-a-tat rhythm of her heartbeat, Frankie pulled off her own shirt and stepped out of her jeans. Oz sat and pulled Frankie close, hooking her ankles around the backs of Frankie's legs. Her breasts were bare before she realized what Oz was doing.

Frankie shivered at the cool room temperature as it tickled over her body. Oz lazed her finger along the goose bumps on Frankie's skin. She followed the path she'd traced with her tongue. Frankie buried her fingers in the soft hair at the back of Oz's neck and held her close.

Oz licked across Frankie's nipple, hardening it. "You like that?"

"If you can't tell, I'm going to reconsider going further."

"You're in good hands." Oz sucked Frankie's nipple fully in her mouth and bit down gently.

Frankie moaned. She didn't realize how much she'd wanted this. Wanted Oz. It was heady to have someone go full superhero protecting you, but this didn't feel like an extension of that. She'd be happy to get rid of the danger and intrigue but keep Oz.

Oz was starting to get a rhythm when her phone rang. "What the fuck!" Frankie groaned in frustration. "InvestBioX won't even let us have this? One simple fuck. Was that too much to ask?"

"I wasn't planning on it being simple, or only once." Oz reached across the bed and grabbed her phone.

Frankie wrapped Oz's discarded towel around herself. Only one person had Oz's phone number and Frankie didn't feel like being naked while Oz was talking to InvestBioX.

She tried not to listen to Oz's half of the conversation and fill in the other half. It was painful waiting for the end of the call, but if they were going to get information from InvestBioX, they needed to think Oz was talking behind her back.

To pass the time she stared at the clock on the wall, counting the seconds as Oz talked next to her. After three minutes and fourteen seconds, Oz hung up.

"I really want to get naked with you, but I think we should put that on hold. I care more about keeping you safe, and InvestBioX is ready to make their move." Oz looked apologetic.

"Can't screw if you're dead." Frankie kissed Oz's cheek. "What's their plan?"

Oz rolled her eyes. "It's hardly sophisticated. I'm supposed to bring you with me to a designated meeting location and then turn you and all the information we've gathered over to them. I assume at that point their plan is to kill both of us."

Frankie recoiled. "Why would they kill you?"

Oz kissed her softly. "Because they're offering me too much money and they know that I know what you know."

It took a minute, but Frankie sorted out what Oz was saying. "I'm sorry I got you into this." Her own life in danger was one thing, now knowing Oz was also in the crosshairs was something else altogether.

"You didn't get me into anything. I'm a grown-ass woman. Besides, they shot up my recliner and that pisses me off." Oz brushed a loose strand of hair behind Frankie's ear.

Frankie leaned into the touch. Oz was steady and confident and strong. Frankie didn't want to consider where she'd be without her. "So, how do we nail these bastards and take all their money?"

Oz's look was predatory. "With this." She pulled a pen from her pocket and set it on the bed between them.

"Is this some kind of 'pen is mightier than the sword' reference?" Frankie was underwhelmed.

"I hadn't thought of that, but yes." Oz clicked the pen. "I guess so." She clicked the pen again twice more. "I guess so" echoed back.

Frankie took the pen and turned it over, inspecting it. "Fox would have loved this."

"I know, right?" Oz retrieved her phone from the head of the bed where she'd thrown it. "I haven't shown you the best part." She clicked through a few screens then held it out to Frankie.

"Bluetooth connectivity too? Where'd you get this?"

"Shipping container. I thought it was a cool-looking pen."

Frankie shook her head. "We were running for our lives and you couldn't resist a souvenir?" Oz didn't look the least bit sorry. "It's going to come in handy now, isn't it?"

"So we get InvestBioX to confess their sins, record it on your fancy gadget, and then die with a ballpoint smoking gun?" Frankie wasn't sure how the pen would help them.

"I can't speak for you, but I'm not ready to die. I want to finish what we started." Oz traced a finger along the top of the towel covering Frankie's chest.

Frankie shivered and her body hummed back to life. Another look at the pen and Oz's phone and her arousal came crashing back to earth. "InvestBioX was kind of a boner killer. I guess you'll have to be my reward for finally nailing these bastards."

"I'll be your reward and anything else you like." Oz's tone was light, but there was something deeper in her eyes that Frankie couldn't quite make out. Devotion? Caring? Love?

She rubbed her eyes. The stress must be getting to her. Now she was seeing things. A small pang of disappointment pinged through her as she dismissed her supposition. She ignored it. Now was not the time for unpacking complicated emotions.

"So they have a basic plan, do we have something better?" Frankie fumbled around for her bra, unsure where Oz had deposited it.

"Honestly? Not really. A fancy plan isn't going to hide the fact that we need multiple miracles to pull this off." Oz looked down at the floor. She looked frustrated.

"So let's not meet them. We can find another way." Frankie's palms were sweating.

Oz shook her head. "We've been lucky so far, but there's only so long we can run from a company with the resources InvestBioX has. I'm not good with computers so hacking into their systems is out. They know what we look like so we can't easily sneak in and steal evidence."

"You said evidence we get illegally won't help us." Frankie's concern was growing.

"That's true. The best option is to get them to confess. It's also the riskiest and I don't like that." Oz looked like a light bulb went off over her head. "They're expecting me to be there, but you don't have to."

Frankie didn't like where Oz was going with this new line of thought. "I'm not letting you go by yourself."

"You need to." Oz looked more confident now. "They might be suspicious if I don't go alone. Of course I'd stash you somewhere and meet them solo. I want to verify I'll get paid. If they try to screw me, I'll get my money from you. Easy peasy."

"Yes, it sounds super easy. I'm still not letting you go alone." What if something happened to Oz because of her? The thought was almost too much to contemplate.

"You have to." Oz took her hand and gave it a squeeze. "Trust me."

Frankie grumbled. She was annoyed that Oz was right and about how much she did trust her. Despite her assurances, Oz could still screw her, but she wouldn't, Frankie was sure of it.

"If it makes you feel better about the arrangement, someone needs to keep an eye on the confession recording. I'll set it up so it automatically uploads to the cloud and you can disseminate as soon as we have it." Even Oz didn't look like she believed things would go that smoothly.

Frankie finished dressing and scooted as close to Oz as she could. They sat together, connected, in silence. Frankie had too many questions and she knew Oz had too few answers.

"It's going to be alright." Oz took Frankie's hand.

She pulled it away. "You have no way of knowing that." Frankie snapped at Oz. "It could all go to shit, probably will, and you'll be there alone. What do I do if you die?"

"Find another down-and-out bounty hunter to protect you?"

Frankie stood from the bed and moved away from Oz. She needed the distance. "You don't get to be a shit right now, Oz. You are not allowed to die. You get the confession and you get yourself back to me." Frankie jabbed a finger in Oz's direction. "Do you understand?"

Oz didn't answer. Instead she closed the distance between them and took Frankie in her arms. Frankie melted into the embrace and held on tight. She didn't want to care about Oz so much it ached, but she did. She didn't want to feel panic at the thought of Oz being taken from her, but she did. She wanted to tell Oz how she felt about her, but she didn't.

CHAPTER THIRTEEN

O z leaned against the third-floor window and looked down on the meeting location InvestBioX had set. It was a patch of concrete buffeted by water and abandoned buildings. It was the kind of place people met to carry out activities not spoken of in polite company. Exactly the kind of activity she would shortly be a part of. Right now it was quiet. She was too high up to make out the rats who were likely the true owners of this part of town, but she assumed they were there.

She checked her phone for the time and felt her pocket ensuring the pen was with her. She'd done the same thing repeatedly over the thirty minutes she'd spent watching. When her phone rang she almost jumped out of her shoes.

"It's not too late to call this off." Frankie sounded as edgy as Oz felt. "We can find another way."

Oz shook her head even though Frankie couldn't see her. "One way or another, this ends today."

"God, you sound like such a badass when you say that."

"I guess I sound more cocky than I am." Oz checked for the pen again. "You keep yourself hidden and safe, like we talked about. I'm going to start the recording to test the transmission. Let me know in the next minute or two if there are any issues."

Oz pressed the record button and ended the call. She tucked her phone in her pocket and made her way down the stairs to the ground floor. She wanted to get another vantage point to wait and watch the arrival of InvestBioX's goons.

No sooner had she opened the door to the stairwell than she was knocked off her feet and thrown to the ground. She gasped for breath after the blow to her stomach and hard landing. She rolled to better face her attackers, hoping she had enough oxygen to parry or strike if given the chance.

Two massive men stood over her, sneering. "Thinking of buying the place?" One of the men pointed around the crumbling building.

"What the fuck is your problem?" Oz stood and did her best to project confidence and strength despite still not being able to take a deep breath.

"Shut up." One of the men hit her before she was able to get her hands up.

Oz's brain was fuzzy when she returned to consciousness. She tasted blood. Her hands were tied and she had a black bag over her head. She concentrated on what she could hear and feel. It was quiet which unnerved her.

She didn't hear her captor approach and wasn't aware of his presence until he smacked her on the back hard enough to knock her from her chair.

"Welcome, Ms. Osborne."

"Funny, I'm not feeling very welcomed." Oz stood blindly and was promptly hit in the back of the knees and brought to the ground again.

"Don't worry, I'm very happy to see you. You are most welcome." Whoever was speaking must have leaned over because his voice was close to Oz's ear.

"How about you allow me to be happy to see you too. Your manners are rubbish." Oz didn't bother standing this time. She was tired of getting knocked down.

Unceremoniously, the hood was pulled off and she was lifted into a chair. Oz blinked against the sudden brightness. A man in an expensive-looking suit and sporting a pinky ring, crouched in front of her. He grabbed her chin roughly and twisted her head, forcing her to look to her right.

"Ms. Osborne, I believe you know Ms. Sender."

Oz wanted to scream every creative curse word she could think of, but she stayed silent. She tried to look unmoved by Frankie's presence even as her insides churned aggressively.

"You spoiled the dramatic moment of my handoff, but okay, whatever." Oz wrenched her face out of the man's hand.

He stood and crossed his arms, looming over Oz. "You expect me to believe you were actually going to hand over your girlfriend?"

"I don't care what you believe. The only thing you need to *know* is I want to get paid. You've got her, hand over my money." Oz couldn't look at Frankie. She needed to come across as cavalier, and if she caught Frankie's eye, she'd be lost.

"It seems to me." The man narrowed his eyes and looked hard at Oz. "That I did all the work. Why should I pay you anything?"

"All the work?" Oz scoffed. "You should pay me double for trying to kill me so many times. You have me to thank for keeping her alive."

The man got into her face again. "The problem is, I don't want her alive."

It took every ounce of composure Oz could muster not to recoil at his words. She held his cruel, predatory look. He averted his eyes first. It was a small victory.

"What did she do to you anyway? Is any of the crap she told me true?" Oz shifted so the pen, which she could still feel in her pocket was closer to the man. She prayed it was still recording.

"You ask too many questions." One of the hunks of muscle lurking in the background made his presence known.

"I have an inquisitive nature." Oz shifted again. "Can I get untied? This isn't necessary. I'm not leaving without my money."

"Shut up." Muscle head spoke up again.

"Tell me what she told you." The man in charge pointed at Frankie.

"Which is it? Shut up or start talking?" Oz took the hint as the man in the suit glared at her. "So serious around here." Oz worked her hands, trying to loosen the rope holding them. "She told me you guys are hyping up a crappy product to drive up your stock prices and then you're going to, I don't remember the word. Squat it? Small it? Something like that."

"So she figured it out. We knew she was smart. Yes, we're driving our stock as high as it will go and then shorting it."

"Shorting. That's the word I was looking for." Oz would have snapped her fingers if her hands weren't bound.

The man looked annoyed which was Oz's goal. The more agitated and frustrated he became, the less likely he'd be as sharp and focused as he needed to be and the more likely he'd run his mouth.

"As I was saying, Ms. Sender is correct, we're going to make a lot of money."

Oz worked the ropes surreptitiously. She didn't want to get caught or make too much noise and muffle the recording. "But what about your fancy new product? If it's so good, why would you bet against it?" The man looked gleeful. "Between friends."

"We're friends now? I'm honored." Oz interrupted again.

The man's irritation was more obvious this time. When he started talking again he seemed determined to explain, which was exactly what Oz was hoping for.

"As I was saying, the new drug's crap. It has a sky-high mortality rate. We only need everyone to think it's the next great drug. She almost ruined it." The man nodded toward Frankie. "So we framed her for murder. Even then you wouldn't take the fucking hint." He raised his voice and pointed to Frankie.

"Why are you telling her all of this?" Frankie sounded angry.

The man moved in front of Frankie and squatted, putting a hand on each of Frankie's knees. "Because neither of you is going to see tomorrow. You have no one to tell and I'm rather proud of my work."

Oz cleared her throat loudly. "I would like to submit a formal complaint about my life expectancy. I never would have taken this side hustle if I knew you were going to get so kill-y at the end."

"Price of doing business, I'm afraid." The man stood and moved back in front of Oz. "You understand."

"Sure, I get it. But I expect you also understand that now I have to hurt you all." Oz worked the last strand of rope and pulled her hands free. "Frankie, get down." Oz flung her chair at the two goons. It caught one in the torso.

He bent over double. His partner, unharmed by the flying furniture, drew his gun. The boss man made no attempt to pull a weapon and in fact looked nervous with Oz loose.

It took three steps to close the distance to the man with the gun. He wasn't able to squeeze off a shot before Oz was on him. She knew these moments were life-or-death so she pummeled him. He was a surprisingly poor fighter given his size and muscle definition. She dispatched him quickly, leaving him unconscious and crumpled on the floor.

His buddy didn't look enthused about fighting her, but she didn't care. She jabbed, weaved, and threw an uppercut-hook combination. He was down before she finished her last punch.

Oz turned to face the next threat, but the only other person in the room was Frankie, lying on her side on the floor, still tied to her chair. Oz jogged to her and started on the ropes.

"Are you okay?" Oz didn't wait for an answer. She pulled Frankie to her feet and then ran her hands up and down Frankie's arms, across her face, and finally, pulled her into a hug. "What happened?"

Frankie returned the embrace, squeezing Oz hard. "I hid like we talked about, but they found me. They broke down the door and grabbed me before I even knew they were outside." Frankie stepped out of Oz's arms and took her hand. "We should go. Do you think we got what we need?"

Oz took the pen from her pocket and turned it over and over. The red "record" light was still illuminated. They still had a chance. "I guess we won't know until we can listen to it. Did you set it up like we talked about?"

Frankie nodded. She looked as if she was all set with this day. "The guy in the expensive suit scampered as soon as he saw you take down the two dump trucks. Should we follow him?"

Oz weighed their options. On the one hand, Mr. Suit was probably well positioned enough to be on a plane to anywhere if he chose, so following might make sense. On the other, he didn't know his words had been recorded, only that Frankie and Oz had gotten loose and therefore had no reason to flee. It didn't seem like pursuit was worth the measly return, especially with the significant risks.

"We can let him go. He's not worth chasing. We should get out of here though. I'm sure these two aren't the only large men around here." Oz checked out the door and motioned Frankie to follow her.

A bullet pinged off the metal doorframe a few inches from Frankie's head as soon as they were both in the hall. Oz felt like her heart skipped a few hundred beats. That was too close.

Frankie looked mad. The shooter appeared around the corner and Frankie pointed at him aggressively. "Stop shooting at me."

By some miracle, he complied, probably so surprised by Frankie's assertive command he defaulted to following directions. Frankie was not so paralyzed with indecision. She stalked down the hall and kicked the shooter hard in the crotch. He groaned weakly and dropped to a knee, cupping himself with both hands.

While he tried to make sure his penis and testicles were still where they belonged and not somewhere in his abdomen, his gun clattered to floor, a secondary concern now. Frankie was quick to pick it up and bring it back to Oz.

"I'm assuming they took yours?" Frankie held it like it was something unsavory and smelly.

"I think I might love you." Oz took the gun in awe. Frankie was amazing.

"I'm sure you say that to all the girls." Frankie batted her eyes flirtatiously.

"Only the ones who kick gunmen in the balls." Oz played along with the joke she'd made, even if the words, once out of her mouth, had taken on a life of their own and were planting roots in her heart.

Oz led them down the hallway hoping to find a quick exit route. It wasn't long until they found a stairwell that led down. They took it, descending as fast as they could. One flight before the first floor, a door crashed open below and two more unfathomably large men lumbered up toward them.

Throwing caution to the wind, Oz charged the men, not waiting to see if they were armed or to identify a tactical advantage. Once in range she planted her hands on the rail and kicked both feet out in front, her body nearly parallel to the ground. She connected solidly with the lead man's chest, knocking him off balance. It seemed like he hung in suspension between climbing and falling a long time before tipping backward and taking out his compatriot as he fell.

"Leave us alone." Oz held out her hand for Frankie and helped her step around the pile of man four steps down.

They reached the ground floor and burst out the door into the blinding light of a beautiful sunlit day. The neighborhood around them was not abandoned and neglected like the one of their original meeting location. When they exited they did so onto a busy sidewalk in the trendy, busy part of town.

Oz held Frankie's hand more tightly and together they eased into the foot traffic and allowed it to carry them away from the danger they'd escaped. Oz's mind whirred as she ran through scenario after scenario to help guide their next move. The options she could think of all seemed like some level of terrible. She had to pick one though. They'd kicked the hornets nest and now they needed someplace safe to avoid getting stung.

CHAPTER FOURTEEN

Frankie held Oz's hand like a lifeline. The further they got from InvestBioX's henchmen, the more terrifying the experience felt. She'd known InvestBioX wanted her dead, that's why she'd hired Oz. The bullets flying her way were also a good indicator. It felt different, though, to listen to someone calmly discuss your execution.

"Do you think they somehow tracked my phone?" Frankie couldn't shake the feelings that surfaced as she was being abducted earlier.

She had felt fear, of course, but also shame, guilt, and a small hint of relief. As Oz had said, "this ends today." Getting caught felt like a "when" not "if" so in a weird way it was nice to have gotten it over with.

"It's possible. We should probably get you a new one to be safe." Oz's face was unreadable, but her tone gave away some of her stress.

They passed a trash can clogged with discarded ice coffee cups and fast food wrappers. Frankie tossed her phone on the ground, stomped on it, then put its remains in the trash. "I don't want to take any chances. When they came for me earlier..." Frankie paused to get ahold of herself. "I wasn't sure I would ever see you again."

Oz gave her a funny look, one Frankie couldn't read. "Weren't you worried about dying?"

"Of course. That too." Frankie looked around. It felt like for the first time since they'd fled, and she tried to get her bearings. "Where are we going?"

"We need to get off the street so we can plan our next move. InvestBioX has never been more dangerous than right now." Frankie hadn't seen Oz worried in all their time together, but she looked concerned now.

Frankie balked. "More dangerous than when they were shooting at us?"

"Afraid so." Oz stopped short and looked around. "They're more dangerous because we're now more dangerous to them. Mr. Fancy Suit ran his mouth so we know things he doesn't want to get out."

"Guess it's time to really give him something to worry about. I love being able to finally fight back." Frankie took Oz's hand again and brushed her thumb along the back. "Why don't we find an alley to hang out in for a little while? We can pick one outside a business with good Wi-Fi."

Oz looked skeptical. "Wouldn't you rather we find a place to sleep and regroup?"

"I'd rather never be caught again. Won't they expect us to find a motel or somewhere to hide for a little while?" Frankie shivered at the thought of being trapped again with nowhere to run.

Oz still didn't look convinced.

"Trust me. You've been doing all the work of keeping us safe, let me take some of the decision-making stress off your shoulders." Frankie cupped Oz's cheek and stroked it softly.

"You can't do that right now." Oz covered Frankie's hand. "It's distracting and I still need to keep you safe."

"I *am* safe, thanks to you. I was so scared, Oz, but I knew you'd get us out of it. I'm incredibly lucky you said yes to my stupid plan." Frankie entwined their hands and kissed each of Oz's knuckles. There was more she wanted to say. She wanted to tell Oz how she felt about her, but this didn't seem like the time.

Oz nodded a couple of times. She looked like she had something on her mind too, but all she said was, "Let's go find a strong wireless signal."

It took longer than Frankie expected to find the perfect hiding place. Oz rejected the first two they scoped out. The more time they were out in the open, the more anxious Frankie got. Finally, Oz found an alley she approved of. They walked around the block twice, Oz checking for tails, before they ducked into the alley and looked for a place to settle down.

They chose a scenic spot next to a large dumpster and a pile of pallets. The smell from the rotting trash was enough to singe off nose hairs, but the large metal bin provided enough cover to give the illusion of safety.

Oz pulled two pallets off the stack and wedged one into the other, forming a very wide V. Frankie took the offered seat and was surprised when it was passably comfortable. The recline was enough to be relaxing but not so much that she felt vulnerable lying down.

"If this bounty hunter thing doesn't work out, you might have a future in furniture design." Frankie laughed when Oz rolled her eyes.

Once they were settled, Oz pulled the pen from her pocket and handed it to Frankie. "Let's see if we got it all."

The air felt especially still, as if the world had taken a breath and held it, as they waited for the audio to replay. As soon as the first, muffled voices came through the tiny pen speaker, Frankie wanted to leap for joy. It was audible and clear enough to make out the conversation. She squeezed Oz's hand in excitement while the rest of the recording played. They needed to make sure the full confession was captured.

When they'd listened to it all, they stared at each other. Frankie had an urge to laugh. The joy and relief threatened to overflow in potentially embarrassing ways. It wasn't out of the realm of possibility that if she started laughing she wouldn't be able to stop. The chance of snort-laughing was high.

"We nailed them." Oz pumped her fist. "Who do we send this to?"

"Leave that to me." Frankie dug in Oz's pocket, her hands searching her thighs and abdomen much more intensely than was strictly necessary. It took effort to stop her exploration, but she finally pulled Oz's phone out and brought it to life.

Oz didn't say anything, but she looked amused. "What are you doing?"

"I'm sending the recording to another short seller I know and every investigative journalist I can find." Frankie didn't look up from the phone.

"That wasn't what I was talking about, but it's always good to know the plan." Oz leaned back against their makeshift recliner and put her hands behind her head. She looked like she could have been settling in for a long afternoon of sunbathing and drinking at a fancy poolside cabana if the reality wasn't so pungent.

Frankie paused. "I don't know what I'm doing." She was surprised at her honesty.

Oz nodded knowingly. "Me either, but I like it. I like you."

"I like you too." Frankie's middle school self from her memories mocked her as she tried to figure out if she like liked Oz. It was none of anyone's business, even Oz's. For now.

Frankie pushed the "send" button for the email she'd composed and flopped back against the pallet couch next to Oz. "It's done."

"Why didn't you post somewhere and let it go viral?" Oz looked tired, but as always, vigilant.

"I don't want any way it can be discredited. A random post isn't verifiable. Let it come from people who have the power to take them down. For now we wait." Frankie said a silent prayer that by the time it took for the story to be picked up they wouldn't have run out of time.

As it turned out, she needn't have worried. By the next morning InvestBioX's stock had fallen twenty percent. It was a massive comfort after a tense, cold, night in the alley. The stock had fallen further by the afternoon. Frankie could have closed her short position and made a lot of money just on the dip thus far, but she wanted to really make InvestBioX hurt. She wasn't selling until the stock reached zero.

"Look at this." Oz held up her phone. "Top story on nearly every news channel. How did they turn the story around so quickly?"

"Do you really want to deep dive journalistic workflows or would you rather kiss me in celebration?" Frankie cocked an eyebrow.

"Kissing please."

Their lips met and as before, Frankie felt like even the tips of her hair were tingling. She pulled Oz to her, desperate for a closer connection. She was lost in the feel of Oz's lips, the blood rushing through her body, and the thrill of acting on emotions she was still too scared to give name to.

After not nearly long enough, Oz pulled away. "I could get lost in you." Oz flopped against their pallet couch, breathing heavily. "But we really need to stop."

"Why in God's name would we want to do that?" Frankie was breathless too.

Oz sighed and looked to the heavens. "It has nothing to do with want. But we're hiding behind a dumpster, hiding from some very bad dudes. I don't want to be looking over my shoulder the next time I kiss you."

Frankie leaned into Oz and rested her head on her shoulder. "As long as there is a next time. Speaking of which, now that the world knows about the recording, aren't we safe?"

Oz put her arm around Frankie and held her closer. "Maybe. Probably. It's hard to say. They're a wounded opponent now and desperate. It would be a bad look if you showed up dead, but then again, there wouldn't be anyone left to air their dirty laundry."

"So what do we do? I don't know about you, but the smell is starting to get to me." Frankie buried her nose in Oz's neck for effect.

"This was your idea. Remember I wanted a hotel room with a bed, running water, and odor control?"

"You can't always get what you want, Osborne."

"Let me guess, we got what we need?" Oz kissed the top of Frankie's head.

"You said it, not me. Seriously though, we need a new place to hang out." Frankie disentangled and stretched. She caught Oz watching and her heart skipped wildly.

"Do you think you'd be safe in jail now?" When Oz looked at Frankie she was all business. "We need to get the charges against you dropped, and entering the recording into evidence might help us as well."

Frankie shuddered. "Is jail negotiable?" Frankie could feel the cold from her last stay behind bars creeping back into her bones. The threadbare sweatshirt she'd received to go with her khaki pants and shirt was laughably inadequate to deal with the frigid temperature. She'd asked why the jail was roughly the same temperature as the arctic, and bug control was the only plausible explanation she'd been given.

"If you don't mind staying here a little while longer, I'll make some calls and see what I can do. I'm not sending you back in if you're in danger. We'll take our chances out here until we clear your name."

Frankie was content to wait, resting against Oz's side, comfortable in the knowledge that as long as she was with Oz, she was safe. Until she thought about kissing Oz, and that felt like much riskier territory. Was it possible to feel so much and have it be the mirage of a life under fire? She wasn't sure anymore. What she was feeling felt as real as the bullets that had been chasing them from the moment they'd met. How much she was willing to risk to find out the answer was something she had to decide, and quickly.

CHAPTER FIFTEEN

O z fidgeted in the courtroom. The court was behind on the day's docket and it was now closing in on the end of business. She couldn't stand the thought of Frankie's case being pushed to the next day. She was, of course, eager for the charges against Frankie to be dismissed, but even more so she was desperate to see Frankie. The days had felt like months since she'd brought Frankie back into custody as an official bail jumper. They'd agreed to follow that path after Oz had secured assurances from people she trusted that Frankie would be kept safe. None of it made it easier to be away from Frankie and not personally responsible for her wellbeing.

Finally, Frankie's case was called and she was led into the courtroom. Oz caught her breath. Despite the setting and circumstances, Frankie was the most beautiful woman Oz had ever seen. She didn't need to give voice to the feelings bubbling through her, not yet and not here, but it was clear to her what they were. Hopefully, Frankie felt the same.

Oz waited impatiently for the legal maneuvering until finally she heard the words she and Frankie had been waiting for. "Case Dismissed."

As the judge gaveled the end of the proceedings, Oz was startled by angry shouting to her left. She watched in horror as the man with the fancy suit burst through the courtroom doors and charged toward Frankie, spitting fire and rage.

Time seemed to stand still as he drew closer. Despite her best efforts, climbing over the gallery seats, and shoving anyone and everyone out of the way, Oz wasn't going to get to Frankie in time.

The man raised his closed fist and lunged, roaring furiously. "You cost me everything, you bitch."

Oz knew she was adding to the cacophony of noise and commotion, but she couldn't hear her desperate cries. Her blood was rushing wildly in her ears and her sole focus was Frankie. Nothing else mattered and she was going to be too late.

While Oz despaired, Frankie calmly picked up her lawyer's briefcase and swung it purposefully at the man's head. It connected with the crack of broken bones. The man stumbled but did not go down, instead kicking out wildly. Oz dove at him, one final, frantic effort to keep Frankie safe. For her part, Frankie parried his attack and stabbed a pen into his thigh. He howled with pain and crumpled to the ground. Oz landed awkwardly next to him staring at Frankie's feet.

Frankie knelt, looking concerned. "Are you okay?" She scooted to the side as the court security personnel swarmed the man.

Oz scrambled to her feet and pulled Frankie into a crushing hug. "You do make life interesting." Oz released her and looked her over, making sure she truly was unharmed.

Frankie grinned. "He attacked me, you can't hold that against me." Frankie leaned over to her lawyer who was standing against the table, knuckles white where he gripped. "Sorry about your pen." She turned back to Oz. "Shall we?"

"I guess so." Oz looked around and didn't see a single reason to stay. "That was an impressive briefcase hook you laid on him."

"I'm not all numbers and money-making, and I was tired of you getting all the glory. I can protect myself, at least from that clown." Frankie took Oz's hand and they picked their way through the mass of people loitering near the action.

"Don't get too good at self-defense or I'll be out of a job. I'd miss you." Oz wanted to blurt out what was in her heart, but the timing was wrong. If Frankie still harbored doubts about the two of them because of their stressful circumstances, spilling her guts right after Frankie was attacked wasn't going to win her points.

The moment the courthouse door opened and the sunshine helped chase some of the darkness of the past few minutes, Frankie was swarmed by reporters. They shouted questions and snapped photo after photo. Frankie froze in the face of the onslaught.

Oz put her arm around Frankie's shoulder and used her other arm to clear a path. At first, Frankie followed meekly. They were almost down the steps and through the crowd when Frankie seemingly changed her mind and stopped. Oz waited. She was happy to follow Frankie's lead.

Frankie surveyed the crowd before pointing to a young female reporter. "You have a question for me?"

"Yes, I do. The same as I'm sure everyone else out here. Is anything on the tape we've all heard true?"

A slow, predatory smile crept across Frankie's face. She was confident and strong. Oz was enamored.

"It's all true." Frankie held eye contact with the reporter. "InvestBioX is corrupt both morally and practically. What you heard on the tape is the tip of the iceberg."

Follow-up questions exploded into the air as soon as Frankie finished speaking. She pointed to another reporter in the crowd and listened intently.

"Ms. Sender, how do you feel now that the charges against you were dismissed?"

"Vindicated, elated, relieved. It's been a long, stressful road to this point. I'm glad I'm personally out from under InvestBioX's thumb, but more importantly, I'm glad the truth about their deception is now known." Frankie pointed to another member of the press. "You with the blue shirt and orange glasses."

"Have you shorted InvestBioX's stock? How much money do you stand to make on InvestBioX's downfall?" The man held a notepad and pen at the ready. He was an anomaly amongst the crowd of cell phones and other recording devices.

"With respect, my business dealings are my own until such time when information becomes public. I think we should focus on the fact that a bad company isn't going to release a killer drug into the market and they will stop stealing money from hard-working people trying to put money away for a happy retirement." Frankie looked over the crowd again. "One last question. You, blond ponytail and black shirt."

The reporter pointed to herself as if to ask "who, me?" Frankie nodded encouragingly.

"Are the rumors true that InvestBioX tried to kill you?"

Frankie laughed. "Multiple times." She grew serious. "And I'd be dead right now if it weren't for this wonderful woman." Frankie put her arm around Oz's shoulders and gave her a squeeze. "In my most desperate moment I asked for her help and with no guarantees or moment of hesitation, she helped me, a perfect stranger, to stay alive."

Oz wanted to roll her eyes at some of the less than truthful aspects of Frankie's retelling, for instance she remembered quite a bit of resistance to their partnership, but she stayed silent. It wasn't her place to interject now. When the reporters turned their attention to her and began the barrage of questions anew, Oz wanted to shrink into the sidewalk. She'd much rather have faced a firing squad than this group of curiosity junkies.

Frankie whispered "get me out of here" just as Oz was beginning to feel hopelessly overwhelmed at the attention.

Oz was more than happy to oblige. She plowed through the crowd, holding Frankie's hand and guiding her protectively. Reporters jumped out of their way, none seemingly eager to try to knock Oz off course.

Once they had cleared the scrum and turned the corner, Oz stopped. For the first time in weeks, she had no idea what the next move should be. Frankie was safe and she'd been paid. Their relationship, as it was originally conceived, was over, but Oz didn't ever want to let go.

"I don't want to part ways and say good-bye." Honesty seemed like the right choice.

"You'd better not." Frankie pulled Oz to her and kissed her with searing passion and desperate wanting. Oz felt it down to her toes and clung to Frankie, desperate to soak up every bit of the feeling in case it was fleeting.

As suddenly as she'd kissed her, Frankie pulled away. She paced down the sidewalk a few feet and returned. She followed that path a few more times before Oz stopped her.

"What are you doing?" Oz wrapped Frankie's pinky finger with her own and swung their arms slowly.

"You've made me do something I hate. I have to admit that I was wrong about you and me."

Anxiety shot painfully through Oz's chest. What was she talking about?

"I told you you'd fall in love with me if you didn't stop flirting. Well, it turns out I'm the one who broke the rules. I love you and not because you saved my life more times than I have any interest in counting. I didn't realize how deeply I love you until we were in this moment. I love you, Oz. I love you." She kissed Oz's nose. "I love you." She kissed her cheek. "I love you." She planted a final chaste kiss on Oz's lips.

Oz cupped Frankie's face between her hands. She rested her forehead on Frankie's and smiled happily. "I love you too."

"Good thing we got that out of the way." Frankie planted a kiss on Oz's cheek.

It was a familiar and possessive gesture. Oz's stomach flipped. "I've never thought of the first 'I love you' as something that has to be gotten out of the way. What's your hurry?"

Frankie took Oz's hand and dragged her down the sidewalk. "You owe me a huge amount of naked time. I'm in a hurry to collect."

Oz's stomach and other parts lower down clenched. "Jesus, woman."

"Yeah, tell me about it. Now, where should we go? My house is too far away. Your house is…" Frankie hesitated.

"Too shot up?" Oz provided.

"Yes. That."

"Leave it to me." Oz took the lead. "I know just the place."

She ordered a ride share and they waited. It was a challenge to keep her hands off Frankie now that they'd brought up topics like love and nakedness. Oz was increasingly impatient to be alone with Frankie.

When their driver pulled up in front of the completely renovated boutique hotel, Oz felt like her energy would measure on the Richter scale. Frankie waited while she secured a room and a bottle of champagne.

They'd been placed in a room on the top floor with a spectacular view of the city. Frankie stood looking out the window, sighing contentedly. Oz wrapped her arms around her from behind and rested her head on Frankie's back.

"You're wearing too many clothes." Oz let her hands wander over Frankie's torso, sides, and chest.

Despite the circumstances of their meeting, Oz was grateful. Frankie was hers and she was Frankie's. Her decidedly solitary existence was a thing of the past. Her life was now filled with Frankie's wit, intelligence, and beauty.

"There's time for deep thoughts later, my love." Frankie turned in Oz's arms. "Right now you have other tasks to attend to."

Oz nodded and licked her lips. She skirted Frankie's breasts and thrilled at her quick intake of breath.

"Yes," Frankie whispered.

That one word was Oz's undoing. She abandoned her plan for a slow build-up and lifted Frankie's shirt over her head and off.

As it drifted to the floor, forgotten as soon as it was off, Oz couldn't remember a time she'd been so happy. This was what and who she wanted and as long as Frankie wanted her, she wasn't ever letting go.

CHAPTER SIXTEEN

Eighteen months later

"Guilty." Frankie watched in happy disbelief as guilty charges were read out, one after the other, in the criminal cases against InvestBioX leadership.

"What did I miss?" Oz skidded to a halt, looking hot as hell in her socked feet, straight cut jeans, and crisp white T-shirt.

"Convictions, across the board." She leapt into Oz's arms. Since she'd been a star witness at the trial, Frankie could have watched the verdict read from the courtroom, but she was happier to be here, away from cameras and other people. It was uncouth to dance in public after the reading of a verdict, but here at home she could dance the night away.

"I'm so proud of you, baby." Oz spun in a circle, holding Frankie tightly.

Frankie wiggled free and moved closer to the television to hear some of the commentary on the verdict. "You know what this means?" She waggled her eyebrows at Oz.

"Victory sex?" Oz looked adorably hopeful.

"Obviously, yes, but that's not what I meant. InvestBioX's stock is about to plunge. Nearly time for us to get filthy rich." Frankie rubbed her thumb and index finger together.

"Not 'us.' You." Oz looked pensive. "You settled your debt when I got the bounty when I turned you in at the courthouse."

"Oh no you don't." Frankie waved her index finger in Oz's direction. "I'd be dead if not for you, and that would be a real shame because then I'd miss out on loving you and on seeing you naked."

Oz shook her head like she was going to argue but stopped. Whatever was on her mind she wasn't ready to share.

Frankie darted into the kitchen and pulled a bottle of wine from the fridge. She rooted around in the junk drawer looking for a corkscrew.

When she returned Oz relieved her of the bottle and twisted off the top. She laughed at what Frankie knew was probably her slack-jawed expression.

"Did you not know wine comes with screw tops?" Oz fetched glasses and poured.

"Move on." Frankie scowled but was sure it would roll off Oz's back like water off a duck. She held her glass aloft. "Here's to new beginnings." Frankie shuffled her feet. "Speaking of which, I was wondering if we could talk about our sleeping arrangements."

Oz looked like she'd gone from elation to devastation and it had been a rough ride. "Tell me more."

"I want to buy a new place." Frankie looked around at the townhouse that had been her home for many years. The thought of leaving didn't leave her aching the way she'd thought it might. It was time to close this chapter and begin another.

"Why?"

"Maybe I should have been more clear. I want us to buy a new place. Together. You're barely at your place now and I want to wake up in your arms every morning." Frankie tried not to sound too eager, but she was excited. "We can get a place together."

A small smile slowly spread across Oz's chiseled features. She was always beautiful, but her smile lit up her face like a bonfire. "I can move in here. You don't have to sell this place."

Frankie shook her head. "I want it to be our place, not mine that you're joining. Besides, maybe I'm ready for more adventure than a townhouse. We could get land, a barn."

"You want to be a farmer now? Don't get me wrong, you'd be damn fine working the land every day." Oz stepped into Frankie's personal space and traced a finger along her collarbone and over her shoulder.

Frankie's pulse quickened and she felt flushed. Oz made her feel things no one else ever had. It was insane to say she'd been lucky InvestBioX had wanted her dead, but she wouldn't have found Oz without them. InvestBioX had stumbled backward into being an excellent matchmaker.

Before Frankie and Oz lost themselves in each other, they were interrupted by the doorbell. Frankie sprang away from Oz and rushed downstairs. "I'll get it." She flung open the door, startling the poor delivery crew. "I'll show you where to put it." She led the way back upstairs and into the living room.

Oz looked curious but didn't ask. It wasn't long before the crew was back carrying a large package wrapped tightly in plastic wrap. Now Oz looked intrigued.

The two men made quick work of the unwrapping and were back down the stairs and gone in minutes.

"What do you think?" Frankie was suddenly nervous. What if she'd made a bad choice or Oz didn't like it? She needn't have worried.

"You got me a new recliner? It looks just like my old one. You said it was ugly." Oz ran her hand reverently along the back of the new chair.

"It still is. But you loved it so I can live with it. And this one's new so I know there isn't a family of mice living in the backing."

Oz looked offended. "Do you think so little of me? It obviously would've been a horde of hamsters."

Frankie put up her hands in mock surrender. "I stand corrected. Still, this chair is rodent-free."

"If you insist." Oz sat in her new chair and pulled the lever to recline. She groaned, a sound of pure contentment. "Thank you." She beckoned Frankie. "Come sit with me."

"Hang on, be right back." Frankie darted into the home office off the living room and grabbed her laptop. When she returned, she settled onto Oz's lap.

"Work wasn't quite what I had in mind." Oz moved Frankie's hair to the side and kissed up and down her neck.

"For the first and last time, I'm going to tell you to keep your hands to yourself. I'm going to make us rock star rich and then we can stay naked as long as we like. You sit there and be studly while I close my short position on InvestBioX." Frankie leaned into Oz's embrace and got to work.

"I'll happily be your eye candy." Oz didn't seem interested in keeping her hands or lips to herself, despite what Frankie said. "God, I love you. Who would have guessed, the bounty hunter and the murderer."

"Exonerated murderer." Frankie poked Oz in the ribs, which drew a chuckle.

When Frankie was finished, she snapped the laptop closed and deposited it on the floor next to the recliner. She curled into Oz and rested her head on Oz's chest. Completing the final chapter on InvestBioX felt anticlimactic, which seemed silly since the last page turn had made them rich beyond measure. In the end though, money wasn't the important thing she took from her experience with InvestBioX. She'd gotten Oz and that was priceless. Some people were forced to choose between love and money, but she'd gotten the bucks and the girl.

She kissed the underside of Oz's jaw and traced her hand along Oz's chest. "What do you say we break in this recliner properly?"

Oz grinned wickedly. "I thought you'd never ask."

They spent the rest of the day tangled in each other, happy to be alive, happy to be together, happy to be in love. Just happy.

About the Authors

NAN CAMPBELL's debut novel, *The Rules of Forever*, is a Lambda Literary Award winner. She grew up on the Jersey Shore, where she first discovered her love of romance novels as a kid, spending her summers at the beach reading stories that were wholly inappropriate for her age. She was, and continues to be, a sucker for a happy ending. Nan lives in New York City.

ALAINA ERDELL lives in Ohio with her partner and their crazy but adorable cats. Prior to writing contemporary sapphic romances, she worked as a chef. She enjoys painting, cooking for friends and family, experimenting with molecular gastronomy, reading, traveling, and spoiling her beloved nephews.

JESSE J. THOMA: Although she works best under the pressure of a deadline, Jesse Thoma balks at being told what to do. Despite that, she's no fool and knows she'd be lost without her editor's brilliance. *Seneca Falls* was a finalist for a Lambda Literary Award in romance. *Data Capture, Serenity,* and *Courage* were finalists for the Golden Crowne Literary Society "Goldie" Award.

Books Available from Bold Strokes Books

And Then There Was One by Michele Castleman. Plagued by strange memories and drowning in the guilt she tried to leave behind, Lyla Smith escapes her small Ohio town to work as a nanny and becomes trapped with an unknown killer. (978-1-63679-688-8)

Digging for Destiny by Jenna Jarvis. The war between nations forces Litz to make a choice. Her country, career, and family, or the chance of making a better world with the woman she can't forget. (978-1-63679-575-1)

Hot Hires by Nan Campbell, Alaina Erdell, Jesse J. Thoma. In these three romance novellas, when business turns to pleasure, romance ignites. (978-1-63679-651-2)

McCall by Patricia Evans. Sam and Sara found love on the water, but can they build a future amid the ghosts of the past that surround them on dry land? (978-1-63679-769-4)

One and Done by Fredrick Smith. One day can lead to a night of passion...and possibly a chance at love. (978-1-63679-564-5)

Promises to Protect by Jo Hemmingwood. Park ranger Maxine Ward's commitment to protect Tree City is put to the test when social worker Skylar Austen takes a special interest in the commune and in Max. (978-1-63679-626-0)

Sacred Ground by Missouri Vaun. Jordan Price, a conflicted demon hunter, falls for Grace Jameson who has no idea she's been bitten by a vampire. (978-1-63679-485-3)

The Land of Death and Devil's Club by Bailey Bridgewater. Special Liaison to the FBI Louisa Linebach may have defied all odds by identifying the bodies of three missing men in the Kenai Peninsula, but she won't be satisfied until the man she's sure is responsible for their murders is behind bars. (978-1-63679-659-8)

When You Smile by Melissa Brayden. Taryn Ross never thought the babysitter she once crushed on would show up as a grad student at the same university she attends. (978-1-63679-671-0)

A Heart Divided by Angie Williams. Emma is the most beautiful woman Jackson has ever seen, but being a veteran of the Confederate army that killed her husband isn't the only thing keeping them apart. (978-1-63679-537-9)

Adrift by Sam Ledel. Two women whose lives are anchored by guilt and obligation find romance amidst the tumultuous Prohibition movement in 1920s California. (978-1-63679-577-5)

Cabin Fever by Tagan Shepard. The longer Morgan and Shelby are stranded together, the more their feelings grow, but is it real, or just cabin fever? (978-1-63679-632-1)

Clean Kill by Anne Laughlin. When someone starts killing people she knows in the recovery world, former detective Nicky Sullivan must race to stop the killer and keep herself from being arrested for the crimes. (978-1-63679-634-5)

Only a Bridesmaid by Haley Donnell. A fake bridesmaid, a socially anxious bride, and an unexpected love—what could go wrong? (978-1-63679-642-0)

Primal Hunt by L.L. Raand. Anya, a young wolf warrior, finds herself paired with Rafe, one of the most powerful Vampires in the Americas, in an erotic union of blood and sex. (978-1-63679-561-4)

Puzzles Can Be Deadly by David S. Pederson. Skip loves a good puzzle. Little does he know that a simple phone call will lead him and his boyfriend Henry to the deadliest puzzle he's ever encountered. (978-1-63679-615-4)

Snake Charming by Genevieve McCluer. Playgirl vampire Freddie is on the run and a chance encounter with lamia Phoebe makes them both realize that they may have found the love they'd given up on. (978-1-63679-628-4)

Spirits and Sirens by Kelly and Tana Fireside. When rumored ghost whisperer Elena Murphy and very skeptical assistant fire chief Allison Jones have to work together to solve a 70-year-old mystery, sparks fly—will it be enough to melt the ice between them and let love ignite? (978-1-63679-607-9)

A Case for Discretion by Ashley Moore. Will Gwen, a prominent Atlanta attorney, choose Etta, the law student she's clandestinely dating, or is her political future too important to sacrifice? (978-1-63679-617-8)

Aubrey McFadden Is Never Getting Married by Georgia Beers. Aubrey McFadden is never getting married, but she does have five weddings to attend, and she'll be avoiding Monica Wallace, the woman who ruined her happily ever after, at every single one. (978-1-63679-613-0)

Flowers for Dead Girls by Abigail Collins. Isla might be just the right kind of girl to bring Astra out of her shell—and maybe more. The only problem? She's dead. (978-1-63679-584-3)

Good Bones by Aurora Rey. Designer and contractor Logan Barrow can give Kathleen Kenney the house of her dreams, but can she convince the cynical romance writer to take a chance on love? (978-1-63679-589-8)

Leather, Lace, and Locs by Anne Shade. Three friends, each on their own path in life, with one obstacle…finding room in their busy lives for a love that will give them their happily ever afters. (978-1-63679-529-4)

Rainbow Overalls by Maggie Fortuna. Arriving in Vermont for her first year of college, an introverted bookworm forms a friendship with an outgoing artist and finds what comes after the classic coming out story: a being out story. (978-1-63679-606-2)

Revisiting Summer Nights by Ashley Bartlett. PJ Addison and Wylie Parsons have been called back to film the most recent Dangerous Summer Nights installment. Only this time they're not in love and it's going to stay that way. (978-1-63679-551-5)

The Broken Lines of Us by Shia Woods. Charlie Dawson returns to the city she left behind and she meets an unexpected stranger on her first night back, discovering that coming home might not be as hard as she thought. (978-1-63679-585-0)

Triad Magic by 'Nathan Burgoine. Face-to-face against forces set in motion hundreds of years ago, Luc, Anders, and Curtis—vampire, demon, and wizard—must draw on the power of blood, soul, and magic to stop a killer. (978-1-63679-505-8)

All This Time by Sage Donnell. Erin and Jodi share a complicated past, but a very different present. Will they ever be able to make a future together work? (978-1-63679-622-2)

Crossing Bridges by Chelsey Lynford. When a one-night stand between a snowboard instructor and a business executive becomes more, one has to overcome her past, while the other must let go of her planned future. (978-1-63679-646-8)

Dancing Toward Stardust by Julia Underwood. Age has nothing to do with becoming the person you were meant to be, taking a chance, and finding love. (978-1-63679-588-1)

Evacuation to Love by CA Popovich. As a hurricane rips through Florida, so too are Joanne and Shanna's lives upended. It'll take a force of nature to show them the love it takes to rebuild. (978-1-63679-493-8)

Lean in to Love by Catherine Lane. Will badly behaving celebrities, erotic sex tapes, and steamy scandals prevent Rory and Ellis from leaning in to love? (978-1-63679-582-9)

Searching for Someday by Renee Roman. For loner Rayne Thomas, her only goal for working out is to build her confidence, but Maggie Flanders has another idea, and neither are prepared for the outcome. (978-1-63679-568-3)

The Romance Lovers Book Club by MA Binfield and Toni Logan. After their book club reads a romance about an American tourist falling in love with an English princess, Harper and her best friend, Alice, book an impulsive trip to London hoping they'll each fall for the women of their dreams. (978-1-63679-501-0)

Truly Home by J.J. Hale. Ruth and Olivia discover home is more than a four-letter word. (978-1-63679-579-9)

View from the Top by Morgan Adams. When it comes to love, sometimes the higher you climb, the harder you fall. (978-1-63679-604-8)